ALSO BY JACQUELINE CAREY

Kushiel's Dart
Kushiel's Chosen
Kushiel's Avatar

Banewreaker
Godslayer

BANEWREAKER

Volume One of The Sundering

Jacqueline Carey

A TOM DOHERTY ASSOCIATES BOOK
NEW YORK

This is a work of fiction. All the characters and events portrayed in this book are either products of the author's imagination or are used fictitiously.

BANEWREAKER: VOLUME ONE OF THE SUNDERING

Copyright © 2004 by Jacqueline Carey

A Tor Book
Published by Tom Doherty Associates, LLC
175 Fifth Avenue
New York, NY 10010

www.tor.com

Tor® is a registered trademark of Tom Doherty Associates, LLC.

ISBN 0-765-34429-7
EAN 978-0-765-34429-8

First edition: November 2004
First mass market edition: August 2005

Printed in the United States of America

0   9   8   7   6   5   4   3   2   1

So farewell hope, and with hope farewell fear,
Farewell remorse: all good to me is lost;
Evil be thou my Good.
                           John Milton, *Paradise Lost*

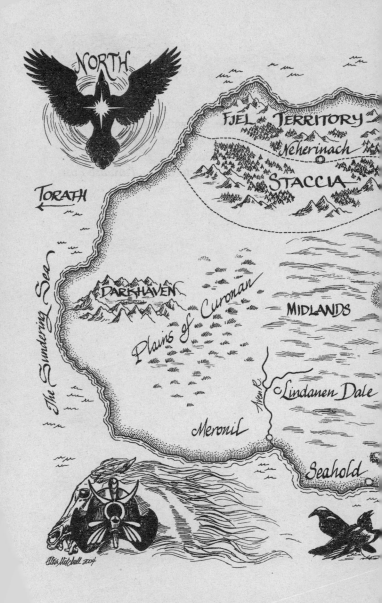

NORTH

FJEL TERRITORY

Neherinach

STACCIA

TORATH

DARKHAVEN

Plains of Curonan

MIDLANDS

The Swarming Sea

Lindanen Dale

Aloeh

Meronil

Seahold

Elisa Mitchell 2004

PELMAR

Beshtanag

Arduan
Delta

UNKNOWN
DESERT

Well of the
World

VEDASIA

Free Fishers

Harrington
Bay

Dvarthorn

URULAT

PROLOGUE

❖

THE PLACE WAS CALLED GORGANTUM.

Wounded once more, he fled there; and having fled, seethed. It was not a defeat, not wholly. No one could say such a thing while he yet lived and held Godslayer in his possession. He was Satoris Third-Born, and from this place, this vale, to the Sundering Sea, the west was his. Two of his Elder Brother's three Counselors were slain, their weapons lost or scattered. The high Lord of the Rivenlost was slain and his son with him, and many others, too. The number of Ellylon who remained would fill no more than a city. There were Men, of course, in ever-increasing numbers, but such discord had been sown on the battlefield as would make for bitter blood between the two races.

It would be long ages before another attempt was made.

But it would happen.

He knew his Elder Brother.

There had not always been enmity between them. Once, the Seven Shapers had dwelled in accord, in the beginning, when Uru-Alat, whom Men called the World God, died to give birth to the world, bringing them forth from the deepest places and giving power unto them.

First-Born among them was Haomane, Lord-of-Thought, for he was brought forth at the place of the Souma, the bright gem, the Eye in the Brow of Uru-Alat.

Second came Arahila the Fair, Born-of-the-Heart, and there was grace in all her ways, and compassion in her fingertips that Shaped the emerging world.

Satoris, once called the Sower, was Third-Born at the juncture of the loins, and in the quickening of the flesh lay his Gift.

Fourth came Neheris, from the northern forelimb, Neheris-of-the-Leaping-Waters, and the high, cold mountains with their sparkling rivers would be her demesne.

From the deep seas came Meronin, where the southern forelimb made harbor, and the Fifth-Born was deep and kept his counsel.

Sixth came Yrinna-of-the-Fruits, Lady of the southern aftlimb, and abundance was in her touch.

Last-Born and seventh was Oronin, the Glad Hunter of the northern aftlimb, and not least, for death rode in his train.

And also, there were dragons.

In those days, the Seven turned their thoughts to the emerging world. Oronin the Youngest gave Shape to wild forests as Yrinna, his sister, brought forth orchards and fields, and Meronin gave form to gentle harbors and deep seas even as Neheris made to rise mountains and rivers. In the Souma dwelled their power, and each drew upon it according to his strength or hers. Haomane First-Born took the brilliance of the Souma itself, the Eye of Uru-Alat, and gave Shape unto light. And the sun shone with bright radiance as it passed; but the night was black, and Arahila took pity upon it, and did Shape a second light called the moon, pale and beautiful, and thousands upon thousands of stars.

This world they called Urulat, after the World God whose death had given birth to it.

And still life emerged from the death of Uru-Alat, those races known as the Lesser Shapers, and each of the Seven did claim a race and Shape their Children according to their strengths and desires.

All save Satoris, who spent his time walking to and fro in the earth, and conversing with dragons; for they came forth from the very bones of Uru-Alat and there was wisdom in them, and cunning, too. Alone among the Seven, Satoris hungered for their knowledge. But his Gift lay in the quickening of the flesh, and he gave it gladly for the asking. Neheris did ask, and Meronin and Yrinna and Oronin, and thus were the children of their Shaping quickened, and the lesser races did increase; Fjeltroll and fish, Were and stag, Dwarf and rabbit alike. Where death entered the world with Oronin's presence, it was countered with Satoris' Gift, and the races did continue.

For the Ellylon, Haomane sought it not, for he had completed their Shaping before the final throes of Uru-Alat's death and time touched them not. He was First-Born, and he drew upon the fullest power of the Souma and wrought his Children of pure thought. Only Arahila's touch did Haomane suffer upon their Shaping, Second-Born and nearest to him of all his brethren. No lesser touch would he abide. Thus did Arahila Shape love into the being of the Ellylon.

In turn, Haomane Lord-of-Thought did place his Shaping on her Children, and those were Men, second among the Lesser Shapers. And they were mightier than all save the Ellylon for they turned the emergent world to their own ends; but they were not outside time and death's touch. Thus did Arahila the Fair seek Satoris' Gift for her children, and Satoris granted it, for he loved her well.

And Haomane was displeased.

For Men were not content, but made war upon the Ellylon, in ever-increasing numbers. And it came to pass in the Fourth Age of Urulat that Haomane First-Born asked Satoris to withdraw his Gift from the race of Men.

Three times, he asked.

Three times, Satoris refused. Out of love for Arahila, he refused; and out of knowledge, the deep and dire knowledge gained from congress with dragons. And, in the discord of his refusal, the Souma, the Eye in the Brow of Uru-Alat, was shattered. In that shattering, a single shard cracked loose from the whole, a shard shaped like a dagger.

Godslayer.

It was Oronin Last-Born who seized the shard and planted it in Satoris' thigh, wounding him so the ichor flowed like blood. Not until then did Satoris call upon the dragons, summoning them to his aid.

So began the Shapers' War.

Though many dragons died and Satoris was held at bay, he might have prevailed in the end, had it not been for Haomane First-Born. The Lord-of-Thought struck the earth a mighty blow, severing the head from the body of Urulat. And, in accordance with the will of Meronin the Deep, the Sundering Sea rushed in to fill the divide.

The Six Shapers were islanded, on that island later called Torath, and the power of the Souma was broken; but Satoris was cast out on the far side of the Sundering Sea, bereft and wounded. The dragons abandoned him, having paid too high a toll for his friendship. This Haomane saw, and the Lord-of-Thought drew upon the might of the shattered Souma. Though he could not Shape the land, he caused the sun above to blaze like a terrible Eye, and Satoris was scorched by the heat of it, and his skin darkened and parched, and the earth did also, until Arahila begged Haomane to relent for mercy's sake.

Northward, Satoris fled, where the mountains cast shadows over the land, and he sought shelter from Haomane's wrath in the deep caverns of the Fjeltroll, Neheris' Children, brutish and strong as mountains, and as solid, too. There he spoke gentle words to them and the Fjeltroll gave an oath to aid him, for they knew naught of the Shapers' War, only that he repaid them in kindness; a kindness Haomane in his pride had never shown them. He sought to heal himself, but ever after his skin bore the mark of Haomane's anger, and the wound dealt by Oronin was unhealed, but ever wept tears of ichor.

And Satoris' Gift was no more.

Still, Haomane would not leave him in peace, but lurked on the isle Torath, and breathed distant rumor into the ears of all on Urulat who would hear. Ellyl and Man were re-united in hatred of Satoris and gave new names to him: Banewreaker, Sunderer and Prince of Lies. And it came to them through Haomane's whispers that if Satoris were defeated, Urulat could be remade, and all would bask in the light of the Souma.

They made war upon him, and when the loyal Fjeltroll honored their pledge and defended him, they made war upon the Fjeltroll.

They made war until Satoris grew weary and bitter and angry, and raised an army of his own; of Fjeltroll, with their brute strength, and the grey Were, Oronin's hunters. All those who felt abandoned by the Six Shapers heeded his words, and he Shaped their will to his and marched against his enemies. What Haomane had named him, he became. Banewreaker, Bringer-of-Doom.

For a time, they laid waste to Urulat, pressing toward the west.

But his Elder Brother was cunning.

Haomane First-Born took three ruby-red chips of the Souma, smoothing them into gems of power: the Soumanië. Three Counselors he Shaped to bear them: Ardrath, Dergail and Malthus. Three weapons he gave them to wield: the Helm of Shadows, the Spear of Light and the Arrow of Fire. And he sent them across the Sundering Sea to raise an army of Ellylon and Men loyal to the Six Shapers to do battle with Satoris.

It had been a near thing.

Not a defeat, no. Not a victory, either.

He was alive and Godslayer was his. Still, he had been wounded anew, twice over, and forced to flee the field. But his enemies, Haomane's Allies, had taken grievous blows. Two Counselors slain, the Arrow of Fire lost, and the Helm of Shadows in Satoris' possession. The war had not ended, but there would be a reprieve, while ages passed and Haomane conceived his next move.

All Satoris could do was make ready for it.

First, he healed the mortal wound. The Ellyl blade that struck him from behind had cut deep, severing the tendons behind his knee. It had surprised him, that; so much so that he had dropped the dagger. And without Godslayer, he was—what? A Shaper, but powerless.

Sundered.

There had been his Gift, once. He smiled with bitter irony as he healed himself, drawing on the power of Godslayer to splice his sinews and knit his flesh. Even if it had not been stripped from him, his Gift would have availed him nothing in this struggle. That time had come and gone in ages past, vanished in an eyeblink.

He had offered his Gift to Haomane's Children.

Haomane had refused it.

The second wound was more difficult, for it had been dealt by a weapon Shaped by his brother. If the first had been a surprise, the second had been a shock. He could see it, still; the Spear of Light, its shaft gleaming under the sullen skies. It extended in a straight line from the place where agony flared, where the shining, leaf-pointed blade was buried in his side. And at the other end, both hands locked fast on the haft, was the last Counselor; Malthus, his brother's final emissary.

It had hurt, a hurt second only to one, as he tore himself loose, a gaffed fish fighting the hook. Such indignity! It was almost worth it to see the Counselor's dumbstruck face. There was only one weapon capable of killing Satoris.

Godslayer.

They had both reached for it at once. The dagger, the shard of the shattered Souma. He grimaced in remembrance, pressing its blade to the ragged lips of the wound in his side. It pulsed there, and light kindled in its rubescent depths. So it had pulsed between their joined hands. Closing his eyes, he called upon its power. Somewhere, beyond the Sundering Sea, the light of the Souma flickered in distant sympathy. His kindred would wonder what he did with it.

Let them wonder, and fear. He drew upon its power for this second healing, so much more difficult than the first. Inch by slow inch, he sealed the wound. It left a scar that shone with a pale light, another memento of his brother's wrath.

When it was done, he was weary.

Not all wounds could be healed.

Always, there was the third wound, the immortal one; there, in the hollow of his thigh, where Oronin had struck him with Godslayer itself. It festered with deep poison and wept unceasing tears of ichor, and where they fell, the land itself was blighted and *changed*.

So be it, he thought. I have fled my brother's wrath, and he has found me. I have challenged his might, and he has thwarted me. My siblings have forsaken me; even Arahila, though her memory makes me weep. Yet I do not regret my choice. If Haomane asked a fourth time, I would refuse him anew. In his pride, the Lord-of-Thought does not see the Shape of what-would-be if my Gift were forever uncoupled from his. I see; all too clearly, I see. Thus in my pride, I name myself my brother's enemy, and not his victim. I did not seek this role, though it has been thrust upon me. Loathe it though I may, it is my lot. I am what I am. I cling to such honor as is left to me. Here I will abide, and make of this place a sanctuary; a stronghold. And when I am done, I will place Godslayer at the heart of it, where no other hand may touch it.

Being whole, or as whole as he might be, he summoned the Fjeltroll.

There, in the vale of Gorgantum, he flung up jagged peaks to surround his place of hiding. He brought forth great slabs of marble from the earth and Shaped them, black and gleaming. And he showed them his plan, the vast citadel with its high towers, its encircling wall, and the se-

cret heart of it like a twin-chambered nautilus. There the
Fjel labored, honoring their ancient oath. Strong and high
they built its walls—and deep, deep below it they delved, in
Gorgantum, the hollow, where the earth's strong bones conjoined.

When they reached the Source, he sighed to see the
marrow-fire.

Godslayer would be safe.

It was a lingering essence of the blazing godhead of Uru-
Alat; a blue-white fire that ran through the bones of the
earth, the spark of which fueled the dragons' fiery bellies at
their emergence. Here, at the Source, it gathered. Nothing
mortal could withstand its touch. He had enough of a
Shaper's power yet to Shape the marrow-fire. It took delicacy, tapping just enough to lace the veined marble of his
citadel, to light the unfaltering torches. For the first time, he
understood the joy his siblings had taken in Shaping the
emerging world, and wondered what it would have been
like to do so in the fullness of power before the Souma was
shattered.

No matter. This would have to be enough.

Of its smoke, he wrought a pall of darkness, and this he
flung like a cloak over the vale of Gorgantum, until the very
skies were shrouded. And at this, too, he smiled, for it
veiled his Elder Brother's prying eyes and sheltered him
from the sun's wrath that had scorched his form to blackness.

The Source itself, he dared not alter, but from it he drew
a steady flow, a Font in which the marrow-fire danced in an
endless coruscation of blue-white flame. In the Font, where
no mortal hands would dare reach, he placed the dagger,
Godslayer. And there it burned, throbbing like an angry
heart; burned, yet was not consumed.

His citadel was complete, and he was pleased.

And he was alone, and lonely.

There were the Fjeltroll, always, faithful to their oath. He had never lied to them. It was true, he treasured them for their very simplicity. But oh, how quickly their lives flickered past, measured against his own! Generations passed in the building of his sanctuary. And in the brute simplicity of their very fidelity, they served as a stark reminder of his complicated, solitary existence. To whom could he turn, when first he heard the whispers of his brother's new Prophecy? It was a cunning plan.

No one.

He turned instead to the prize the Fjeltroll had seized from the battlefield and brought him like a trophy at his summons. The Helm of Shadows, Men had named it.

It hurt to look upon it, even for him. His Elder Brother, who had Shaped the sun of the Souma's light, had Shaped this thing of its absence, from the lightless cracks of its shattering. On the battlefield, Men had averted their eyes, and even the Ellylon had wept to behold it. It held the darkness of all things lost and broken beyond repair—of the Souma, of the concord of the Shapers, of the Sundered World itself.

I am one of those things, he thought, turning the Helm in his hands. Broken beyond repair. Abandoned and bereft, cast out by those who once loved me.

And so thinking, he set about tuning its darkness to his own despair.

In it he placed his abiding frustration at his Elder Brother's stubborn pride, and his own hatred of the role he had been condemned to play. He placed into it his anguish at his siblings' betrayal, shaded with profound sorrow and honed keen with rage—for they had all betrayed him, all of them. He gave Shape to his own self-loathing, to the memory of futile defiance, to that moment, that terrible moment, when the world was Sundered and the seas rushed into the chasm, and he knew himself defeated and alone.

Of helpless torment he Shaped it, of the memory of

crawling upon the heaving earth, clutching at it in his pain while the long arm of his brother's wrath pursued, shifting the very sun until his skin blackened and cracked, and he was forced, bellowing, to flee once more. Of countless days and nights of bitter convalescence he Shaped it, of the awareness of his lost Gift and the dire knowledge that he was maimed beyond repair, that his name had become a curse on the lips of his brother's Children. He Shaped it of sheer loathing at the cowardice of his Elder Brother, who dared not cross the Sundering Sea, but worked ever at a distance.

Of the grief at all fair things lost, he Shaped it, and the bittersweet pleasures he found to fill their place—of vengeance and rancorous triumph, of the dawning knowledge that he was well and truly abandoned, a rebel Shaper casting a threatening shadow over his siblings' dearest labors. Of a faint, desperate thread of hope, he Shaped it; and the sure knowledge that hope was doomed.

Of searing pain he Shaped it, of impotent fury, of the remorseless agony of his wounded flesh, of the slow drip of ichor that bled from his wound, of the slow drip of malice that poisoned his heart, fed by generation upon generation of hatred endured.

Of unflinching truth, he Shaped it.

When it was done, he donned the Helm of Shadows and gazed through the eye-slits of his own dark vision, gazing across the land and hoarding his dwindling energies to peer into the hearts and minds of all living beings blessed with his Elder Brother's Gift of thought; for yes, oh yes, that had been his brother's Gift, in all the mingled curse and blessing it entailed.

Somewhere, in the far reaches of the Sundered World, there must be others who shared the pain of betrayal, who understood what it was to rage against an unfair destiny. Mortals, it was true, with brief, flickering lives—but with Godslayer to hand, it need not be so.

Three emissaries his Elder Brother had sent to destroy him. He would summon three of his own; comrades, commanders, keepers of his citadel.

He would find them.

He would make them his.

He would make them immortal.

ONE

❖

TANAROS WALKED DOWN THE HALLWAY, black marble echoing under his bootheels.

It was like an unlit mirror, that floor, polished to a high gleam. The archways were vast, not built to a human scale. All along the walls the marrow-fire burned, delicate veins of blue-white against all that shining blackness. In both, his reflection was blurred and distorted. There was Tanaros; there, and there and there.

A pale brow, furrowed. A lock of dark hair falling, so.

Capable hands.

And a stern mouth, its soft words of love long since betrayed.

It had been a long time, a very long time, since Tanaros had thought of such matters, of the sum total the pieced-together fragments of his being made; nor did he think of them now, for his Lord's summons burned like a beacon in his mind. And beneath his attire, beneath the enameled armor that sheltered him, his branding burned like marrow-fire on his flesh, white-hot and cold as ice, throbbing as his heart beat, and piercing.

So it was, for the Three.

"Guardsman," he said in greeting.

"General Tanaros, sir." The Havenguard Fjeltroll on duty grinned, showing his eyetusks. His weapons hung about him like boulders on the verge of avalanche; he hoisted one, a sharp-pointed mace, in salute as he stood aside. Beyond him, the entrance to the tower stair yawned like an open mouth. "His Lordship awaits you in the observatory."

"Krognar," Tanaros said, remembering his name. "Thank you."

"My pleasure, Lord General." The Fjeltroll saluted again.

It was a long way to the observatory, to the very top of the utmost tower of Darkhaven. Tanaros climbed it step by step, feeling his heartbeat increasing as he labored. A mortal heart, circumscribed by the silvered scar of his branding. When all was said and done, he was a Man, nothing more. It was his Lordship who had made him one of the Three, and deathless. He heard his breath labor, in and out. Mortal lungs, circulating blood. How long had they been at that task? It had been a thousand years and more since Tanaros had answered his Lord's first summons, his hands red with the lifeblood of one he had once loved, his heart filled with rage and anguish.

It felt longer.

He wondered, briefly, how Vorax made the long climb.

Darkness spiraling on darkness. Broad steps, wrought by Fjeltroll, made to endure their broad, horny feet. Tanaros reached out, touching the spiraling wall of the tower, fingers trailing. It should have burned, the marrow-fire; it did burn, but faintly. Here the veins branched and branched again, growing ever thinner and fainter as the tower thrust upward into the darkness.

It was always dark here.

Tanaros paused in the entrance to the observatory, letting his eyes adjust. Dark. It was always dark. Even the windows opened onto darkness, and the night sky. There, the stars, that never shone in cloud-blotted daylight.

"My Lord." He bowed, crisp and correct, as he had bowed for centuries on end.

"Tanaros." The voice rumbled, deep as mountains; it soothed, easing his joints, loosening the stiffness of centuries, of honor betrayed and never forgotten. It always had. In the darkness, the Shaper was silhouetted in the windows of night, vast shoulders occluding the stars. A pair of eyes glinted like crimson embers. "You have come."

Tanaros took a breath, feeling his lungs loosen. "Always, my Lord Satoris."

"It is well."

In a carven chair in the corner sat Vorax, his thick legs akimbo, fanning himself and breathing hard. Long ago he had been a lord of the race of Men, dwelling in the cool clime of Staccia, far to the north. Gluttony, greed and a ruthless pragmatism had moved him to answer the Shaper's summons, becoming one of the immortal Three. He grinned at Tanaros from where he sprawled, his beard fanning over his massive chest. "Grave doings, cousin! Is it not so?"

"If you say so, cousin." Tanaros did not sit in his Lord's presence. Long ago, he had stood vigilant in the presence of his King as he stood now, in the presence of one far greater. Loyalties changed; protocol did not. He inclined his head in deference. "We await the Dreamspinner, my Lord?"

"Yes." His Lord turned to the westernmost window, gazing out at the night. "Tell me, Tanaros. What do you see, thence?"

He made his way to his Lord's side. It was like standing beside a stoked forge, the might of the Shaper beating against his skin in waves. In the air a scent, coppery and sweet, like fresh-spilled blood, only *stronger*. "Where, my Lord?"

"There." Satoris pointed to the west, the line of his arm unerring.

It could not be otherwise, of course, for westward lay Torath and the Souma, the Eye in the Brow of Uru-Alat—and Lord Satoris was a Shaper. Though his brethren had cast him out, though their allies reviled him and called him Sunderer, Banewreaker and Prince of Lies, he was a Shaper.

Day or night, above the earth or below it, he knew where the Souma lay.

Beyond the Sundering Sea.

Tanaros gripped the edge of the casement and looked west into the night. The low mountains surrounding Darkhaven rose in ridges, silvered by a waning moon. Far, far beyond, he could see the faintest shimmer of surging darkness on the distant horizon where the sea began. Below, it was quiet, only an occasional clatter to be heard in the barracks of the Fjeltroll, a voice raised to break the silence.

Above there was the night sky, thin clouds scudding, scattered with pinpricks of stars and the waning moon. As it was since time had begun, since Arahila the Fair had Shaped them into being that the children of Men might not fear the darkness.

No.

There . . . *there*. Low on the horizon, a star.

A red star.

It was faint, but it was there. Its light throbbed, faint and fickle, red.

Leather and steel creaked as Vorax levered his bulk to his feet, his breathing audible in the tower chamber; louder, as he saw the star and sucked his breath between his teeth with a hiss. "Red star," he said. "That wasn't there before."

Tanaros, who had not known fear for many years, knew it now. He let go the edge of the casement and flexed his hands, tasting fear and wishing for his black sword. "What is it, my Lord?"

The Shaper watched the red star flicker low in the distance. "A warning."

"Of what, my Lord?" The taste of fear in his mouth. "From whom?"

"My elder sister." The voice was as soft as a Shaper's could be, touched with ages of sorrow. "Oh, Arahila!"

Tanaros closed his eyes. "How can that be, my Lord? With the Souma shattered and Urulat sundered . . . how can it be that Arahila would Shape such a thing?"

"Dergail," said Vorax. "Dergail's Soumanië."

A chip of the Souma, long since shattered; a chip, Shaped by Haomane First-Born, Chief of Shapers, into a gem, one of three. It had been lost even before Tanaros was born, when Haomane sent his three Wise Counselors to make war upon his Lordship. The Counselor Dergail, who had borne the Arrow of Fire, had known defeat and flung himself into the sea rather than allow the gem or the weapon to fall into enemy hands. For over a thousand years, both had been lost.

"Yes," said Satoris, watching. "Dergail's Soumanië."

Tanaros' mouth had gone dry. "What does it mean, my Lord?"

Satoris Third-Born watched the red star, and the faint light of the waning moon silvered his dark visage. Calm, so calm! Unmoving, he stood and watched, while ichor seeped like blood from the unhealing wound he bore, laying a glistening trail down the inside of his thigh, never ceasing.

"War," he said. "It means war."

Footsteps sounded on the tower stair, quick and light, announcing Ushahin's arrival. The half-breed entered the chamber, bowing. "My Lord Satoris."

"Dreamspinner," the Shaper acknowledged him. "You have news?"

In the dim light, there was beauty in the ruined face, the mismatched features. The half-breed's smile was like the edge of a knife, deadly and bitter. "I have passed across the plains of Curonan like the wind, my Lord, and walked in the dreams of Men while they slept. I have news. Cerelinde of the Ellylon, granddaughter of Elterrion, has agreed to wed Aracus Altorus of the children of Men."

When a daughter of Elterrion weds a son of Altorus . . .

It was one of the conditions of Haomane's Prophecy, those deeds by which the Lord-of-Thought vowed Satoris would be overthrown and defeated, and Urulat reclaimed by the Six Shapers who remained.

Vorax cursed with a Staccian's fluency.

Tanaros was silent, remembering.

Aracus Altorus.

There had been another of that House, once; there had been many others, and Altorus Farseer first among them, in the First Age of the Sundered World. For Tanaros, born in the years of dwindling glory, there was only one: Roscus Altorus, whom he had called "King," and "my lord." Roscus, dearer to him than any brother. Red-gold hair, a ready smile, a strong hand extended to clasp in friendship.

Or in love, as his hand had clasped that of Tanaros' wife. Claiming her, possessing her. Leading her to his bed, where he got her with child.

Tanaros trembled with hatred.

"Steady, cousin." Vorax's hand was heavy on his shoulder, and there was sympathy in the Staccian's voice. They knew each other well, the Three, after so long. "This concerns us all."

Ushahin Dreamspinner said nothing, but his eyes gleamed in the dark chamber. Near black, the one, its pupil fixed wide; the other waxed and waned like the moon, set in a pale, crazed iris. So it had been, since the day he was beaten and left for dead, and Men said it was madness to meet his eyes. What the Ellylon thought, no one knew.

"My Lord Satoris." Tanaros found his voice. "What would you have of us?"

"Readiness." Calm, still calm, though it seemed the ichor bled faster from his wound, the broad trail glistening wider. "Tanaros, command of the armies is yours. Those who are on leave must be recalled, and each squadron rendered a full complement. There must be new recruits. Vorax, see to our lines of supply, and those allies who might be bribed or bought. Ushahin . . . " The Shaper smiled. "Do as you do."

They bowed, each of the Three, pressing clenched fists to their hearts.

"We will not fail you, my Lord," Tanaros said for them all.

"My brave lieutenants." Satoris' words hung in the air, gentle. "My brother Haomane seeks my life, to end the long quarrel between us. This you know. But all the weapons and all the prophecies in the Sundered World avail him not, so long as the dagger Godslayer remains safe in our charge, and where it lies, no hands but mine may touch it. This I promise you: for so long as the marrow-fire burns, I shall reign in Darkhaven, and you three with me. It is the pact of your branding, and I shall not fail it. Now go, and see that we are in readiness."

They went.

On the horizon, the red star of war flickered.

"SO IT'S WAR, THEN."

For all his mass, the Fjeltroll's hands were quick and deft, working independent of their owner's thoughts.

"So it seems." Tanaros watched Hyrgolf's vast hands shape the *rhios,* using talons and brute force to carve the lump of granite. It was in its final stages, needing only the smoothing of the rounded surfaces and the delineation of the expressive face. "You'll order the recall? And a thousand new recruits drafted?"

"Aye, General." His field marshal blew on the stone, clearing granite dust from the miniature crevices. He held the *rhios* in the palm of his horny hand and regarded it at eye level. A river sprite, rounded like an egg, an incongruous delicacy against the yellowed, leathery palm. "What think you?"

"It is lovely."

Hyrgolf squinted. His eyes were like a boar's, small and fierce, and he was of the Tungskulder Fjel, broad and strong and steady. "There's some will be glad of the news."

"There always are," Tanaros said. "Those are the ones bear watching."

The Fjeltroll nodded, making minute adjustments to the

figurine's delicate features, shearing away infinitesimal flakes of granite. "They always are."

Brutes, Men called them; delvers, sheep-slaughterers, little better than animals. Tanaros had believed it himself, once. Once, when the sons of Altorus ruled a powerful kingdom in the southwest, and he had been Commander of the Guard, and held the borders of Altoria against the forces of Satoris; the deadly Were, the horrid Fjeltroll. Once, when he had been a married man deep in love, a husband and faithful servant, who had called a bold, laughing man with red-gold hair his lord and king.

Roscus. Roscus Altorus.

Aracus Altorus.

Oh, love, *love!* Tanaros remembered, wondering. How could you do that to us?

Somewhere, an infant drew breath into its lungs and bawled.

So much time elapsed, and the wound still unhealed. His heart ached with it still, beat and ached beneath the silvery scar that seared it, that made the pain bearable. It had cracked at her betrayal; cracked, like the Souma itself. And in that darkness, Satoris had called to him, and he had answered, for it was the only voice to pierce his void.

Now . . . now.

Now it was different, and he was one of the Three. Tanaros, General Tanaros, Tanaros Blacksword, and this *creature,* Hyrgolf of the Fjeltroll, was his second-in-command, and a trusted companion. For all that he massed more than any two Men combined, for all that his eyetusks showed when he smiled, he was loyal, and true.

"You think of *her,*" Hyrgolf said.

"Is it so obvious, my friend?"

"No." Hyrgolf blew dust from the *rhios* and studied it again, turning it this way and that. "But I know you, General. And I know the stories. It is best not to think of it. The dead are the dead, and gone."

Her neck beneath his hands, white and slender; her eyes,

bulging, believing at the last. A crushing force. And some-where, an infant crying, wisps of red-gold hair plastered on its soft skull. An infant he had allowed to live.

Tanaros remembered and flexed his hands, his capable hands, hunching his shoulders under the weight of memory. "I have lived too long to forget, my friend."

"Here." Broad hands covered his, pressing something into them. Dirt-blackened talons brushed his wrists. An object, egg-sized and warm. Tanaros cradled the *rhios* in his palms. A sprite, a river sprite. Her delicate face laughed at him from between his thumbs. A rounded shape, comfort-ing, bearing streaks of salmon-pink. It made him think of backwater currents, gentle eddies, of spawning-pools rife with eggs.

"Hyrgolf . . . "

"Keep it, General." The Fjeltroll gave him a gentle smile, a hideous sight. "We carry them to remember, we who were once Neheris' Children. One day, if the Sundered World is made whole, perhaps we will be again."

Neheris Fourth-Born, Neheris-of-the-Leaping-Waters, who had Shaped the high mountains of the north and the bright waters that tumbled down them, and Shaped the Fjel-troll also. Tanaros rubbed the *rhios,* the curving stone pol-ished smooth as satin and warm from Hyrgolf's touch. It felt good in his hand.

"That's it." His field marshal nodded. "Keep it in your pocket, General, and it will always be with you."

He stowed the figurine. "Thank you, Hyrgolf."

"Welcome you are, General." Picking up a battle-axe, the Fjel rummaged for a whetstone and began honing the edge of his weapon with the same attentive patience. The whet-stone made a rhythmic rasping sound in the snug cavern, fa-miliar and soothing. "Regular weapons inspections from here out, you reckon?"

"Yes." Tanaros rubbed his temples. "We'll double up on drills as soon as the recalled units arrive. And I want scout-ing patrols in the tunnels, reporting daily. Establish a post at every egress between here and the Unknown, with runners between them. I want daily reports."

"Aye, sir." Hyrgolf tested the edge of the blade with a thick-calloused thumb and resumed his efforts. "Pity for the lads due leave."

"I know." Restless, Tanaros stood to stretch his legs, pacing around the confines of the field marshal's chamber. Like all the barracks, this one was built into a stony ridge. The Fjeltroll had constructed Darkhaven to their own scale, but Lord Satoris was its genius and its architect, and the convoluted magnificence of it echoed its creator. For themselves, the Fjeltroll had eschewed walls and towers, delving into the bones of the earth and carving out the simple caverns they preferred, laid out to flank and protect the mighty edifice. Most dwelled in common chambers; Hyrgolf, due to his rank, had his own. It held a sleeping pallet covered in sheepskin, his weapons and gear, a few simple things from home. Tanaros stopped before a niche hollowed into the wall, containing the stump of a tallow candle and a crudely carved *rhios*.

"My boy's first effort," Hyrgolf said behind him. There was pride in his voice. "Not bad for a mere pup, eh General?"

Tanaros touched the cavern wall, bowing his head. "You were due leave."

"In two months' time." The sound of the whetstone never slowed. "That's the luck, isn't it? We always knew this day might come."

"Yes." He looked back at the Fjeltroll. "How do your people tell it?"

"The Prophecy?" Hyrgolf shook his massive head. "We don't, General."

No, of course not. In the First Age of the Sundered World, when Satoris was sore wounded and at his weakest, when Haomane First-Born, the Lord-of-Thought, had called upon the Souma and brought the sun so near to earth it scorched the land and brought into being the Unknown Desert, the Fjeltroll had sheltered Satoris and pledged their loyalty to him. After his Counselors had been defeated, Haomane First-Born uttered his Prophecy into the ears of his allies. The Prophecy was not shared with the Fjel.

Instead, it doomed them.

"And yet you still honor Neheris," Tanaros said, fingering the *rhios* in his pocket. "Who sided with Haomane, with the Six, against his Lordship. Why, Hyrgolf?"

"It's Shapers' business," Hyrgolf said simply, setting down his axe. "I don't pretend to understand it. We made a pact with his Lordship and he has honored it, generation after generation. He never asked us to stop loving Neheris who Shaped us."

"No," Tanaros said, remembering his Lord's cry. *Oh, Arahila!* "He wouldn't."

And he fingered the *rhios* in his pocket again, and longed for the simplicity of a Fjeltroll's faith. It was not granted to Men, who had been given too many gifts to bear with ease. Oh, Arahila! Second-Born among Shapers, Arahila the Fair, Born-of-the-Heart. Would that you had made us less.

"How do your people tell it?" Hyrgolf asked. "The Prophecy, that is."

Tanaros relinquished the *rhios,* his hands fisted in his pockets as he turned to face his field marshal. "In Altoria," he said, and his voice was harsh, "when I was a boy, it was told thus. 'When the unknown is made known, when the lost weapon is found, when the marrow-fire is quenched and Godslayer is freed, when a daughter of Elterrion weds a son of Altorus, when the Spear of Light is brought forth and the Helm of Shadows is broken, the Fjeltroll shall fall, the Were shall be defeated ere they rise, and the Sunderer shall be no more, the Souma shall be restored and the Sundered World made whole and Haomane's Children shall endure.'"

It grieved him to say it, as if the Fjeltroll might hold him in some way responsible. After all, if he had killed the babe . . . *if he had killed the babe*. The House of Altorus would have ended, then, and there would have been no Prophecy.

Blue eyes, milky and wondering. Red-gold hair plastered to a damp skull.

He hadn't been able to do it. The babe, the child of his cuckolded marriage bed, had succeeded Roscus in the House of Altorus.

"Aye," Hyrgolf said, nodding. "That's as I heard it. The Sundered World made whole, but the cost of it our lives. Well, then, that's only a piece of it, this wedding. There's a good deal more needs happen before the Prophecy is fulfilled, and who knows what the half of it means?"

"His Lordship knows," Tanaros said. "And Malthus."

Their eyes met, then; Man and Fjel, hearing a common enemy named.

"Malthus," Hyrgolf rumbled, deep in his chest. The Wise Counselor, Wielder of the Soumanië, last of three, last and greatest of Haomane's Shapings. "Well, there is Malthus, General, I don't deny you that. But he is only one, now, and we have among us the Three."

Tanaros, Vorax, Ushahin.

"Pray that we are enough," Tanaros said.

"That I do, General," said the Fjeltroll. "That I do."

Tanaros Blacksword, Commander General of the Army of Darkhaven, walked alone to his quarters, a stone the size of an egg in his pocket.

From time to time, he touched it for reassurance.

ELSEWHERE IN THE LAND OF Urulat, flames burnt low and dwindled in their lamps in the archives of Meronil, housed in the Hall of Ingolin, where an elderly figure in scholar's robes bent over a hide-bound tome, muttering. The lamplight caught in his grey, tangled beard, cast shadows in the deep lines of his face, marking them in contrast to the

splendid treasures that gleamed about him, housed in the
archives for safekeeping.

Footsteps, slow and measured, quiet on the elegant carpets.

"Old friend," said Ingolin, the last Lord of the Ellylon.
"You should rest."

The head lifted, sharp nose pointing, eyes fierce under
heavy brows. "You know why I do not."

"It is a day for rejoicing, old friend," the Ellyl reminded
him.

Malthus the Counselor laughed without mirth. "Can you
tell me how to quench the marrow-fire, Ingolin the Wise?
Can you render the unknown known?"

"You know I cannot." There was calm acceptance in the
Ellyl's reply. In the manner of his people he had lived a
long time, and knew the limits of his own knowledge. "Still,
Cerelinde has unbent at long last, and Aracus Altorus has
bowed his House's ancient pride. Love, it seems, has found
them. A piece of the Prophecy shall be fulfilled, and the
Rivenlost endure. May we not rejoice in it?"

"It is not enough."

"No." Ingolin glanced unthinking to the west, where Dergail's Soumanië had arisen. "Old friend," he asked, and his
voice trembled for the first time in centuries. "Do you hold
the answers to these questions you ask?"

"I might," Malthus the Counselor said slowly, and
pinched the bridge of his nose, fixing the Lord of the Ellylon with a hawk's stare. "I might. But the way will be long
and difficult, and there are many things of which I am unsure."

Ingolin spread his hands. "The aid of the Rivenlost is
yours, Malthus. Only tell us how we might serve."

"You can't, old friend," said Malthus the Counselor.
"That's the problem."

* * *

In another wing of the Hall of Ingolin, a fire burned low in the great hearth. Cerelinde, the granddaughter of Elterrion, gazed at it with unseeing eyes and thought about the deed to which she had committed herself this day.

She was the Lady of the Ellylon, the last scion of the House of Elterrion. By the reckoning of her people, she was young, born after the Sundering of the world, after the grieving Ellylon had taken the name Rivenlost unto themselves. Her mother had been Erilonde, daughter of Elterrion the Bold, Lord of the Ellylon, and she had died in childbirth. Her father had been Celendril of the House of Numireth the Fleet, and he had fallen in battle against Satoris Banewreaker in the Fourth Age of the Sundered World.

If the courage of Men had not faltered that day, her father might have lived. Haomane's Allies might have triumphed that day, and the world been made whole.

She had never known the glory of the Souma and Haomane's presence, only the deep, enduring ache of their absence.

That bitter knowledge had dwelled in her while generations were born and died, for, by the reckoning of Men, she was timeless. She had watched, century upon century, the proud Kings of Altoria, Altorus' sons, as they grew to manhood and took their thrones, made love and war and boasts, withered and died. She had watched as they disdained their ancient friendship with the Ellylon, watched as Satoris Banewreaker calculated his vengeance and shattered their kingdom. She had stopped watching, then, as the remnants of a once-mighty dynasty dwindled into the Borderguard of Curonan.

Then Aracus had come; Aracus Altorus, who had been tutored by Malthus the Counselor since he was a lad. Like her, he was the last of his line.

And he was different from those who had come before him.

She had known it the moment she laid eyes upon him.

Unlike the others, the Kings of Altoria in all their glory, Aracus was aware of the brevity of his allotted time; had measured it against the scope of the Sunderer's plan and determined to spend it to the greatest effect. She had seen it in his face, in the wide-set, demanding gaze.

He understood the price both of them would have to pay.

And something in her had . . . quickened.

In the hall outside the hearth chamber she heard the sound of his bootheels striking the white marble floors, echoing louder than any Ellyl's tread. She heard the quiet murmur of words exchanged with Lord Ingolin's guards. And then he was there, standing before the hearth, the scent of horses and leather and night air clinging to his dun-grey cloak. He had ridden hard to return to her side. His voice, when he spoke, was hoarse with weariness.

"Cerelinde."

"Aracus."

She stood to greet him. He was tall for a Man and their eyes were on a level. She searched his face. In the dim fire-light, it was strange to see the glint of red-gold stubble on his chin. He was Arahila's Child, and not of her kind.

"Is it done?" she asked.

"Aye," he said. "The Borderguard carry word of our betrothal."

Cerelinde looked away. "How long before it reaches the Sunderer's ears?"

"It has done so." He took her hand. "Cerelinde," he said. "The Sunderer flaunts his defiance. The red star of war has risen. I saw it as I rode."

Her fingers trembled in his grasp. "So quickly!"

His voice grew softer. "You know what is said, my lady. One of the Three stalks the dreams of mortal Men."

"The Misbegotten." Cerelinde shuddered.

Aracus nodded. "Aye."

Cerelinde gazed at their joined hands. His fingers were warm and calloused, rough against her soft skin. It seemed she could feel his lifeblood pulse through them, urgent and mortal, calling to her. She tried not to think of Ushahin the Misbegotten, and failed.

"Our children . . . " she murmured.

"No!" Aracus breathed the word, quick and fierce. His grip tightened, almost painful. Lifting her head, she met his eyes. "They will not be like that one," he said. "Wrenched forth from violence and hatred, cast out and warped. We honor the Prophecy. Our children will be conceived in love, in accordance with Haomane's will, and Arahila's."

She laid her free hand upon his chest. "Love."

"Aye, lady." He covered her hand with his own, gazing at her. "Never less. I swear it to you. Though my heart beats to a swift and mortal tune, it beats true. And until I die, it lies in your keeping."

"Ah, Aracus!" His name caught in her throat. "We have so little time!"

"I know," he murmured. "All too well, I know."

ELSEWHERE ON URULAT, NIGHT CREPT westward.

Slowly, it progressed, a gilt edge fading to the blue of twilight, drawing a cloak of darkness behind it. Where it passed—over the fields and orchards of Vedasia, over the dank marshes of the Delta, over Harrington Inlet, across the Unknown Desert and Staccia and Seahold and Curonan—the stars emerged in its wake.

It came to the high mountains of Pelmar, where a woman stood on the steep edge of a cavern, and a gem bound in a circlet at her brow shone like the red star that flickered low, low on the far western horizon.

Her name was Lilias, though Men and Ellylon called her the Sorceress of the East. She had been a mortal woman, once; the daughter of a wealthy Pelmaran earl. The east was the land of Oronin Last-Born, in whose train death rode, and his lingering touch lay on those Men, Arahila's Children, who settled in Pelmar as their ever-increasing numbers covered the earth. It was said those of noble birth could hear Oronin's Horn summon them to their deaths.

Lilias feared death. She had seen it, once, in the eyes of a young man to whom her father would have betrothed her. He was a duke's son, well made and gently spoken, but she had seen in his eyes the inevitability of her fate, old age and generations of children yet unborn, and she had heard the echo of Oronin's Horn. Such was the lot of Arahila's Children, and the mighty Chain of Being held her fast in its inescapable grip.

And so she had fled into the mountains. Up, she went, higher than any of her brothers had ever dared climb, scaling the height of Beshtanag Mountain and hiding herself in its caverns. It was there that she had encountered the dragon.

His name was Calandor, and he was immortal after his kind. If he had hungered, he might have swallowed her whole, but since he did not, he asked her instead why she wept.

Weeping, she told him.

Twin jets of smoke had risen from his nostrils, for such was the laughter of dragons. And it was there that he gave a great treasure into her keeping: One of the lost Soumanië, Ardrath's gem that had been missing for many centuries. It had been plucked from the battlefield by a simple soldier who thought it a mere ruby. From thence its trail was lost until it ended in the hoard of a dragon, who made it a gift to a mortal woman who did not wish to die.

Such was the caprice of dragons, whose knowledge was vast and unfathomable. Calandor taught her many things, the first of which was how to use the Soumanië to stretch the Chain of Being, keeping mortality at bay.

She was no longer afraid.

It had been a long time ago. Lilias' family was long dead, her lineage forgotten. She was the Sorceress of the East and possessed great power, which she used with neither great wisdom nor folly. She allowed Oronin's Children, the Were, to hunt freely in the forests of Beshtanag, though elsewhere they were reviled for aiding Satoris the Sunderer in the last great war. The regents of Pelmar feared her and left her in peace, which was her sole desire.

And, until now, the Six Shapers had done the same.

Lilias regarded the red star on the horizon and felt uneasiness stir in her soul for the first time in many centuries. Dergail's Soumanië had risen, and change was afoot. Behind her in the mammoth darkness a vast shadow loomed.

"What does it mean, Calandor?" she asked in a low voice.

"Trouble." The word emerged in a sulfurous breath, half lost in the heights of the vaulted cavern. Unafraid, she laid one hand on the taloned foot nearest her. The rough scales were warm to the touch; massive claws gleaming like hematite, gouging the stone floor. On either side, forelegs as vast and sturdy as columns. Somewhere above and behind her head, she could hear the dragon's heart beating, slow and steady like the pulse of the earth.

"For whom?"

"Usssss." High above, Calandor bent his sinuous neck to answer, the heat of his exhalation brushing her cheek. "Uss, Liliasss." And there was sorrow, and regret, in the dragon's voice.

I will not be afraid, Lilias told herself. I will not be afraid!

She touched the Soumanië, the red gem bound at her brow, and gazed westward, where its twin flickered on the horizon. "What shall we do, Calandor?"

"Wait," the dragon said, laying his thoughts open to her. "We wait, Liliasss."

And in that moment, she *knew,* knowledge a daughter of Men was never meant to bear. The sorceress Lilias shook with knowledge. "Oh, Calandor!" she cried, turning and hiding her face against the plate-armor of the dragon's breast, warm as burnished bronze. "Calandor!"

"All things must be as they are, little sister," said the dragon. "All thingsss."

And the red star flickered in the west.

TWO

TENS OF THOUSANDS OF FJELTROLL awaited his command.

It was the first full assembly since the troops had been re-called, and there were seasoned veterans and raw recruits alike in their ranks. All of them had labored hard through the winter at the drills he had ordered, day in and day out, put to the test this spring afternoon.

Whatever reservations he had, Tanaros' heart swelled to behold them. So many! How long had it been since so many had assembled under his Lord's command? Since the fall of Altoria, centuries ago, when he had led a vast army across the plains of Curonan, breaking the rule of the House of Altorus forevermore in the southwest of Urulat, establishing the plains as no-man's-land. If they could not hold it, neither would they cede it to the Enemy.

Who threatened them once again.

"Hear me!" he shouted, letting his voice echo from the hillsides. "A red star has risen in the west! Our Enemy threatens war! Shall they find us ready, my brothers?"

A roar answered, and his mount danced sideways beneath him; black as pitch, a prince among stallions, frothing at the bit. The strong neck arched, hide sleek with sweat. At his side, Vorax chuckled deep in his chest, sitting comfortably in his deep-cantled saddle. Unlike Tanaros in his unadorned field armor, the Staccian wore full dress regalia, his gilded armor resplendent as a lesser sun beneath the heavy clouds.

"Steady," Tanaros murmured to his mount, shortening the reins. "Steady." A breed apart, the horses of Darkhaven. The stallion calmed, and he raised his voice again. "Let us do, then, what we do, my brothers! Marshal Hyrgolf, on my orders!" And so saying, he gave the commands in common parlance. "Center, hold! Defensive formation! Left flank, advance and sweep! Right flank, wheel! Attack the rear!"

Under a sullen sky, his orders were enacted. In the center, bannermen waved frantically, conveying his commands to the outer battalions, even as Hyrgolf roared orders, repeating them in common and in the rough tongue of the Fjel-troll, taken up and echoed by his lieutenants. The chain of command, clear-cut and effective.

The central mass of the army swung into a defensive formation, a mighty square bristling with pikes and cudgels. The left flank strung itself out in a line, spears raised. There, to the right, the third unit swung away, retreating and regrouping, forming a wedge that drove into the rear of the central square, shouting Staccians at the fore. In his own tongue, Vorax exhorted his kinsmen with good-natured cries.

Mock battle raged, with wooden swords and cork-tipped spears, and the hills resounded with the clash of armor and grunting effort, and the terrifying roars of the Fjel. Tanaros rode the length of the battle-lines, back and forth, approving of what he saw.

There, he thought, the cavalry would go when they had them, augmenting the left flank; two units of Rukhari, the swift nomads who dwelt on the eastern outskirts of the desert. Long ago, when Men had begun to disperse across the face of Urulat, the Rukhari conceived a love of wandering and disdained the notion of settling in one place. As a result, other Men viewed them with distrust.

The Rukhari were fierce and unpredictable and owed allegiance to no nation, but their culture was based on trade, and they could be persuaded to battle for a price. Vorax had promised them, and Vorax always delivered. As to what was to be done with them—that was Tanaros' concern.

That was his genius. He had done it here.

In their native terrain, the Fjelltroll were strong, cunning adversaries, relying on individual strength and their ability to navigate the steep mountainsides, luring their opponents into traps and snares, fighting in small bands knit with fierce, tribal loyalties. It had worked, once—in the Battle of Nêherinach, in the First Age of the Sundered World, when Lord Satoris had fled to the isolated north and gone to earth to heal.

There Elderran had fallen, and Elduril too, sons of Elterrion the Bold.

And the dagger Godslayer, a shard of the Souma itself, had returned to Satoris.

It was the only weapon that could kill him.

And in the Fourth Age of the Sundered World, it had nearly been lost again, after Satoris had retaken the west and made his stronghold at Curonan, the Place-of-the-Heart, when Haomane First-Born sent his Wise Counselors across the sea, and Men and Ellylon alike had raised an army, a mighty army the likes of which had never been seen before or since. On the plains of Curonan, they had overrun the Fjeltroll—outfought them, *outstrategized* them.

Well, there were other forces at play, then; Tanaros knew it, though it was long before he had lived. There was Ardrath the Counselor, mightiest of them all, and the Helm of Shadows had been his, then, until his Lordship slew him. And there was Malthus, who bore the Spear of Light, who stepped into the gap when Ardrath fell, and so very nearly prevailed. Well and so; what of it? If the Fjeltroll had held, Tanaros thought grimly, his Lordship would never had to take the field, never lost Curonan, never been forced to retreat here, to Darkhaven.

And so he had trained the Fjel, whose numbers ever increased; trained them, dividing them into battalions, units and squadrons, each according to its own strength. He taught them to fight as Men, capable of holding their own on level ground, of working in consort with one another, of shifting and *adapting* at their commander's order. Together, they had brought down Altoria and held their own on the plains of Curonan.

That was what he could do.

That was why Lord Satoris had summoned him.

It had been his idea to outfit the Fjeltroll who held the center with round bucklers, little though they had liked it. The Fjel went into battle laden like carters' horses, leather harnesses over their vast shoulders, hung about with every manner of weapon: two battle-axes crossed at the back, cudgel and mace at the waist, a spear in either hand. All of these they were quick to discard, fighting at the end with tusk and talon. Shields had gone against their nature—yet they endured longer with them, holding formations that would have broken down into milling chaos.

Now, they took pride in their discipline.

Other innovations were his, too, some of them newer than others. The Gulnagel squadron of the left flank, Fjel from the lowlands of Neherinach; they were his. Smaller and more agile than their highland brethren, adept at leaping from crag to crag, they could keep pace with a running horse on level ground. Tanaros had found a way to make use of their speed. In a real battle, they would sow chaos in an unready cavalry.

Wood rang on steel, promising bruises and broken bones to the careless. Tanaros winced to hear the latter. When a Fjeltroll went down, howling in agony, one knew the damage was serious. Still, he kept them at it.

Better sick-leave in Darkhaven than dying at the point of an Ellyl sword.

The mock battle raged on, turning grim as the Fjeltroll in the center dug in and held their positions. Inside the square, Hyrgolf stomped, waving his arms and shouting orders, strengthening his troops. Tanaros allowed himself a brief smile. It was well that the center had held. When all was said and done, the strength of Satoris' army was in its infantry.

"Enough, cousin." Vorax came alongside him, laid a heavy hand upon his forearm. Emeralds and other gems winked on the cuffs of his gilded gauntlets. In the shrouded daylight, his features were blunt-carved and unsubtle, only the shrewd eyes hinting at a mind that thought. "Reward them, and keep their loyalty."

Tanaros nodded. "Well done!" he called to them, to the tens of thousands assembled in the valley of Darkhaven, as they laid up their weapons and listened, gasping, to his approbation. "Oh, bravely done, my brothers! Your night's rest is well earned."

"And a measure of *svartblod* to anyone on his feet to claim it!" Vorax bellowed.

They gave a ragged cheer, then.

They knew, the Fjeltroll did, that it was Lord Vorax who filled their trenchers and tankards, who gave them to eat and to drink, understanding the simple hungers that drove their kind. And yet they knew, too, what General Tanaros brought to the battlefield, and what he had made of them. Neheris had Shaped them, and Neheris had given them such Gifts as were in her keeping—a love of mountains and high places, and the hidden places within them, knowledge of stone and how it was formed, how it might be shaped, how a swift river might cut through solid rock.

Tanaros made them a disciplined fighting force.

"A fine skirmish!" Vorax clapped a powerful hand on his back. Tanaros coughed at the force of it, his highstrung mount tossing its head. The Staccian only grinned, revealing strong, white teeth. Some said there was Fjeltroll blood in the oldest Staccian lines; Vorax had never denied it. "I'm off to the cellars to count kegs against unkept promises. You'll keep them hard at it in days to come, cousin?"

General Tanaros, half-breathless, fought not to wheeze. "I will," he said as the Staccian saluted him, wheeling his

deep-barreled charger toward the cellars of Darkhaven.
What they contained, only Vorax knew; as with the larders,
as with the treasury. *More,* was the Staccian's motto; *more
and more and more,* a hunger as vast as all Urulat. And only
his Lord Satoris had granted him indulgence for it.

As he had given Tanaros an army to command.

Thus the desires of two of the Three.

He stayed on the field, watching and waiting as the troops
filed past him and saluted, here and there greeting a Fjel by
name, commending his performance. Vorax's Staccian unit
passed, too, laughing and saluting with fists on hearts, eager
for their reward; *svartblod* and gold, Vorax would have
promised. He knew them, too. It mattered. He was their
general, their commander. He had commanded soldiers before, and he knew their hearts.

And they had hearts; oh, yes. Arahila Second-Born,
Arahila the Fair, had given them that Gift. She had given
her Gift to all the Shapers' Children, and she had not stinted
in the giving.

Thus do we love, Tanaros thought, watching the Fjeltroll
parade past him, bantering and jesting in their own guttural
tongue, canny veterans dressing down the embarrassed recruits, mocking their bruises and pointing out their journey-
man errors. And thus do we hate, for one begets the other.

Once, he had loved his wife and his liege-lord, and despised the Fjeltroll with all the rancor in his passionate
heart. And yet it was the betrayal of that very love that had
led him to this place, and made the Fjel his boon companions.

A pair of veterans passed, Nåltannen Fjel of the Needle
Teeth tribe, bearing along an injured youngster, his meaty
arms slung over their shoulders as he hobbled between
them. They were laughing, showing their pointed teeth, the
lad between them wincing every time his left foot made
contact with the ground. "What think you, General?" one
called in the common tongue, saluting. "Can we make a soldier of this one?"

"Mangren," Tanaros said, putting a name to the young Fjel's battered face, remembering where he had stood in the battle-lines. This one had worked hard in the drills. Dark bristles covered his hide and rose like hackles along the ridge of his spine; one of the Mørkhar Fjel, injured and glowering and proud. "You held your ground when the Gulnagel overran your position. Yes, lads, I think he'll do. Get a measure of Lord Vorax's *svartblod* in him, and you'll see."

The veterans laughed, hurrying toward their reward.

Between them, the lad's face relaxed into a grin, still-white tusks showing against his leathery lips as he hobbled toward the barracks, aided by his comrades. He had done well, then; his general was pleased.

And on it went, and on and on, until it was done.

"They did well, eh, General?" Hyrgolf rumbled, planting himself before him.

The Fjeltroll was dusty with battle, dirt engrained in the creases of his thick hide. Scratches and dents marred the dull surfaces of his practice-weapons, the blunt iron. Tanaros shifted in his saddle, his mount sidling beneath him.

"They did well," he agreed.

Once upon a time, he had been the Commander of the Guard in Altoria. Once upon a time, he had taught Men to master their instinctive fear at the sight of the hideous, bestial visages of the Fjeltroll, taught them to strike at their unprotected places. Now, he taught the Fjeltroll to carry shields, and those hideous visages were the faces of his friends and brethren.

Hyrgolf's small eyes were shrewd beneath the thick shelf of his brow-bone. "Shall I report to debrief, General?"

"No." Tanaros shook his head. "The lads fought boldly, Hyrgolf. I saw it myself. Go, then, and claim Lord Vorax's reward. We'll return to regular drills on the morrow, and work on such weaknesses as I perceived."

"Aye, General!" Hyrgolf saluted smartly and set off for the barracks.

Tanaros sat his horse and watched him go. A rolling gait, better suited for the steep crags of the highlands than the floor of this stony hollow. The Fjeltroll's broad shoulders rocked from side to side as he marched, bearing lightly the burden of his battle-harness, the badges of his rank. Such loyalty, such courage!

It shamed him, sometimes.

Above his heart, the mark of his branding burned.

Bloody rays from the setting sun sank low under the overhanging clouds, striking a ruddy wash of light across the Vale of Gorgantum. Following in the wake of his troops, Tanaros shuddered out of habit. Haomane's Fingers, they called it here, probing for Lord Satoris' pulse. Somewhere, in the depths of the mighty edifice of Darkhaven, Satoris cowered, fearing his Elder Brother's wrath that had once made a desert of his refuge.

It angered Tanaros. Flinging back his helmeted head, he watched the dim orb of the setting sun in the west; watched it, issuing his own private challenge. He was a Man, and should not fear the sun. Come, then, Haomane First-Born! Send your troops, your Children, your Ellylon with their bright eyes and sharp blades, your allies among Men! We are not afraid! We are ready for you!

The sun sank behind the low mountains, the challenge unanswered.

A red star flickered faint warning on the western horizon.

Tanaros sighed, and turned his horse toward home.

LINDANEN DALE HELD THEM LIKE a cupped hand, green and inviting. It was ringed with stalwart oaks that stood like sentries, their leaves not yet fully fledged. In the distance, Cerelinde could hear the Aven River, a sound evocative of Meronil and home. Overhead, the sky was clear and blue, Haomane's sun shining upon them like a blessing.

"What think you, my lady?" Aracus smiled at her. He sat

at ease on his mount, one of the Borderguard, his second-in-command, a half pace behind him. Sunlight made his hair blaze, copper threaded with gold. "Your kinsmen and mine once met to take counsel in this place, when Altoria ruled the west."

"Then it is fitting." Cerelinde smiled back at him. "I would fain wed in a place of such beauty."

"Duke Bornin of Seahold has pledged a company," he said. "It will be witnessed by Men and Ellylon, that all may know what we do."

A shadow passed over the greensward. Aracus shaded his eyes with one hand, gazing at the sky. It was limpid and blue, empty. Amid the oaks, a raven's hoarse call sounded once, then was silent.

"This is not without risk," Cerelinde said quietly.

"No." He glanced at her. "But it must be witnessed, Cerelinde. It must be done openly. Haomane's Prophecy will never be fulfilled unless we fire the hearts and minds of Men. Is Lord Ingolin willing to admit hundreds upon hundreds of us to Meronil?"

She shook her head. "You know he is not. Our magic has grown weak in this Sundered World. The wards would not hold. We must be able to defend our last stronghold."

"Here, then." His smile returned. "We will put our faith in mortal steel."

Cerelinde inclined her head, turning in the saddle to address Aracus' companion. "I do not doubt my lord Blaise is capable," she said.

The two Men exchanged an uneasy glance.

Cerelinde raised her brows. "Will you not be in attendance?"

Blaise Caveros bowed briefly in the saddle. "Lady, forgive me, but I will not."

She studied his face. He returned her regard steadily, his dark gaze haunted by the shadow of his lineage. Once upon a time, his distant kinsman Tanaros Caveros had served as second-in-command to a scion of the House of Altorus; served and betrayed, becoming one of the Three. The enormity of his betrayal had tainted the name of all who bore it, and all their descendants thereafter. Aracus had been the first in a thousand years to set aside the ancient mistrust the Caveros name engendered, and Blaise was willing to spend his lifetime in atonement for his ancestor's sin. His loyalty was fierce, defiant and beyond question, and Aracus would never spare him unless grave doings were afoot.

"What," she asked, "is Malthus plotting?"

"Cerelinde." Aracus leaned over to touch her arm. "Nothing is certain and much is yet unknown. I pray you, ask me no questions I cannot answer. Malthus has bidden me keep his counsel, at least until we are wed."

"Even from me?" Anger stirred in her. "Am I not the Lady of the Ellylon? Does the Wise Counselor find even me unworthy of his trust?"

"No." It was Blaise who answered, shaking his head. "Lady, I know not where I am bound, nor does Aracus. It is Malthus who asks that we trust him."

"Malthus." Cerelinde sighed. "Haomane's Weapon keeps his counsel close; too close, perhaps. Haomane's Children do not like being kept in ignorance."

"It is for a short time only, my lady. Malthus knows what he is about." Aracus gazed at her. His eyes were a stormy blue, open and earnest, filled with all the passion of his belief. "Will you not abide?"

Cerelinde thought about all they risked, and the pain both of them would suffer. Time would claim him, leaving her untouched. There would be pain enough to spare, and no need to inflict more upon them, here and now, at the beginning. For the sake of what brief happiness was theirs to claim, she was willing to set aside her pride.

"So be it," she said. "I will abide."

* * *

THE EDIFICE OF DARKHAVEN EMBRACED the whole of the
Vale of Gorgantum.

The fortress itself loomed at the center, black and gleaming, veined throughout with the marrow-fire. Its steep walls
and immaculate lines had a stark beauty, tempered here and
there with an unexpected turret, a hidden garden, an elabo-
rate gable. To the west rose the Tower of the Observatory,
where Satoris had met with the Three. In the east, there
arose the Tower of Ravens, seldom used, though to good effect.

Between and below lay the Chamber of the Font, and
Godslayer, where Lord Satoris dwelt.

Deeper still lay the Source.

Of *that,* one did not speak.

Tanaros had been there, in the Chamber of the Font. He
had beheld Godslayer, pulsing like a heart in the blue-white
flames. And he had knelt, gasping his allegiance, while the
Lord Satoris had reached into the marrow-fire and taken
Godslayer for his own, reversing the dagger, the Shard of
the Souma, and planting its hilt above Tanaros' heart, searing his mortal flesh.

What lay beneath the Font?

The Source.

One did not speak of that which might be extinguished.

And from the Source at its center, Darkhaven spiraled
outward to encompass the Vale entire, a double spiral with
the two Towers as opposite poles. At its outermost perimeter, black walls coiled up the mountainsides, here and there
punctuated by sentry posts, lit with watch-fires emerging
visible in the dusk. There, to the east, a gap where the
watchtowers flanked the Defile, their signal fires burning
low and steady. Tanaros noted them as he rode, numbering
them like a merchant counting coin. All was as it should be
in the realm of Lord Satoris.

Inside the inner walls of the sanctuary, Tanaros made his
way to the stables, dismounting with a groan. He had grown

stiff in the saddle, stiff in the service of his Lord. A young stablehand came for the stallion, shadowy and deft, eyes gleaming behind the thatch of his forelock. One of Ushahin's madlings. The lad bobbed a crooked bow, then crooned to the stallion. It arched its neck, flaring its nostrils and huffing in gentle response.

"You needn't walk him long," Tanaros said in the common tongue, laying a hand on the stallion's glossy hide and finding it cool. "He's had his ease since the skirmish."

The madling sketched him a second bow, eyes bright with knowing.

What did he hear, Tanaros wondered; what did he understand? One never knew, with the Dreamspinner's foundlings. This one understood the common tongue, of that he was sure. Most of them did. A few did not. The madling led his mount away, still crooning; the stallion bent his head as if to listen, sleek black hide rippling under the light of the emerging stars. This one, Tanaros thought, loved horses. So much he knew, and no more. Only Ushahin, who walked in their dreams, knew them all.

With stiff fingers, Tanaros unbuckled his helm and approached the postern gate.

"General Tanaros!" The pair of Fjeltroll on duty saluted smartly, slapping the butts of their spears on the marble stair. "We heard the exercise went well," one added cunningly. "Too bad the Havenguard weren't there, eh?"

Pulling off his helm and tucking it under his arm, Tanaros smiled at the ploy. "I'll match Lord Vorax's offer, lads. A measure of *svartblod* to all who stood duty, and see it sent round to the lads on the wall, a full skin to each sentry-post. Send word to the quartermaster that it's on my orders."

They cheered at that, standing aside to let him pass. In some ways, the Fjel were like children, simple and easy to please. Loyalty was given, and loyalty was rewarded. No more could be asked, no more could answer.

Indeed, Tanaros thought as he entered Darkhaven proper, what more is there? He ran his hand through his dark hair, damp with sweat from confinement in his padded helm. Once, he had given his loyalty for the asking. Given it to Roscus Altorus, blood-sworn comrade and liege-lord, he of the red-gold hair and ready grin, the extended hand.

Given it to Calista, his wife, whose throat was white like the swan's, whose doe-eyes had bulged at the end, beseeching him; *oh love, forgive me, forgive me!*

Wary madlings skittered along the hallways, scattering at his passage, reforming behind to trail in his wake. Tanaros, lost in his memories, swung his helm from its leather strap and ignored them. There was food cooking in the great kitchens of Darkhaven, its savory odor teasing the hallways. He ignored that, too. They would serve the barracks, bringing platter upon platter heaped high with mutton, steaming in grey slabs. What Lord Vorax demanded in his quarters was anyone's guess. Tanaros did not care.

Fjeltroll mate for life, Hyrgolf had told him. Always.

He thought about that, sometimes.

"Lord General, Lord General!"

A lone madling, more daring than the rest, accosted him at the doors to his quarters. Tangled hair falling over her face, peering where her work-reddened hands pushed it away to reveal a darting eye.

"Yes, Meara?" Tanaros knew her, made his voice gentle.

She cringed nonetheless, then flexed, arching the lines of her body. "Lord General," she asked with satisfaction, "will you dine this evening? There is mutton and tubers, and Lord Vorax ordered wine from Pelmar."

The madlings behind her sighed, envying her boldness.

"That would be pleasant," he said, inclining his head. "Thank you."

"Tubers!" cried one of the madlings, a hulking figure with a guileless boy's eyes in a man's homely face, hopping up and down. "Tubers!"

Meara simpered, tossing her tangled hair. "I will bring a tray, Lord General."

"Thank you, Meara," he said gravely.

In a rush they left him, following now in Meara's wake, their voices whispering from the walls. Left in peace, Tanaros entered his own quarters.

It was quiet here, in the vast rooms he inhabited. A few lamps burned low, flickering on the gleaming black walls and picking out veins of marrow-fire. Tanaros turned up the wicks until the warm illumination offset the blue-white glimmer of the marrow-fire, lending a human touch to his quarters. Thick Rukhari carpets muffled his footsteps, their intricately woven patterns muted by lamplight. One of his few concessions to luxury. He undid the buckles on his corselet, removed his armor piece by piece, awkward without assistance, hanging it upon its stand. Sitting on a low stool, Tanaros sighed, tugging off his boots, the point of his scabbard catching on the carpet as he bent, the sword's hilt digging into his side.

War. It means war.

Standing and straightening, Tanaros unbuckled his swordbelt. He held it in his hands, bowing his head. Even sheathed, he felt the blade's power, the scar over his heart aching at it. Black it was, that blade, tempered in the marrow-fire and quenched in the ichor of Satoris himself. It was the gift he had received at the pact of his branding, and it had no equal.

Tanaros Blacksword, he thought, and placed the weapon in its stand.

Without it, he felt naked.

There was a scratching at the door. Padding in stocking feet across the carpets, Tanaros opened it. The madling Meara cringed, then proffered a silver tray, other madlings peeping from behind her. Fragrant aromas seeped from beneath the covered dishes.

"Thank you, Meara," he said to her. "Put it on the table, please."

Hunched over her burden, she slunk into the room, setting the gleaming tray on the ebony dining-table with a clatter. Triumphant, she straightened, beckoning to the others. Whispering to one another, they crept into his quarters like shadows, taking with reverent hands his dusty, sweated armor, his dirty boots. In the morning these would be returned, polished and gleaming, the buckles cleaned of grime, straps fresh-oiled, boots buffed to a high gloss.

Tanaros, who had beheld this drama many, many times over, watched with pity. "No," he said gently when one, scarce more than a lad, reached for the black sword. "That I tend myself."

"I touch?" The boy threw him a hopeful glance.

"You may touch it in its scabbard, see?" The Commander General of the Army of Darkhaven went to one knee beside the madling lad, guiding his trembling hand. "There."

The boy's fingers touched the scabbard and he groaned deep in his throat, his mouth soft with ecstasy. "My Lord! My Lord's blood!"

"Yes," Tanaros said softly, as he had done many times before, with this lad and others. "It was tempered in the marrow-fire, and cooled in his blood."

The madling cradled the hand that had touched it. "His blood!" he crowed.

"His blood," Tanaros agreed, rising to his feet, knee-joints popping at the effort. Always, it was so; the young men, the youths, drawn to the blade.

"Enough!" Emboldened by the success of her mission, Meara put her hands upon her hips, surveying Tanaros' quarters, finding nothing amiss. "Will you want a bath, Lord General?"

"Later," Tanaros said. The odor of mutton roast teased the air and his stomach rumbled at it. "Later will suffice."

She gave a firm nod. "Ludo will bring it."

"Thank you, Meara." Tanaros made her a courtly half-bow. She shuddered, a rictus contorting her face, then whirled, summoning the others.

"Come! You and you, and you. Algar, pick up the Lord General's greaves. Come, quickly, and let the Lord General eat!"

Tanaros watched them go, hurrying under Meara's command, laden with their burdens. Where did Ushahin find them? The unwanted, the misbegotten, the castoffs of Urulat. Damaged at birth, many of them—slow, simple, ill-formed. Others, the world had damaged; the world, and the cruelty of Men and the Lesser Shapers. Beaten by jealous lovers, shaken by angry parents, ravaged by conquest, they were victims of life, of circumstance or simple accident, fallen and half-drowned, until wits were addled or sanity snapped like a fine thread and darkness clouded their thoughts.

No wonder Ushahin Dreamspinner loved them.

And in their dreams, he summoned them, calling them to sanctuary in Darkhaven. All through the ages, they had come; singly, in pairs, in groups. In this place, they were sacrosanct. Lord Satoris had decreed it so, long, long ago, upon the day Ushahin had sworn the allegiance of his branding. No one was to harm them, upon pain of death.

Vorax had his indulgences.

Tanaros had his army.

Ushahin had his madlings.

Mutton roast steamed as Tanaros removed the covering domes and sat to his dinner. He carved a slab of meat with his sharp knife, juices pooling on the plate. The tubers were flaky, and there were spring peas, pale green and sweet. Sane or no, the madlings of Darkhaven could cook. Tanaros chewed slowly and swallowed, feeling the day's long efforts—the long efforts of a too-long life—settle wearily into his bones.

A warm bath would be good.

"WELL DONE, COUSIN."

A voice, light and mocking. Tanaros opened his eyes to

see Ushahin in his drawing-room. The wicks had burned low, but even so the lamplight was less kind to the half-breed, showing up his mismatched features. One cheek bone, broken, sank too low; the other rode high, knotted with old pain.

"Do you jest, cousin?" Tanaros yawned, pushing himself upright in the chair. "How came you here?"

"By the door." The Dreamspinner indicated it with a nod of his sharp chin. "I jest not at all. Readiness, our Lord asked of us; readiness, you have given, Tanaros Blacksword. A pity you do not ward your own quarters so well."

"Should I not trust to the security of Darkhaven, that I myself have wrought? You make mock of me, cousin." Tanaros stifled a second yawn, blinking to clear his wits. A bath had made him drowsy, and he had dozed in his chair. "What do you seek, Dreamspinner?"

The half-breed folded his knees, dropping to sit cross-legged on Tanaros' carpet. His mismatched gaze was disconcertingly level. "Malthus is plotting something."

"Aye," Tanaros said. "A wedding."

"No." Ushahin shook his head, lank silver-gilt hair stirring. "Something *more*."

Tanaros was awake, now. "You've heard it in the dreams of Men?"

"Would that I had." The Dreamspinner propped his chin on folded hands, frowning. "A little, yes. Only a little. Malthus the Counselor keeps his counsel well. I know only that he is assembling a Company, and it has naught to do with the wedding."

"A Company?" Tanaros sat a little straighter.

"Blaise of the Borderguard is to be in it," Ushahin said softly, watching him. "Altorus' second-in-command. He has dreamed of it. He's your kinsman, is he not?"

"Aye." Tanaros' jaw clenched and he reached, unthinking, for the *rhios* in the pocket of his dressing-robe. The smooth surfaces of it calmed his mind. "Descended on my father's side. They are mounting an attack on Darkhaven? Even now?"

"No." Ushahin noted his gesture, but did not speak of it. "That's the odd thing, cousin. It's naught to do with us, or so it would seem."

"The Sorceress?" Tanaros asked.

Ushahin shrugged unevenly. "She holds one of the Soumanië, which Malthus the Counselor would like to reclaim. Beyond that, I cannot say. Those who have been chosen do not know themselves. I know only that a call has gone out to Arduan, to ask the mightiest of their archers to join the Company."

"Arduan," Tanaros said slowly. Relinquishing the *rhios*, he ran a hand through his hair, still damp from his bath. The Archers of Arduan, which lay along the northern fringes of the Delta, were renowned for their skill with the bow. "Does his Lordship know?"

"Yes." Ushahin's eyes glittered in the lamplight. "He knows."

The taste of fear was back in Tanaros' mouth, the triumph of the day's exercise forgotten. "Does he think it has to do with—"

"The lost weapon of the Prophecy?" the half-breed asked bluntly. "How not?"

Both were silent, at that.

Dergail's Soumanië had risen in the west.

Dergail the Counselor had been one of three, once; three that Haomane First-Born had sent against Satoris in the Fourth Age of the Sundered World. And he had been armed, as they all had. Armed with the Soumanië, polished chips of the Souma with the force to Shape the world itself—and armed also with weapons of Haomane's devising. One, they knew well; the Helm of Shadows, that Ardrath the Counselor had borne, which had fallen into Lord Satoris' grasp, and been *changed*. One other, they knew and feared; the Spear of Light, that Malthus had hidden.

But the last was the Arrow of Fire, that had vanished when Dergail was defeated and flung himself into the sea, and no one knew where it was.

"Ravens bore it away," Tanaros said at length. "Do they know?"

Ushahin shook his head again. "They are as they are, cousin," he said; gently, for him. "Brief lives, measured against ours; a dark flash of feathers in the sun. They do not know. Nor do the Were, who remember. Ravens bore it east, but it did not reach the fastholds of Pelmar."

When it came to the Were, Ushahin alone among Men—or Ellylon—would know. Oronin's Children had raised him, when no one else would. Tanaros considered. "Then Malthus knows," he said.

"Malthus *suspects,*" Ushahin corrected him. "And plots accordingly."

Tanaros spread his hands. "As it may be. I command troops, cousin. What would you have me do?"

"Do?" The half-breed grinned, his mood as mercurial as one of his madlings. "Why, cousin, do as you do! I have come to tell you what I know, and that I have done. You spoke, also, of ravens."

"Ravens." Tanaros smiled. "Is it time?"

"Time, and more." Ushahin uncoiled from the carpet, straightening as he rose. "There is a wedding afoot, after all, and the ravens have come home to roost, with their eyes filled with visions. Your friend is among them. Will you come with me to the rookery on the morrow, ere his Lordship summons them?"

"I will," Tanaros said, "gladly."

THREE

❖

A LIGHT MIST WREATHED THE beech wood, and their steps were soundless on the mast of fallen leaves, soft and damp after winter. New growth was greening on the trees, forming a canopy overhead.

It was a deeper green than the beeches Tanaros had known as a boy, the leaves broader, fanning to capture and hold the cloud-filtered sunlight. The trunks of the trees were gnarled in a way they weren't elsewhere, twisted around ragged boles as they grew, like spear-gutted warriors straining to stand upright.

They were old and strong, though, and their roots were deep.

Blight, the Ellylon said; Satoris the Sunderer blighted the land, the ichor of his unhealing wound seeping like poison into the earth, tainting it so no wholesome thing could grow.

Tanaros had believed it, once. No longer. Wounded, yes. The Vale of Gorgantum had endured the blow of the Shaper's wound, as Lord Satoris himself endured it. Deprived of sunlight, it suffered, as Lord Satoris suffered, driven to earth by Haomane's wrath. Yet, like the Shaper, it survived; adapted, and survived.

And who was to say there was no beauty in it?

Ahead, a rustling filled the wood. There was no path, but Ushahin Dreamspinner led the way, at home in the woods. From behind, he looked hale, his spine straight and upright, his step sure. His gilt-pale hair shone under the canopy. One might take him, Tanaros thought, for a young Ellyl poet, wandering the wood.

Not from the front, though. No one ever made that mistake.

There, the first nest, a ragged construction wedged in the branches high overhead. Others, there and there, everywhere around them as they entered the rookery proper, and the air came alive with the sound of ravens. Ushahin stopped and gazed around him, a smile on his ruined face.

Ravens hopped and sidled along the branches, preening glossy black feathers. Ravens defended their nests, quarreled over bits of twig. Ravens flew from tree to tree, on wings like airborne shadows.

"*Kaugh!*"

The sound was so close behind him that Tanaros startled. "Fetch!"

There, on a low branch, a raven; *his* raven. The wounded fledgling he had found half-frozen in his Lord's garden six years gone by, grown large as a hawk, with the same disheveled tuft of feathers poking from his head. The raven cocked its head to regard him with one round shiny eye, then the other. Satisfied, it wiped its sharp, sturdy beak on the branch.

Tanaros laughed. "Will he come to me, do you think?"

Ushahin gave his uneven shrug. "Try it and see."

The ravens were the Dreamspinner's charges, a gift not of Lord Satoris, but of the Were who had reared him. Elsewhere, they were territorial. It was only here, in Darkhaven, that they gathered in a flock—and only when summoned, for Ushahin Dreamspinner had made them the eyes and ears of Lord Satoris, and sent them throughout the land.

This one, though, Tanaros had tended.

"Fetch," he said, holding out his forearm. "Come."

The raven muttered in its throat and eyed him, shifting from foot to foot. Tanaros waited. When he was on the verge of conceding, the raven launched himself smoothly into the air, broad wings outspread as he glided to land on

Tanaros' padded arm, an unexpectedly heavy weight. Bobbing up and down, he made a deep, chuckling sound.

"Oh, Fetch." At close range, the bird's feathers shone a rich blue-black, miniscule barbs interlocking, layered in a ruff at his neck. Tanaros smoothed them with the tip of one finger, absurdly glad to see him. "How are you, old friend?"

Fetch made his chucking sound, wiped his beak on Tanaros' arm, then uttered a single low "*Kaugh!*" and bobbed expectantly. Tanaros reached into a pouch at his belt and drew forth a gobbet of meat, fed it to the raven, followed by others. In the trees, the others watched and muttered, one raising its voice in a raucous scolding.

"He's very fond of you." Ushahin sounded amused.

Tanaros smiled, remembering the winter he'd kept the fledgling in his quarters. A foul mess he'd made, too, and he was still finding things the raven had stolen and hidden. "Do you disapprove?"

The half-breed shrugged. "The Were hunt with ravens, and ravens hunt with the Were. It is the way of Men, to make tame what is wild. If you had sought to cage him, I would have disapproved."

"I wouldn't." Finding no more meat forthcoming, the raven took his leave, strong talons pricking through the padded leather as he launched himself from Tanaros' arm, landing on a nearby branch and preening under the envious eyes of his fellows, the tuft of feathers atop his head bobbing in a taunt. Tanaros watched his mischief with fond pleasure. "Fetch is his own creature."

"It's well that you understand it. The Were sent them, but the ravens serve Lord Satoris of their own choosing." Ushahin rubbed his thin arms against the morning's chill. "You've a need in you to love, cousin. A pity it's confined to birds and Fjel."

"Love." Anger stirred in Tanaros' heart. "What would you know of love, Dreamspinner?"

"Peace, cousin." Ushahin raised his twisted, broken

hands. "I do not say it in despite. The forge of war is upon us, and all our mettle will be tested. Once upon a time, you loved a son of Altorus. And," he added, "once upon a time, you loved a woman."

Tanaros laughed, a sound as harsh as a raven's call. "Altoria lies in ruin because of that love, *cousin,* and the sons of Altorus are reduced to the Borderguard of Curonan. Do you forget?"

"No," Ushahin said simply. "I remember. But it was many years ago, and hatred burned in you like the marrow-fire, then. Now, there is yearning."

The calm, mismatched regard was too much to bear, undermining his anger. What was his suffering, measured against the half-breed's? Ushahin Dreamspinner had been unwanted even before his birth. It was an ill-gotten notion that had sent an embassy of the Ellylon of the Rivenlost to Pelmar in the Sixth Age of the Sundered World; an ill-gotten impulse that had moved a young Pelmaran lordling to lust.

A son of Men had assaulted a daughter of the Ellylon.

And Ushahin was the fruit of that bitter union, which had dealt the Prophecy a dire blow. Ushahin the Unwanted, whose birth ruined his mother—though he'd had no name, then, and hers was hidden from history. In their grief, the Ellylon laid a charge upon the family of the nameless babe's father, bidding them raise him as their own.

Instead, they despised him, for his existence was their shame.

Even in the Dreamspinner's story, Tanaros thought, he could not escape the sons of Altorus, for one had been present. Prince Faranol, Faranol Altorus, who had accompanied the Ellylon embassy on behalf of Altoria. A mighty hunter, that one, bold in the chase. He'd ridden out in a Pelmaran hunting-party, hunting the Were who savaged the northernmost holdings of Men. Oronin's Children were deadly predators, a race unto themselves, as much akin to wolves as Men. And if they hadn't found the Grey Dam herself, they'd found her den—her den, her cubs and her mate.

Prince Faranol had slain the Grey Dam's mate himself, holding him on the end of a spear as he raged forward, dying, the froth on his muzzle flecked with blood. They still told the story in Altoria, when Tanaros was a boy.

A mighty battle, they said.

Was it a mighty battle, he wondered, when Faranol slew the cubs? In Pelmar they had lauded him for it, even as they had turned their backs upon the family of Ushahin's father. Still, the damage was done, and no treaty reached; the Ellylon departed in sorrow and anger, Faranol Altorus' deeds went unrewarded, and in the farthest reaches of Pelmar, the Sorceress of the East remained unchallenged.

Such was the outcome of that embassy.

And seven years later, when a nameless half-breed boy, the shame of his family, starveling and ragged, was set upon and beaten in the marketplace of the capital city, who remarked it? When he staggered into the woods to die, the bones of his face shattered, his limbs crooked, his fingers broken and crippled, who remarked it?

Only the Grey Dam of the Were, still grieving for her slain mate, for her lost cubs, who claimed the misbegotten one for her own and named him in her tongue: Ushahin. And she reared him, and taught him the way of the Were, until Lord Satoris summoned him, and made of his skills a deadly weapon.

Tanaros watched the ravens, *his* raven. "Do you never yearn, cousin?"

"I yearn." The half-breed's voice was dry, colorless. "I yearn for peace, and a cessation to striving. For a world where the Were are free to hunt, as Oronin Last-Born made them, free of the encroachments of Men, cousin. I yearn for a world where ones such as I are left to endure as best we might, where no one will strike out against us in fear. Do you blame me for it?"

"No." Tanaros shook his head. "I do not."

For a moment, Ushahin's face was vulnerable, raw with ancient pain. "Only Satoris has ever offered that hope. He has made it precious to me, cousin; this place, this sanctuary. Do you understand why I fear?"

"I understand," Tanaros said, frowning. "Do you think I will fail his trust?"

"I do not say that," the half-breed replied, hesitating.

Tanaros watched the raven Fetch, sidling cunningly along the low branch, bobbing his head at a likely female, keeping one eye cocked lest he, Tanaros, produce further gobbets of meat from his pouch. "Ravens mate for life, do they not, cousin?"

"Yes." Ushahin's eyes were wary.

"Like the Fjel." Tanaros turned to face the Dreamspinner, squaring his shoulders. "You need not doubt me, cousin. I have given my loyalty to his Lordship; like the Fjeltroll, like the ravens, like the Were." Beneath the scar of his branding, his heart expanded, the sturdy beating that had carried him through centuries continuing, onward and onward. "It is the only love that has never faltered."

Love, yes.

He dared to use that word.

"You understand that what you see this night may pain you?" Ushahin asked gently. "It involves your kindred, and the sons of Altorus."

"I understand." Tanaros inclined his head. "And you, cousin? You understand that we are speaking of a union between Men and Ellylon?"

Ushahin grimaced, baring his even teeth. "I understand, cousin. All too well."

"Then we are in accord," Tanaros said.

The raven Fetch chuckled deep in his throat, shifting from foot to foot.

* * *

THREE WERE EMERGED FROM THE dense forest at the base of Beshtanag Mountain, drifting out of the foliage like smoke. They rose from four legs to stand upon two, lean and rangy. Oronin's Children, Shaped by the Glad Hunter himself. They were vaguely Man-shaped, with keen muzzles and amber eyes, their bodies covered in thick pelts of fur.

One among them stood a pace ahead of the others. He addressed Lilias in the Pelmaran tongue, a thick inflection shading his words. "Sorceress, I am the ambassador Kurush. On behalf of the Grey Dam Sorash, we answer your summons."

"My thanks, Kurush." Lilias inclined her head, aware of the weight of the Soumanië on her brow. Her Ward Commander, Gergon, and his men flanked her uneasily, hands upon weapons, watching the Were. In the unseen distance, somewhere atop the mountain, Calandor coiled in his cavern and watched, amusement in his green-slitted eyes. Lilias did not fear the Were. "I seek to affirm our pact."

Kurush's jaws parted in a lupine grin, revealing his sharp white teeth. "You have seen the red star."

"I have," she said.

"It is Haomane's doing," he said, and his Brethren growled low in their throats.

"Perhaps," she said carefully. "It betokens trouble for those who do not abide by the Lord-of-Thought's will."

Kurush nodded toward the mountain with his muzzle. "Is that the wisdom of dragons?"

"It is," Lilias said.

Turning to his Brethren, Kurush spoke in his own tongue, the harsh sounds falling strange on human ears. Lilias waited patiently. She did not take the alliance of the Were for granted. Once, the east had been theirs; until Men had come, claiming land, driving them from their hunting grounds. In the Fourth Age of the Sundered World, the Were had given their allegiance to Satoris Banewreaker, who held the whole of the west. Haomane's Counselors had arrived from over the sea, bearing the three Soumanië and the weapons of Torath, the dwelling-place of the Six Shapers: the Helm of Shadows, the Spear of Light, the Arrow of Fire.

There had been war, then, war as never before. Among the races of Lesser Shapers, only the Dwarfs, Yrinna's Children, had taken no part in it, taking instead a vow of peace.

While Men, Ellylon and Fjel fought on the plains of Curonan, the Were had lain in wait, on the westernmost shore of Urulat—the last place they would be expected. When the ships of Dergail the Counselor and Cerion the Navigator made landfall, thinking to assail Satoris from the rear, the full force of the Were met them and prevailed. Dergail flung himself into the sea, and his Soumanië and the Arrow of Fire were lost. Cerion the Navigator turned his ships and fled, vanishing into the mists of Ellylon legend.

And yet it was no victory.

If the Were had remained in the west, perhaps. Though Satoris had been wounded and forced to take refuge in the Vale of Gorgantum, there he was unassailable. But no, Oronin's Children returned east to the forests of their homeland, flowing like a grey tide, and the wrath of Men was against them, for Haomane's Counselors and the army of Men and Ellylon they led had failed, too. And Men, always, increased in number, growing cunning as they learned to hunt the hunters, waiting until spring to stalk Were-cubs in their dens, while their dams and sires foraged.

Not in Beshtanag. Many centuries ago, Lilias had made a pact with the Grey Dam, the ruler of the Were. Oronin's Children hunted freely in the forests of Beshtanag. In return, they held its outer borders secure.

Concluding his discussion with his Brethren, the ambassador Kurush dropped into a crouch. Gergon ordered his wardsmen a protective step closer to Lilias, and the two Brethren surged forward a pace.

"Hold, Gergon." Lilias raised her hand, amused. It had been more than a mortal lifetime since she had cause to summon the Were. Betimes, she forgot how short-lived her Ward Commanders were. "The ambassador Kurush does but speak to the Grey Dam."

With a dubious glance, Gergon shrugged. "As my lady orders."

Kurush crouched, lowering his head. His taloned hands dug into the forest loam, the lean blades of his shoulders protruding like grey-furred wings. His eyes rolled back into his head, showing only the whites, as he communed with the Grey Dam.

Oronin's Children possessed strange magics.

A gratifyingly short time passed before Kurush relaxed and stood. With another sharp grin he extended his hand. "Yea," he said. "The Grey Dam Sorash accedes."

Lilias clasped his hairy hand. His pads were rough against her palm and his claws scratched lightly against the back of her hand. She recited the ritual words of their alliance. "Thy enemies shall be mine, and my enemies shall be thine."

"My enemies shall be thine, and thy enemies shall be mine," Kurush echoed.

Dipping his muzzle to her, the Were ambassador turned, his Brethren following. In the space of a few heartbeats, they had melted back into the forest from which they had come. The pact had been affirmed. Beshtanag's defenses were secure.

From his distant eyrie, Calandor's thoughts brushed hers, tinged with warm approval.

Well done, Lilias.

IT WAS THE DARK OF the moon, and dark in the Tower of Ravens.

There was no view, here, though the windows stood open

onto the night. The rooftops of Darkhaven fell away beneath them, illuminated faintly by starlight.

All of them were there, all of the Three.

And in the center of them stood the Shaper.

"They are ready, Dreamspinner?" he asked.

Ushahin bowed low and sincere, starlight glimmering on his moon-pale hair, "They are, my Lord."

"Come," Lord Satoris whispered, his voice carrying on the night breeze "Come!" And other words he added, uttered in the tongue of the Shapers, tolling and resonant, measured syllables that Shaped possibilities yet unformed.

Beating wings filled the air.

Through every window they came, filling the tower chamber; ravens, the ravens of Darkhaven, come all at once. They came, and they flew, round and around. Silent and unnatural, swirling in a glossy-black current around the tower walls—so close, wings overlapping like layered feathers, jet-bright eyes gleaming round and beady. Around and around they went, raising a wind that tugged at Vorax's ruddy beard, making the Staccian shudder involuntarily.

Still, they held their positions, each of the Three.

Where are you, Tanaros wondered, *which* are you? To no avail he sought to pick a raven, his raven, from the dark, swirling tide that enveloped the tower walls, looking to find a mischievous eye, an errant tuft of pin-feathers, from among them. Darkness upon darkness; as well pick out a droplet of water in a rushing torrent.

"The Ravensmirror is made," Ushahin announced in a flat tone.

In the churning air, a scent like blood, sweet and fecund.

Satoris the Shaper spread his hands, drawing on ancient magic—the veins of the marrow-fire, running deep within the earth; the throbbing heart of Godslayer, that Shard of the Souma that burned and was not consumed.

"*Show!*"

The command hung in the air with its own shimmering

darkness. Slowly, slowly, images coalesced, moving. Sight made visible. Only fragments, at first—the tilting sky, a swatch of earth, an upturned face, a scrabbling movement in the leaf-mold. A mouse's beady eye, twitching whiskers. A drawn bow, arrow-shot and an explosion of feathers, a chiding squawk.

Such were the concerns of ravens.

Then; a face, upturned in a glade. A thread for Lord Satoris to tease, drawing it out. What glade, where? Ravens knew, ravens kept their distance from the greensward. One flew high overhead, circling; their perspective diminished with lurching swiftness to an aerial view. There. Where? A greensward, ringed about with oak, a river forking to the north. And in it was a company of Ellylon.

There was no mistaking them for aught else, Haomane's Children. Tall and fair, cloaked in grace. It was in their Shaping, wrought into their bones, in their clear brows where Haomane's blessing shone like a kiss. It was in the shining fall of their hair, in the touch of their feet upon the earth. If their speech had been audible, it would have been in the tenor of their voices.

"What is this place?" Ushahin's words were strained, a taut expression on his ravaged face. Always it was so. More than the children of Men who had shunned him, he despised the Ellylon who had abandoned him.

"It is called Lindanen Dale," said the Shaper, who had walked the earth before it was Sundered. "Southward, it lies."

"I know it, my Lord," Tanaros said. "It lies below the fork of the Aven River. Betimes the Rivenlost of Meronil would meet with the sons of Altorus, when they ruled in the west. Or so my father claimed."

"But what are they *doing?*" Vorax mused.

In the shifting visions, Ellyl craftsmen walked the greensward, measuring, gauging the coming spring. Banners were planted, marking the four corners of the Dale;

pennants of white silk, lifted on the breeze, showing the device of Elterrion the Bold, a gold crown above the ruby gem of the Souma, as it had been when it was whole. The Ravensmirror churned and circled, showing what had transpired.

A Man came riding.

The weak ounlight of early spring glinted on his hair, red-gold. His eyes were wide-set and demanding, his hands steady on the reins as he guided his solid dun mount. Tanaros felt weak, beholding him.

Aracus Altorus.

It was him, of course. There was no denying it, no denying the kingship passed down generation upon generation, though the kingdom itself was lost. It did not matter that he wore no crown, that his cloak was dun-grey, designed to blend with the plains of Curonan. What he was, he was. He looked like Roscus. And he looked like Calista, too—Tanaros' wife, so long ago. The set of the eyes, last seen believing. How not? He was of their blood.

And at his side, another, dark-haired and quiet, with scarred knuckles. Unlike his lord, he was watchful as he rode, stern gaze surveying the wood as they emerged into the glade. Ravens took wing, the perspective shifting and blurring as they withdrew, resolving at a greater distance.

Once, Tanaros had ridden just so, at the right hand of his lord.

Strange, that his memory of Roscus' face as he died was so vague. Surprised, he thought. Yes, that was it. Roscus Altorus had looked surprised, as he raised his hand to the sword-hilt protruding from his belly. There had been no time for aught else.

In the churning Ravensmirror, in Lindanen Dale, Aracus Altorus halted, his second-in-command beside him. Behind them, a small company of Borderguard sat their mounts, silent and waiting in their dun-grey cloaks.

The Ellyl lord in command met him, bowing low, a ges-

ture of grace and courtesy. Aracus nodded his head, accepting it as his due. Who is to say what the Ellyl thought?
There was old sorrow in his eyes, and grave acceptance. He
spoke to the Altorian king-in-exile, his mouth moving
soundlessly in the Ravensmirror, one arm making a sweeping gesture, taking in the glade. There and there, he was
saying, and pointed to the river.

Such a contrast between them! Tanaros marveled at it.
Next to the ageless courtesy of the Ellyl lord, Aracus Altorus appeared coarse and abrupt, rough-hewn, driven by
the brevity of his lifespan. Small wonder Cerelinde Elterrion's granddaughter had refused this union generation after generation. And yet . . . and yet. In that very roughness
lay vitality, the leaping of red blood in the vein, the leaping
of desire in the loins, the quickening of the flesh.

Satoris' Gift, when he had one.

It was the one Gift the Ellylon were denied, for Haomane
First-Born had refused it on his Children's behalf, who
were Shaped before time came into being and were free of
its chains. Only the Lord-of-Thought knew the mind of
Uru-Alat. The slippery promptings of desire, the turgid
need to seize, to spend, to take and be taken, to generate life
in the throes of an ecstasy like unto dying—this was not for
the Ellylon, who endured untouched by time, ageless and
changeless as the Lord-of-Thought himself.

But it was for Men.

And because of it, Men had inherited the Sundered
World, while the Ellylon dwindled. Unprompted by the
goads of desire and death, the cycle of their fertility was as
slow and vast as the ages. Men, thinking Men, outpaced
them, living and dying, generation upon generation, spreading their seed across the face of Urulat, fulfilling Haomane's fears.

"A wedding!" Vorax exclaimed, pointing at the Ravensmirror. "See, my Lord. The Ellyl speaks of tents, here and
here. Fresh water from thence, and supplies ferried upriver,
a landing established *there*. From the west, the Rivenlost

will come, and Cerelinde among them. They plan to plight their troth here in Lindanen Dale."

Lord Satoris smiled.

Above, the stars shuddered.

"I think," he said, "that this will not come to pass."

And other things were shown in the Ravensmirror.

The ravens of Darkhaven had flown the length and breadth of Urulat, save only the vast inner depths of the Unknown, where there was no water to sustain life. But to the south they had flown, and to the east and north. And every place they had seen, it was the same.

Armies were gathering.

In the south, the Duke of Seahold increased his troops, fortifying his borders. Along the curve of Harrington Inlet, where gulls cried above the sea, the Free Fishers laid aside their nets and sharpened their long knives. The knights of Vedasia rode in stately parties along the orchard roads and, here and there, Dwarfs appeared along the roadside, giving silent greeting as they passed. In Arduan, men and women gathered in knots to speak in the marketplace, full quivers slung over their shoulders. The streets of Pelmar City were filled with soldiers, and long trains of them wound through the woods. Along the eastern verge of the desert, the Rukhari whetted their curving swords. To the north, the stone fortresses of Staccia were shut and warded.

"What do they dream, Dreamspinner?"

"War, my Lord," Ushahin said briefly. "They dream of war. They dream of a red star arisen in the west, and the rumor of a wedding-to-come. They dream, in fear, of the rumor of Fjeltroll moving in the mountains, in such numbers as none have seen in living memory."

"Do they dream of the Arrow of Fire?"

Ushahin paused, then shook his head. "In Arduan, they do. All Arduans dream of Oronin's Bow and the Arrow of Fire. But they do not know where it is."

Satoris Third-Born, whom the Ellylon named Banewreaker and Men called Sunderer, watched the swirling images, motionless as a mountain. "Haomane," he murmured, then again, "Haomane!" He sighed, gathering himself. "They will not strike, not yet. Not unless this wedding occurs, and fills them with the courage of my Elder Brother's Prophecy, such as they understand it." A glare lit his eyes. "Then they will bring war to my doorstep."

"Not Staccia, my Lord," Vorax promised. "They guard their own, but they have pledged their loyalty on gold, and sent a company in earnest token. As long as we may ward the tunnels, our lines of supply shall remain open. And the desert Rukhari may be bought for swift horses, for they love fine steeds above all else, and despise the Pelmarans."

"Loyal Vorax," the Shaper said gently. "Your heart is as vast as your appetite. What you have done, I know well, and I am grateful for it. It the unknown that I fear."

When the unknown is made known . . .

Tanaros shivered, brushed by the feather-touch of the Prophecy.

"My Lord." Ushahin pointed at the Ravensmirror. "There is more."

Around and around, the dark maelstrom whirled, fleeting visions forming against the black gloss of feathers, the gleam of round eyes pricking like stars. Around and around, inevitable as time, link upon link in the Chain of Being, circling like the ages.

When the companies parted in Lindanen Dale, Blaise Caveros of the Borderguard—Aracus' second-in-command—went with the Ellylon. He spoke at length with a lieutenant in his company, a young man who saluted him firmly, his jaw set. Aracus Altorus gripped his wrists, gazing into his eyes. And they parted. Blaise rode with the Rivenlost to Meronil, and did not look back, bound to a greater mission.

Tanaros watched him hungrily.

What need could be so great that it would part the second-in-command from his sworn lord? None, in his lifetime, in his mortal lifetime. And yet it was so. Blaise

Caveros, who was his own kinsman many times removed, left his lord without glancing back, his grey-cloaked back upright.

"What are you up to, Malthus?" Lord Satoris whispered.

To that, there was no answer. The Ravensmirror swirled onward, giving only taunting glimpses. A contest, and bow-strings thrumming. Fletched arrows, a silent thud. Feathers, scattering. A lone Arduan, setting forth on a journey, coiled braids hidden beneath a leather cap.

On the verges of his journey—hers, as it transpired—there was the Unknown Desert, glimpses assayed by fearful ravens, wary of the lack of water.

Malthus the Counselor keeps his counsel well . . .

"Enough!" The Shaper's fists clenched, and the Ravens-mirror dispersed, trembling, breaking into a thousand bits of darkness. Roosts were found, bescaled and taloned bird-feet scrambling for perches, bright eyes winking as the Shaper paced, the Tower trembling beneath his footfalls. A single raven, with a tuft of feathers atop his head, croaked a tremulous query. In the air hung the copper-sweet smell of blood.

"It shall not be," Lord Satoris said. "Though I have left my Elder Brother in peace, still he pursues me, age upon age. I grow weary of his enmity. If it is war Haomane wishes, my Three, I shall oblige him. And I shall not wait for him to bring it to my doorstep." He turned to Tanaros. His gaze burned, ruddy coals in the night. A line of seeping ichor glistened on his inner thigh, reeking of blood, only stronger. "My General, my rouser of Men. Are you fit to travel the Marasoumië?"

Tanaros bowed.

Tanaros could not do aught else.

"I am yours to command, my Lord," he said, even as a single raven dispatched itself from the horde, settling on his shoulder. He stroked its ruffled feathers with a fingertip. "Only tell me what you wish."

Satoris did.

FOUR

❖

LILIAS KNEW.

It came as a stirring, a tensing of her brow, as if the circlet she ever wore had grown too tight. Awareness tickled the base of her skull, and the Soumanië on her brow warmed against her skin, rendering her feverish.

She paced the halls of her fasthold of Beshtanag, restless and uneasy, curt with her body-servants, her pretty ones, when they sought to soothe her. Calandor had shown her long ago how to Shape the hearts and minds of those who served her, and they were her one indulgence. Some of them sulked, but not all. She had always tried to choose them wisely. Little Sarika wept, curling into a ball, damp hair clinging to her tear-stained cheeks. Pietre dogged her steps, squaring his shoulders in a manful fashion until she snapped at him, too. It wasn't their fault, and she felt guilty at it.

"Calandor," she whispered, *reaching*. "Oh, Calandor!"

I am here.

At the touch of the dragon's thoughts, the Sorceress of the East relaxed, obliquely reassured. "One is coming, traveling the Marasoumië."

Yes, little sister. One of the Branded.

Lilias grasped the railing of the balustrade and stared down the mountainside.

It was secure, of course. The grey crags, the pine mantle spread like a dark green apron below. Gergon and his wardsmen held it for her and the Were defended its borders, but the mountain was hers, hers and Calandor's. With the power of the Soumanië, they had made it so. No creature moved upon it, not squirrel nor bat, wolf nor Were, and least of all Man, but that Calandor knew it. And what the dragon knew, the sorceress knew.

So it had been, for a long, long time.

"I shall have to meet him, won't I?" she asked aloud. "Which one is it?"

The Soldier.

Lilias grimaced. It would have been easier, in a way, had it been one of the others—the Dreamer, or the Glutton.

The Dreamer, she understood. When all was said and done, they were both Pelmaran. The Were had raised him, and although their ways were strange, she understood them better than anyone else of mortal descent.

And as for the Glutton, his wants were simple. Gold, mayhap; a portion of the fabled dragon's hoard. Or flesh, carnal desire. Lilias touched the curves of her body, the ample, swelling flesh at her bodice. That too, she understood.

What the Soldier asked would be harder.

The summons at the base of her skull shrilled louder, insistent. Lilias hurried, taking a seldom-used key from the ring at her waist and unlocking the door that led to the caverns and the tunnels below. The ancient steps were rough-hewn, carved into the living rock. She held her skirts, descending swiftly. If not for Calandor's wisdom, she would never have known such things existed.

Now, little sister. He comes now.

Down, and down and down! All beneath the surface of Urulat, the tunnels interlaced, carved out in ages past, before the world was Sundered. Calandor knew them, for it was his brethren who had carved them, long ago, when there were dragons in the earth. And along those passages lay the Ways of the Marasoumië, the passages of the Souma, along which thought traveled, quick as a pulse. Though they were Sundered from Torath and the Souma itself, still they endured; dangerous, yet passable to those who remembered them and dared.

Dragons remembered, as did the Shaper. No others

would dare the Ways, save perhaps Malthus the Counselor, who wielded a Soumanië of his own.

Lilias reached the bottom, hurried along the passageway.

Ahead lay the node-point, and blood-red light beat like a heart, bathing the rocky walls. A vaulted chamber, and a tunnel stretching away westward into darkness. Lines of light, the forgotten Ways, pulsed along it, bundled fibers laid in an intricate network, all linked back to the severed bond of the Souma.

The Marasoumië of Uru-Alat, whom Men had once called the World God. Though Uru-Alat had died to give birth to the world, remnants of his power yet existed. The Marasoumië was one.

A figure was coming, dark and blurred, moving at a walking pace with inhuman speed, each motion fanning in her vision, broken into a thousand component parts. Lilias pressed her back to the stony walls of the cavern, reaching desperately for Calandor.

All is well.

The node-light flared, red and momentarily blinding. Lilias cried out as a figure stumbled into the chamber, his body stunned by the transition to a mortal pace.

A Man, only a Man.

Lilias the Sorceress pulled herself away from the cavern wall and stood upright to acknowledge him, summoning her dignity and the might of the Soumanië she wore. "Greetings, Kingslayer."

He flinched at the title, straightening as though his back pained him, pushing dark hair back from his brow. "Greetings, Sorceress."

A quiet voice, low and husky with exhaustion. He spoke Pelmaran well, with only a trace of a southerner's accent. It was not what Lilias had expected; and yet it was. Calandor had known as much. He was tall, but not nearly as tall as the stories made him, when he had ridden to battle on the plains of Curonan, wearing the Helm of Shadows. A Man, nothing more, nothing less.

"Your Lord has sent you."

"Yes." The Soldier bowed, carefully. "He would beg a favor, my lady. You know that Dergail's Soumanië has risen in the west?"

"I know it." A mad laugh rose in Lilias' throat; she stifled it. It tasted of despair. "I have known it these many weeks, Tanaros Blacksword."

His eyes were weary. "Shall we speak, then?"

Lilias inclined her head. "Follow me."

She was aware of him on the stair behind her, his steps echoing hers, following at a respectful distance. The skin of her back crawled and her throat itched, when she remembered how his wife had died.

He offered no threat.

Even so.

"My lady!" Her Ward Commander, Gergon, was waiting at the top of the stair. He took a step forward, frowning. "You should have sent for—" Her stalwart, grizzled commander forgot what he was saying, staring in hushed awe. "General Tanaros!"

"Commander." The Soldier bowed courteously.

Gergon's gaze slid to the hilt of the black sword, hanging inconspicuously at Tanaros' side. He blinked, his mouth working, no words emerging. Behind him, a pair of junior warders clad in the colors of Beshtanag, forest-green and bronze, jostled one another and craned to see over their commander's shoulder.

Always the blades, with Men.

The dragon's voice sounded amused, by which token Lilias knew there to be no danger. She sighed inwardly, and exerted the power of the Soumanië. "Commander Gergon, I thank you for your concern. I will summon you if there is need."

Gergon stood aside, then, having no choice; his junior warders scrambled to fall in beside him. Lilias swept past them, leading Tanaros Blacksword to her private chambers. He followed her without comment, more patient than she would have guessed. His hands hung loose at his sides, and she tried not to think what they had done.

I have killed, little sister. I have eaten Men whole.

"None that you loved," Lilias said aloud.

Tanaros looked quizzically at her. "Sorceress?"

The dragon chuckled. *What is love?*

Lilias shook her head. "It is nothing," she said to Tanaros.

Calandor's question was too vast to answer, so she ignored it, escorting Tanaros to her drawing-room. A woman's room; she had chosen it deliberately. A warm fire burned in the grate, chasing away the spring chill. Soft rose-colored cushions adorned the low couches, and tapestries hung on the walls, illustrating scenes from Pelmar's past. There was a rack of scrolls along one wall, and shelves with curiosities from Calandor's hoard. In one corner stood a spinning-wheel, dusty for lack of use. The lamps were hooded with amber silk, casting a warm glow. Lilias sank into the cushions, watching Tanaros, lamplight glancing off the lacquered black of his armor.

He was uneasy in the room.

"Sit," she said, indicating a chair. "You must be in need of refreshment, after your journey."

He sat, clearing his throat. "The Ways of the Marasoumië are not easy."

Lilias pulled a bellcord of bronze cabled silk, soft to the touch. Pietre was there almost before she released it, half-belligerent in his eagerness to serve.

"My lady?" He bowed low.

"Pietre." She touched his luxuriant brown hair, caught in a band at the nape of his neck. The silver collar about his neck gleamed. He shivered with pleasure at her touch, and she repressed a smile. "Bring us wine and water, a terrine with bread and cheese, and some of the Vedasian olives."

"My lady." He shivered again before departing.

Tanaros Blacksword watched, expressionless.

"You do not approve?" Lilias raised an eyebrow.

He released his breath in a humorless laugh, pushing at his dark hair. "Approve? I neither approve nor disapprove. It is the way of Men, and the daughters of Men, to make tame what is wild."

Lilias shrugged. "I Shape only those whose natures it is to serve, as mine was not. Some are more willing than others. I try to choose wisely. Pietre has pride in his labors."

"And your army?" He leaned forward, hands on his knees, greaves creaking.

"You have seen my Ward Commander, Kingslayer." Lilias eyed him. "Gergon learned his task at his father's knee, as did his father before him. Though Dergail's Soumanië has risen in the west, Beshtanag is secure. You have done as much for Darkhaven, since before his grandfather drew breath. Do you doubt his pride in it?"

"No." He exhaled, met her gaze. "How long has it been, lady?"

Such a question! She knew what he meant, and tears, unbidden, stung her eyes. "Over a thousand years. How long for you?"

"Twelve hundred." He bowed his head, touching some unknown talisman in his pocket. His dark hair fell to curtain his features. It was ill-cropped, and there was not a trace of grey in it. "Over twelve hundred."

Neither of them spoke.

The door opened for Pietre's return, with Sarika at his heels, a pitcher of water in one hand and wine in the other. They served the refreshments with exquisite, sullen grace. Sarika knelt at her feet, grey-blue eyes pleading mutely for reassurance. Lilias caressed her cheek, finding her voice.

"Thank you, child."

Sarika was pleased; Pietre shot a triumphant glance at the Soldier, who nodded courteously at him, studiously ignoring his bared chest, and how it gleamed by lamplight, oiled and taut below his servant's collar. Lilias poured the wine herself, and waited until Tanaros had filled his mouth with bread and cheese.

"So," she asked him then, "what does your Lord Satoris wish of me?"

Swallowing crumbs, he told her.

I WILL NOT BE AFRAID.

I will not be afraid.

Calandor!

And he was there, with her, as he had been for a thousand years and more, a reassuring presence coiled around the center of her being. Lilias touched the Soumanië at her brow and breathed easier, turning to face the Soldier. When had she risen to pace the room, when had her hands become fists? She did not remember.

"You will bring war to Beshtanag."

"Aye, lady." There was regret in his voice. "A war to prevent a war."

Bring him to me, Lilias. I would hear his Master's words.

"You understand," Lilias said to him, "the decision is not mine alone to make."

"The dragon." There was fear in his eyes, and exultation, too.

"Yes." Lilias nodded. "We are as one in Beshtanag."

Tanaros rose, bowing. "It will be my honor. I bear him greetings from my Lord Satoris."

"Come," Lilias said.

Outside, the air was thin, gold-washed in the afternoon sun. Once again, she led him herself, through the rear entrance her wardmen guarded, out of the castle and upward, up the lonely, winding path where her own people feared to tread. The mountain of Beshtanag ran both deep and high. His breath labored in the thin air. Holding her skirts, the Sorceress cast glances behind her as she climbed.

His face was rapt, and he paused at every chance to gaze

at the sun as it gilded the peaks of the trees below. Seeing her notice, he smiled with unexpected sweetness. "Forgive me, my lady. We do not see the unveiled sun in Darkhaven, save as an enemy."

Of course.

Haomane First-Born had Shaped the sun, wrought it of the light of the Souma before the world was Sundered. Lilias knew it, as every schoolchild did. And after the world was Sundered, when Satoris fled into the depths of Urulat, Haomane sought to destroy him with it, withdrawing only when the sun scorched the earth, threatening to destroy all life upon it.

And Satoris had escaped; and in his wake, the Unknown Desert.

Still, it had marked the Sunderer, cracking and blackening his flesh, weakening him so that he could not bear the touch of the sun. A whole Age he had hidden himself in the cold, cavernous fastnesses of Neherinach, among the Fjel, seething and healing, until he was fit to emerge and forge his way west, wreaking vengeance upon the world.

Of course the sun did not shine full upon Darkhaven.

"Your pardon, General," Lilias said. "I did not think upon it."

"No mind." Tanaros smiled again, drawing a deep breath of mountain air. "I have missed it."

Lilias paused, tucking a wind-tugged strand of hair behind her ear. The height was dizzying and the crags fell away beneath their feet, but she was at home, here. "Then why do you serve him?" she asked curiously.

"You know what I did?" His gaze flicked toward her.

She nodded.

She knew; the world knew. Twelve hundred years gone by, Tanaros Caveros had been the Commander of the King's Guard in Altoria, sworn to serve Roscus Altorus, his kinsman. His wife had betrayed him, and lain with the King, giving birth to a babe of Altorus' get. For that be-

trayal, Tanaros had throttled his beloved wife, had run his
sworn King through on the point of a sword and fled,
bloody-handed. And that was all Urulat had known of him
until he returned, four hundred years later, at the head of the
army of Darkhaven and destroyed the kingdom of Altoria.

"Well." Tanaros stared into the distant gorge at the base
of the mountain. "Then you know. My Lord Satoris . . ." He
paused, fingering the unseen talisman. "He needed me, my
lady. He was the only one who did, the only one who gave
me a reason to live. A cause to fight, an army to lead. He is
the only one who allowed me the dignity of my hatred."

Small wonder, that.

Lilias knew something of the Sunderer's pain, of the betrayal that had Shaped him; but that was between her and
the dragon. She wondered how much Tanaros knew. It was
difficult to imagine him committing the deeds that had
driven him to the Shaper's side, and yet he had not denied
it. She wondered if he regretted them, and thought that he
must. Even in the bright sunlight, there was a shadow that
never left his eyes. "Come," she said. "Calandor is waiting."

And she led him, then, to the mouth of the cavern, scrabbling up the lip of the plateau, all dignity forgotten. It didn't
matter, here. The opening yawned like a mouth, and something *moved* within it, high above them. Stalagmites rose
from the cavern floor, towering in the air in fantastic, taper-
ing columns. Beyond, distant heaps of treasure glinted, gold
and trinkets and sorcerers' gewgaws, books and chalices
and gems, all bearing the impress of their once-owners'
touch.

A smell of sulfur hung in the air, and Lilias laughed for
pure joy.

"Calandor!"

"Liliasssss."

One of the stalagmites moved, then another, equidistant.
Something scraped along the cavern floor. Vast claws
gouged stone, and a bronze-scaled breast hove into view

like the keel of a mighty ship. High above, a snort of flame lit the vaulted roof sulfur-yellow. Tanaros took a step backward, reaching unthinking for the hilt of his sword, then held his ground as the dragon bent his sinuous neck downward, scales glinting in the slanting light from the opening.

"Tanaross Caverosss."

The mighty jaws parted as the dragon spoke, lined with rows of pointed teeth, each one as large as a man's hand. Forge-breath ruffled the Soldier's hair, but he stood unflinching though the dragon's head hovered above his own, incomprehensibly vast. Thin trickles of smoke issued from the dragon's nostrils and its eyes were green, green and cat-slitted, lit with an inner luminescence.

"Calandor." Tanaros bowed, unable to conceal the awe in his face. "Eldest, I bear you greetings from my Lord Satoris, whom you once called friend."

A nictitating membrane covered the dragon's eyes in a brief blink; a smile, though Tanaros could not have known it. "I am not *the* Eldessst, Blackssword. Your Masster knows as much. What does he want, the Sssower?"

"He wants our aid, Calandor," Lilias said aloud what the dragon already knew. "He wants to lay a false trail to our doorstep for the Ellylon to follow."

Calandor ignored her, dragging himself past them step by slow step to the verge of the cavern, positioning his immense claws with care. His plated underbelly rasped on the stone. The crest of spines along his neck became visible, the massive shoulders. His wings, folded at his sides, the vaned pinions glittering like burnished gold. Outspread in the sky, they would shadow the mountainside. Lilias heard Tanaros stifle a gasp.

The dragon scented the air through nostrils the size of dinner-plates. "Sheep," he said, sounding satisfied. "In the northeast meadow. Three have lambed this day. I am hungry, Liliasss."

"Then you shall feed, Calandor."

"At nightfall," the dragon said. "I will take wing. Two ewes, and one lamb."

"It shall be so, Calandor." Lilias had conferred with her head herdsman, as she did each spring. They knew, to a lamb, what losses the flock could sustain. The dragon knew it, too. She wondered at what game he played.

Calandor's head swung around, swiveling on that sinuous neck, green eyes fixing on the Soldier. "You were to have been my rightful prey, Man! You whose numbers have overrun the earth."

Tanaros shuddered and held fast. "I represent my Lord, not my race, Calandor."

Twin jets of smoke emerged in a laugh. "The Shaper."

"Yes," Tanaros said. "The Shaper."

The dragon lifted his massive head and stared westward, eyes slitting in the sun. "We aided Sssatoriss when the Sssouma was shattered, because he was a friend. Many of usss died for it, and Haomane became our Enemy. No more, we sssaid. But it was too late, and we too few, and I, I am one of the lasst. Do you asssk me now to die, Ssoldier?"

"No," Tanaros said. "No! Eldest Brother, we will lay a trail to the doorstep of Beshtanag, yes. And when the Ellylon follow it, and the sons of Altorus and whatever allies they might gather, we will fall upon them from behind, the army of Darkhaven in all its strength, and it shall be ended. This I swear to you. Do you doubt it?"

Why, Lilias wondered, did she want to weep?

Calandor blinked, slowly. "I am not the Eldessst, Kingsslayer."

"Nonetheless." Tanaros' voice hardened. "My lord Calandor, Dergail's Soumanië has risen, and the signs of the Prophecy have begun. In a week's time, Cerelinde of the Ellylon will plight her troth with Aracus Altorus, and across the land, Urulat prepares for war. Haomane himself only knows what mission Malthus the Counselor has undertaken. Where will you be, if Darkhaven falls? If Godslayer falls into the Counselor's hands, if Urulat is made whole on

Haomane's terms? Do you think one mortal sorceress with a chip of the Souma can resist the Six Shapers? Where will you be then, Elder Brother?"

"Enough!" Lilias clapped her hands over her ears.

But the dragon only sighed.

"Then let them come, Kingssslayer," he said. "You ss-peak the truth. If I will not ssserve your cause, neither will I oppose it. Lay your falssse trail. Let them come, and make of uss the anvil on which your hammer may ssstrike. Does this please you?"

"My lord Calandor," Tanaros said. "I am grateful. My Lord is grateful."

"Yesss," the dragon said. "Now go."

FIVE

THE OLD MAN SQUATTED ON his haunches, gazing at the stars.

Even in the small hours of night, the rock held enough sun-captured heat to warm his buttocks, though the naked soles of his feet were calloused and immune to warmth or cold. He watched the stars wheel slowly through their nocturnal circuit, counting through the long telling of his ancestors. There was a smell of water in his nostrils, iron-rich and heavy. Something scrabbled in the spiny thorn-brush. It might have been a hopping-mouse or a hunting lizard, though it was not. He was an Elder of the Yarru-yami, and he knew every sound in the Unknown Desert.

"Can you not leave me in peace, old woman?" the old man grumbled.

"Peace!" She emerged from the night to place herself before his rock, folding arms over withered dugs, her long, grey-white hair illuminated by starlight. "You would squat on this rock all night, old man, chewing *gamal* and watching the stars. You call that peace?"

After all these years, she was as spirited as the day he had met her. He smiled into his beard. "I do, old woman. If you'll not let be, then join me."

With a snort of disapproval, she clambered up the rock to squat at his side, groaning a little as her hipbones popped and creaked. He shifted to make room for her, digging into the worn pouch that hung at his waist and passing her a pinch of *gamal*. Her jaws worked, softening the dried fibers, working her mouth's moisture into them. Eighty-three years old, and her teeth still strong, working the *gamal* into a moist wad to tuck into her cheek.

Side by side, they squatted and watched the stars.

Especially the red one low on the western horizon.

Her voice, when she spoke, was sombre. "It's the choosing-time, isn't it?"

He nodded. "Coming fast."

"The poor boy." She shook her head. "Poor boy! There's no fairness in it. He's not fit to make such a choice. Who is?"

He shrugged. "Doesn't stop it from coming."

She eyed him acerbically. "And how would you choose, old one?"

"Me?" He turned his hands over, examining his palms. Paler than the rest of his skin, they were leathery and creased, tanned like an old hide. Age had marked them, and wear, and the lines of mortality. Nothing else. "It's not mine to choose."

"I know," she whispered. "Poor boy! I pray he chooses aright."

The old man squatted and listened to the sounds of the desert, while the stars wheeled slowly overhead. He felt the slow, steady beat of his heart, winding down to its inevitable faltering, the blood coursing through his veins, as water coursed through the earth far, far below them. In the heart of the Unknown Desert, there was water, water from the deepest place, the oldest place.

Birru-Uru-Alat, the Navel, the Well of the World.

It had been forgotten by all save the Yarru, who had cause to remember. Long ago, Haomane's Wrath had driven them beneath the earth, where they fled for shelter and in turn were given a trust. The Elders had kept the wisdom of Uru-Alat. When the boy was born with the markings on his hands, they had known. He was the Bearer, one who could carry the Water of Life, though it weighed heavier than stone or steel, as heavy as the burden of choice itself.

The Water of Life, which could extinguish the marrow-fire.

It would not be forgotten forever. A red star had risen and the Bearer was nearing manhood. The choosing-time would be upon him.

It was coming.

TANAROS CHOKED BACK A GASP as he emerged in the Chamber of the Marasoumië beneath Darkhaven, his heart constricting with a sharp pain as the node-point closed, hurling his form back into the framework of mortality, stumbling and shaken, his senses blurred with the speed of his passage.

"Steady, cousin." Vorax's deep voice reassured him, a solid hand on his elbow, anchoring him in time and place. Tanaros blinked, waiting for his vision to clear, every bone in his body aching at the abrupt transition. The world seemed preternaturally *slow* after traveling the Ways. He stared at the Staccian's beard, feeling he could number each auburn hair of it while the fleshy lips formed their next sentence. "Did the Sorceress consent?"

"Aye." Seizing upon the question, he managed an answer. His chest loosened, normal breathing returning. "The lady and the dragon consented alike."

"Well done." Forgetting himself, Vorax thumped his

shoulder with a proud grin. "Well done, indeed! His Lordship will be pleased."

Tanaros winced as the edge of his spaulder bruised his flesh. "My thanks. What has transpired here, cousin?"

"General." A Fjeltroll stepped forward, yellow-eyed in the pulsing light of the chamber. One of the Kaldjager, the Cold Hunters, who patrolled the vast network of tunnels. "We have scouted passage to Lindanen Dale. We may pass below the Aven River. An entrance lies less than a league to the north. Kaldjager hold it secure. We took pains not to be seen."

"Good." Tanaros collected his wits, which were beginning to function once more. "Good. And Vorax, on your end?"

The Staccian shrugged. "I am in readiness. A chamber has been prepared, fit for a Queen. As for the rest, there's a fast ship awaiting in Harrington Bay, and a company of my lads ready to outrace the Ellylon to it, posing as Beshtanagi in disguise."

"Good," Tanaros repeated. "And the Dreamspinner? Did he succeed?"

"Well . . . don't go a-walking in the wood, cousin." Vorax grinned. "Does that answer it for you?"

It did.

IT WAS A PLAN, A simple plan.

Tanaros considered it as he lay in his bath.

The difficulty lay in gaining access, for the full might of the Rivenlost would be turned out to safeguard this wedding; aye, and the Borderguard of Curonan, too. And unless Tanaros missed his guess, the Duke of Seahold would have a contingent present as well. Every inch of ground within a dozen leagues of Lindanen Dale would have been scouted and secured.

Except the tunnels.

It was a pity they could not make use of the Marasoumië, but that would come later. Merely to hold the Ways open for so many would require two of the Three, taxing them to their utmost, and Ushahin was needed for this plan. The tunnels would be slower, but they would suffice.

It was a pity, a grave pity, that he could not bring the entire army through them with sufficient time to assemble. That would put an end to it. The army of Darkhaven was not so vast as Men believed it; that was Ushahin Dreamspinner's work, who walked in the dreams of Men and magnified their fears, playing them into nightmares. But it was vast enough, Tanaros thought, to win in a pitched battle. Under Lord Satoris' protection, the numbers of the Fjel had grown steadily throughout the centuries. Not enough to rival Men, who held nearly the whole of Urulat as their domain, but enough. And Tanaros had trained them.

On level ground, on the open field . . . ah, but the Ellylon and the sons of Altorus were too clever for that gambit. Once, it had worked. Long ago, on the plains of Curonan. He had donned the Helm of Shadows, and led the army of Darkhaven against the forces of Altoria, bringing down a nation, securing a buffer zone.

Altoria had had a Queen, then. He had never met her, never seen her. He wondered, sometimes, if she had resembled his wife. In the adamance of her pride, at the urging of her advisors, she had poured all the resources of her realm into that war, until nothing was left. In the end, Altoria lost Curonan and the throne, leaving the remnants of the sons of Altorus to patrol the verges of the lost plains.

Now, it was different. They needed to draw their Enemy out into the open. And they needed bait to do it. That was where the tunnels came into play, and Beshtanag, and above all, the Were that Ushahin had brought to Darkhaven.

The bath-water was growing cool. Tanaros stood, dripping.

"Here, Lord General."

Meara, the madling, slunk around the entrance to his bathing-chamber, proffering a length of clean linen toweling and eyeing him through her tangled hair. She had never done such before.

"Thank you, Meara." He dried himself, self-conscious for the first time in many decades. Physically, his body was unchanged. Save for the mark of his branding, it was little different than it had been on his wedding night, strong and lean and serviceable. Only the puckered, silvery scar on his breast gave evidence of his nature; that, and the deep ache of years.

"Does it hurt?" She pointed at his chest.

"Yes." He touched the scar with his fingertips, feeling the ridged flesh, remembering the searing ecstasy he'd felt when his Lord took Godslayer from the blazing marrow-fire and branded him with it, using the force of the Souma to stretch the Chain of Being to its limits to encompass him. "It hurts."

Meara nodded. "I thought so." She watched him don his robe. "What was she like, Lord General?"

"She?" He paused.

Her eyes glittered. "The Sorceress."

"She was . . . courteous."

"Was she prettier than me?" she asked plaintively.

"Prettier?" Tanaros gazed at the madling, who squirmed away from his scrutiny. He thought about Lilias, whose imperious beauty softened only in the presence of the dragon. "No, Meara. Not prettier."

She followed him as he left the bathing-chamber, tossing back her hair and glaring. "Another one is coming, you know. Coming *here*."

"Another one?"

"A *lady*." She spat the word. "An *Ellyl* lady."

"Yes." He wondered how she knew, if they all knew. "Such is the plan."

"It is a mistake," Meara said darkly.

"Meara." Tanaros rumpled his hair, damp from the bath. He remembered the Sorceress, and how the wind on the mountainside had tugged at her hair, that had otherwise fallen dark and shining, bound by the circlet, the red Soumanië vivid against her pale brow. He wondered what the other would be like, and if it were a mistake to bring her here. "The lady is to be under our Lord's protection."

The madling shuddered, turned and fled.

Bewildered, Tanaros watched her go.

THERE WAS NEVER ENOUGH TIME to prepare, when it came to it.

The Warchamber was packed with representatives of three of the races of Lesser Shapers, all crowded around the map-table and listening intently to the Commander General of the Army of Darkhaven. It was a simple plan. Tanaros wished he liked it better. Nonetheless, it was his Lord's will, and he continued, carrying it out to the letter. "And here,"—he pointed at the map—"is the mouth of the tunnel. Here, and here and here, there will be sentries posted, guarding the perimeter of Lindanen Dale. Those,"— Tanaros glanced at the Were Brethren—"will be yours to dispatch, as we agreed."

A flat voice spoke, passionless and grey. "And here they plight their troth?"

"Aye." The skin at the back of his neck prickled. With an effort, Tanaros made himself meet the gaze of Sorash, the Grey Dam of the Were, who rested one clawed forefinger upon the heart of Lindanen Dale. "That is where you will strike, honored one, if you be willing."

The Grey Dam gave him a terrible smile. "I am willing."

There was no telling her age. The Were had used the strange magics bequeathed them by Oronin Last-Born to circumvent the very Chain of Being, at least for the Grey Dam. Tanaros knew only that she was ancient. Ushahin

Dreamspinner had been a boy when Faranol, Crown Prince of Altoria, had slain the Grey Dam's cubs and her mate in a hunting excursion, heaping glory upon his kindred during a state visit to Pelmar.

"You are brave, honored one," Tanaros said.

The ancient Were shook her head. "My successor is chosen."

Grey her voice, grey her name, grey her being. One year of their lives, that was what each of the Were surrendered that the Grey Dam might endure. So it had been, in the beginning; now, it was more, for their numbers had dwindled. Five years, ten, or more. Tanaros knew naught of what such ceremonies might entail, how it was enacted. Only that the Grey Dam endured, until the mantle was passed, and endured anew.

It had been many centuries since that had happened.

"You know you will die, old mother?"

Ushahin's voice, raw and aching. It was not the first time he had asked it.

"Little Man-cub, little son." The old Were's amber gaze softened, and she patted his misshapen cheek with her padded, hairy palm. "You have assuaged my pain these many years, but the time has come to make an end. It is a good way to die. If the Glad Hunter wills it, my teeth will meet in the flesh of an Altorus before the finish."

He bowed his head. The Were Brethren growled softly.

Tanaros cleared his throat. "Then you will strike here, honored one, and your Brethren will clear the way. In the confusion, we will make our move, here." He traced a pathway on the map. "Under my command, a company of Lord Vorax's men will seize Cerelinde of the Rivenlost, and fall back to the meeting point, where the switch will be made. From thence, they will flee east, with the decoy. Lord Ushahin, weave what visions you may. The remaining men and I will hold them as long as we dare, before we retreat to the tunnels and the Kaldjager Fjel hide our passage."

And there it was, the first phase of it, in all its risky totality.

"General." Hyrgolf's shrewd eyes met his with a soldier's frankness. "The Fjel are ready to serve. It would be better if you did not command the raid yourself."

"It must be," Tanaros said bluntly. "It is his Lordship's will, and there is no room for error. Hyrgolf, I would trust you to lead it, and I would trust any lieutenant of your appointing. But if we are to convince the Ellylon and the Altorians that this raid originated in Beshtanag, there can be no hint of the presence of Fjeltroll."

"Cousin, I would command my own—" began Vorax.

Ushahin cut short his words, his tone light and bitter. "You can't, fat one. Your bulk can't be concealed under Pelmaran armor, as can the rest of your beard-shorn Staccians, and Tanaros, too." With a twisted smile, he raised his crippled hands that could grip nothing heavier than a dagger. "I would do it myself, if I could. But I think my skills do not avail in this instance."

"Enough!" Tanaros raised his voice. "It is mine to do." For a moment, he thought they would quarrel; then they settled, acceding to his command. He leaned over the maptable, resting his hands on the edges, the southwestern quadrant of Urulat framed between his braced arms. "Are we in accord?"

"We are, brother," whispered the Grey Dam. "We are."

No one disagreed.

HIS DREAMS, WHEN HE HAD them, were restless.

Tanaros slept, and awoke, restless, tossing in his bedsheets, and slept only to dream anew, and twist and wind himself into shrouds in his dreaming.

Blood.

He dreamed of blood.

An ocean of it.

It ran like a red skein through his dreams, wet and dripping. Red, like the Souma, like Godslayer, like the star that had arisen in the west and the one that adorned the Sorceress' brow. It dripped like a veil over the features of his wife, long-slain, and over his own hands as he looked down in horror, seeing them relinquish the hilt of his sword, the blade protruding from his King's chest.

Tanaros tossed, and groaned.

It went back, further back, the trail of blood; far, so far. All the way back through the ages of the Sundered World, blood, soaking into the earth of a thousand battlefields, clots of gore. Back and back and back, until the beginning, when a great cry rent the fabric of Urulat, a mighty blow parted the world, and the Sundering Seas rushed in to fill the void, warm and salty as blood.

Tanaros awoke, the mark of his brand aching in summons.

He dressed himself and went to answer it.

Downward he went, through one of the three-fold doors and down the spiraling stairs that led to the Chamber of the Font, down the winding way where the walls shone like onyx, and the veins of marrow-fire were buried deep and strong. At the base of the spiral stair a blast of heat greeted him.

"My Lord."

Some distance from the center of the chamber, in a ringed pit, the marrow-fire rose from its unseen Source to surge like a fountain through a narrow aperture, blue-white fire rising up in a column, falling, coruscating. And in the heart of it—ah! Tanaros closed his eyes briefly. There in midair hung the dagger Godslayer, that burned and was not consumed, beating like a heart. Its edges were as sharp and jagged as the day it had been splintered from the Souma, reflecting and refracting the marrow-fire from its ruby facets.

"Tanaros." The Shaper stood before the Font, a massive form, hands laced behind his back. The blazing light played over his calm features, the broad brow, the shadowed eyes that reflected the red gleam of the Souma in pinpricks. "Tomorrow it begins."

He knew not what to say. "Yes, my Lord."

"War," mused the Shaper, taking a step forward to gaze at the Font. The preternatural light shone on the seeping trail of ichor that glistened on his thigh, and the marrow-fire took on an edge of creeping blackness, like shadow made flame. "My Elder Brother gives me no peace, and this time he wagers all. Do you understand why this must be, Tanaros? Do you understand that this is *your* time?"

"Yes, my Lord." His teeth chattered, his chest ached and blazed.

"I was stabbed with this dagger." Lord Satoris reached out a hand, penetrating the blue-white fountain, and the flames grew tinged with darkness. "Thus." His forefinger touched the crudely rounded knob that formed Godslayer's hilt. Tanaros hissed through his teeth as the dagger's light convulsed and the scar of his branding constricted. "To this day, the pain endures. And yet it is not so great as the pain of my siblings' betrayal."

"My Lord." Tanaros drew a deep breath against the tightness in his chest. On the eve of war, he asked the question none of the Three had voiced. "Why did you refuse Haomane's request?"

"Brave Tanaros." The Shaper smiled without mirth. "There is danger in conversing with dragons. I saw too clearly the Shape of what-would-be if my Gift were withdrawn from Men, uncoupled forever from the Gift of thought. Out of knowledge, I refused; and out of love, love for Arahila, my Sister. Still." He paused. "What did Haomane see, I wonder? Why did he refuse my Gift for his Children? Was it pride, or something more?"

"I know not, my Lord," Tanaros said humbly.

"No." Considering, Lord Satoris shook his head. "I think not. My Elder Brother was ever proud. And it matters not, now." His hand tightened on Godslayer's hilt. "Only this. Haomane seeks it, my General. That is what it comes to, in the end. Blood, and more blood, ending in mine—or his."

"My Lord!" Tanaros gasped, tearing at his chest.

"Forgive me." The Shaper withdrew from the marrow-fire, his hands closing on Tanaros' upper arms. The power in them made Tanaros' skin prickle. "Would you know what is in my heart?" he asked in a low voice. "I did not choose this, Tanaros Blacksword. But I will not go gently, either. Any of them . . . *any* of them!" He loosed his hold and turned away. "Any of them could cross the divide," he said, softly. "Any of the Six. It is theirs to do, to defy Haomane's will, to risk mortality. If they did . . ." He smiled sadly. "Oh, Arahila! Sister, together, you and I . . ."

Catching his breath, Tanaros bowed, not knowing what else to do before such immeasurable sorrow. "My Lord, we will do our best to deliver you Urulat."

"Urulat." The Shaper gathered himself. "Yes. Urulat. If I held Urulat in my palm, would it be enough to challenge Haomane's sovereignty?" His laughter was harsh and empty. "Perhaps. I would like to find out."

"It shall be yours, my Lord!" Tanaros said fiercely, believing it, his heart blazing within him like the marrow-fire. "I will make it so!"

Blood yet unshed dripped between them.

"Tanaros." His name, nothing more; everything. The touch of the Shaper's lips on his brow, chaste and burning. It had been his Gift, once. The quickening of the flesh, joyful blood leaping in the loins. A crude Gift, but his, cut short by Godslayer's thrust. "May it be so."

"My Lord," Tanaros whispered, and knew himself dismissed.

As he took his leave, Lord Satoris turned back to the marrow-fire, gazing at it as if to find answers hidden in the ruby shard. The Shaper's features were shadowed with unease, a fearful sight of itself. "Where is your weapon Malthus, Brother, and what does he plot?" he murmured. "Why must you force my hand? I did not Sunder the world.

And yet I have become what you named me. Is that truly what must come to pass, or is there another way?" He sighed, the sound echoing in the Chamber. "If there is, I cannot see it. Your wrath has been raised against me too long. All things must be as they must."

Tanaros withdrew quietly, not swiftly enough to avoid hearing the anguish in the Shaper's final words.

"Uru-Alat!" Lord Satoris whispered. "I would this role had fallen to another."

SIX

"COUNSELOR, FORGIVE ME," THE ARDUAN croaked, falling to her knees.

The Company of Malthus halted beneath the hammer of the sun, a merciless, white-hot blaze in the vivid blue sky. All around them, the scorched landscape extended farther than the eye could see in any direction, red earth baked and cracking, broken only by the strange, towering structures of anthills.

"I told you it was no journey for a woman." Although his face was drawn beneath beard-stubble, the former Commander of the Borderguard kept his feet, wavering only slightly. "We should have sent her back."

"Peace, Blaise." Even Malthus' voice was cracked and weary. "Fianna is the Archer of Arduan. It is as it must be. None of us can go much farther." Drawing back his sheltering hood, the Counselor bowed his head and took the Soumanië from its place of concealment beneath his robes, chanting softly and steadily in the Shaper's tongue. The gem shone like a red star between his hands.

Ants scurried on the cracked earth as it stirred beneath them, departing in black rivulets. Dry spikes of thorn-brush rattled, trembling.

"Look!" It was the young Vedasian, Hobard, who saw it first, pointing. A green tendril of life emerging from the cracks in the desert floor, questing in the open air. "A drought-eater! Yrinna be blessed!"

It grew beneath the Counselor's fraying chant, thc green stalk thickening, branches springing from the trunk with a thick succulent's leaves; grew, and withered, even as flowers blossomed and fruited, seeds swelling to ripe globes. A drought-eater, capable of absorbing every drop of moisture within an acre of land and producing fruit that was almost wholly water. Water, held within a tough greenish rind.

They fell upon it, ripping the fruit from its stems even as the branches shriveled. Hobard split his with both thumbs, sucking at the pulpy interior. Blaise Caveros, for all his harsh words, had a care with the Arduan woman, cutting the fruit and feeding it to her piece by dripping piece. Malthus the Counselor leaned wearily on his walking-staff and watched them, and among all his Company only Peldras of the Rivenlost, whose light step left no tracks on the red, dusty soil, waited his turn until the rest were sated.

Thirst could not kill Haomane's Children; only steel.

Peldras shaded his eyes, gazing at the endless vista of baked red earth. If the Counselor's wisdom were true, they should have found the ones they sought long before; the Charred Ones, who had hidden from the scorching fire of Haomane's wrath.

"What do you see, my long-sighted friend?" Malthus asked in a low tone.

The Ellyl shook his head. "Nothing."

"Hush."

Staring at the vine-curtained opening, Tanaros lifted a hand for silence. To a fellow, Men and Fjel obeyed him alike. No need to caution the Were, who were silence itself. Only the shuffle and stamp of the horses disturbed the quiet, and even that was minimal. Green light filtered into the tunnel, and beyond the opening he could hear birdsong.

"Go." He motioned to the Were brethren. "Clear the perimeter, and report."

They went, both of them, like arrows shot from the bow, low to the ground and sleek, traveling at an inhuman gait, muzzles pointed forward, ears pricked and wary.

"Good hunting, brothers," the Grey Dam murmured.

Tanaros repressed a shudder.

Always, the waiting was the hardest. He felt awkward in the unfamiliar Pelmaran armor; steel plates laced onto boiled leather, and an ill-disguised conical helmet. Their arms had been chosen with care, to give a semblance of Beshtanagi troops in disguise. Tanaros rolled his shoulders, loosened his sword in its sheath. A borrowed sword, not his own, with a Pelmaran grip.

Behind him, Vorax's Staccians whispered in excitement. This was their moment, the role only they could play. Among them, Vorax had chosen the youngest, the fiercest, the swiftest. They had trained hard, and rehearsed their roles to perfection. They had shaved their beards and stained their skin with walnut dye. Tanaros turned in the saddle to survey them, feeling the battle-calm settle over him.

Their lieutenant met his eye; Carfax, a steady fellow. They exchanged nods. And there, in the vanguard, Turin, the yellow-haired decoy, swallowing hard. *Choose one who is fair,* his Lordship had said, *fair as morning's first star.* He was a youth, still beardless, his skin undyed and pale, clad in bridal silks. The troops had laughed, to see him thus. Now, none laughed.

"We strike a blow this day, brothers," Tanaros said in a soft, carrying voice, jostling his mount to face them. "A mighty blow! Are you ready?"

They gave a whispered cheer.

"Field marshal." His gaze roamed past the Staccians, falling upon Hyrgolf, who stood with the massed Fjeltroll at the rear. "Are you ready?"

Hyrgolf of the Tungskulder Fjel stood like a boulder, stolid and dependable. "We are ready, General," he rumbled. "Bring us the Ellyl lady, and we will conduct her in all speed to Darkhaven."

"Dreamspinner." Tanaros bent his gaze upon the half-breed, who crouched at the entrance to the tunnels, holding the Helm of Shadows in his trembling hands. "Are you ready, cousin?"

"I am ready." Ushahin bared his teeth, the enlarged pupil in one eye glittering. In the green light, his face looked ghastly. The thing in his hands throbbed with a darkness that ached like a wound, unbearable to behold. "Upon your command!"

As if summoned by his words, one of the Were brethren dashed through the hanging vines that curtained the entrance, eyes glowing amber, bloodstains upon his muzzle. "The way is clear," he said, the words thick and guttural in his throat. Sharp white teeth showed as he licked blood from his chops. "Why do you wait? In the Dale, they wed. Go now, now!"

Sorash the Grey Dam lifted her muzzle and keened a lament for her long-slain cubs.

The moment had come.

Tanaros drew his sword, and though it was not his, still it sang as it cleared the scabbard, a high, piercing sound that echoed inside his head. "Go!" he shouted, digging his heels into his mount's sides, feeling the surge of muscle as the black horse lunged up the sloping tunnel for the entrance. "Go, go, go!"

Lashed by green vines, Tanaros burst through the tunnel entrance, bounding into a forest in the full foliage of spring. A grey form hurtled past him, bound at speed for Lindanen Dale.

Altorus!

The word was a battle-paean in his head, igniting the ancient hurt, the ancient hatred. Altorus! He took a deep breath, filling his lungs with it. Rage, cleansing rage. Tanaros wheeled the black horse, his mind clear and sharp. There, the Staccians, emerging in formation. There, the dim figures of the Kaldjager Fjel, slipping through the trees. There, by the opening, Ushahin Dreamspinner, lowering the Helm of Shadows onto his head.

"Ride!" Tanaros shouted. "Men, *ride!*"

They rode, pounding through the oak wood, the ancient holdings of Altoria, and the mounts they rode were the horses of Darkhaven, swift-hooved and high-spirited, their glossy coats disguised with mud and burrs. They rode, and the trees passed in a blur, and behind them slid Fjeltroll with yellow eyes and sharp axes, laying a trap for those who would follow—and there four of their number paused, waiting. Here and there lay corpses, Ellylon and Men alike, sentries who grinned in death at the innocent spring leaves. They rode, and death ran before them, Oronin's Children, grey and implacable.

A league, a league, less than a league.

Ahead, the trees thinned, bright sunlight shining on Lindanen Dale. Tanaros glanced left and right, wind-sprung tears blurring his vision. In the periphery of his gaze, he could see the Staccians following, falling into a wedge formation. The Were had vanished. Let them be there, he thought, a desperate prayer. Oh my Lord, let them be there! Drawing his sword, he loosed a wordless cry as they emerged into the Dale.

Greensward, and flowers hidden in the grass.

Silk tents, with pennants fluttering.

And the host, the nuptial host, milling on the lawn, chaos sown in their midst, with rent garments and blood flowing freely. A harpist, moaning and pale, cradled a torn forearm; others lay unmoving, and their blood spread on the grass, darkening. This, they had not expected. Not the grey hunters of the Were, not Oronin's Children, who could pen-

etrate any defense not raised behind walls. Ah, and even so!
So many, so many of Haomane's Allies, gathered in one
place. Lindanen Dale seethed like a kicked anthill. Unready
and unmounted they might be, but they had not come unarmed. Already, the soldiers were gathering their wits.
There was one of the Were brethren, dying, his hairy belly
slit, entrails dragging on the greensward. And there, the
other, brought to bay by the Duke of Seahold's men, closing
in with spears.

Tanaros thundered past, ignoring them.

There . . . *there*.

Before the bower, wrought with Ellylon craftsmanship,
enwrapped with flowers—*there*. A man, bare-headed,
danced with death in a bridegroom's finery, and the sunlight
gleamed on his red-gold hair and the naked steel of his
blade. A grey, shadowy figure lunged at his throat, teeth
snapping in a hunger that had honed itself for centuries.
Around and around they went in a deadly pavane. After a
thousand years, the Grey Dam of the Were sought to avenge
the deaths of her mate and cubs. And all around them, the
Altorians stood in a ring, the Borderguard of Curonan,
holding their blades for fear of striking awry, shouting
fierce encouragement to their king-in-exile, so grievously
assaulted on his wedding day.

Not there. No.

To the left, where an Ellyl woman stood, clad in bridal
silks. There was fear in her face, and pride. Oh yes, Haomane knew, there was pride! She shone like a flame, lending courage to the women who attended her and cowered at
her side, strengthening the hearts of her Rivenlost guards
who bristled about her, swords and spears at the ready.

It took all his strength not to howl his Lord's name, be-
traying the origin of their attack; though in truth, it would
not have mattered if he did, for at that moment the Dreamspinner's subtle influence began to manifest, warping sight
and sound, and Men turned in confusion toward imagined
attackers where there were none. Such was Ushahin's illu-

sion, augmented by the Helm of Shadows, that even the Ellylon believed with utter certitude that an involuntary Beshtanagi warcry was uttered in the mêlée.

"Now!" Tanaros shouted to his men. "Now!"

They followed as he led them in a charge against the personal guard of Cerelinde, granddaughter of Elterrion the
Bold, Lord of the Rivenlost. Young men—boys, some of
them—sworn to fat Vorax. Why? He didn't dare ask, but
must trust them to be there, fighting on horseback at his side
as his sword rose and fell, rose and fell, dripping with Ellyl
blood. The cries of the dying rang in his ears, his and theirs.
Proud Ellyl faces, eyes bright with Haomane's favor, swam
in his vision; he cut them down, cleaving a path through
them, again and again and again, until his sword-arm grew
tired.

And then . . .

Only fear, in her beautiful face; fear and disbelief.

"Lady, come!" he gasped, discarding his buckler and
hauling her across his pommel with one strong arm.

The weight of her—oh Lord, oh my Lord Satoris!

Tanaros gritted his teeth, feeling her struggle, her flesh
against his; Ellyl flesh, a woman's flesh, warm and living.
Her hair spilled like gleaming silk over his left knee, tan-
gling in his Pelmaran greaves, his stirrup. Pale, her hair, like
cornsilk. The surviving Staccians closed around him,
swords flashing as they fought, checking their mounts
broadside into the bodies of her defenders. Across the Dale,
cavalry units scrambled to assemble and an Ellyl horn blew,
a sound of silvery defiance, summoning the Host.

"Lady, forgive me," Tanaros muttered and, raising his
sword, brought the hilt down sharply on the base of her
skull. Her weight went still and limp, quiescent.

A cry of rage and fury shattered the air.

"Cerelinde! CERELINDE!"

Tanaros turned his head and met Aracus Altorus' gaze.

In that instant, the Grey Dam of the Were made her final
lunge; one last, desperate attack, carrying the onus of the

battle to her opponent, spending her life upon it. Altorus'
sword came up between them, spitting her, and he wept
with futile anger as her weight bore him down, jaws seeking
his throat even as her eyes filmed.

"Go!" Tanaros shouted, wheeling the black. "*Go!*"

TANAROS CLUNG TO HIS MOUNT like grim death, one hand on
the reins, one clutching the limp burden athwart his pommel,
the Staccians surrounding him as they raced for the treeline.
The greensward of Lindanen Dale was churned to mud beneath the pounding hooves of the horses of Darkhaven.

And behind them, Haomane's allies were closing fast,
astride and racing, and in the vanguard was the cavalry of
Ingolin the Wise, Lord of the Rivenlost, moved to hot-
blooded wrath for the first time in centuries; and close at
their heels were the Borderguard of Curonan in their dun-
colored cloaks. Thirty paces to the forest, twenty . . .

With Cerelinde to carry, he couldn't outrun them.

"Now, Dreamspinner," Tanaros whispered under his
breath. "Now!"

Madness broke.

Like a wave, a vast black wave, it crashed down upon
them, and the sound in his skull was an atonal howl of grief,
as if the whole of Oronin's Children mourned at once, as if
every Were in Urulat opened throat in lament. And so it
was, in a fashion, for Ushahin Dreamspinner unleashed the
full force of his power and gave voice to the grief of them
all, and the form of his grief was madness, given shape by
the Helm of Shadows.

It halted the armies of Haomane; horses balking, throwing riders, Men clapping hands over ears and falling to
writhe on the ground, while the Ellylon sought in vain to
control mortal steeds that plunged and pitched in terror.
Only the horses of Darkhaven, tended from their foaling by
the hands of madlings, were untouched by it.

"Ride, damn you!" Carfax, the Staccian lieutenant, exhorted his troops, almost weeping. "Ride, you sons of whores!"

A flurry of ravens arose as they entered the forest.

Branches, breaking at their passage. Tanaros bent low over the black stallion's neck, clinging with his knees, concentrating on the limp form of the Ellyl woman. The horse's mane stung his eyes. Oh, brave heart! Hooves pounded the loam, massive trunks rushed past them. How long, until Haomane's Allies gathered themselves to follow?

A league, less than a league to the meeting place.

In a dappled glade surrounded by dense thickets and tall oaks, he drew rein, sawing at the black's lathered neck. Turin the decoy was there waiting, and three others, helping as he dismounted, easing the Ellyl noblewoman to the ground. She moaned faintly, stirring against the loam. Tanaros reached down, unclasping her outer garment; a cloak of white silk, embroidered in gold thread and rubies with an interlacing pattern of crown and Souma. It came loose with surprising ease, and he straightened with it.

"That would be for me, Lord General." The young Staccian settled the cloak over his shoulders and fastened the clasp, tossing his yellow locks back. He nodded at a round Pelmaran buckler propped against a rock. "In thanks, I give you my shield."

Tanaros clasped his hand. "Lord Satoris' blessing on you, Turin."

The Staccian spared him a brief grin. "And you, General. Buy us time."

With that, he turned away, and one of his comrades, astride a black horse, gave him a hand, slinging him across the pommel where he landed with a grunt. The decoy was in place.

"Lord General!" Carfax saluted.

"Go," Tanaros said softly. "We'll hold them long enough for you to cross the Aven. Cut the bridges if you can. After that, you're on your own. Lord Vorax's ship awaits you in Harrington Bay."

Carfax smiled. "We'll see you in Beshtanag."

With that, he gave the command, wheeling; the bulk of the Staccians thundered with him, heading eastward through the forest, toward the River Aven, Turin the decoy jouncing athwart the pommel of one.

"General," a deep voice rumbled, as Hyrgolf stepped between the trees, massive and deliberate. Lowering his thick head, he stared under his brow-ridges at the inert form of the Ellyl woman. "This is her?"

"Aye."

"Well, then." The Fjeltroll stooped, gathering Cerelinde of the Ellylon in his thick-hided arms. Her body sagged, pale hair trailing earthward on one end, slipper-shod feet twitching at the other. "Poor lass," Hyrgolf murmured.

"Take her to Darkhaven!" Tanaros snapped, swinging astride his mount.

"Aye, General." The Fjel's tone was mild as he turned away, bearing his burden. "We will do that," he said over his shoulder. "Hold the glade, as long as you dare. The Kaldjager are ready with their axes. Do not wait too long."

Tanaros nodded and settled Turin's buckler on his left arm.

He was ready.

THEY WERE FEW, SO FEW.

Tanaros did not count the losses; he did not dare. Even now, after so many, it hurt to number them. He merely waited, with Vorax's Staccians, and knew that a dozen were left to him. Bold lads, to a man. Their teeth gleamed white against their dyed skin as they awaited the onslaught. This time, there would be no help from the Dreamspinner; Ushahin was spent. Only them, with mortal steel against innumerable odds.

It came quickly.

The passage into the glade was narrow. Tanaros took the lead position, with a soldier a pace behind him on either side, the rest arrayed in ranks of three behind them, ready to move up should any fall. The forest resounded with the sound of enemy pursuit. Through the trees, he saw them coming, and a lord of the Ellylon led the charge, checking when he saw the narrow gap with its defenders. Horns blew, ordering a halt, but even so Haomane's Allies continued to come by the hundred; the Borderguard of Curonan, blue-clad men of Seahold, massed behind the Ellylon.

"Yield, defiler." The Ellyl lord's voice was implacable. "Return the lady."

Tanaros shook his head.

The Ellyl drew his sword, and dappled sunlight shone silver on it; silver was his armor, and worked on his shield a thistle-blossom, marking him of the House of Núrilin. "Then you will die."

Nudging his mount forward, Tanaros drew his Pelmaran sword in salute.

They engaged.

The Núrilin's first blow reeled him in the saddle, nearly cracking the borrowed buckler with its force. This was no mere guardsman taken unaware and on foot, but a lord of the Ellylon fighting on horseback, equal to equal. Tanaros' shield-arm went numb to the shoulder. Anger rose in him like a tide. With a wordless shout, he pressed the attack, driving the Ellyl back by main force. The heaving sides of their mounts jostled one another as they grappled, too close for either to get a solid blow. On the left and right, the sounds of battle arose.

"You're too few," the Núrilin lord said. "Surrender, and be spared."

Tanaros gritted his teeth and raised his aching shield-arm, shoving the buckler hard into the Ellyl's body, gaining a few inches of space. Obedient to the command of his knees, the black horse wheeled and Tanaros brought his sword around in a flashing arc, landing a solid blow to the helm. The Núrilin retreated a pace, shaking his head, but to his left, one of the Staccians cried out and fell back, wounded. Even as another struggled to take his comrade's place, battle surged, pressing toward the glade. Tanaros cut across, driving them back, gasping as the tip of a blade scored his unprotected side, piercing the leather seam of his armor. Blood trickled down his ribcage.

"How long, defiler?" the Núrilin lord called. "Until all your men are dead?"

From the corner of his eyes, Tanaros could see movement in the massed ranks behind the Ellylon. Dun-colored cloaks, moving through the trees. He swore under his breath. The Borderguard of Curonan was spreading out, seeking another passage, trying to come around and flank them. It was what he would have ordered. They would do it, in time; and worse, they would find the decoy's trail, too soon.

"How long, General?" one of the Staccians muttered behind him as the onslaught redoubled its efforts, forcing them back another pace.

Tanaros pressed his elbow against his bleeding side. "We will—"

At the rear of the massed Allies, something stirred, the troops of the Duke of Seahold parting to admit a handful of men, spearheaded by one who uttered a single cry. "*Curonan!*"

In the woods, the dun-colored cloaks turned back in answer.

The Ellylon halted their attack, waiting.

In the gap, the Staccians held, panting, Tanaros at their head. One was dead, two direly wounded. Tanaros pressed his wound and watched as Aracus Altorus made his way through the ranks. Pride, he thought, as Aracus drew nearer. Always pride. His armor had been donned in haste, flung over his bridegroom's finery. He held his helmet under one arm, and his wide-set eyes were filled with fury.

"Now," Tanaros whispered.

His blow caught the Núrilin lord unaware, the sword finding a gap in the Ellyl's armor. With cries of wrath, the Ellylon surged to the attack. Everywhere, silvered armor, fair Ellyl faces, eyes bright and fierce behind visors, horse-flesh churning as they pressed through the gap, forcing the Staccians backward. Aracus Altorus and the Borderguard of Curonan were lost in the center of the mêlée.

One more step, Tanaros thought, wielding his Pelmaran sword with desperate energy, guarding their retreat and trying to save as many of Vorax's men as he might. The Ellylon were fearful in their wrath, and he could feel the Staccians' courage ebbing, turning to terror. It was why he had needed to lead the raid himself. Battle-trained, the black horse retreated, obedient to his commands, turning this way and that to allow him room to swing his blade.

One more step, one . . . more . . . step . . .

With a sound like cracking thunder, trees began to fall; ancient trees, mighty oaks, the sentinels of Lindanen Wood. And the first to fall toppled like a giant across the gap, smashing the enemy vanguard, shattering bone and crushing flesh, the earth shuddering at its impact. The way was blocked, for now, and above the moans of the enemy rose the screaming of injured horses.

The Kaldjager Fjeltroll had done their job.

Weary and sore, Tanaros turned his mount and ordered his Men back to the tunnels. There should have been joy in the victory, and yet there was none. Once, he would have been on the other side of this battle, defending his liege-lord. Those days were long gone, and yet. . . . Destroying the happiness of one Son of Altorus did not bring back the love Tanaros had lost, the life that had once been his. Nothing would, ever. With his own hands, he had destroyed it, and chosen Lord Satoris' dark truth over the bright lie of love that he had once cherished.

If it had been true before, it was true twice over this day. He had sealed that path as surely as the Kaldjager

Fjel had blocked their retreat. There was no merit in regretting what was done, and no choice but to continue onward.

Darkhaven was all that was left to him.

SEVEN

❖

CERELINDE OPENED HER EYES ONTO a nightmare.

Fjeltroll.

She was the Lady of the Ellylon and, to her credit, she did not cry aloud, though the face that hovered over hers was immense and hideously ugly, covered in a thick, grey-green hide. It was so close she could smell its musk, feel its breath on her skin. Its nostrils were the size of wine goblets. Tiny eyes squinted down at her beneath the bulge of an overhanging brow. A broad mouth stretched its width, yellowing tusks protruding above and below the leathery lips.

Even as she blinked in uncomprehending fear, its maw opened. A voice emerged, deep and rumbling, speaking in the common tongue. "The Lady wakes."

Cerelinde sat up, seeking to scramble backward. A sharp pain lanced her skull, and a wave of sickness clutched her stomach.

"Peace, lass." The squatting Fjeltroll held up one enormous hand. The hide was thick and horny, the dangerous talons grimy. It was not a reassuring sight. "You will come to no harm here."

"No harm?" With an effort of will, she quelled the sensation of sickness. Memories of Lindanen Dale rose in its place and overwhelmed her; the grey Were in their midst, her kinsmen slain and Aracus fighting for his life, the mounted figure in Pelmaran armor bearing down upon her, blood dripping from his blade. "Ah, Haomane! There is naught but harm in this day!"

"As you say, lass." The vast shoulders moved in a shrug. "It is Haomane's Prophecy you sought to fulfill this day. Still, I tell you, you will not be harmed by my Lordship's hand."

"Your Lordship." Cerelinde glanced at her surroundings. She was underground in a vast tunnel, tall and wide. A handful of Fjel carrying heavy packs squatted in waiting, their fearsome features further distorted by wavering torch-light. She repressed a shudder. Beyond them, another figure stood, dismounted beside a restless horse, a bundle under one arm. His head was bowed, his face in shadow. The torchlight glinted on his pale hair, which shone like that of her own people. Through the anguish in her heart and the throbbing pain in her head, slow realization of her plight dawned. It was not Beshtanagi who had attacked her wedding. It was worse, far worse. "Who are you?" she asked, already fearing the answer. "What is this place?"

The Fjeltroll smiled with hideous gentleness. "Lady, I am Hyrgolf of the Tungskulder Fjel, field marshal of the Army of Darkhaven," he said. "And this place is merely a waystation."

"Darkhaven," she whispered. "*Why?*"

He looked at her a moment before speaking. "Surely you must know."

Cerelinde closed her eyes briefly. "Your master seeks to destroy us."

"Destroy?" The Fjeltroll gave a rumbling snort. "Haomane's Wrath brings destruction upon us. His Lordship wishes to survive it." He rose, extending one horny hand. "Come, lass. Can you travel? I will bear you if you cannot."

"I pray you, Marshal Hyrgolf, do not." Cerelinde took a shallow breath, conscious of the limited air, of the weight of the earth pressing above them. It was a sickening sensation.

Her head ached and her heart felt battered within her breast. Her flesh retained a vague, horrible memory of being borne in the Fjeltroll's arms. She had been right; there was risk, too much risk.

Lindanen Dale had been a mistake.

"It is no hardship," Hyrgolf said, misunderstanding her hesitation. His talons brushed her fingertips.

"*No!*" Cerelinde shrank from his touch. She found the wall of the tunnel at her back and levered herself upright. "If I must walk," she said, summoning her dignity and gathering it around her, "I shall walk."

"Lady." Hyrgolf uttered a few words in the guttural Fjel tongue, and the others shook off their apparent torpor. The light of their torches receded as they began to trot down the tunnel at a steady pace. The other figure, beside the horse, stood unmoving. Hyrgolf gestured for her to precede him. "As you will."

The rocky floor of the tunnel was harsh beneath her feet, clad in the embroidered slippers of her wedding finery. As they passed the motionless figure with the pale hair, she glanced sidelong.

Ushahin the Misbegotten raised his head, his mismatched eyes glittering with unshed tears and hatred. His combined heritage was stamped on his face, as clearly as the marks of violence left by those who had sought to erase his existence.

"Ah, Haomane!" She breathed the word like a prayer, faltering.

"Come, Lady," Hyrgolf said low in his throat. His talons were on her arm, hurrying her past. "Leave the Dreamspinner to his grief."

She went without arguing.

Behind them, she heard the sound of hooves shuffling and stamping, a horse's snort. And then hoofbeats, following in their wake. When she dared glance behind once more, he was there, riding astride with the leather case in his lap. He stared hard at her, his twisted face a parody of Haomane's Children, of almost all she held dear.

And there were no more tears in his eyes, only hatred.

She was alone among the Sunderer's minions.

The Fjel were not swift, but they were steady and tireless. They spoke little, keeping to their pace, and the Misbegotten spoke not at all. Cerelinde walked among them for hours, feeling Ushahin's hatred at her back, as palpable as the heat of a blazing hearth. The tunnel sloped downward, and with each step she felt herself taken further from the surface, from Aracus and her kinfolk, from clean air and the light of Haomane's blessed, life-giving sun. The air within the tunnels was dank and close, growing ever more so the further they went. Only a handful of shafts pierced the stifling darkness, providing barely enough air to keep them alive, to keep the torches alight.

Within the first hour, they passed beneath the Aven River.

The sound, a deep, muffled rushing sound, announced it. The walls of the tunnel thrummed and groaned. Cerelinde started in terror even as the Fjel tramped onward, unperturbed.

"Peace, lass," Hyrgolf rumbled. "It is only the river above us."

"Above us?" Cerelinde echoed the words, feeling ill. The weight of all that water, rushing overhead, was incomprehensible. She knew the river well. Some leagues to the south, Meronil, the white city, sat on its banks.

"Aye, far above." Hyrgolf regarded her. "The Fjel know tunnels, lass. You're safe with us. You've no need to fear."

"Lass!" A despairing laugh escaped her. "Ah, Marshal! So you call me, and yet I have lived long enough for ten score of your generations to toil and die in the Sunderer's name. Have you any idea what it is you do here?"

He gave another shrug, as though her words glanced off his impervious hide. "As you will, Lady. Can you continue?"

"Yes," Cerelinde whispered.

Onward they tramped, and the sound of the Aven River grew louder and more terrifying, then faded and vanished. Cerelinde thought of Meronil, of her home, passing steadily beyond her reach, and fought against despair.

After many hours, they reached a vast, open cavern where Hyrgolf called a halt. Cerelinde stood on battered and aching feet, watching as his Fjel made camp, dispersing the supplies they bore. There were food and water, as well as bedrolls and fodder for horses. Others, it seemed, were anticipated. Only the Misbegotten took no part in the preparations, retreating to a dark alcove and crouching in misery, arms wrapped around the case he carried.

Cerelinde was too weary to care. Whatever ailed him, there was no room in her heart for compassion, save for those she had left behind. When Hyrgolf pointed to a hide tent his Fjel had erected for her, pounding tent-pegs into rock with sheer might, she crawled into it without a word, drawing the flap closed behind her. There she lay, staring open-eyed at the tent's peak, and reliving the bloody memories of Lindanen Dale.

Hours passed.

The hoofbeats, when they came, were weary and slow. Cerelinde lay tense and quiet, listening to the sounds of the camp. There was a Man's voice speaking in the common tongue, tired, yet filled with command. "How is she?"

"Quiet, Lord General," answered Hyrgolf's deep tone.

The voice spoke in Staccian, giving orders. For a moment, Cerelinde relaxed; then came the sound of booted feet drawing near her tent.

"Lady," the Man's voice said. "I bring you greetings from my Lord Satoris."

Her fingers trembled as she drew back the tent's flap. He averted his gaze as she emerged, allowing her to study him. The sight made her stomach clench. His was the face she had seen through the opening of a Pelmaran helm, bearing down upon her, a bloody sword in his fist.

Not until she stood did he meet her eyes, and she knew, then, that she had seen his likeness elsewhere, in the shadow of features worn by his distant kinsman. The dark hair was the same, falling over his brow; the stern mouth, the face, austere and handsome by the standards of Men. Only the eyes were different, weary with the knowledge of centuries beyond mortal telling.

Her voice shook. "*You!*"

"Lady." He bowed, correct and exacting. "I am General Tanaros of Darkhaven, and I mean you no harm."

"Harm!" Cerelinde passed her hands over her face, another wild laugh threatening to choke her. "O blessed Haomane, Arahila the Fair, what does such a word *mean* to you people? I know you, Tanaros Kingslayer, Banewreaker's Servant."

"So you name me." A muscle in his jaw twitched. "I did not choose such names, Lady. Is this how you return a greeting fairly given?"

"You cut down my guardsmen where they stood, sent one of Oronin's Hunters against my husband-to-be, unarmed in his wedding bower. How can you say you mean me no harm?" Anger set her words ablaze. "What happens to me matters naught, Kingslayer. I am resolved to die. But do not slay my kinsmen and tell me you mean no harm! In cold blood, unprovoked—"

Tanaros interrupted her. "Why did you agree to wed him?"

Cerelinde looked away, gazing past him, through the impenetrable cavern walls.

"*Why?*"

She flinched at his tone; the granddaughter of Elterrion the Bold. Yet there was steel in her—courage, and heart. Oh yes, Haomane's Children had heart. It had been Arahila's Gift to them, the only one Haomane had permitted. "You need to ask?" Her backbone rigid, she stood straight and tall. "There is valor in him, and a noble spirit. I am a woman, Tanaros Kingslayer, Ellyl or no." Color flushed her cheekbones. "And there is naught in him a woman would not—"

He cut her short. "You sought to fulfill the Prophecy."

Cerelinde opened her mouth, then closed it.

Tanaros laughed, a dry sound. "You sought to fulfill the Prophecy. Make no mistake. It was an act of war."

"I seek to preserve the lives of my people, Tanaros Blacksword." Her grey eyes were somber. "Can you say the same?"

"Aye, I can and do. You are a pawn, Lady, in a war of Haomane First-Born's devising." He raked a hand through his hair; it was greasy, after days under a helm. "Who talked you into the wedding? Ingolin the Wise? Malthus the Counselor, Haomane's Servant and Weapon?" Tanaros gave a bitter smile at her expression. "See how their wisdom availed them! Well, now I have taken you, and you are Lord Satoris' pawn. At least he is honest about it. And as his emissary, I tell you this: He means you no harm."

"I have been abducted." Cerelinde's voice trembled, with anger and the effort of holding her fear at bay. "Abducted by force, brought here against my will, held captive by—" Catching sight of Ushahin huddled against the far wall, she pointed with a shaking finger. "By *creatures,* by Fjeltroll and that foul Misbegotten—"

"Enough!" Tanaros struck her hand down, a sharp, shocking blow.

Too close for comfort, they stared at one another.

"Your people abandoned Ushahin, Lady," Tanaros said to her. "Remember that. Such as he is, your own children would have been, had you wed Aracus Altorus."

"Never!" She flung the denial out in defiance, his words touching on her darkest fear. "They will be conceived in love, in accordance with Haomane's Prophecy." Cerelinde shook her head. "It is not the same, not the same at all. Why do you think we name him thusly? It is not for the mixing of the races. Ushahin the Misbegotten was conceived in lust, in base desire." She pronounced the words with distaste.

"The Sunderer's *Gift,* not fair Arahila's."

Tanaros raised his brows. "Thus you hold him account-able for his birth?"

"Not his birth, but what he has made of the ill-conceived life he was given," Cerelinde said evenly. "And my folk gave him into the care of yours, Tanaros Kingslayer. We are not to blame for the cruelty wrought by the children of Men."

"No." He looked away from her, gazing at Ushahin. "And yet you were quicker to abandon him than the children of Men were to assail him. Only Oronin's Children rose above such pettiness. The Were took him in when none other would." His gaze returned to hers. "Leave him be. He lost more than any of us in Lindanen Dale."

She remembered the grey forms in their midst, Aracus engaged in combat. Her breath was quick and shallow. "The one who attacked my betrothed . . ."

"The Dreamspinner called her 'mother,'" Tanaros said quietly. "Remember that, when you condemn us in Hao-mane's name, Lady. You have my word as surety: No harm will come to you here."

Bowing stiffly, he took his leave.

Cerelinde watched him go. A part of her heart soared, for if his words were true, it meant that Aracus lived. As dire as her prospects appeared, while they both drew breath, hope must not be abandoned. Haomane's Prophecy might yet be fulfilled, and Satoris Banewreaker destroyed through his own folly.

And yet she was troubled.

Tanaros moved through the encampment, greeting the Fjel, checking on his injured Men, making his way to Ushahin's side. There he squatted on his heels, speaking in low tones, one hand on the Misbegotten's shoulder.

He was her enemy, one of the Three. He had killed his wife and slain his King. He was the servant of Satoris Banewreaker.

He was not at all what she had expected.

* * *

THE WHITE SLIVER OF THE new moon was bright enough to cast shadows.

The old man shook his head, watching the strangers stumble into the Stone Grove. Half dead, most of them, past caring that they entered a sacred place. One crumpled, unable to walk another step; another knelt beside her, breathing hard through his mouth. Foolish, wasting his breath's moisture in the desert, but what else were they to do with those tiny nostrils?

One stayed upright through sheer will, glancing at the tall rocks surrounding the empty circle, eyes suspicious by moonlight. The old man smiled. Stubborn, that one. He must be the appointed guardian. And the others . . .

"Ngurra!" His wife's whisper tickled his ear with delight. "Look! One of the Haomane-gaali."

And so it was, tall and fair, wrought with such grace that thirst and hunger only stripped him to a translucent beauty, his Shaper's intended essence. Ngurra clicked his tongue. Fair, yes, but could Haomane's Children find water in the desert? No.

One of the strangers could, though; their old one—or at least, where he could not find it, he could compel it. And he'd done so, the old wizard. From Dry Basin to Lizard Rock, across the Basking Flats, he'd done it, calling drought-eaters from barren sand. The desert was leached where they had passed, struggling for survival. The old man felt it, himself; there, above his third rib, a dull ache where Thornbrake Bore had run dry.

"Did you see—?" his wife whispered.

"Shhh." He hushed her. "Watch. They have found it."

It was their old one, their wizard. He leaned on his staff, bowing his head. One hand fumbled beneath the moonlit spill of his beard, drawing forth the Soumanië. It shone like a red star in his hand. The wizard raised his head, gazing at the pile of rocks in the center of the Stone Grove. "It is here," he said softly. "Ah, Haomane! The Unknown made Known. Blaise, Peldras, come."

Together, they clambered over the rocks. What they found there, every member of the Yarru knew full well. A cleft, ringed round with rocks, opening onto unfathomable depths, and from it emerging a breath of water, heavy, with a strong mineral tang. A battered tin bucket, sitting atop an endless coil of rope. A faint sigh whispered around the Stone Grove.

"Is it . . . ?" asked the one called Blaise.

"It is the Well of the World and the Navel of Uru-Alat." The wizard's voice held awe. *"Try though they may, one and all, by no hand save the appointed Bearer . . . "* He halted his recitation. "Let us try, then, and see."

Among the rocks surrounding Stone Grove, the Yarru chuckled, a soft, soughing sound, like the shifting of desert sands. Ngurra rested on his haunches, watching as the strangers fed the tin bucket into Birru-Uru-Alat, the hole at the center of the world. Down and down and down it went, on a coiling rope of thukka-vine. He counted the heartbeats, waiting as the rope uncoiled.

Down . . .

Down . .

Down.

Almost, the strangers gave up after long minutes, for there seemed no end to the coiling rope. Ngurra knew how long it was. He had measured it, cubit by cubit, all the days of his life. That was his charge, as chieftain of the Stone Grove Clan. His grandmother, who had been chieftainess before him, had passed it to him, along with her knowledge. Maintain the rope, inch by inch. It was one of his charges.

A faint splash in the night.

"Water," said Peldras the Haomane-gaali, lying prone above the opening. His ears were sharper than those of Men. "The bucket has struck water, Counselor."

One after another, they tried it. Blaise, the appointed

guardian, tried it first, grunting in the moonlight, muscles straining as he sought to raise the bucket. Then the Haomane-gaali Peldras tried, and fared no better. The wizard tried, too, muttering spells that availed him naught, but earned a silent chuckle from the watching Yarru. In the end, they all tried, the whole of Malthus' Company, even the thirsting Archer and the bone-weary Knight, laying hands on the rope together and hauling as one. Yet, even as a whole, bone and muscle and sinew cracking, they failed.

The laden bucket was too heavy to raise.

"Enough," whispered their old one, their wizard. "We have tried, one and all, and fulfilled the letter of the Prophecy." Laying down his staff, he cupped the Soumanië in both hands. His voice grew strong as he spoke the words of the choosing, and the ruddy glow of the chip of the Souma grew, spilling from between his cupped hands to illuminate the Stone Grove. "Yarru-yami! Charred Ones! Children of Haomane's wrath! I call upon you now in his name. Lend us your aid!"

"Time and gone he asked," Warabi muttered.

"Hush, old woman!" Ngurra glared at her. She wouldn't understand the common tongue if he hadn't taught it to her himself. "Kindle the torch."

Still muttering, she obeyed, striking flint to iron. The oil-rich fibers of the bugy-stick sputtered and lit, sending a signal. All around the perimeter of the Stone Grove, bugy-stick torches caught and kindled as, one by one, members of the Six Clans of the Yarru revealed themselves.

Ngurra stepped before the torches, gazing down at the small figures gathered around the Birru-Uru-Alat, their shadows stark on the sand. "The Yarru are here," he called in the common tongue, the language his grandmother had taught him. "As we have always been, since before the earth was scorched. What do you seek?"

Malthus the Counselor opened his arms, showing himself weaponless, offering himself as surety. The Soumanië shone like a red star upon his breast. "Speaker of the Yarru, I greet you. We come seeking the Bearer."

In the night, someone gasped.

FOR TWO MORE DAYS, THEY traveled through the tunnels.

Truth be told, Tanaros had never been comfortable in them. They reminded him, too acutely, that Urulat was old, older than his lifespan, unnatural as it was, could reckon. Dragons had carved them, it was said; whether or not it was true, dragons did not acknowledge. Still, they served their purpose for the armies of Darkhaven.

It was harder, with the Lady of the Ellylon.

Vast as they were—broad enough at all times for two horses to ride abreast, and sometimes three—the tunnels were dark and stifling, a mass of earth pressing above at all times. At times, when it was far between vents, the air grew thick and the torches guttered, burning low. Then it was worse, and even Tanaros fought panic, his chest working to draw air into his lungs.

The Fjel, rock-delvers by nature of their Shaping, were untroubled. Their eyes were well suited to darkness and they could slow the very beat of their hearts at need, breathing slow and deep, moving unhurried at a steady pace, carrying heavy packs of supplies. Brute wisdom, mindless and physical, attuned to survival. Even the horses, bred in the Vale of Gorgantum to fear no darkness, endured without panic.

It was different for Men, who thought overmuch.

It was worst of all for the Ellyl.

Tanaros saw, and sympathized against his will. It was simpler, much simpler, to despise her. Ushahin Dreamspinner managed it without effort, his face twisted with pure and absolute despite when he deigned glance her way. By all rights, the Dreamspinner should have hated the tunnels, being human and Ellyl, a creature of open skies. But he was a child of the Were as well, and at home underground.

Not so the Lady Cerelinde.

Her face, by torchlight, was pale, too pale. Skin stretched taut over bones Shaped like lines of poetry, searing and gorgeous. Haomane's Child. Even here, her beauty made the heart ache. Her eyes were wide, swallowed up by darkness. From time to time her pale fingers scrabbled at her throat, seeking to loosen the clasp of a rough-spun wool cloak someone had loaned her on the first day; Hyrgolf, at a guess.

On the second day, Tanaros could bear it no longer.

An escort of marching Fjel surrounded her as she rode, seated on one of the fallen Staccian's mounts. Tungskulder Fjel, Hyrgolf's best lads, their horny heads at a level with her shoulder even as she rode astride. She bore it well, Cerelinde of the Ellylon, only a faint tremor giving evidence to her fear, until the air grew thick once more and she clutched her throat, gasping.

"Give way," Tanaros murmured to the rearguard.

"General!" A Fjeltroll grinned and saluted, dropping back.

He made his way to her side, maneuvering the black horse. "Lady," he said, and her stricken gaze met his. "All is well. There is air, see?" He inhaled deeply, his chest swelling, detecting a waft of fresh air from an unseen vent. His brand pulsed like bands of marrow-fire around his heart. "We will survive, and endure."

"I am afraid." Her frightened eyes were like stars.

Once, Calista had said that to him; his wife. He hadn't know, then, what she meant. Hadn't known of her past-dawning attraction to his blood-sworn kinsman, his king, Roscus Altorus, or the affair it had engendered. He had laughed at her fears, laughed and embraced her, protecting the child that grew in her belly with his own strong arms, believing them strong enough to fend off aught that might harm them.

Now, he didn't laugh.

"I know," he said instead, somber. "Tomorrow we ride aboveground."

Cerelinde of the Ellylon shuddered with relief. "You might die, Kingslayer," she said in her low, musical voice. "If the tunnel fell, deprived of air, you would die and your comrades with you. It would be terrible, but swift. My death would be slow, for such is Haomane's Gift. I would die by inches, and my mind last of all. Though my body held the semblance of death, I would endure. Days, or weeks, alive in the crushing darkness, aware. Think on that, before you name me a coward."

"I would not." He felt embarrassed. "I would not say such a thing."

Her gaze slid sideways, touching him. "What of him?" She indicated the Dreamspinner, who rode before them in the vanguard, trailing the Cold Hunters, the Kaldjager Fjel, who scouted before them to ensure the way was secure. "The blood of Men and Ellylon runs in his veins, yet he knows no fear."

"There is little Ushahin Dreamspinner fears."

"He is mad."

"Yes and no." Tanaros regarded her. "He has reason to hate your kind, Lady. And mine. If it is madness that warps him, it is of our people's devising."

She looked away, showing her profile, clear-cut as a cameo. "So you have said," she said quietly. "And yet, did he come to us, Malthus would heal him. He is wounded in body and mind. It could be done, by one who knew how to wield the Soumanië. Such is the power of the Souma, to Shape and make whole. Even in the merest chip, it abides. In the dagger Godslayer, it abides tenfold. Satoris Banewreaker is cruel to deny him."

"Deny?" Tanaros laughed aloud.

"You are quick to speak of his pain!" Cerelinde's voice rose with her temper. "And the Sunderer was quick to turn it to his ends. Did you never think that Ushahin the Misbegotten might be better served by kindness?"

"Kindness?" Tanaros drew rein, halting their progression. Behind them, the Fjel chuckled, amused by their exchange. "Lady, my Lord Satoris has offered healing to the Dreamspinner more times than I can number." He smiled grimly at her reaction. "Aye, indeed. Do you think the Lord of Darkhaven does not know how to wield Godslayer? He is a Shaper, one of Seven, no matter that Haomane abjures him. It is Ushahin's choice, to wear this broken face, these crippled hands. He was not denied. He chose to keep his pain, his madness. Again and again, he has chosen."

"It is not right." She was shaken.

"Why? Because you say so?" Tanaros shook his head, nudging his mount to a walk. "You understand nothing."

"Tanaros." The fear in her voice and the fact that she spoke his name made him turn in the saddle. Her face was pale against the darkness of the tunnel, and her upraised chin trembled. "What does he want of me, the Sunderer? Why was I taken and yet not slain? It makes no sense. When you attacked . . ." Cerelinde closed her eyes briefly. "When you attacked, I thought you were Beshtanagi in disguise. Haomane help me, I would have sworn to it. Then I awoke, surrounded by Fjeltroll . . ." She shuddered, swallowing. "Why?"

Pity stirred in his heart, a dangerous thing. "Lady, I cannot say. Only trust that you will be unharmed. My Lord has sworn it."

There was despair in her face, and disbelief.

"Be we moving or no, Lord General?" Hyrgolf's rumbling voice called.

"Aye!" Tanaros tore his gaze away and dug his heels smartly into the black's sides. It snorted, moving at a trot through the ranks of the Fjel, who offered good-natured salutes. "Call the march, Field Marshal!"

"March!" Hyrgolf shouted.

Onward they marched. Tanaros let them pass, falling in beside Ushahin Dreamspinner, who regarded him with an unreadable gaze. "You play a dangerous game, cousin," he said.

Tanaros shook his head. "There is no game here."

Ushahin, still clutching the case containing the Helm of Shadows to his belly, shrugged his crooked shoulders. "As you say. Were the choice mine, I would waste no time in killing her."

"The choice is his Lordship's." Tanaros' voice hardened. "Would you strip all honor from him?"

"In favor of survival?" Ushahin looked bleak. "Aye, I would."

Tanaros reached over to touch his crippled hand where it rested on the case. "Forgive me, cousin," he said. "The Grey Dam of the Were is due all honor. She spent her life as she chose and died with her eyeteeth seeking her enemy's throat."

"Aye." Ushahin drew a deep breath. "I know it." In the torchlit tunnel, his mismatched eyes glittered. "Do you know, cousin, my dam afforded you a gift? Even as she died. You will know it ere the end."

"As you say, cousin." Tanaros withdrew his hand, frowning in perplexity. Perhaps, after all, the Dreamspinner's grief had worsened his madness. "Her life was gift enough."

Ushahin bared his teeth in a grimace. "It was for me."

THE SIX CLANS OF THE Yarru-yami, the Charred Ones, Children of Haomane's Wrath, debated the matter for two days. In the cool hours of the early morning and the blue hours of dusk they debated, each member given his or her allotted length of time to speak in the center of the Stone Grove, atop the rocks that marked the Well of the World.

The debate hinged on a single Yarru, the one who must choose.

He was young, the Bearer, still a youth. Of average height for one of his folk, his head scarce reached the Counselor's shoulder, with coarse black hair falling to his shoulders and liquid-dark eyes in an open, trusting face, struggling manfully to listen and weigh all that was said. He was quick and agile, as the Yarru were, with bare feet calloused by the desert floor, and brown-black skin. It was the mark of his people, the Charred Ones, unwitting victims of Haomane's wrath—save his palms, that were pinkish tan, creased with deep-etched lines.

And when he pressed them together and made a cup of his hands, those lines met at the precise base of the hollow to form a radiant star, for such was the sign of the Bearer.

He was seventeen years old and his name was Dani.

"Can he hoist the bucket?" Blaise Caveros had asked bluntly.

"Yes, Guardian." The old man Ngurra had shifted a wad of *gamal* into the pocket of his cheek, regarding the Altorian. "He is the Bearer. It is what he was born to do, to carry the water of Birru-Uru-Alat, that weighs as heavy as life. But whether or not he does is his choosing."

And so there was debate.

It began with Malthus the Counselor. "Dani of the Yarru," he said, leaning upon his staff. "You have seen the red star, the signal of war. In the west, the Sunderer's army grows, legion upon legion of Fjeltroll streaming to join him. Soon he will move against us like a mighty tide, for it is his will to lay claim to the whole of Urulat and challenge his brother, Haomane First-Born, Lord-of-Thought, the Will of Uru-Alat." The Counselor scowled, his bushy eyebrows fierce. "We can fight, and die, we who are loyal to Haomane and the light of the Souma, who would see Urulat made whole. We *will* fight, and die. But in the end, only one thing can halt Satoris Banewreaker."

With his staff he pointed to the rock-pile in the center of the Stone Grove. "Therein," he said, "lies the Water of Life. It alone can quench the marrow-fire that wards the dagger

Godslayer. And you alone can draw it, Dani of the Yarru. You alone can carry it. You are the vessel, a part of the Prophecy of Haomane, the Unknown made Known." The Counselor opened his arms. The Soumanië gleamed red upon his breast, nestled amid his beard. "It is a grave matter," he said. "To bear the Water of Life into the Vale of Gorgantum, inside the walls of Darkhaven itself, and extinguish the marrow-fire. We who stand here before you, the Company of Malthus, are pledged to aid you in every step of the way. Yet in the end, the fate of Urulat rests in your hands, Bearer. Choose."

Such was the beginning.

Many others spoke, and among the Company of Malthus, only the Counselor understood the tongue of the Yarru; for many years had he studied it in his quest to unravel the Prophecy. And what he understood, he kept to himself over the days that followed.

When all was said, Dani the Bearer chose.

EIGHT

❖

"YES?" LILIAS RECLINED ON SILK cushions, raising her brows at the page.

"My lady," he said and gulped, glancing sidelong at pretty Sarika in her scanty attire, kneeling at her mistress' side and wafting a fan against the unseasonal heat of a late Pelmaran spring. "My lady . . . there is an ambassador to see you. From the Were."

"Well?" Lilias arched her carefully plucked eyebrows a fraction higher, watching the page stutter. "Are the Were not our allies? See him in!"

He left in a rush. Sarika ceased her fanning. "You should bind him to you, my lady," she murmured, lowering her head to press her lips to the inside of Lilias' wrist. "He would be quicker to serve."

"I've no need of fools and imbeciles, dear one." She stroked the girl's hair. "Enough surround me without binding."

Head bent, Sarika smiled.

Calandor?

Abide, little sister.

The Were ambassador, when he came, entered the room like grey smoke, flowing around corners, low to the ground. Only when he stood and bowed did his form become fixed in the mind's eye. Sarika let out a squeak, huddling close to her mistress' couch. "Sorceress of the East." The Were dipped his muzzle in acknowledgment. "I am Phraotes. I bring you greetings from the Grey Dam of the Were."

Lilias frowned. "Where is Kurush to whom I spoke a fortnight ago? Has he fallen out of favor with the Grey Dam Sorash?"

Phraotes grimaced, lips curling back to show his sharp teeth. "The Grey Dam is dead. The Grey Dam lives. Vashuka is the Grey Dam of the Were."

"Ahhh." A pang ran through her. For as long as Lilias had lived—far longer than the allotment of Arahila's Children—Sorash had been the Grey Dam. "I grieve for your loss, Phraotes," she said in formal response, rising from her couch and extending her hand. "I give greetings to the Grey Dam Vashuka, and recognize the ancient ties of alliance. Thy enemies shall be mine, and my enemies shall be thine."

"Sorceress." He bowed his head, but his amber eyes glowed uneasily at her. "The Grey Dam values the friendship of Beshtanag."

The words were a blow. "Friendship." Lilias withdrew her outstretched hand, regarding Phraotes. "Not alliance."

The ambassador's keen, pointed ears tightened against

his head. "War comes to Beshtanag. We do not desire war. Only to hunt, and live."

"You helped to set these forces in motion, Phraotes."

"Yes." His muzzle dipped in a nod. "The Grey Dam So-rash had cause for vengeance. Two Brethren accompanied her. All are dead. The debt is paid. The Grey Dam Vashuka does not desire war."

"Why?" she asked him.

His lip curled. "Once was enough, Sorceress."

Lilias paced her drawing-room, ignoring the clatter of Gergon's wardsmen arriving in a panic, waving them back when they sought to enter the room. Phraotes watched her with wary patience. "You prevailed in that war, Phraotes."

The Were shook his head. "We won our battle, Sorceress. We lost the war."

It is so, Lilias.

Lilias sighed. "You should have stayed in the west," she said to Phraotes. "The children of Men would not hunt you beneath the Sunderer's protection. He commands a vaster territory than I do."

His amber eyes shone. "Our home is in the east, Sorceress. We are Oronin's Children and it is here he Shaped us."

"Oronin should have better care for his Children," Lilias said sharply.

"No." Phraotes' shoulders moved in a shrug. "He is the Glad Hunter. He Shaped us in joy. The Grey Dam Vashuka believes we were foolish to listen to Satoris Banewreaker, who spoke smooth words and roused our ire against Hao-mane First-Born for denying us the Gift of cleverness. Only Yrinna's Children were wise."

"The *Dwarfs?*" She laughed. "The Dwarfs are content to till the soil and tend the orchards of arrogant Vedasian no-bles, ambassador, accepting humility as their lot. You call that wisdom?"

"No one slaughters their young," said Phraotes. "There is merit in Yrinna's Peace. So the Grey Dam Vashuka be-

lieves. I am sorry, Sorceress. You have been a good friend to
the Were. In Beshtanag, we have been safe. No longer, if
war comes." He paused, then added, "We do not abandon
you. The Grey Dam pledges a scouting-pack of yearling
Brethren to range the western borders, reporting to you. But
we will not join in battle. We are too few."

It is their right, Lilias.

"I know," she said aloud, replying to the dragon. "I
know." Reluctantly, Lilias inclined her head to the Were
ambassador. "I hear your words, Phraotes. Though I am disappointed, they are fair-spoken. Tell the Grey Dam Vashuka
that the Sorceress of the East values her friendship. So long
as Beshtanag is under my rule, the Were are welcome in it."

"Sorceress." He bowed with obvious relief, ears pricked
at a more confident angle. "You are wise and generous."

In the hallway, one of the warders coughed. Lilias sup-
pressed a surge of annoyance. Her wardsmen enjoyed an
easy life, and greater freedom than they might elsewhere in
Pelmar, subject to the whims of the Regents. With the aid of
the Were, she and Calandor defended the boundaries of
Beshtanag. All she had done was to forge a holding where
she might live in peace, as she chose.

All she asked was loyalty.

Her indulgences were few. There were her attendants, her
pretty ones, but what of it? She liked to be surrounded by
beauty, by youth. It was a precious and fleeting thing, that
span of time wherein youth attained the outer limits of
adulthood and reckoned itself immortal, refusing to acknowledge the Chain of Being. It reminded her of why she
had chosen to become what she was, the Sorceress of the
East.

Most of them served of their own volition. And the
rest . . . well. She tried to choose wisely, but perhaps there
were a few exceptions. It was a small Shaping, a minor
binding at best. None of them took any harm from it, and
Lilias dowered them generously, lads and maids alike, when
the freshness of their youth began to fade and she dismissed

them from her service to go forth and lead ordinary, mortal lives, shaded by the glamor of being part of a story that had begun before they were born, that would continue after their deaths.

None had any right to complain.

And none of them were wise enough to shudder under the shadow of what had occurred here this day, hearing in Grey Dam Vashuka's stance the echo of what was to transpire in the promise of Haomane's Prophecy. Lilias heard its echo, and knew, once more, the taste of fear.

The Were shall be defeated ere they rise . . .

"Thank you, ambassador," she said. "You have leave to go."

He left, belly low to the ground, flowing like smoke.

"BESHTANAG HAS NEVER DEPENDED ON the Were, little ssissster."

"No." Lilias leaned back against the strong column of the dragon's left foreleg, watching blue dusk deepen in the cavern mouth. "But it's a blow nonetheless. Even if all goes as Tanaros Blacksword claimed, we have to be prepared to keep Haomane's Allies at bay for a day, perhaps longer. Beshtanag won't fall in a day, but it would have helped to have the Were in reserve."

"Yesss."

On the horizon, the red star winked into visibility. "Calandor?"

"Yess, Liliasss?"

"What if he's right?" She craned her neck to look up at him. "What if the Dwarfs *did* choose wisely in choosing Yrinna's Peace? Might we not do the same? Are we wrong to defy the will of Haomane?"

A nictitating membrane flickered over the dragon's left eye. "What is *right*, Liliasss?"

"Right," she said irritably. "That which is not wrong."

"In the beginning," Calandor rumbled, "there was Uru-

Alat, and Uru-Alat was all things, and all things were Uru-Alat—"

"—and then came the Beginning-in-End, and the Seven Shapers emerged, and first of all was Haomane, Lord-of-Thought, who was born at the place of the Souma and knew the will of Uru-Alat," Lilias finished. "I *know*. Is it true? Does Haomane speak with the World God's voice? Are we wrong to defy him?"

The dragon bent his sinuous neck, lowering his head. Twin puffs of smoke jetted from his nostrils. "You quote the catechism of your childhood, little ssisster, not mine."

"But is it *true?*"

"No." Calandor lifted his head, sighing a sulfurous gust. "No, Liliasss. You know otherwise. These are things I have shown you. The world began in ending, and it will end in beginning. Thisss, not even Haomane Firsst-Born undersstands. What he grasspss is only a portion of Uru-Alat'ss plan, and his role in it is not as he thinksss. All things mussst be Ssundered to be made whole. It is not finished . . . yet."

"Calandor," she said. "Why did you tell such things to Satoris Third-Born, yet not to Haomane First-Born?"

"Because," the dragon said. "He asssked."

For a long moment, neither spoke. At length, Lilias said, "Is that why Haomane despises him?"

The dragon shifted. "Perhapss, Liliasss. I cannot sssay."

"Between them, they will tear the world asunder anew," she said in a low voice.

"Yesss," Calandor agreed. "One in his pride, one in his defiansse. Sso it musst be. All things change and transsmute, even Shapers. They play the roles they mussst."

"Do they know?" she asked.

Calandor blinked once, slowly. "Sssatoriss knows."

In the unseasonal warmth she shivered, wrapping her arms about herself, pressing her body against the scaled forelimb. Even the forge-heat of the dragon's body could not dispel her chill. "Calandor, what of us? What happens if we fail?"

"Fail?" There was amusement in the dragon's deep voice. "What is *failure?*"

"RIGHT." THE CAPTAIN OF THE *Ilona's Gull* scratched his stubbled chin, running a calculating eye over Carfax' company. "My bargain was for twenty men, not horses. 'Specially not *these* horses. Reckon they'll wreak right hell in my hold if the crossing's rough, won't they?"

In the bright sunlight of Harrington Bay, the measures taken to disguise the horses of Darkhaven held up poorly. Even with burred manes and ill-kept coats, their eyes gleamed with preternatural intellect, muscles gliding like oil under their bunching hides.

"Look, man." Carfax struggled for calm, finding his hand reaching for his sword-hilt. Nothing on earth was more frustrating than dealing with the Free Fishers of Harrington Inlet. They owed allegiance to no mortal ruler, and their independence was legendary. "A bargain was made. My understanding is that it was for passage for my men and their mounts . . . and for the lady. Will you keep it or no?"

A crowd was gathering on the quai, which was to the good. They wanted witnesses who could testify that a group of armed men, likely Pelmaran, had departed on the *Ilona's Gull,* escorting a woman garbed in a cloak of white silk wrought by Ellylon, the gold-embroidered crowns and ruby Souma glinting in the sunlight.

What they *didn't* want was witnesses who crowded close enough to note that the supposed Pelmarans spoke the common tongue with a Staccian accent, the horses they rode were found nowhere else on earth, and beneath the shadow of her exquisite hood, the Ellyl noblewoman sported blond beard-stubble.

"I might . . ." the captain drawled, winking at his mates. "For a price. A damage tax, y'see."

"Fine," Carfax snapped. If he'd had the luxury of time, he'd have showed the Free Fisherman what it meant to bargain with a disciple of mighty Vorax, whose appetite was matched only by his shrewdness. But somewhere behind them—hours, at best—a host of Haomane's Allies pursued them. "Name your price."

The Free Fisher captain pursed his wind-chapped lips. "I might do it for a pair of those fine steeds you ride, goodman."

"Two horses?" Carfax raised his hand, cutting off a protest from his comrades.

"Two." The captain nodded. "Aye, two will do it. Reckon they'll fetch a good price in Port Calibus." He grinned, revealing strong white teeth. "They do like to cut a fine figure astride, those Vedasian knights."

"Done."

The bargain struck, the planks were laid, and Carfax's company began boarding the *Ilona's Gull*. The horses of Darkhaven permitted themselves to be led down the ramps with wary dignity, eyes rolling as they descended into the ship's hold. Turin in his Ellyl cloak was hustled aboard, surrounded by an escort. Carfax breathed a sigh of relief as he disappeared.

"Lieutenant." One of his men, young Mantuas, tugged at his elbow. "Lieutenant," he hissed in Staccian, "we *can't* part with any of the horses! 'Twill leave a trail pointing straight to Darkhaven!"

"Peace, lad," Carfax muttered out of the side of his mouth. "At least speak in common, if you must. Hey!" he added, shouting at the pressing crowd, affecting a Pelmaran accent rather well, he thought. "You and you, get back! This is important business, and none of yours!"

They withdrew a few paces, the Free Fishers; net-men and fish-wives, curious children with bright eyes. A few paces, no more. Carfax hid a smile. Lord Vorax had a fondness for the Free Fishers of Harrington Inlet, truth be told. Stubborn as they were, they had the pride of their self-interest, unabashed and free—some, like this captain, even willing to strike deals with agents of suspect origin.

But when it came to war, the Free Fishers would side with Haomane's Allies, believing Lord Satoris would strip away their independence. Mantuas was right, of course. They couldn't afford to lose the horses.

If there were more time, Carfax thought, he might try to sway the captain and his crew. They seemed like shrewd men who understood profit and would listen to reason, who could be brought to understand that Lord Satoris offered a greater freedom than they knew existed; freedom from the yolk of Haomane's will, under which they labored unknowing, trudging like a miller's oxen in endless circles.

But given the time constraints, it would be much simpler to kill them at sea.

Carfax hoped he remembered how to sail a ship. It had been a long time since he had summered on the shores of Laefrost Lake with his mother's kin, the clear, ice-blue waters swollen with snowmelt. Well, he thought, crossing the ramp, standing at the railings as the planks were drawn aboard and the mainsail hoisted, the winch grinding as the anchor was raised; we will find out.

The sail bellied full, showing the proud insignia of the Free Fishers of Harrington Inlet, the stone anchor and fish-hook. Crewmen scrambled here and there, obeying the captain's shouted orders. A wedge of open water divided them from the shore, growing steadily as the *Ilona's Gull* nudged her prow seaward.

NINE

❖

THEY EMERGED FROM THE TUNNELS in the outskirts of a ruined city.

Once, there had been walls and towers of white onyx, proud spires rising from the plains. Now, the walls were breached and broken, and plain-hawks nested in the toppled towers. Sturdy heart-grass grew in the empty streets, cracking the marble flagstones, and the wind made a mournful sound in the ruins.

The entrance to the tunnel was partially blocked by great slabs of blue chalcedony, and they picked their way out one by one. Cerelinde, emerging into the cloud-shrouded daylight, reached out from her saddle to touch the cracked walls of the adjacent structure from which slabs of precious stone had slid, revealing the granite beneath. "Ellylon made this."

"Careful, Lady," Tanaros muttered. "It is unstable."

"What is this place?" She shivered. "There is sorrow in its bones."

Hyrgolf glanced backward, his massive head silhouetted against the lowering sky. "Your people called it the City of Long Grass, Lady of the Ellylon," he answered in his guttural voice. "A long time ago."

"Ah, Haomane!" Cerelinde flung herself from her mount's back, kneeling at the base of one chalcedony slab. *"Cuilos Tuillenrad."* Her fingers brushed the moon-blue surface with delicate reverence, revealing lines of Ellylon runes therein engraved. "This city belonged to Numireth the Fleet," she breathed.

"Yes." Tanaros caught the reins of her mount, glancing around uneasily. The city, or what remained of it, was a desolate place. It had been conquered long ago, in the Third Age of the Sundered World, when Lord Satoris had led the Fjeltroll out of the fastness of the north and swept westward, driving the Ellylon before him. The plains had reclaimed it since. No one else wanted it. "Lady Cerelinde, we must ride."

"A moment," she whispered, tracing the runes with her fingertips. "I beg you."

He glanced at Hyrgolf, who shrugged. The Fjel were engaged in hauling supplies from the tunnel, assessing what must be ported, what could be left behind. There would be ample grazing now that they were on the open plains. It had been carefully chosen, this site; close enough to Darkhaven to ensure a safe return, far enough to ensure that the Lady of the Ellylon did not guess the extent of the tunnel system that lay beneath Urulat, which led to the door of Darkhaven itself.

And, of course, there was the history, which was supposed to remind her of the folly of opposing Lord Satoris' will. All of these matters were well considered, which did naught to assuage the prickling sensation at the back of Tanaros' neck.

Why had the plains gone wind-still?

"Cousin." Ushahin sidled his mount close to Tanaros. His good eye squinted tight. "I mislike this stillness. Something is wrong."

The Fjel had paused in their labors, broad nostrils sniffing the air. Vorax's Staccians were huddled together, crowding their mounts' flanks. Pressure built all around. At the base of the chalcedony slab, the Lady Cerelinde traced runes, whispering under her breath.

"Dreamspinner!" Tanaros grabbed the half-breed's wrist. "What is she doing?"

"You do not know?" Ushahin's smile was sickly. "This is

the crypt where the fallen of the House of Numireth were interred. The tunnels lie beneath it. Where she kneels?" He nodded toward Cerelinde, whose bridal skirts lay spread in a pool. "It is where their kin offered prayers for vengeance against the Sunderer. I imagine she does the same."

Every blade of heart-grass stood motionless, waiting, in the gaps of the walls, the cracked and desolate streets. There was only the whisper of Cerelinde's voice.

Tanaros swore.

"Put on the helm," he said, his fingers tightening hard on the half-breed's wrist. "Dreamspinner! *Don the Helm of Shadows!*"

Too late.

From everywhere and nowhere they came at once; wraiths, the host of the House of Numireth. Misty riders on misty horses, converging from all quarters of the forsaken city. With hollow eyes filled with white flame, the Ellylon dead heeded Cerelinde's prayer, and the clamor of ancient battle rose as they rode, a grief-stricken wail riding above it all.

"Tungskulder Fjel!" Somewhere, Hyrgolf was roaring. "Form a square! Kaldjager! To the hunt!"

Tanaros swore again, having lost his grip on the reins of Cerelinde's mount and on Ushahin. He drew his Pelmaran sword as a ghostly warrior bore down upon him, swinging hard. His blade cleaved only mist, and Ellyl laughter pealed like bells, bright and bitter. Again, and again. The Host of Numireth encircled him, pale mocking in their unsubstantial beauty, riding past to swipe at him with ghostly blades. Filled with unreasoning terror, Tanaros dug his heels into the black's sides, turning him in a tight circle, lashing out with his sword.

Everywhere he turned, the wraiths surrounded him, riding in a ring, swirling into mist when his steel passed through them, only to coalesce unharmed. White fire filled the hollows of their eyes, and death was written in it. Some yards away through the wraith-mist, Ushahin Dreamspinner had fallen writhing to the ground, clutching his twisted hands over his ears. And then one of the riding wraiths brushed close enough to touch him, and Tanaros heard the voices of the dead whispering in his own mind.

. . . because of you we were slain whom the Lord-of-Thought made deathless, because of you the world was Sundered, because of you we are bound here . . .

"No!" Tanaros shouted to silence the rising chorus. "It's not true!"

. . . dwelled in peace until the Enemy came from the north and hordes upon hordes of Fjeltroll tore down our walls and slaughtered our armies . . .

"It's not true!"

Numireth, Valwe, Nandinor . . . names out of legend, slain before his birth. Tall lords of the Ellylon with eyes of white fire, and on their breastplates the insignia of their House, the swift plains elbok, picked out in sable shadow. Numireth the Fleet, whose silver helm was crowned with wings. They closed around him, wraith-mist touching his living flesh, the tide of their litany rising in his straining mind.

. . . plains of Curonan ran red with blood and the screams of the dying, and we were driven from our homes, we who are the Rivenlost . . .

"No." Tanaros shut his eyes against them in desperate denial, putting up his sword. Under his right elbow, he felt the lump of Hyrgolf's *rhios* in its pouch. A familiar rage rose in his heart. "Dwelled in peace, my arse! You marched against him in Neherinach!"

Elsewhere, the sound of battle raged; but the voices fell silent in his mind.

Without daring open his eyes, Tanaros dismounted, letting the reins fall slack. Crawling, he groped his way across the cracked marble and tufted heart-grass toward the sound of Ushahin's agonized keening. There, a few paces from the half-breed, his hands found what he sought—the leather case that held the Helm of Shadows.

"Cousin." He reached out blindly to touch Ushahin. "I'm taking the Helm."

"Tanaros!" A breath hissed through clenched teeth. *"Get them out of my head!"*

"I will try." With fingers stiff from clutching his hilt, Tanaros undid the clasps and withdrew the Helm. It throbbed with pain at his touch and he winced at the ache in his bones. His hands trembled as he removed the Pelmaran helmet and placed the Helm of Shadows on his head, opening his eyes.

Darkness.

Pain.

Darkness like a veil over his vision, casting the plains and the ruined city in shadow; pain, a constant companion. The ghost of a wound throbbed in his groin, deep and searing, pumping a steady trickle of ichor down the inside of his leg. Such was the pain of Satoris, stabbed by Oronin Last-Born before the world was Sundered, and the darkness of the Helm was the darkness in his heart.

Once it had been Haomane's weapon. No longer.

Tanaros rose. Before him, the wraiths of the House of Numireth arrayed themselves in a line, silent warriors on silent horses. In the Helm's shadowed vision they had taken on solidity, and he saw bitter sorrow in their eyes instead of flames, and the marks of their death-wounds upon their ageless flesh.

Across the plains and throughout the city, other battles raged. Westward, the surviving Staccian riders fled in full-blown terror, not even the horses of Darkhaven able to outrun the wraiths. In a deserted plaza where once a fountain had played, Hyrgolf's Fjel fought shadows, their guttural cries hoarse with exhaustion and fear. Here and there in the streets, the stalking Kaldjager waged battle with the dead.

And to the south, a lone rider streaked in flight, unpursued.

"Numireth." Tanaros gazed steadily through the eyeslits of the Helm of Shadows. "I claim this city in the name of

Satoris the Shaper. This quarrel is older than your loss, and your shades have no power in Urulat. Begone."

The Lord of Cuilos Tuillenrad, the City of Long Grass, grimaced in the face of the Helm's dark visage; held up one hand, turned away, his figure fading as he rode. One by one, the wraith-host followed, growing insubstantial and vanishing.

"Well done." Breathing hard, Ushahin struggled to his feet. His mouth was twisted in self-deprecation. "My apologies, Blacksword. I've walked in the dreams of the living. I've never had the dead enter mine. It was . . . painful."

"It doesn't matter." Tanaros removed the Helm, blinking at the sudden brightness. The piercing throb in his groin subsided to a vestigial ache. "Can you summon her horse? I've not the skill for it."

"Aye." Donning the Helm of Shadows, Ushahin faced south, sending out a whip-crack of thought. In the distance, the small, fleeting figure of a horse balked. There was a struggle between horse and rider; a brief one. The horses of Darkhaven had strong wills and hard mouths. This one turned in a sweeping loop, heading back for the ruined city at a steady canter, bearing its rider with it.

Tanaros watched long enough to be certain Cerelinde would not throw herself from the saddle, then turned his attention to his company. To the west, the Staccians had regrouped, returning shame-faced at their flight. Singly and in pairs, the Kaldjager loped through the streets, irritable at the false hunt. But Hyrgolf's Fjel . . . ah, no!

They came slowly, carrying one of their number with uncommon care.

"General Tanaros." Hyrgolf's salute was sombre. "I am sorry to report—"

"Jei morderran!" It was a young Tungskulder Fjel, one of the new recruits, who interrupted, hurling himself prone on the cracked marble, offering his bloodstained axe with both hands. "Gojdta mahk åxrekke—"

"Field marshal!" Tanaros cut the lad short. "Report."

"Aye, General." Hyrgolf met his gaze. "Bogvar is wounded. I do not think he will live. Thorun asks you to take his axe-hand in penance."

"He asks *what?* No, never mind." Tanaros turned his attention to the injured Fjeltroll, laid gently on the ground by the four comrades who carried him. "Bogvar, can you hear me?"

"Lord . . . General." Bogvar's leathery lips parted, flecked with blood. One of his eyetusks was chipped. A dreadful gash opened his massive chest, and air whistled in it as he struggled for breath, blood bubbling in the opening, gurgling as he spoke. "You . . . were . . . right." The claws on his left hand flexed, and he forced his lips into a horrible smile. "Should have held . . . my shield higher."

"Ah, curse it, Bogvar!" Kneeling beside him, Tanaros pressed both hands hard over the gash. "Someone bring a— ah, no!" A rush of blood welled in the Fjel's open mouth, dribbled from one corner. Bogvar of the Tungskulder Fjel lay still, and bled no more. Tanaros sighed and ran a hand through his hair, forgetful of the blood. "You should have held your shield higher," he muttered, clambering wearily to his feet. "The lad Thorun did this?"

"Aye." Hyrgolf's voice came from deep in his chest. "An accident. The dead came among us, and some broke ranks. Thorun was one. He thought he struck a blow at an Ellyl wraith. My fault, General. I reckoned him ready."

"Gojdta mahk åxrekke . . . " The young Fjel struggled to his knees, holding his right arm extended and trembling, clawed fist clenched. "Take my axe-hand," he said thickly in the common tongue. "I kill him. I pay."

"No." Tanaros glanced round at the watchful Fjeltroll, the chagrined Staccians straggling back on their wind-blown mounts. "The first fault was mine. I chose this place without knowing its dangers. Let it be a lesson learned, a bitter one. We are at war. There are no safe places left in the world, and our survival depends on discipline." He bent and retrieved Thorun's axe, proffering it haft-first. "Hold ranks," he said grimly. "Follow orders. And keep your shields up. Is this understood?"

"General!" Hyrgolf saluted, the others following suit.

The young Fjel Thorun accepted his axe.

THE TASTE OF FREEDOM WAS sweet; as sweet as the Long Grass in blossom, and as fleeting. She felt the Host of Numireth disperse, its bright presence fading. She felt the Misbegotten's thought flung out across the plains, a thread of will spun by an unwholesome spider of a mind.

If he had reached for her, Cerelinde might have resisted. Even with the Helm of Shadows, he was weak from the ordeal and here, on the threshold of Cuilos Tuillenrad, she was strong. The old Ellylon magics had not vanished altogether.

But no, he was cunning. He turned her mount instead.

She had dared to hope when it had raced willingly at her urging; another of Haomane's Children's ancient charms, the ability to sooth the minds of lesser beasts. But the horses of Darkhaven were willful and warped by the Sunderer's Shaping, with great strength in their limbs and malice in their hearts. It fought against her charm and the bit alike, its eyes roiling with vile amusement as it turned in a vast circle to answer the Misbegotten's call.

She let it carry her back to the ruined city, its path carving a wake through the long grass. There Tanaros stood, watching and awaiting her return. Her dark-dappled mount bore her unerringly to him then stopped, motionless and quiescent.

"Lady," Tanaros said, bowing to her. "A noble effort. Bravely done."

Cerelinde searched his face for mockery, finding none. "Would you have done otherwise?" she asked.

"No," he said simply. "I would not."

Behind him, grunting Fjel wielded their maces with mighty blows, breaking the chalcedony slabs into rubble, demolishing forever the inscriptions upon them. They were porting massive chunks of moon-blue stone and heaping them atop a fallen comrade to form a cairn. Cerelinde felt herself turn pale at the sight. "They are destroying the resting-place of my ancestors!" Her voice shook. "Ah, Haomanc! Is it not enough the city was destroyed long ago? Must you permit this desecration?"

Tanaros' expression hardened. "Lady," he said, "Your *ancestors* marched against theirs long before the City of Long Grass fell. Marched into Neherinach, and took arms against Neheris' Children in the high mountains. Do you blame them?"

Two spots of color rose on her cheeks. "They chose to shelter the Sunderer!"

"Yes." He held her gaze. "They did."

Cerelinde shook her head. "I do not understand you," she said in a low tone. "I will never understand. Why do you serve one such as Satoris Banewreaker, who exists only to destroy such beauty?"

Tanaros sighed. "Lady, these ruins have stood untouched for centuries. It was you who sought to make a weapon of them," he reminded her. "For that, I do not blame you. Do me the courtesy of understanding that I must now destroy them in turn."

Though his words were just, her heart ached within her breast. The Fjel maces swung onward, breaking and smashing, each blow further diminishing the presence of the Rivenlost in the Sundered World. Never again would the wraiths of the valiant dead of the House of Numireth ride the plains of Curonan. "You did not have to choose this," Cerelinde whispered. "My paltry effort caused you no harm."

"No harm?" Tanaros stared at her. "Lady Cerelinde, I do not begrudge you either your valor or your vengeance, but I pray you, spare me your hypocrisy. One of my lads lies dead, and that is harm aplenty." Contempt laced his voice. "Unless that is not what such a word *means* to your people."

Without another word, he walked away.

Cerelinde bowed her head, weary and defeated. It was true, she had forgotten about the slain Fjeltroll. Until this moment, she had not known it was possible for a Man to mourn the passing of such a creature.

It seemed it was.

She did not understand.

USHAHIN DREAMSPINNER SLEPT, AND DREAMED.

On the plains of Curonan, the wind blew low and steady, soughing through the heart-grass. The city of Cuilos Tuillenrad lay three leagues to the south, and the dead lay quiet in it, including Bogvar of the Tungskulder Fjel, who slept the sleep of the dead beneath a cairn of Ellylon rubble.

On the plains, the Cold Hunters stood sentry, watching the grass bow in the wind through yellow eyes that could see in the dark. Even so, Field Marshal Hyrgolt walked the perimeter with heavy steps, peering into the night. No Fjel were to have died on this mission, and his heart was uneasy.

General Tanaros slept, fitful in his bedroll.

In a simple hide tent, Cerelinde of the Ellylon did not sleep, and her eyes were open and wakeful onto the world.

These, the Dreamspinner passed over.

Over and over, ranging far afield. Outside the warded valley of Meronil, he sifted through the sleeping thoughts of Altorian warriors, flinching at their violence as they dreamed of a council of war in the halls of the Rivenlost. On the rocking waters of Harrington Bay, he brushed the mind of a dozing Staccian lieutenant, filled with reef-knots and mainsails and a dagger stuck in a Free Fisherman's throat.

Further.

Further.

A dry land, so dry the ravens feared it.

There, he found seven minds sheltered, warded against incursions in one manner or another. One, that shone like a red star, he avoided like plague. One was Ellyl, and made him shudder. One was wary, bound with suspicion. One dreamed only of the bow's tension, the drawn string quivering, the arrow's quick release.

One dreamed of water, following the veins of the earth, carrying a digging-stick.

One dreamed of marrow-fire and clutched his throat.

But one; ah! One seethed with resentment and dreamed of what displeased him, and his envy made brittle the wardings that protected him until his thoughts trickled through the cracks and he might be known, his place located and found upon the face of Urulat, his destination discerned. Hobard of Malumdoorn was his name, and he was Vedasian. A young knight, given his spurs only because of his family's long association with the Dwarfs and the secret they guarded. Were it not for that, he would never have been knighted, never sent to Meronil to confer with the wise.

Never chosen for the Company of Malthus.

In the darkness, Ushahin smiled, and woke.

Sitting cross-legged, he summoned the ravens of Darkhaven.

TEN

SUNLIGHT FLOODED THE GREAT HALL of Meronil, streaming through the tall windows. The slender panes of translucent blue flanking the clear expanses of glass laid bars of sapphire light across the polished wood of the long table.

Ingolin the Wise surveyed those assembled.

"There are tidings," he said to them. "Good and ill."

"Give us the bad news." It was Aracus Altorus who spoke. The loss of Cerelinde had struck him hard, etching lines of sorrow and self-blame into his features. No longer did the ageless Ellylon behold the Altorian king-in-exile and reckon him young for one of his kind.

"The Lady Cerelinde's abductors elude us," Ingolin said. "Even now, we pursue them across the waters. But hope dwindles."

"Why?" Aracus' voice was grim. "Do our allies fail us?"

Duke Bornin of Seahold cleared his throat. "Kinsman, I have bargained with the Council of Harrington Bay on our behalf, and all aid they have given us. This much is known. The miscreants booked passage to Port Calibus aboard the *Ilona's Gull*. Witnesses in the harbor attest to the fact that the Lady Cerelinde was with them, and seemingly unharmed. But," he said somberly, "ships returning from Vedasia report passing no such vessel en route. I fear they changed their course at sea."

There was silence in the great hall.

"So we have lost them?" A single frown-line knit the perfect brow of the Lady Nerinil, who spoke for the surviving members of the House of Numireth.

"Yes." Ingolin bowed his head to her. "For now. If they are bound for Port Calibus, we will intercept them there. If not—"

"Lord Ingolin, we know where they are bound. All signs point to Beshtanag." Aracus Altorus flattened his hands in a patch of blue light atop the table. "The question is whether or not the Rivenlost and our allies dare to challenge the Sorceress of the East." His face was hard with resolve. "Ingolin, I fear the Sorceress and the Soumanië she wields, that we must face without the aid of Malthus the Counselor. I fear the Dragon of Beshtanag in his ancient lair. But I fear more hearing you say, 'hope dwindles.'" He raised his chin an inch, sunlight making a brightness of his red-gold hair.

"Cerelinde lives, Ingolin. The Prophecy lives, and where there is life, there is hope. The Borderguard of Curonan will *not* despair."

"Nor do I suggest it," Ingolin said gently. "Son of Altorus, did I not say there were glad tidings among the sorrowful?" Turning in his chair, the Lord of the Rivenlost beckoned to an attendant, who came forward to set a gilded coffer on the table before him. It was inlaid with gems, worked with the device of the Crown and Souma.

"That is the casket Elterrion the Bold gave to Ardrath, Haomane's Counselor, is it not?" the Lady Nerinil inquired."

"Yes." Ingolin nodded. "And it passed to Malthus, who gave it to me. 'Ward it well, old friend,' he told me, 'for I have attuned the humble stone within it to the Gem I bear. If it kindles, you may know we have succeeded.'"

And so saying, he opened the casket.

It blazed.

It blazed with light, a rough shard of tourmaline, spilling pale blue light across the polished surface of the table like water in the desert. Incontrovertible and undeniable, the signal of Malthus the Counselor shone like a beacon.

"The Unknown," said Ingolin, "is made Known."

And he told them of the Water of Life.

STRIPPED TO THEIR BREECHES AND sweating, the riders straggled along the riverbank, each picking his path through sedge grass. Insects rose in buzzing clouds at their passage, and even the horses of Darkhaven shuddered, flicking their tails without cease. Little else lived along the lower reaches of the Verdine River, which flowed torpid and sluggish out of the stagnant heart of the Delta itself.

"Sweet Arahila have mercy! I'd give my left stone for a good, hard frost."

Snicker, snicker. "Might as well, Vilbar. It's no use to *you*."

"A sodding lot you know! I've had girls wouldn't give you a drink in the desert."

"Wishing don't make it so."

"Wish we *were* in the desert. At least it would be dry."

"Wish I had a girl right now. This heat makes me pricklish."

"Have a go at Turin, why don't you? He's near pretty enough."

"Sod you all!"

"*Quiet!*" At the head of their ragged column, Carfax turned to glare at his men. They drew rein and fell into muttering silence. "Right," he said. "It's going to get worse before it gets better. If you think this is bad, wait until we get into the Delta. In the meantime, save your breath and keep your flapping jaws *shut.*"

"Who's going to hear us out here, lieutenant?" Mantuas gestured, indicating the broad expanse of sedge grass, the open sky. "The local frog-hunters? There's not a living soul in shouting distance! Vedasian patrols wouldn't bother getting their gear muddy this close to the stinking Verdine. Look around you, there's . . . " He stopped, staring.

To the west, three specks in the sky.

"Ravens," someone breathed.

"Hey!" Turin dragged the Lady Cerelinde's cloak from his saddlebag, waving it in the air. "The Dreamspinner must have sent them to find us, lieutenant. Mayhap they carry a message. Here!" he shouted, waving the white cloak. Gilt embroidery and tiny rubies flashed in the sun. "We're over here!"

High above, a half league to the west, the ravens paused, circling.

"Over here!" Turin shouted. "Here!"

"Idiot!" Carfax jammed his heels into his mount's sides, plowing through the sedge grass to snatch the cloak away. "They're not looking for us."

"Then what—" Turin shoved his fist against his teeth. "Ah, no!"

A faint streak, tipped with a spark of sunlit steel; one, two, three. Arrows, shot into the sky, arcing impossibly high, impossibly accurate. A burst of feathers, small bundles of darkness plummeting; one, two, three.

"Haomane's Allies." Mantuas swallowed. "You think they found the ship, lieutenant? Are they after us?"

"They couldn't have found the damned ship." It had been near dusk on the second day at sea when Carfax had dispatched the captain of the *Ilona's Gull*, planting a dagger in the side of his throat. An ignoble death, but a swift one. His men had seen to the crew, and together, under cover of darkness, they'd gotten the ship headed north, making landfall the next day at the fetid, uninhabited mouth of the Verdine. "Why would they look there?"

Turin retrieved the Ellyl cloak and folded it away, not meeting his eyes. "We were seen crossing the Traders' Road, lieutenant."

"We were *supposed* to be seen. Heading north, overland to Pelmar." Carfax passed a hand over his face, found it oily with sweat. If he looked anything like his men, he looked a mess, the walnut dye darkening his skin to a Pelmaran hue streaking in the humid heat. That had been the last effort of their pretense, crossing the old overland trade route that ran between Seahold and Vedasia. Since then, they'd seen no other travelers and had let their guises fail. "We've made good time. They couldn't have followed that quickly."

"Well, someone did."

They watched him, waiting; waiting on *him*, Carfax of Staccia. His comrades, his countrymen. There was no one else in command in this desolate, humid wasteland. What, Carfax thought, would General Tanaros do if he were here?

"Right," he said smartly. "Someone did. Let's find out who."

THEY HAD REACHED THE DEFILE'S Maw.

It was aptly named, a dark, gaping mouth in the center of

the jagged peaks that reared out of the plains, surrounding and protecting the Vale of Gorgantum. They looked to have been forced out of the raw earth by violent hands, those mountains; in a sense, it was true, for Lord Satoris had raised them. It was his last mighty act as a Shaper, drawing on the power of Godslayer before he placed the shard of the Souma in the flames of the marrow-fire. It had nearly taken the last reserves of his strength, but it had made Darkhaven into an unassailable fortress.

Tanaros breathed deep, filling his lungs with the air of home. All around him, he saw the Fjel do the same, hideous faces breaking into smiles. The Staccians relaxed, sitting easier in the saddle. Even Ushahin Dreamspinner gave a crooked smile.

"We are bound *there?*"

He studied the Lady Cerelinde, noting the apprehension in her wide-set eyes. They were not grey, exactly. Hidden colors whispered at the edges of her pleated irises; a misty violet, luminous as the inner edge of a rainbow. "It is safe, Lady. Hyrgolf's Fjel will not let us fall."

She clutched the neck of her rough-spun cloak and made no answer.

Kaldjager Fjel ran ahead up the narrow path, bodies canted forward and loping on knuckled forelimbs, pausing to raise their heads and sniff the wind with broad nostrils. They climbed the steep path effortlessly, beckoning for their comrades to follow.

"Lady," Hyrgolf rumbled, gesturing.

One by one, they followed, alternating Fjel and riders. The horses of Darkhaven picked their way with care, untroubled by the sheer drops, the steep precipice that bordered the pathway. Below them, growing more distant at each step, lay the empty bed of the Gorgantus River. Only a trickle of water coursed its bottom, acrid and tainted.

At the top of the first bend, one of the Kaldjager gave a sharp, guttural call.

A pause, and it was answered.

It came from the highest peaks, a wordless roar, deep and deafening. Thunder might make such a sound, or rocks, cascading in avalanche. It rattled bones and thrummed in the pits of bellies, and Tanaros laughed aloud to hear it.

"Tordenstem Fjel," he shouted in response to the panicked glance Cerelinde threw him over her shoulder. "Have no fear! They are friends!"

She did fear, though; he supposed he couldn't blame her. It had taken him hard, a thousand and more years gone by. A Man in his prime, with blood on his hands and a heart full of fury and despair, riding in answer to a summons he barely understood.

Bring your hatred and your hurt and serve me . . .

Then, he had shouted in reply; had faced the Tordenstem as it crouched atop the peak with its barrel chest and mouth like a howling tunnel, and shouted his own defiant reply, filled with the fearless rage of a Man to whom death would be a welcome end. And the Tordenstem, the Thunder Voice Fjel, had laughed, barrel chest heaving, ho! ho! ho! Maybe you are the one his Lordship seeks, scrawny pup!

And it had been so, for he was; one of the Three, and the Tordenstem had led him along the treacherous passage to Darkhaven, where he pledged his life to Lord Satoris, who had withdrawn Godslayer from the marrow-fire and branded him with its hilt, circumscribing his aching heart. A haven, a haven in truth, sanctuary for his wounded soul . . .

"What?" Echoing words penetrated his reverie; the Tordenstem sentry—kinsman, perhaps, of the long-dead Fjel who had intercepted him, was shouting a message, incomprehensible syllables crashing like boulders. Tanaros shook himself, frowning, and called to his field marshal. "What did he say?"

"General." Hyrgolf trudged back to his side, stolidly unafraid of the heights. "Ulfreg says they captured a Man in the Defile, two days past. One of your kind, they think. He made it as far as the Weavers' Gulch. They took him to the dungeons."

"Aracus!" Cerelinde breathed, her face lighting with hope.

It struck him like a blow; he hadn't believed, before now, that the Lady of the Ellylon could love a Son of Altorus. "Not likely," Tanaros said sourly, watching the light die in her lovely face. "He'd have been killed thrice over. Dream-spinner?"

Ushahin, huddled out of the wind with his mount's flank pressed to the cliff wall, shrugged. "Not one of mine, cousin. I alert the sentries when a madling comes. Those with wits to seek shelter have already fled the coming storm." He touched the case that held the Helm of Shadows with delicate, crooked fingers. "Do you want me to scry his thoughts?"

"No." Tanaros shook his head. "Time enough in Dark-haven."

Onward they continued, winding through the Defile. After the first peak, the path widened. The Kaldjager continued to lope ahead, scouting. Periodically, one would depart from the path to scale a crag, jamming sharp talons on fist and foot into sheer rock, scrambling with four-limbed ease. There they would perch, yellow eyes glinting, exchanging calls of greeting with the Tordenstem sentries, who replied in booming tones.

Hyrgolf explained it to Cerelinde with Fjel patience.

". . . worked together, you see, Lady. Used to be the Tor-denstem—Thunder Voices, you call them—would herd game for the Cold Hunters, driving them to the kill. They'd flee the sound, you see, and there would be plenty for all. When your folk invaded the Midlands, they did the same. It worked, too."

Her face was pinched. "You herded my people to slaughter."

"Well." Hyrgolf scratched the thick hide on his neck,

nonplussed. "Aye, Lady. You could see it as such. The Battle of Neherinach. But your folk, your grandsire's sons and the like, were the ones brought the swords."

"You sheltered the Sunderer!"

Cerelinde's voice, raised, bounced off the walls of the Defile, clear and anguished. A sound like bells chiming, an Ellylon voice, such as had not been heard within a league of Darkhaven for ten centuries and more. The Kaldjager crouched yellow-eyed in the heights, and the Tordenstem were silent.

"Aye, Lady," Hyrgolf said simply, nodding. "We did. We gave shelter to Lord Satoris. He was a Shaper, and he asked our aid. We made a promise and kept it."

He left her, then, trudging to the head of the line, a broad figure moving on a narrow path, pausing here and there to exchange a word with his Fjel. Tanaros, who had listened, waited until they rounded a bend, bringing his mount alongside hers when there was room enough for two to ride abreast. Side by side they rode, bits and stirrups jangling faintly. The horses of Darkhaven exchanged wary glances, snuffled nostrils, and continued. The Lady Cerelinde sat upright in the saddle and stared straight ahead, her profile like a cut gem.

"I do not understand," she said at length, stiffly.

"Cerelinde." Tanaros tasted her name. "Every story has two sides. Yours the world knows, for the Ellylon are poets and singers unsurpassed, and their story endures. Who in Urulat has ever listened to the Fjeltroll's side of the tale?"

"You blame us." Cerelinde glanced at him, incredulous. "You blame us! Look at them, Tanaros. Look at *him*." She pointed at the Fjel Thorun, marching in front of them in stoic silence. He had spoken seldom since Bogvar's death. His broad, horny feet spread with each step, talons digging into the stony pathway. The pack he bore on his wide shoulders, battle-axe lashed across it, would have foundered an ox. "Look." She opened her delicate hands, palm-upward. "How were we to stand against *that?*"

Ahead, the path veered left, an outcropping of rock jutting into the Defile. Thorun lingered, pausing to lead first Cerelinde's mount, then Tanaros', around the bend. Though he kept his eyes lowered, watching the horses' hooves, unsuited for the mountainous terrain, his hand was gentle on the bridle.

"He speaks Common, you know," Tanaros said.

The Lady of the Ellylon had the grace to blush. "You know what I mean!"

"Aye." Tanaros touched the *rhios* in its pouch. "Neheris-of-the-Leaping-Waters Shaped the Fjel, Lady. Fourth-Born among Shapers, she Shaped them to match the place of her birth; with talons to scale mountains, strong enough . . . " he smiled wryly, " . . . to carry sheep across their shoulders, enough to lay up meat to stock a larder against a long winter."

"Strong enough," she retorted, "to tear down walls, General. You saw Cuilos Tuillenrad! Do you deny the dead their due?"

"No." He shook his head. "Only their version of truth, Lady." He nodded at the axe that jounced against Thorun's pack. "You see that weapon? Until the Battle of Neheri-nach, it was unknown among the Fjel. We taught them that, Cerelinde. Your people, and mine."

Her face was pale. "Satoris Banewreaker armed the Fjel."

"It is what your people claim," Tanaros said. "Mine too, come to it. But I have learned better in a thousand years, Lady. My Lord armed them, yes; after the Battle of Neheri-nach, after hundreds of their number fell defending him with tusk and talon. Yes, he taught them to smelt ore, and gave them weapons of steel. And I, I have done my part, Cerelinde. I taught them to use those weapons and such gifts as Neheris gave them in the service of war. Why?" He touched one forefinger to his temple. "Because I have the gift of intellect. Haomane's Gift, that he gave only to his children, and Arahila's. And that, Lady, is the Gift the Fjel were denied."

Cerelinde raised her chin. "Was their lot so terrible? You said it yourself, General. The Fjel were content, in their mountains, until Satoris Banewreaker convinced them otherwise."

"So they should have remained content with their lot?"

"They *were* content." Her gaze was unwavering. "Haomane First-Born is Chief among Shapers, Lord of the Souma. Satoris defied him, and Sundered the world with his betrayal. He fled to Neherinach in fear of Haomane's wrath, and there he enlisted the Fjel, swaying them to his cause, that he might avoid the cost of his betrayal. Did he reckon the cost to *them?*"

Beneath her horse's hooves, the edge of the path crumbled, sending stones tumbling into the Defile. Tanaros checked his black violently, and it shied against the cliff wall. Ahead of them, Thorun whirled into action, spinning to grab at Cerelinde's bridle, wedging his bulk between her and the sheer drop. Pebbles gave way as his taloned toes gripped the verge of the path and his eyetusks showed in a grimace as he urged her mount to solid ground by main force, shoving his shoulder against its flank, hauling himself after it.

"My thanks," Cerelinde gasped.

Thorun grunted, nodding, and resumed his plodding pace.

For a time, then, Tanaros rode behind her, watching the shine of her hair, that hung like an Ellyl banner down her spine. Downward wound the path, then upward, winding around another peak. And down again, where the river-basin broadened. Soon they would enter the Weavers' Gulch. He dug his heels into the black's sides, jogged his mount alongside hers.

"How does it feel, then, to owe your life to a Fjeltroll?" he asked her.

Cerelinde did not spare him a glance. "You brought me here, Tanaros."

"Of course." He bowed from the saddle, mocking. "Proud Haomane will suffer no rivals. Like the Fjel, my Lord Satoris should have remained *content* with his lot."

Ahead, the low river-bottom opened onto a narrow gorge. It was flat, as flat as anything might be in the Defile. The dank trickle of water intensified. This was water tainted by the ichor of Satoris the Shaper, seeping slow and dark. It reeked of blood, only sweeter. The walls of the gorge loomed high on either side, strung across with webs like sticky veils.

One by one, the Kaldjager Fjel parted the veils and entered. Ushahin Dreamspinner passed into the gorge, seemingly unperturbed. At the rear of the company, the Staccians mingled with Hyrgolf's Tungskulder Fjel and made uneasy jests in their own tongue, awaiting their turn.

"What is this place?" Cerelinde asked, her voice low.

"It is the Weavers' Gulch." Tanaros shrugged. "There are creatures in Urulat upon whom the Shapers have not laid hands. Lady. In these, my Lord is interested. Do you fear them? They will do us no harm if we leave them undisturbed."

At the entrance, Thorun waited for them, holding back the skeins of sticky filament so they might pass untouched. A small grey spider scuttled over the gnarled knuckles of his hand. Another descended on a single thread, hovering inches above his head, minute legs wriggling.

Cerelinde looked at what lay beyond and closed her eyes. "I cannot do this."

"I'm sorry, Lady." It had turned his stomach, too, the first time. Tanaros touched his sword-hilt. "But willing or unwilling, you will go."

At the threat, she opened her eyes to regard him. She was Ellylon, and the fineness of her features, the clear luminos-

ity of her skin, were a silent reproach, a reminder that he as-
pired to that which was beyond him.

Tanaros clenched his teeth. "Go!"

Drawing her hood, the Lady Cerelinde entered the
Weavers' Gulch.

ELEVEN

◆

"HERE'S A GOOD SPOT, LIEUTENANT."

Crawling on his belly, Carfax made his way to Hunric's
side. Saw-toothed blades of sedge grass caught at him,
sweat trickled into his eyes and midges buzzed in his ears.
He fought the urge to swat at them.

"Hear that, sir?" The tracker laid his ear flat to the
ground. "They'll be along presently. It's a small company,
I'm thinking."

Carfax rubbed at the sweat on his brow with the heel of
his hand, leaving a grimy streak. "As long as they can't see
us."

"Not here." Hunric glanced at him. "Long as we stay
quiet. It's tall grass, and we've a clear sight-line to the
verge, there. Lay low and you'll see, Lieutenant."

Overhead, the sun was relentless. One forgot, in Darkhaven, how bright it could be—and how hot. It had made
him squint at first and, despite many days on the road, he
had not fully adjusted to it. A moist heat arose from the
earth, smelling of roots. Carfax was aware of his own odor,
too, rank as a badger, and Hunric no better. A good tracker,
though, the best in the company. In Staccia, he could track a
snow-fox through a blizzard. Pity there wasn't a blizzard
here. The place could use one. Or a good hard frost, like

Vilbar had said. It wouldn't be so bad, hoar-frost glistening
on the sedge grass, every blade frozen . . .

"Sssst!"

Hoofbeats, and a single voice raised in tuneless song, the
words unfamiliar. Plastered to the earth, Carfax squinted
through the tall grass and caught himself before he whistled
in amazement.

"What the sodding hell?" Hunric whispered.

Seven strangers, traveling in company, led by a bearded
old man in scholars' robes, astride what was clearly the best
horse in the lot. An Ellyl, who traveled on foot, stepping
lightly, with that annoying air of his kind. A young man
sweltering in the armor of a Vedasian knight, ill-fitting and
much-mended. Another, older, dun-cloaked and watchful.

"Borderguard," Carfax muttered. "That one's from Curonan."

"Blaise Caveros?" Hunric's eyes widened. Everyone in
Darkhaven knew that General Tanaros' distant kinsman was
second-in-command among the Borderguard.

"Could be."

"Then that's—"

"Malthus' Company." Carfax studied the remaining
three. One, to his surprise, was a woman; clad in leathers, a
quiver and an unstrung bow at her back. An Archer of Arduan. And good, too. She would have to be. The carcasses of
three ravens dangled from her saddle, tied by their feet, a
sad bundle of black feathers. But the others . . . he frowned.

"Charred Folk," Hunric murmured. "Heard tell of those,
Lieutenant."

Indeed they were, their skins a scorched shade of brown.
It was one of the two who was singing tunelessly, riding
astride a pack mule, clad only in a threadbare breechclout.
From time to time he patted his brown, swelling gut, punc-
tuating his song. Carfax, listening to the incomprehensible
words, found himself thinking of water, flowing the hidden
pathways of Urulat, coursing like blood in the veins, racing

from the leaping snowmelt of a swollen Staccian river to sink torpid in the Delta, bearing life in all its forms . . .

"One's scarce more'n a boy," Hunric observed.

Last among them, a wide-eyed youth, wiry and dark as sin, perched uneasily atop a pony. Something hung about his throat; a flask of fired clay, strung on corded vine. He was the one the Borderguardsman shadowed, unobtrusively wary in his dun cloak.

Small hairs stirred at the back of Carfax's neck.

He felt a chill, like a wish granted.

"Hunric," he whispered, his mouth dry. "They're not following us, and they didn't come from the Traders' Road. Or if they did, it was only long enough to buy mounts. They came from the Unknown. This is the Prophecy at work. And whoever sent the ravens, whether it was the Dreamspinner or Lord Satoris, they failed."

Side by side in the sedge grass, they stared at one another.

"What do we do, Lieutenant?"

It was a gift, an unlooked-for blessing. Malthus' Company, crossing their path unaware. Three dead ravens, tied by their feet; it meant no one in Darkhaven knew anything of this. Carfax licked his dry lips. There were only seven of them, and two, surely, were no warriors. What about the Counselor? Malthus had fought at the Battle of Curonan, had nearly slain Lord Satoris himself. If the news of Dergail's fall had not caused the armies of Men to falter, he might even have prevailed.

But he had borne the Spear of Light, then.

He wasn't carrying it now.

And where was the Soumanië? Mayhap he didn't bear it, either. It would be foolish, after all, to risk such a treasure on an ill-protected journey. Mayhap, Carfax thought, Malthus had entrusted the Soumanië to the keeping of Ingolin the Wise, who would keep it safe in Meronil. After all, this mission was undertaken in secrecy. And if it were so . . .

"Regroup!" he hissed to Hunric. "We need to plan an attack!"

USHAHIN DREAMSPINNER GAZED ABOUT HIM as he rode.

It was a wondrous place, the Weavers' Gulch, though few appreciated it. Everywhere he looked, gossamer filaments were strung, filtering the few rays of cloud-muted sunlight that pierced the gulch with its inward-leaning cliff walls.

And the patterns, ah!

Intricate, they were; and vast. Some, incomprehensibly so. He watched the grey spiders shuttle to and fro, the weavers at their loom. How long did it take for a single spider to spin a web that crossed the Defile? One lifetime? Generations? With delicate thread that broke at a hand's careless wave. But it was strong, too. Given time, Satoris' weavers could spin a cocoon that would render a strong man immobile. And small though they were, their sting was paralyzing.

It could be done, in time.

No wonder Satoris was interested in them.

It saddened him, that so few people understood this. There was a pattern at work in the Sundering of Urulat, one would take many ages to come to fruition. Ushahin, born unwanted to two races of the Lesser Shapers, raised by a third, understood this in his ill-mended bones. He wished that Tanaros understood it, too. It would have been good if he had. But Tanaros, when all was said and done, was a Man, burdened with the short sight of his race. Even now, after so long.

Among all the Lesser Shapers, only Men had found no way to make provision for the shortness of memory. Oronin's Children had done so. What the Grey Dam had known, the Grey Dam knew, and it encapsulated all that every predecessor before her had known. So it was among the Fjel, who passed their memory into the bone and bred it among their descendants. It was why they had remained loyal to Lord Satoris after so many generations, remembering that first promise.

A single thread, Ushahin thought, descending through time.

A pity, after all, that they lacked the scope—the *wit*—to discern the pattern. That was what Haomane had denied them. A single spider, shuttling on the loom of Weavers' Gulch, had more perspective.

Of course, no one had Shaped them.

Tanaros *should* have seen it. After so many centuries in Darkhaven, he had learned to see its underlying beauty. Was that not enough? Ah, but he was a Man, and ruled by his heart. Arahila's Child, in whom love and hatred grew intertwined. Look at him now, solicitous of the Lady of the Rivenlost. Haomane's Child, whose people had no need of a remembrance born in the flesh, for their flesh was untouched by time. Of their fallen, they told *stories,* shaping history in their image. And the Children of Men, who emulated them in all things, learned to do the same though their lives were as the passage of shooting stars measured against the span of the Ellylon.

Yet their numbers increased, while the Ellylon dwindled.

The Lady Cerelinde gave a choked cry, beating at her cloak. Ushahin watched with a cynical gaze as Tanaros aided her, brushing hurriedly at the woolen fabric with his gauntleted hands. Small grey figures dropped, scuttling on the rocks. One of the Tungskulder Fjel stamped after them, squashing them beneath the impervious hide of his feet. It wouldn't do to have their prize arrive in a state of paralysis.

"This land breeds foulness!" The Lady was pale. "It is the taint of the Sunderer!"

Foul is as foul does, Ushahin thought in silence. What harm did the weavers do before you blundered through their webs? If they did not feed, we would have a pestilence of flies in Darkhaven, because yes, Lady, this land is tainted with Lord Satoris' blood, which has seeped into the very ground, which taints the waters we drink. He bleeds and bleeds anon, for the wound that was dealt him with the Godslayer, the wound that destroyed his Gift, is unhealing.

And why was he wounded?

Smiling to himself, Ushahin gazed at the delicate spans of webbing. Hanging veils, swags of filament, finespun and milk-white. The vast network filled him with delight. What architect could have wrought such a thing? A tendril of thread, flung out into empty space, meets another. Is it chance, or destiny? Will the weavers defend their territory in jealous battle, or will they knit their threads together to span the void?

The Ellylon would dwindle, while Men increased.

Lord Satoris was wounded because he defied Haomane's will.

He had refused to withdraw his Gift from Men.

And Ushahin was one of the Three and madness was his moiety, because he had his roots in three worlds and saw too clearly that which none of the Lesser Shapers were meant to know. What sanity he possessed was instilled in a thin strand of pain; the ache of bones ill-set and ill-mended, the sharp pang of light piercing his skull through a pupil unable to contract. Walking this fine-spun thread of pain, Ushahin knew himself sane in his madness.

Not even Lord Satoris, who would have healed him, who had kindled in his soul a fierce ache of love and pride, understood that part.

It didn't matter, though.

Ahead, a narrow aperture, marking the end of the Weavers' Gulch. The Kaldjager scrambled around it, drawing back the hanging veils of webbing with unexpected care. They, at least, understood that the little weavers were as much a part of the defense of Darkhaven as the strong walls beyond; not for nothing were they called the Cold Hunters. Ushahin, passing through, approved. Of all the

Fjel, he understood them best, for they were most like the Were who had raised him.

The thought was accompanied by pain.

Oh, Mother!

She had died well, her jaws snapping at her enemy's throat, Ushahin reminded himself for the hundredth time. It was what she had chosen. And if he could not inherit her memories, still, he would carry the memory of her in his heart. Of the gentleness she had shown, finding him in the Pelmaran forest where he had crawled in blind agony. Of the touch of her rough-padded hands as she cradled his child's body, protecting his broken face, his shattered hands. Of her harsh grey pelt warm against his skin as she carried him to safety, grieving for her own lost ones.

The Grey Dam is dead. The Grey Dam lives.

Beyond the aperture, the Defile opened onto the Vale of Gorgantum. Ushahin, who passed this way more often than most, was inured to it. He heard a gasp as the Lady Cerelinde beheld it for the first time: the rearing towers that flanked the Defile Gate, the vast wall winding league upon league up the low mountains, the massive edifice of Darkhaven itself.

Marvel at it, Ellyl bitch, he thought; marvel at it and fear. Your visit here has been paid for in blood, with the life of one I held dear. What do you know of kindness and compassion? Your kinfolk left me to die, for I was a shame to them, a reminder of the dark underbelly of the Gift they were denied; Lord Satoris' Gift, which Haomane spurned. And yet he seeks it now, on his own terms. Do you truly believe your offspring would be so different from me? I would be otherwise had your people embraced me.

Atop a high peak, one of the Tordenstem Fjel crouched. As the last of the company emerged from the Weavers' Gorge, he announced them, filling his mighty lungs to bursting and hurling words aloft in his thunderous voice. Boulders shuddered in their stony sockets. Shouts of greeting answered from the sentry-towers, and Tanaros rode forward to salute them and give the password.

The Defile Gate was wrought of black granite, carved with scenes from the Battle of Neherinach. The central panel showed the death of Eldarran and Elduril; the sons of Elterrion the Bold, Cerelinde's uncles. Once the bar was lifted, it took two teams of four Fjel each to shift the massive doors, and it creaked as it opened.

Darkhaven stood open for their victorious entry.

"Dreamspinner." It was one of the Kaldjager, yellow-eyed, who pointed to the specks of darkness circling the spires. "The ravens are restless."

Victorious cries rained down from the sentry-towers and the walls as they entered Darkhaven. The Lady Cerelinde kept her chin aloft, refusing to show the terror that must be coursing her veins. She had courage, Ushahin had to give her that. Tanaros stuck close by her side, clearly torn between reveling in his triumph and protecting his trophy. How not? If he'd had the heart for it, Ushahin would have appreciated the irony. The Lady of the Riven-lost had given her love to a Son of Altorus, even as Tanaros' wife had done so long ago. It must gall the mighty General.

Poor Tanaros.

They must be something, those Sons of Altorus, to command such passion.

Being a portion of the Prophecy and bespeaking as it did the union of Men and Ellylon, it would have interested Ushahin more had the ravens of Darkhaven not been circling. As the cheers rained down, he clutched the case that held the Helm of Shadows close to him, longing only for a quiet place where he could free his mind to roam the length and breadth of Urulat.

If victory was theirs, why were the ravens restless?

* * *

"SO THIS IS IT." LILIAS held the mirror in both hands. It was small and tarnished, reflecting dimly in the low-burning torchlight that augmented the diffuse light of dawn. The dragon did not like any fire save his own to illuminate his lair. "We do it now?"

"It is time, Liliasss." Calandor's claws flexed, sifting through gold coins, jeweled goblets. High above her, his eyes winked like emeralds in the torchlight. "Elterrion's granddaughter has arrived in Darkhaven."

"How can you be sure?"

The emerald eyes stared unwinking. "I am sure."

Outside the mouth of the cavern, a troop of Gergon's wardsmen and her personal attendants huddled, waiting. What Lilias attempted this morning would draw strength from her, even with the aid of the Soumanië. It was Ellylon magic, and not meant to be undertaken by a Daughter of Men. "If we used only the eyes, if we watched them longer, we might learn more of their plans."

Calandor snorted smoke in a laugh. "Can you read the speech of their lipsss, little ssisssster? Neither can I."

"I know." Lilias flicked the mirror with a fingernail in annoyance. "Haergan the Craftsman should have crafted ears onto his creation, instead of eyes and a mouth. It would have been more useful."

"Indeed." A nictitating membrane blinked over the dragon's eyes. "I might not have eaten him if he had been more ussseful."

"I would feel better if Lord Satoris' decoy had arrived in Beshtanag."

"Sso would I, little ssisssster." Calandor sounded regretful. "But there is risssk in waiting. I would have gone, if you wished, to ssseek them."

"No." Lilias covered the mirror with her palm. On that point she had been adamant. Calandor was one of the last of his kind, the last known to the Lesser Shapers. In the Shapers' War, scores of dragons had died defending Satoris from his kin; after the Sundering, the Ellylon had hunted them mercilessly, slaying the weak and wounded. She would not allow Calandor to risk himself for a Shaper's machinations. "My spies have laid a trail of rumor from Pelmar to Vedasia, swearing the Dragon of Beshtanag was seen aloft and heading south. It is enough."

"Then it is enough," the dragon said gently. "Haomane's Allies will believe I ferried the Lady here on dragonback. If you ssspeak now, they will be ssertain of it. If you delay, it may be proved a lie."

"All right." Lilias sighed again. "It's time, it's time. I understand. I'll do it."

"You know the way . . . ?"

"Yes," she said shortly. "I know it."

She knew it because Calandor had showed her, as he had done so many times before. What the dragon consumed, he consumed wholly, knowledge and all. And long ago, in the First Age of the Sundered World, he had consumed Haergan the Craftsman, who had built a folly into the great hall of Meronil.

It was a head, the head of Meronin Fifth-Born, Lord of the Seas; Haomane's brother and chiefest ally, patron of Meronil. And it adorned a marble pediment atop the doorway into the great hall, his hair wrought into white-capped waves. When the world was Sundered, Meronin had brought the seas to divide the body of Urulat from Torath, the Souma-crowned head of the world.

But truth be told, there was precious little to be seen in the great hall of Meronil. Lilias knew, having looked into the mirror, Haergan's mirror, through the sculpture's eyes. Ingolin the Wise convened his assembly, day in and day out. One day, he brought forth a stone in a casket. It blazed with a pale blue light, which seemed to impress those assembled. Well and good; what did it mean?

"I know not," Calandor had said, though he sounded uneasy, for a dragon. "But it is nothing to do with Beshtanag. This I ssswear, Liliasss."

She believed him, because she had no choice. If Calandor was false . . . ah, no. Best not to think of such things, for she would sooner die than believe it. Lilias gripped the mirror, letting her vision diffuse, sinking into its tarnished surface, sensing the marble eyes wrought by Haergan the Craftsman open.

There.

There.

A skewed view, seen from the pediment. Ingolin the Wise, Lord of the Rivenlost, presiding over the argumentative assembly. Had it ever been otherwise? There, Bornin of Seahold, stout in his blue livery. There, Lord Cynifrid of Port Calibus, pounding the table with his gauntleted fist. There, two representatives of the Free Fishers of Harrington Bay, clad in homespun. And there, Aracus Altorus, taut with energy, willing the Council of War onward.

So few women, Lilias thought, gazing through the marbled eyes. So few!

"Liliassss."

"I know. I know." Drawing on the power of the Soumanië, feeling the fillet tighten on her brow, and speaking the words of invocation set forth by Haergon the Craftsman, who had left his knowledge in a dragon's belly.

In Meronil, Haomane's Allies gaped.

It was hard, at such a distance. Her flesh was mortal, and not meant to wield a Shaper's power nor Ellylon magics. Lilias closed her eyes and willed the marble lips to speak, stiff as stone, forming words that boomed in the distant hall.

"GREETINGS . . . TO . . . HAOMANE'S . . . ALLIES!"

Her face felt rigid and unfamiliar, inhabiting the sculpted relief more thoroughly than ever she had dared. She forced open the dense marble lids of her eyes, gazing down at the assembly. They were all on their feet, staring upward at the pediment, giving her a sense of vertigo.

"YOU SEEK . . . THE LADY . . . CERELINDE. SHE IS . . . SAFE . . . IN BESHTANAG." The words made a

knot in her belly. It was the end of deniability, the beginning
of blame. "SHE WILL BE RESTORED TO YOU . . . FOR
A PRICE."

There was squabbling, then, in the great hall of Meronil.
Lilias watched them through marble eyes, dimly aware that
in a Beshtanagi cavern, the edges of a small mirror bit into
her clutching palms. Some were shouting as if she could
hear them. She watched and waited, and wished again that
Haergan the Craftsman had given ears to his creation.

One knew better.

Ingolin the Wise, Lord of the Rivenlost. Ignoring the
chaos, he approached to stand beneath the pediment, his
ageless face tilted upward.

Among the Ellylon, the best and brightest had stood
nearest to the Souma. When the world was Sundered and
the seas rushed in to fill the divide, they remained upon the
isle Torath, and there they dwelt, singing the praises of
Haomane and the Six Shapers. It was only those who dwelt
upon the body of Urulat who were stranded, separated forever from Haomane First-Born who Shaped them.

They were the Rivenlost.

And Elterrion the Bold had been their Lord, once; but he
was dead, and with him Cerion the Navigator and Numireth
the Fleet, who were also Lords of the Rivenlost. Only Ingolin was left, who was called the Wise.

Lilias gazed down upon him and felt pity, which she had
not expected. A simple fillet of gold bound his shining hair
and his brow was marked with worry. His eyes were grey as
a storm, and deep with sorrow. How not, when they bore the
shadows of centuries unnumbered? Urulat had not been
Sundered when Ingolin first walked the earth. Perhaps, if he
had been Lord of the Rivenlost in the First Age of the Sundered World and not Elterrion the Bold, it might have been
different. Ingolin the Wise spread his arms, his lips shaping
words clear enough for her to read: What do you want?

Her marble lips moved, forming the answer.

"I WANT MALTHUS ... AND HIS SOUMANIË.
BRING THEM TO BESHTANAG." Chaos followed on the
heels of her words. How they quarreled, the Sons of Men!
Lilias kept her stone eyes fixed on the Lord of the Rivenlost. "THE LADY IS YOURS IN TRADE."

A flash of red-gold, caught in periphery. Aracus Altorus
had leapt upon the table, his boot-heels scarring the polished wood, his sword-arm cocked. His face was lit with
fury and in his hand he held the haft of a standard, snatched
from a wall. With a soundless cry, he hurled it at her like a
javelin.

A pennant fluttered in midflight. An argent scroll, half
open upon a field of sage; the device of the House of Ingolin.

So much and no more did Lilias see before the pointed
iron finial that tipped the standard struck, marble shattering
at the force of the blow. She cried out loud, feeling her
brow-bone splinter at the bridge of her nose, clapping both
hands over her face.

"Aaahhhh!"

The pain was unspeakable. Dimly, Lilias was aware that
in the great hall of Meronil, blow after blow was struck at
the pediment, gouging chunks of marble, destroying forever
the head of Meronin, Haergan's creation. For the most part,
she was aware only of agony, of splintered bones piercing
her flesh as she writhed on the floor of the dragon's cavern,
the bronze mirror forgotten beside her.

"My lady, my lady!" It was Gergon's voice, uncharacter-
istically terrified. Her Ward Commander's strong hands
covered hers, trying to draw them away from her face. "Are
you injured? Lady, let me see!"

"Hurts," Lilias managed to whisper. "Oh blessed Haomane, it hurts!"

Lilias. Lilias, it is only an illusion.

"Calandor, help me!"

The dragon's bulk shifted, rasping on the stony floor.

One mighty claw reached, talons closing delicately on the round mirror. "Ssstand back, Ssson of Man!"

Gergon scrambled backward, holding her against his chest with one strong arm. With pain-slitted eyes, Lilias peered through her fingers as the dragon bent his sinuous neck. Scales glinted dully as he lowered his head to the object he held in the talons of one uplifted claw. The pale armor of his underbelly expanded as he drew breath.

The dragon roared.

Fire shot from Calandor's gaping jaws; blue-hot at its core, the flames a fierce orange shading to yellow. Gripped in his talons, Haergan's mirror *melted,* droplets of bronze falling molten and sizzling to the cavern floor.

The connection was broken.

The pain stopped.

Cautiously, Lilias felt at her face. It was whole and intact, no bone-splinters piercing her smooth skin. No pain, only the ghost of its memory. There, on her brow, was the Soumanië, nearly lifeless. "Calandor?"

"Forgive me, Liliasss." The dragon sounded contrite. "I did not . . . antissssipate . . . such violence."

"You're all right then, my lady?" Gergon asked with gruff solicitude.

"My lady!" Pietre burst into the cavern, flinging himself to his knees. There were tears in his eyes. "I thought you were killed!"

"Not yet, sweetling." She smiled at him through deep-rooted exhaustion. They were there, they were all there, her pretty ones, crowding behind Pietre. Not wholly willing, not all of them, no, she had not always chosen wisely— there was Radovan, scowling, near time to release him, and sullen Marija—but there was worried Stepan, dusky-eyed Anna, and dear Sarika biting her trembling lip. "Only tired, now."

"I'll take you to your quarters, my lady." Without waiting for permission, Pietre scooped her into his arms and stood.

To his credit, he only shivered a little at the dragon's amused regard.

Too weary to object, Lilias allowed it. Gergon snapped orders, his wardsmen falling in around them. It was a frightening thing, to be this weak, even with a Soumanië in her possession. Now, more than ever, Beshtanag needed her.

Rest, Lilias. Recover.

She nodded in silent answer, knowing the dragon understood. Beneath her cheek, the bare skin of Pietre's chest was warm and resilient. Such a heady elixir, youth! Lilias felt her thousand years of age. It came at a price, cheating death. If her flesh did not show it, still, she felt it in her bones, now as never before. Had she invoked Haomane's name in her agony? Yes, and there was something fearful in it. Pietre murmured endearments under his breath, walking as though he held something precious in his arms. *I should let him go,* Lilias thought. *I should let them all go, before danger comes. But I am old, and I am afraid of being alone.*

Calandor?

I am here, Lilias.

It was enough. It had to be enough. It was the bargain she had made, a thousand years ago. And it had always, always endured. As long as it did, nothing else mattered. The thing was done, the die cast. Why, then, this foreboding?

Calandor?

Lilias, you must rest.

Calandor, where are Lord Satoris' men?

"RIGHT." CARFAX SURVEYED HIS MEN with a sharp eye. "Vilbar, scrub your face again. Use marsh-root if you have to. You're still spatch-cocked with dye."

"That river water stinks, Lieutenant!"

"I don't care," he said ruthlessly. "Scrub it! Turin, Mantuas, Hunric—you understand your mission?" There was silence in answer. Mantuas, holding his mount's reins, kicked stubbornly at a clump of sedge grass. "You understand?"

"Don't worry, sir." Hunric leaned on his pommel. "I'll see 'em through the Delta and on to Beshtanag."

"Good. With luck, we'll be no more than a day behind you. But whatever happens here, you need to report what we've seen to the Sorceress of the East. Now,"—Carfax drew a deep breath—"are the rest of you ready?"

They shouted a resounding yes. With the last remnants of dye washed from their skin, and beards beginning to grow, they looked more like Staccians, members of the boldest nation on earth; Fjel-friends, frost-warriors, allies of the Banewreaker himself. Had they not slain scores of the enemy at Lindanen Dale? And if they could do this thing, if they could capture Malthus' Company and prevent the Prophecy from being fulfilled . . .

A grin stretched Carfax's face. Lord Satoris would be pleased, mightily pleased. Mayhap pleased enough to consider making the Three into Four. Immortality would be a fine thing, indeed.

He drew his sword. "For the honor of Darkhaven!"

TWELVE

❖

THE GARRISON HAD TURNED OUT for their return, rank upon rank of Fjel flanking the approach to Darkhaven, holding formation with military discipline, issuing crisp salutes.

It was an imposing sight. It was meant to be.

All the tribes were represented; Tungskulder, Mørkhar, Gulnagel, Tordenstem, Nåltannen, Kaldjager. Tanaros gazed over a sea of Fjel, with thick hides of smooth grey, of a pebbled greenish-brown, or black with bristles. His troops, his men. They wore their armor with pride, pounding the butts of their spears in steady rhythm. They kept their shields raised.

"So many!" Cerelinde whispered.

Tanaros bowed from the saddle. "Welcome to Darkhaven, Lady."

Before them loomed the edifice itself, twin towers rearing against an overcast sky, dwarfing the entrance until they drew near enough to see that the portal itself was massive; thrice the height of any Fjel. The bar had been raised and the brass-bound inner doors flung open.

In the entrance stood Vorax of Staccia, gleaming in ceremonial armor.

"Lady Cerelinde of the Rivenlost!" he called. "Lord Satoris welcomes you."

At his words, a stream of madlings spewed forth from the interior of the fortress, surging into their midst to lay hands on the bridles of their horses. Tanaros dismounted, and helped the Lady down. He felt her trembling underneath his touch.

Her gaze was locked with the Staccian's. "This hospitality is a gift unwanted, Lord Glutton."

Vorax shrugged. "It is a gift nonetheless, Lady. Do not disdain it. Hey! Dreamspinner!" He clapped Ushahin on the shoulder. "Still sky-gazing? I hear you did well in the Dale, wielding the Helm of Shadows."

The half-breed muttered some reply, moving away from the Staccian's touch, the helm's case clutched under his arm. Tanaros frowned. Why were the ravens circling? He spared a thought for Fetch as he approached the entrance, hoping the scapegrace was unharmed.

"Blacksword." The Staccian clasped his forearm.

"Vorax. Your men did well. Commend them for me."

"I'll do that." Vorax paused, lowering his voice. "His Lordship awaits you, Blacksword; you and the Ellyl. Come see me when he's done."

"The captive?"

"Aye."

"I'll be there." An escort of Mørkhar Fjel stood waiting just inside the vast doors; four brethren all of a height, the silver inlay on their weapons-harnesses contrasting with their dark, bristling hides. "Dreamspinner?"

"You go, cousin." Ushahin thrust the helm's case into his unready arms. "You took the risks, not I. Tell Lord Satoris . . . tell him I am in the rookery. I will make my report anon."

"All right." Tanaros frowned again. It should have been a glorious homecoming, this moment; it *was* a glorious homecoming. The Prophecy had been averted, and the Lady of the Ellylon was theirs. She didn't look it, though. As frightened as Cerelinde was—and she *was* frightened, he'd felt it in his fingertips—she held herself with dignity. "Lady. Are you ready?"

Wide, her eyes; wide and grey, luminous as mist. "I do not fear the Sunderer."

"Then come," Tanaros said grimly, "and meet him."

THE SEDGE GRASS APPEARED TO bow at their approach, flattening as if a great wind preceded them. Carfax, sword in hand, found a Staccian battle-song on his lips as he rode. He sang it aloud, heard other voices echoing the words.

To battle, to battle, to battle! What a glorious thing it was! The horses of Darkhaven, who had borne them so faithfully, were bred to this purpose. His mount sensed it, nostrils flaring, the broad chest swelling with air as its hooves battered the marshy plains.

And there, ahead: The Enemy.

Malthus' Company had heard their approach, the hooves drumming like thunder. They prepared, as best they could, making a stand on the open sedge. Carfax watched them encircle the Charred Ones, back to back to back.

"Fan out!" he cried, seeking to pick his target.

The Staccian riders divided, two wings opening to encompass the tight-knit company, which they outnumbered nearly three to one. Which one, which one? The old Counselor, staff in hand? The Vedasian, glaring defiance? The Archer, coolly nocking arrows? The Ellyl lordling with his bright eyes, sword braced over his shoulder?

Ah, no, Carfax thought. You, Borderguardsman. You, in your dun cloak and false modesty. Unless I am much mistaken, I think you are charged with the protection of this Company, Blaise Caveros, my General's kinsman. We are of an age, you and I; but I am Tanaros' disciple, and you are Altorus' dog. Let us cross steel, shall we?

He swung close, close enough to exchange blows. His round Pelmaran shield rang with the force of the Borderguard's strength; rang, and held true. Carfax kneed his mount and swung away, exultant. In the center of their circle, the Charred lad looked wild-eyed, clutching a flask at his throat. Only his kinsman, the fat one, stood at his side, wielding a digging-stick like a quarterstaff, huffing as he did.

Carfax laughed aloud.

Thrum, thrum, thrum.

Arrows, flying level as a bee to clover. Two Staccians cried out, fell. The Archer of Arduan had dismounted, kneeling on the marshy soil; the Vedasian knight protected her, swinging his father's sword with ferocious blows.

"Take the Archer!" Carfax cried, readying for another pass at the Borderguard.

He was aware, distantly, of his men closing in on Malthus' Company, overwhelming them by sheer force; surging past the old Counselor, peeling the Vedasian away from the Archer and surrounding her, penetrating the silvery circle of defense the Ellyl wove with the point of his blade. A surprise, there on the inside, how deftly the fat one wielded his digging-stick, protecting his young kinsman.

It didn't matter, though. They were too few, and Carfax's

men too many. He watched Blaise Caveros angle for position, setting his sword a touch too high. A good trick, that, good for luring in an overconfident enemy. General Tanaros had devised it a thousand years ago and taught it to his troops, as well as how to evade it.

All those hours on the practice-field paid a reward.

Carfax shifted his grip on his sword, digging his heels into his mount's sides. *Let him believe,* he thought, bearing down on his dun-cloaked opponent. *Let him believe I have taken the gambit, and at the last moment, I shall strike high where he looks for low . . .*

"Enough!"

It was Malthus who spoke, and the Counselor spread his arms, his staff in his right hand. There, gleaming through the parted strands of his beard, was the Soumanië. Red, it was, like a star, and it shone upon his breast, until no one could look away. A ruddy glow rippled in the air and a force struck like a hammer.

And the world . . . changed.

Carfax felt it, felt his mount's knees buckle beneath him, shifting and . . . *changing.* He hit the ground, hard, flung from the saddle. Like a vast wave, the might of the Souma overtook them all. Horses fell, and Men. The Counselor closed his eyes as if in pain, wielding the Soumanië. In the space of a shrieked breath, Staccian and equine flesh crumbled to loam, fingers sprouted tendrils and strands of hair sank rootlets into the earth. Shaped from their bodies, hummocks arose on the flat marshes, marking the territory forevermore.

Where they fell, sedge grass grew.

Except for Carfax.

He tried to move, the cheek-plates of his Pelmaran helmet scraping the rich loam. No more could he do; the strength had left his limbs. Only his senses worked. Through helpless eyes, he watched as the Borderguardsman's booted feet approached. Ungentle hands rolled him onto his back and patted him down, taking his belt-knife. His sword had been lost when he fell. Lying on his back, Carfax stared helpless at a circle of empty sky.

"Is he . . . dead?" A soft voice, an unplaceable accent.

"No."

A face hovered above him; young and dark, rough-hewn, with wide-set eyes. Sunlight made a nimbus of his coarse black hair and an earthenware flask dangled around his neck, swinging in the air above Carfax.

"Stand back, Dani." It was a weary shadow of the Counselor's voice. "It may yet be a trap."

The face withdrew. A boot-tip prodded his side. "Shall I finish him?"

"No." Unseen, Malthus the Counselor drew a deep breath. "We'll bring him with us. Let me regain a measure of strength, and I'll place a binding upon him. There may be aught to learn from this one."

Unable even to blink, Carfax knew despair.

MADLINGS SKITTERED ALONG THE HALLS of Darkhaven, their soft voices echoing in counterpoint to the steady tramp of the Fjel escort's feet. Old and young, male and female, they crept almost near enough to touch the hem of the Lady Cerelinde's cloak before dashing away in an ecstasy of terror.

It had been a long time, Tanaros realized, since he'd seen Darkhaven through an outsider's eyes. It must seem strange and fearful.

Inward and inward wound their course, through hallways that spiraled like the inner workings of a nautilus shell. There were other passageways, of course; secret ones, doors hidden in alcoves, behind tapestries, in cunning reliefs. Some were in common usage, like those that led to the kitchens. Some were half-forgotten, and others existed only as rumor. Madlings used many, of course, taking care not to be seen. Vorax disdained them, and Ushahin preferred them. Tanaros used them at need. The Fjel used them not at all, for the passages were too winding and narrow to admit them. No one knew all their secrets.

Only Lord Satoris, who conceived them—or their beginnings.

And so the main halls spiraled, vast curving expanses of polished black marble, lit only by the veins of marrow-fire along the walls. It was a winding trap for would-be invaders, Fjel guards posted at regular intervals like hideous statues. It should have awed even the Lady of the Ellylon.

Tanaros stole a sidelong glance at her to see if it did.

There were tears in her luminous eyes. "So many!" she whispered, and he thought she meant the Fjel again; then he saw how her gaze fell on the madlings. She paused, one hand extended, letting them draw near enough to touch and turning a reproachful look upon him. "Merciful Arahila! What manner of cruelty is this, Tanaros? What has been done to these folk?"

"Done?" He stared at her. "They sought sanctuary here."

"Sanctuary?" Her brows, shaped like birds' wings, rose. "From *what?*"

"From the world's cruelty, which drove them to madness." Tanaros reached out, grabbing the arm of the nearest madling; by chance, it was one he knew. A woman, young when she came to Darkhaven, elderly now, with a birthmark like a dark stain that covered half her wrinkled face. "This, my Lady, is Sharit. Her parents sold her into marriage to a man who was ashamed of her, and beat her for his shame. Do you see, here?" He touched her skull beneath wispy hair, tracing a dent. "He flung her against a doorjamb. Here, no one will harm her, on pain of death. Is that *cruelty?*"

"You're frightening her," Cerelinde said softly.

It was true. Repentant, he released the madling. Sharit keened, creeping to crouch at Cerelinde's skirts, fingers plucking. The Mørkhar escort waited, eyeing Tanaros. "I didn't mean to," he said.

"I know." She smiled kindly at the madling, laying a gentle hand on the withered cheek, then glanced at Tanaros. "Very well. I do not deny the world's cruelty, General. But your Lord, were he compassionate, could have healed her suffering. You said as much; he offered to heal the halfbreed." Her delicate fingers stroked Sharit's birthmark, and the madling leaned into her touch. "He could have made her beautiful."

"Like you?" Tanaros asked quietly.

Cerelinde's hands fell still. "No," she said. "Like *you*."

"Like Arahila's Children. Not Haomane's." Shifting the Helm of Shadows under one arm, Tanaros stooped, meeting the old woman's eyes. They were milky with cataracts, blinking under his regard. "You don't understand," he said to Cerelinde, gazing at Sharit. "To Lord Satoris, she *is* beautiful."

There was magic in the words, enough to summon a smile that broke like dawn across the withered face. Taking his hand, she rose, proceeding down the hall with upright dignity.

Tanaros bowed to Cerelinde.

Her chin lifted a notch. "It would still be kinder to heal her. Do you deny it?"

"You have charged my Lord with Sundering the world," he said. "Will you charge him now with healing it?"

One of the Mørkhar shifted position, coughing conspicuously into a taloned fist.

"It's in his power, Tanaros." Passion and a light like hope lit Cerelinde's eyes. "It *is*, you know! Did he but surrender to Haomane and abide his will——"

Tanaros laughed aloud. "And Haomane's Children accuse his Lordship of pride! Be sure to tell him that, Lady."

She drew her cloak around her. "I shall."

* * *

USHAHIN DREAMSPINNER STEPPED AS LIGHTLY as any Ellyl
under the canopy of beech leaves, grown thicker and darker
with the advent of summer. Setting loose his awareness, he
let it float amid the trunks and branches, using the ancient
magic the Grey Dam Sorash had taught him so long ago.

Ah, mother!

Tiny sparks of mind were caught in his net; feathered
thoughts, bright-eyed and darting. One, two, three . . . five.
Folding his legs, Ushahin sat in the beech loam, asking and
waiting. *What is it, little brothers? What has befallen your
kin?*

A raven landed on a nearby branch, wiped its beak twice.
Another sidled close.

Three perched on the verge of an abandoned nest.

Thoughts, passed from mind to mind, flickered through
his awareness. Not a thing seen, no; none who had *seen*
lived to show what had happened in the dark shimmering of
the Ravensmirror. Only these traces remained, drifting like
down in the flock's awareness. Marshes, an endless plain of
sedge grass. A high draft, warm under outspread wings. A
target found, a goal attained. One two three four seven, circling lower, a good draft, good to catch, wings tilting, still
high, so high, only close enough to see—

Arrow!

Arrow!

Arrow!

And death, sharp-pointed and shining, arcing from an
impossible distance; the *thump* of death, a sharp blow to the
breast, a shaft transfixed, wings failing, a useless plummet,
down and down and down, blue sky fading to darkness,
down and down and down—

Earthward.

Death.

The memory of the impact made his bones ache. Ushahin
opened his eyes. The living ravens watched him, carrying
the memories of their fallen brethren, waiting and wondering. *I am sorry, little ones. It was dangerous, more danger-*

ous than I reckoned. Malthus was clever to bring an Archer.

What was the Company of Malthus doing in the Vedasian marshes?

Ushahin stared at the cloud-heavy sky, seen in glimpses through the beech canopy. It was early yet, too early for the dreams of Men to be abroad. He sighed, flexing his crippled hands. Tonight, then. When the moon rode high over the Vale of Gorgantum, darkness would be encroaching on the marshes.

Time to walk in their dreams.

THE DOORS TO THE THRONE Hall stood three times higher than a tall man, wrought of hammered iron. On them was depicted the War of the Shapers.

The left-hand door bore the Six: Haomane, chiefest of all; Arahila, his gentle sister; Meronin, lord of the seas; Neheris of the north; Yrinna the fruitful; and Oronin, the Glad Hunter. Haomane had raised his hand in wrath, and before him was the Souma—an uncut ruby as big as a sheep's heart, glinting dully in a rough iron bezel.

On the right-hand door were Lord Satoris, and dragons. And they were glorious, the dragons depicted in lengths of coiling scales, necks arching, vaned wings outreaching, the mighty jaws parted to issue gouts of sculpted flame. At the center of it all stood the wounded Satoris, a glittering fragment of ruby representing Godslayer held in both hands like a prayer-offering.

"General!" The Fjeltroll on guard saluted. "His Lordship awaits."

"Krognar. You may admit us."

As ever, Tanaros' heart constricted as the massive doors were opened, parting Torath from Urulat, mimicking the Sundering itself; constricted, then blazed with pride. Beyond was his Lord, who had given him reason to live. The Throne Hall lay open before them, a vast expanse. Unnatural torches burned on the walls—marrow-fire, tamed to the

Shaper's whim, casting long, crisscrossing shadows across the polished floor. A carpet of deepest black ran the length of the Hall, a tongue of shadow stretching from the open maw of the iron doors to the base of the Throne. It was carved of a massive carnelian, that Throne, the blood-red stone muted in the monochromatic light.

There, enthroned, sat a being Shaped of darkness with glowing eyes.

"Tanaros." Cerelinde's voice, small and dry.

"Don't be afraid." There was more, so much more he wanted to tell her, but words fell short and his heart burned within him, drowning out thought. Settling the Helm of Shadows under his left arm, he offered the right in a gesture half-remembered from the Altorian courts. "Come, Lady. Lord Satoris awaits us."

How long? Ten paces, twenty, fifty.

Thrice a hundred.

The torches burned brighter as they traversed the hall, gouts of blue-white flame reaching upward. The Mørkhar Fjel paced two by two on either side of them, splendid in their inlaid weapons-harnesses that glittered like quicksilver.

Always, the Throne, looming larger as they drew near, Darkness seated in it. Fair, once; passing fair. No longer. A smell in the air, the thick coppery reek of blood, only *sweeter.* The brand that circumscribed Tanaros' heart blazed; Cerelinde's fingertips trembled on his forearm, setting his nerves ablaze. Directly beneath the Throne Hall lay the Chamber of the Font, and below it, the Source itself. In the dazzling light, she might have been carved of ivory.

"Tanaros."

He drew a deep breath, feeling his tight-strung nerves ease at the Shaper's rumbling voice. Home. "My Lord Satoris!" The bow came easily, smoothly, a pleasing obeisance. He relinquished Cerelinde's arm, placing the Helm's case atop the dais. "Victory is ours. I restore to you the

Helm of Shadows, and present the Lady Cerelinde of the Rivenlost, the betrothed of Aracus Altorus."

Gleaming eyes blinked, once, in the darkness of the Shaper's face; one massive hand shifted on the arm of the Throne. His voice emerged, deep and silken-soft. "Be welcome to Darkhaven, Elterrion's granddaughter, daughter of Erilonde. Your mother was known to me."

Her chin jerked; whatever Cerelinde had expected, it was not that. "Lord Satoris, I think it is not so. Your hospitality has been forced upon me at the point of a sword, and as for my mother . . . my mother died in the bearing of me."

"Yes." A single word, solemn and bone-tremblingly deep. "Erilonde, daughter of Elterrion, wife of Celendril. I recall it well, Cerelinde. In the First Age of the Sundered World, she died. She prayed to me ere her death. It is how I knew her."

"No." Delicate hands, clenched into fists. "I will not be tricked, Sunderer!"

Laughter, booming and sardonic. The rafters of the Throne Hall rattled. The Mørkhar Fjel eyed them with pragmatic wariness. "Is it so hard to believe, Haomane's Child? After all, it was my Gift . . . once. The quickening of the flesh. Generation." The air thickened, rife with the sweet scent of blood, of desire. Satoris' eyes shone like spearpoints. "Do you blame her? Many women have prayed to me in childbirth. I would have saved her if I could."

"Then why didn't you?"

The words were flung, an accusation. Tanaros shifted uneasily between his beloved Lord and his hostage. The Shaper merely sighed, disturbing the shadows.

"My Gift was torn from me, pierced to the heart by Oronin Last-Born, who drove a shard of the Souma into my thigh. I had nothing to offer your mother. I am sorry. If Haomane had not disdained my Gift when I had it, it might have been otherwise. I grieve that it was not. Your people will dwindle for it, and die, until you pass forevermore from Urulat's memory."

Cerelinde eyed him uncertainly. "You lie, Lord Sunderer."

"Do the Ellylon not dwindle in number?"

"Yes." She held his gaze, a thing few mortals could do unflinching. "And so we shall, until you relent or the Prophecy is fulfilled. Haomane has pledged it."

"Haomane," the Shaper mused, plucking the case that held the Helm of Shadows from the dais. "My Elder Brother, the Lord-of-Thought. Do you not find him an absent parent to his children, Lady Cerelinde?"

"No." She stared, transfixed, as his dark fingers undid the case's clasps.

"This was his weapon, once." Satoris lifted the Helm and held it before him, its empty eye-sockets gazing the length of the hall. "It contained in its visage the darkness of Haomane's absence, the darkness that lies in the deepest cracks of the shattered Souma, those things which all the Children of Uru-Alat fear most to look upon. To Ardrath the Counselor my Elder Brother gave it, and Ardrath called me out upon the plains of war." He smiled, caressing the worn, pitted bronze of the Helm. "I prevailed, and now it is mine. And I have Shaped into it my own darkness, of truth twisted and the shadow cast by a bright, shining lie, of flesh charred to blackness by the wrath of merciless light. Will you gaze upon it, Haomane's Child?"

So saying, he placed the Helm upon his head.

Cerelinde cried out and looked away.

"My Lord," Tanaros whispered, stretching his hands helplessly toward the Throne. Pain, so much pain! "Oh, my Lord!"

"It is enough." Satoris removed the Helm and regarded it. "Send for Lord Vorax," he said to the Mørkhar Fjel, "that he might conduct the Lady to the quarters prepared for her. I will speak more with her anon. General Tanaros." The gleaming eyes fixed him. "Tell me of Lindanen Dale, and what transpired thereafter."

* * *

A SULLEN CAMPFIRE BURNED. ARMFULS of dried sedge grass were thrown upon it, sending sparks into the starry skies. Carfax watched them rise. He was able, now, to move his eyes. He could move his limbs, too, so long as he did not contemplate violence against his companions. The mere thought of it brought retching nausea.

"You are safe, here." It was the Counselor who spoke, his voice calm and soothing. He pointed around the perimeter of an invisible circle with the butt-end of his staff. "Inside this ring, nothing can harm you; not even Lord Satoris. Do you understand?"

He did. All too well, he understood. He had failed.

"It is dangerous to keep him." Firelight played over Blaise Caveros' face; spare features, like the General's, yet somehow stirring.

"He is no danger to us now."

It was true. Carfax's tongue was sealed, stuck to the roof of his mouth by force of will and the oath he had sworn. Silence was his only protection, his only weapon. His hands lay limp, upturned upon his thighs. Yet if he had the chance . . .

"Who are you? Why were you sent?"

He could have laughed; he would have laughed, if the binding had permitted it. Faces, arrayed around the campfire. Such a tiny company, to threaten the foundations of Darkhaven! He knew their names, now. Not just the Counselor and the Borderguardsman, but the others. Fianna, the Archer; a tenderness there despite the lean sinews of her arms. He saw it when she looked at Blaise. Peldras, the Ellyl; of the Rivenlost, Ingolin's kindred, young and ancient at once. Hobard, proud and angry in his hand-me-down armor, his every thought writ on his face.

You were the one, weren't you? The Dreamspinner found you and sent his ravens . . .

But not the boy, ah, Arahila! What was his role? Fingering the flask that hung about his neck on corded twine. Dani, they called him. A cruel fate, to summon one so young. If he'd been Staccian, Carfax would have sent him back to gain another summer's age. Small wonder his uncle had accompanied him. Thulu, that one was called. Unkempt black hair, thick and coarse. A broad belly, spilling over his crude breechclout. Lord Vorax would have understood this one, whose eyes were like raisins in the dark pudding of his face.

"Why were you sent?"

Why? Why, indeed? To secure the world against your machinations, Haomane's tool! Carfax suffocated his laughter, biting his tongue. Red foam spilled from the corners of his mouth. Why? Why are you *here,* in these Shaper-forsaken marshes? What do you want in Vedasia? What does the boy Dani carry in his flask, that you guard so fearfully?

"Why doesn't he answer?"

"He is afraid, Dani." It was Peldras the Ellyl who answered in gentle tones. "He has served a cruel master. Give him time, and he will come to see we mean him no harm."

"Can you not compel him, wizard?" Hobard challenged the Counselor.

"No." Malthus shook his head wearily, taking a seat on a grassy tussock. "Satoris' minions swear an oath bound by the force of Godslayer itself. I can compel his flesh, but not his loyalty. Not even the Soumanië can undo that which is bound to a shard of the Souma." His deep-set gaze rested on Carfax. "That, he must choose himself."

"He's bleeding." The boy poured water from a skin into a tin cup, approaching Carfax and squatting to proffer the cup. In the firelight, the tin shone like a ruddy star between his palms. "Would you like a drink to rinse your mouth?" he asked.

Carfax reached for it with both hands.

"Dani," Blaise cautioned. "Don't go near him."

"Let him be, swordsman." Fat Thulu spun his digging-stick with deceptive ease. "'He's the Bearer, and that's water he bears. Let him do it."

Cool tin, sweet water. It stung his tongue and turned salty in his mouth. Carfax spat pink-tinged water onto the marshy soil, then drank, his throat working. Water, cool and soothing, tasting of minerals and hidden places deep in the earth. "Thank you," he whispered, returning the cup.

The boy smiled, an unexpected slice of white in his dark face.

"Malthus." Blaise raised his brows.

The Counselor, watching, shook his head. "Thulu is right, Blaise. Whether he knows it or not, the boy does Haomane's work in ways deeper than we may fathom. Let it abide. Mayhap his kindness will accomplish what the Soumanië cannot. Any mind, I have spent too deeply of myself to pursue it further this night." Yawning with weariness, he let his chin sink onto his chest, mumbling through his beard. "In the morning, we will continue on toward Malumdoorn. Peldras, the first watch is yours."

Overhead, the stars wheeled through their courses.

One wouldn't expect a wizard to snore, but he did. One might expect it to loosen his bindings, but it didn't. Carfax struggled against them, testing of his circumscribed thoughts and constrained flesh. The Ellyl watched him, not without pity, an unsheathed blade across his knees. All around them, starlight shone on the hummocks and knolls that had been Carfax's companions when dawn had risen on that day. Now it was night and they were earth and grass, nourished by his bloody spittle, glimmering beneath the stars and a crescent moon.

"She Shaped them, you know." The Ellyl tilted his perfect chin, gazing at the night sky. "Arahila the Merciful took pity on night's blackness and beseeched Haomane to allow her to lay hands upon the Souma, the Eye of Uru-Alat that she might Shape a lesser light to illume the darkness." He smiled compassionately at Carfax's struggle. "It is said among the Rivenlost that there is no sin so great that Arahila will not forgive it."

It was dangerous to match words with an Ellyl; nonetheless, Carfax left off his efforts and replied, the words grating in his throat. "Will she forgive Malthus what he did to my men?"

"It does not please him to do so, Staccian." The Ellyl's voice held sorrow. "Malthus the Wise Counselor would harm no living thing by his own choice. You sought to slay us out of hand."

"What do you seek, Rivenlost?"

"Life." The Ellyl's hands rested lightly on his naked blade. "Hope."

Carfax bared his bloodstained teeth. "And Lord Satoris' death."

Peldras regarded the stars. "We are Haomane's Children, Staccian. It is the Sunderer's choice to oppose him and it is the Rivenlost, above all, who will die for this choice if we do not take it from him." He looked back at Carfax, his gaze bright and direct. "Torath is lost to us and, without the Souma to sustain us, we diminish. Our numbers lessen, our magics fading. If Satoris Banewreaker conquers Urulat, it will be our end. What would you have us do?"

Dangerous, indeed, to match words with an Ellyl. This time, Carfax held his bitten tongue. Better to keep silent and hope against hope for rescue or a clean death that would place him beyond his enemies' reach.

If either could find him here.

On and on the night sank into darkness, the fire settling to embers. Carfax dozed in exhaustion. A mind, borne on dark wings, beat desperately at the outskirts of the Counselor's circle; beat and beat, skittering helpless away. The Vedasian groaned in his sleep, untouchable. In the sedge grass, a saddle sat empty, three dead ravens tied by their feet. Waking, dimly aware, Carfax strained against the Counselor's binding.

Dreamspinner, I am here, here!
Nothing.

THIRTEEN

It took you long enough, cousin." Standing before the dungeon stair with a smoldering torch in one hand, Vorax raised his bushy red brows. "Was it a hard reckoning?"

"No harder than it ought to be," Tanaros said. "His Lordship wanted the details."

"Twenty-three lost in Lindanen Dale."

"Aye. Yours." He met Vorax's gaze. "Good men. I'm sorry for it."

The Staccian shrugged. "They knew the price, cousin. Battle-glory, and fair recompense for the fallen. The couriers will leave on the morrow, bearing purses. At least every man's widow, every man's bereaved mother, will know the cost to a coin of her husband or son's life."

Tanaros touched the pouch where Hyrgolf's *rhios* hung, thinking on the death of Bogvar in the City of Long Grass, and how Thorun had begged him take his axe-hand. "Do they reckon it enough, in Staccia?"

"They reckon it a fairer trade than any Haomane offered." Vorax raised the torch, peering. Light glittered on the rings that adorned his thick fingers; topaz, ruby, emerald. "Cousin, this can wait until you're rested."

"No." Tanaros gathered himself with an effort. "I want to see the prisoner."

Keys rattled as Vorax sought the proper one to open the door to the lower depths. Tanaros held the torch while he fumbled. The Fjel guard stood at attention. Dank air wafted from the open door, smelling of mold and decay. Below, it was black as pitch. No marrow-fire threaded the veins of the dungeon's stone.

"Phaugh!" Tanaros raised the torch. "I forget how it stinks."

"No point in a pleasant prison," Vorax said pragmatically.

Stepping onto the first stair, Tanaros paused. "You didn't put the Lady Cerelinde in such a place, I hope."

"No." Torchlight made a bearded mask of the Staccian's face. "She's our *guest*, cousin, or so his Lordship would have it. Her quarters are as fine as my own; more so, if your taste runs to Ellylon gewgaws."

"Good," Tanaros said shortly. The winding stairs were slippery and he took them with care, one at a time. It would be a bitter irony indeed if he slipped and broke his neck here and now, in the safe confines of Darkhaven. Something moved in the reeking darkness below; there was a sound of chains rattling, a phlegmy cough. "Tell me of the prisoner. He was captured in the Weavers' Gulch?"

Behind him, Vorax wheezed with the effort of descending. "Trussed like a goose in spider-silk and glaring mad at it. He bolted like a rabbit when the Thunder Voice challenged him at the Maw. They let him go to see how far he'd get."

In the darkness, Tanaros smiled. "You put him to the questioning?"

"Aye." Vorax bent over, resting his meaty hands on his knees. "Some of Hyrgolf's lads gave him a few love-taps when he struggled. Otherwise, we held his feet to the fire." Seeing Tanaros' expression, he straightened. "Only the usual, not enough to cripple. He might be missing a few fingernails."

"And?" Tanaros waited mid-stair.

"Nothing." The Staccian shrugged. "Says he's a Midlander, a horse-thief. Says he's here to offer his service. Doesn't appear to be mad. We waited for you, otherwise."

"My thanks, cousin." Descending the final steps, his boots squelched in the damp. There must have been an inch of standing water on the floor, seeping through the dungeon's foundation. Tanaros crossed the cell and thrust the torch into a waiting sconce. "Let's see what we have."

It took a moment for his eyes to adjust. Wavering torchlight reflected on the standing water and the dark, moisture-
slick walls. On the far wall, a single prisoner hung, knees
sagging, resting his weight on the chains that held his arms
upraised. Under Tanaros' regard, he hauled himself upright,
his blistered feet disturbing the stagnant water. "General
Tanaros Blacksword." A broad Midlander accent placed his
origin in the fertile territories south of Curonan. He was
young, not out of his twenties, with light brown hair falling
matted and greasy over his brow. "A fine welcome you give
those who would serve you."

"Count yourself lucky for it, boyo," Vorax muttered,
making his way to the bottom of the stair, one hand on the
wall for balance. "The Tordenstem Fjel could have killed
you as easily as not."

"Lucky me." The prisoner smiled crookedly. His lips
were split and swollen, one of his front teeth a ragged
stump, broken by a Fjel love-tap. "What do you say, General? Could you use one such as me?"

Tanaros folded his arms. "Who are you?"

"Speros of Haimhault. I'd make a proper bow, Lord General, but . . ." The prisoner twitched his hands, dangling
limp in their iron manacles. His fourth and fifth fingers
ended in raw wounds. "Well, you see."

"And you seek to offer your service?" Tanaros raised his
brows. "Others in your position might complain of such
treatment."

The prisoner Speros shrugged, causing his chains to rattle. "I came unannounced. Darkhaven has cause for suspicion. Shall we say as much and begin anew?"

Vorax stifled a yawn and settled his bulk on a three-
legged stool left by the prisoner's questioners. Tanaros ignored him, eyeing the young man. "Lord Vorax says you
claim to be a horse-thief."

"I have done." Brown eyes glinted through matted hair.
"Stole a Seaholder lordling's mount, once, when I was em-
ployed at a blacksmith's forge. Cut purses, wooed women

I'd no intent to wed. Served as second-in-command to the volunteer militia of Haimhault, for a time. I've done lots of things, Lord General. I've lots of ideas, too. I'm chock full of ideas."

"Have you shed innocent blood?" Tanaros asked brusquely.

There was a pause, then, punctuated only by another stifled Staccian yawn.

"Aye." The prisoner's voice was soft. "That, too."

Tanaros paced the narrow cell, his boot-heels splashing in the standing water. In the wavering torchlight, Vorax watched him without offering comment. As it was, as it should be. It was true, this was one of his, one of his own. He fetched up before the prisoner, peering at his bruised face. "You do know where you are? This is Darkhaven, lad. Beyond the wall, the world is our enemy. If you swear loyalty to Lord Satoris—for it is him you will serve, and not me—it will be your enemy, too. Your name will become poison, a symbol of the worst betrayal a man may commit."

"Aye, Lord General." Speros straightened in his chains. "I know."

"Then why?"

An inch could have closed the space between them; even in chains, Speros could have flinched. He didn't, clenching his manacled fists instead. Blood fell, drop by drop, from his wounded fingertips. It made a faint splashing sound as it struck the water. "You need to ask?"

Tanaros nodded. He could smell the prisoner's suppurating wounds. "I do."

"I'm tired of paying for my sins." Speros smiled, taut and bitter. "I never set out to become a thief and a killer, but it's funny the way things go. You make enough mistakes, comes a day when no one will take a chance on you. Arahila may forgive, General Blacksword, but her Children do not. I am weary to the bone of courting their forgiveness. Lord Satoris accepted your service. Why not mine?"

Had he been that young, that defiant, twelve hundred

years ago? Yes, Tanaros thought; he had been. Twenty-and-eight years of age, hunted and despised throughout the realm. Kingslayer, they had called him. Wifeslayer, some had whispered. Cuckold. Murderer. He had yearned for death, fought for life. A summons tickling his fevered brain had led him to Darkhaven.

Still, he shook his head. "You're young and angry at the world. It will pass."

The brown eyes glinted. "As yours did?"

Tanaros awarded him a slight smile. "Anger is only the beginning, Midlander. It does not suffice unto itself."

"What, then?" Speros shifted in his chains, but his gaze never left Tanaros' face. "Tell me, General, and I will answer. Why do *you* serve him? For gold and glory, like the Staccians? Out of mindless loyalty, like the Fjeltroll?"

On his stool, Vorax coughed. Tanaros glanced at him.

"The Staccians' bargain grants peace and prosperity to the many at a cost to the few," he said. "And the Fjel are not so mindless as you think."

"Yet that is not an answer," Speros said. "Not your answer."

"No." Tanaros faced him. "I serve my Lord Satoris because, in my heart, I have declared myself the enemy of his enemies. Because I despise the hypocrisy and cowardice of the Six Shapers who oppose him. Because I despise the tyranny of certitude with which Haomane First-Born seeks to rule over the world, placing his Children above all others." His voice grew stern. "Make no mistake, lad. For many years, his Lordship sought nothing more than to live unmolested, but great deeds are beginning to unfold. I tell you this, here and now; if you swear yourself to Lord Satoris' service, you are declaring yourself an enemy of the Lord-of-Thought himself, and a participant in a battle to Shape the world anew."

The prisoner grinned with his split, swollen lips. "I am not fond of the world as I have found it, General. You name a cause in which I would gladly believe."

"Haomane's Wrath is a fearsome thing," Tanaros warned him.

Speros shrugged. "So was my Da's."

It was a boy's comment, not a Man's; and yet, the glint in the lad's eyes suggested it was deliberate, issued as a reckless dare. Against his better judgement, Tanaros laughed. He had found fulfillment and purpose in service to Lord Satoris, in seizing his own warped destiny and pitting himself against the will of an overwhelming enemy. If it afforded him the chance to play a role in Shaping the world that had betrayed him, so much the better.

Did the lad deserve less?

"Vorax," Tanaros said decisively. "Strike his chains."

THE LAMPS BURNED LOW IN her quarters.

There was a veneer of delicacy overlaying the appearance of the rooms to which she had been led. Tapestries in shades of rose, celadon and dove-grey hid the black stone walls; fretted lamps hung from the buttresses, their guttering light casting a patterned glow. These elements had been added, tacked atop the solid bulwark of the fortress in an effort to disguise the brooding mass of Darkhaven.

Cerelinde was not fooled.

This prison had been made for her.

She paced it, room by room, her feet sinking deep into the cloud-soft carpets that concealed the polished floor. What halls had they adorned? Cuilos Tuillenrad? A faint scent arose at her passage. Heart-grass, bruised and crushed by her feet. Oh, this was Ellylon craftsmanship, to be sure! Her kinfolk had woven it in ages past, with fingers more nimble than any son or daughter of Man could hope to emulate. The wool would have been culled from the first coats of yearling lamb, washed with an effusion of the delicate flowers of heart-grass that bloomed for three days only in the spring. Journeymen would have carded it, singing under the open skies, but the spinning, ah! That would have been done by Ellylon noblewomen, for they alone had the nicety of touch to spin wool thread as fine as silk.

Her own mother might have touched it . . .

Your mother was known to me.

Cerelinde closed her eyes. Unfair; oh, unfair!

It was not true. It could *not* be true. Time and time again, Malthus had said it: Satoris Banewreaker is cunning, he Shapes truth itself to his own ends. Her father . . . her father Celendril, she remembered well, for he had died in the Fourth Age of the Sundered World, slain upon the plains of Curonan amid the host of Numireth.

And left her alone.

No. That, too, was a lie; this place bred them like flies. Lord Ingolin had opened the gates of Meronil to all the Rivenlost who had fled the Sunderer's wrath. Always her place there had been one of honor, even during the long centuries she had refused to hear their arguments. Malthus had been the first to say it, his wise old eyes heavy with grief at the death of his comrades. It is your duty and destiny, Cerelinde.

When a daughter of Elterrion weds a son of Altorus . . .

What a bitter irony it was!

At first, she had refused out of anger. It was a son of Altorus who had cost them dear on the plains of Curonan; Trachan Altorus, who received the news of Dergail's defeat, who saw Ardrath the Counselor fall. Too soon he had sounded the retreat, and in that moment Satoris Banewreaker regained the dagger Godslayer and fled.

Long years it had taken for her people to overcome the bitterness of that blow and the ill-will it engendered between their races. Indeed, there were many among the Rivenlost who blamed Men for all the woes of their people; jealous, short-lived Men, who had long ago made war upon the Ellylon, coveting the secret of immortality. None of the House of Altorus, no, but others. And the ill-will flowed both ways, for the descendents of those Men who had kept

faith with the Ellylon blamed them for repaying loyalty by
drawing them into dire war against the Sunderer.

It was not their fault, not entirely. The lives of Men were
brief, flickering like candles and snuffed in a handful of
years. How could they hope to compass the scope of the
Sunderer's ambition when Satoris Banewreaker was content to wait ages for his plan to unfold? It was the second
reason Cerelinde had refused to hear the arguments of
Malthus and Lord Ingolin. Though she was young by Ellylon reckoning, she remembered ages preserved only in the
dusty memories of parchment for the sons and daughters of
Men.

How would it be, to wed one whose life passed in an eyeblink? One in whose flesh the seeds of death already took
root? For century upon century, Cerelinde had never contemplated it with aught but a sense of creeping horror.

And then Aracus had come.

Oh, it was a bitter irony, indeed.

What lie, she wondered, would the Sunderer make of it?
The truth was simple; He had won her heart. Aracus Altorus, a King without a kingdom, had ridden into Meronil
with only a handful of the Borderguard to attend him. By
the time he left, she had agreed to wed him.

Now she knew better the machinations behind that meeting, the long planning that had gone into it. By whatever to-
kens and arcane knowledge he used to determine the mind
of Haomane, the Wise Counselor had divined that the time
of reckoning was coming and Aracus Altorus, last-born
scion in a line that had endured for five thousand years,
must be the one to fulfill the Prophecy. Malthus had begun
laying the groundwork for it when Aracus was but a child,
visiting the boy in the guise of an aged uncle, filling his ears
with portents.

With one wary eye on Darkhaven, for nearly thirty years
he had exerted his subtle influence, laying seeds of thought
and ambition in the boy that came to fruition in the man.

And he had done his work well, Cerelinde thought with rue. The Wise Counselor had set out to Shape a hero.

He had done so.

For all the dignitaries assembled in the Hall of Meronil, they might have been alone, they two. It had passed between them, a thing understood, undetermined by the counsels of the wise. He reached out to grasp his destiny like a man grasping a burning brand. He would love her with all the fierce passion of his mortal heart. And she, she would love him in turn, in a tempestuous blaze. There was sorrow in it, yes, and grief, but not horror. Love, fair Arahila's Gift, changed all.

And while it lasted, the fate that overshadowed them would be held at bay. Oh, the price would be high! They knew it, both of them. Death would come hard on its heels, whether by sickness or age or the point of a sword. Oronin Last-Born, the Glad Hunter, would blow his horn, summoning the hero home. And Cerelinde would be left to endure in her grief. Even in victory, if the Sunderer were defeated at last and Urulat healed, her grief would endure. But their children; ah, Haomane! Mortal through their father's blood, still they would be half-Ellylon, granted a length of days uncommon to Men, able to reckon the vast span of time as no mortals among the Lesser Shapers had done before them. Their children would carry on that flame of hope and passion, uniting their races at last in a world made whole.

The image of the half-breed's crooked face rose unbidden in her memory, Tanaros' words echoing dryly. *Such as he is, your own children would have been . . .*

A lie; another lie. Surely children conceived in love would be different, would be accepted by both races. Was that not the intent of Haomane's Prophecy? Cerelinde sat upon the immense bed that had been prepared for her, covering her face with both hands. If she could have wept, she would have, but Ellylon could only shed tears for the sorrow of others. A storm of terror raged in her heart and mind. After five thousand years of resistance, she had relented, had accepted her fate. A moment of joy; an eternity of grief. It was enough; merciful Arahila, was it not enough?

This was not supposed to happen.

"Aracus," she whispered.

DAWN ROSE ON THE DELTA, and with the return of the light came swarms of gnats. They were merciless, descending in dark clouds, settling on sweat-slick skin already prickling in the heat, taking their measure of blood and leaving itching welts in trade. Turin waved his arms futilely and swore.

It didn't matter.

Nothing mattered. Mantuas, quick-witted, loud-mouthed Mantuas, was dead, drowned in a sucking mudpool. It happened so fast. Even Hunric, who could track his way through a Staccian blizzard, hadn't seen it coming. There hadn't been a thing they could do. Slithering on their bellies, poking branches; Mantuas, take hold, take hold! He couldn't free his arms from the muck, could only blink, desperately, as it covered his nostrils. He sank fast. Turin had turned away when the mud reached his eyes. By the time he dared look, only a few locks of hair lay atop the burbling muck.

Farewell, Mantuas.

A good job they'd turned the horses loose.

Lord Satoris might be wroth, but Lord Satoris should have *known*. This was the place that had engendered him. Had it been fair, once? Hunric said old trackers' tales claimed as much. Well, it was foul, now. All the muck and foetor that fouled the Verdine River crawled straight from the stinking heart of the Delta.

"Hold." Ahead of him, Hunric paused, probing the watery passage with a long stick he'd cut from a mangrove tree. "All right. Slide along here."

"I'm coming." Turin followed his lead, slogging through

waist-deep water along the edge of a clump of mangroves. His waterlogged boots were like lead weights on his feet, slipping on the slick, knotted roots that rose above the swamp. Only fear of snakes kept him from removing them. A few feet away, a basking lizard blinked at him and slithered rapidly in his direction, flicking a blue tongue. "Gah!" Turin recoiled, flailing his arms as the heavy pack strapped across his shoulders overbalanced him.

"Steady!" Hunric caught his flailing wrist, bracing him. "It's just a lizard, lad. It won't harm you."

"All right, all right, I'm all right!" Turin fought down his panic and shook off the tracker's hand. Was his gear secure? Yes, there was his sword, lashed sideways atop his pack. He reached behind him, felt the reassuring bulk of the supplies he carried. There was gold coin there, Lord Vorax's gift, useless in this place. Arahila willing, the bannock-cakes were secure in their oilcloth wrappings and they would not starve just yet. "All right. Let's go."

"Here." Hunric scooped a handful of muck from the bottom of the swamp. "Plaster it on your skin. It will help keep the gnats off."

He pushed away the proffered hand, dripping mud. "I don't want it on me."

"Turin." There was a despairing note in the tracker's voice. "Don't make it harder. I'm sorry about Mantuas, truly. I don't know the terrain and the Delta is harder than I thought. I'm doing my best."

"Hunric?"

"Aye?"

"They're not coming, are they?" Turin swallowed, hard. The words were hard to say. "Lieutenant Carfax, the others . . . you've been scoring trees, marking the safest route, ever since Mantuas died. I've watched you. If they were following, we'd have heard them by now."

"Mayhap." The tracker's eyes were shuttered in the mask of drying mud that coated his face. "If they captured Malthus' Company . . . if they did, lad, it may be that they found more pressing business lay elsewhere. Mayhap they seek to catch the Dreamspinner's thoughts, aye, or his ravens, to make a report to General Tanaros, aye, or Lord Satoris himself."

"Mayhap." Waist-deep in water, Turin tilted his chin and gazed at the sky, a heated blue against the green leaves of the mangroves. Birds roosted in the treetops, but only the kind that were born to this place. High above, the sun blazed like a hammer. Haomane's Wrath, beating down incessantly on the birthplace of Satoris Third-Born, who had defied his will. Banewreaker, the world named him, but he had always honored his word with Staccia, ever since Lord Vorax struck his bargain over a thousand years ago. What other Shaper had done as much since the world was Sundered? If matters went awry now, it meant something had gone grievously wrong. And Turin had a bad feeling that it had. "I don't think so, Hunric."

Water splashed as the Staccian tracker shifted, settling his own pack on his shoulders. "Well, then," he said, his voice hardening. "We'll have to press on, won't we?"

FOURTEEN

❖

A HUNDRED BANNERS FLEW IN Seahold.

There was the trident of Duke Bornin, of course, argent on a sea-blue field. And there were others; a dozen of his liege-lords, the barons and earls who held fiefdoms in the Midlands. There was the spreading oak of Quercas, the gilded stag of Tilodan, the harrow of Sarthac, all declaring their allegiance with pride. All had been seen in the city of Seahold, though never at once.

Not the Host of the Ellylon.

It had been a long time, since the Fourth Age of the Sundered World. Altoria had reigned and the Duke of Seahold had sworn fealty to its Kings when last these banners had been seen in the city.

It was a glorious sight.

Pennants and oriflammes hung from every turret, overhung every door of Castle Seahold. In the marketplaces, merchants displayed them with pride, hoping to stake some claim by virtue of symbolism to Ellyl patrons. In the streets, companies of Ellylon passed, carrying their standards with sombre pride. There was the argent scroll of Ingolin, the thistle-blossom of Núrilin, the gilded bee of Valmaré, the sable elbok of Numireth, the shipwright's wheel of Cerion . . . all of these and more, many more, representing the Houses of the Rivenlost, personified by their living scions and grieving kin alike.

Above them all hung the Crown and Souma of Elterrion the Bold.

No company dared bear this standard, no merchant dared display it. It hung limp in the summer's heat from the highest turret of Castle Seahold, gilt and ruby on a field of virgin white, a dire reminder of what was at stake.

Cerelinde.

And one other standard flew, plain and unadorned, taking place of precedence above the Duke of Seahold. It was dungrey, this banner; a blank field empty of arms. From time to time, the summer breezes lofted its fabric. It unfurled, revealing . . . nothing. Only dun, the dull-yellow color of the cloaks of the Borderguard of Curonan, designed to blend with the endless plains of heart-grass.

Once, Altoria had reigned; once, the King of Altoria had born different arms. A sword, a gilt sword on a field of sable, its quillons curved to the shape of eyes. It was the insignia of Altorus Farseer, who had been called friend by the Ellylon and risen to rule a nation in the Sundered World of Urulat.

No more.

Aracus Altorus had sworn it. Not until his Borderguard opposed Satoris Banewreaker himself would he take up the ancient banner of his forefathers. But he did not doubt—did not doubt for an instant—that the Sunderer was behind the Sorceress' actions. Once Cerelinde was restored, he would turn his far-seeing gaze on their true Enemy.

Rumor ran through the city. Citizens and merchants and freeholders assembled in Seaholder Square, gazing up at the Castle, waiting and murmuring. Opportunistic peddlers did a good trade in meat-pies wrapped in pastry; winesellers prospered, too. At noon, Duke Bornin of Seahold appeared on the balcony and addressed them. Possessed of a good set of lungs, he spoke with volume and at length.

It was true, all true.

The Prophecy, the wedding-that-would-have-been, the raid on Lindanen Dale. Oronin's Children, the Were at hunt. An abduction; the Lady of the Ellylon. Pelmaran soldiers in guise, falling trees. A message, an impossible ransom, delivered at a magical distance; rumors of the Dragon of Beshtanag, seen aloft.

Oh, it was all true, and the Sorceress of the East had overreached.

There was cheering when Duke Bornin finished; cheering, rising en masse. He had ruled long enough to be clever. He waited for it to end. And when it was done, he introduced to them Aracus Altorus, naming him warleader of the Allied forces of the West.

Primed for it, they cheered all the louder.

War was declared on Beshtanag.

WASHED, SALVED AND RESTED, CLAD in the armor of slain a Staccian warrior, Speros of Haimhault looked much improved by daylight. Despite his travail, his eyes were clear and alert and he moved as smoothly as his bandaged wounds allowed, a testament to the resilience of youth.

He hadn't lied, either; he knew how to handle a sword. At his insistence, Tanaros tested the former prisoner himself on the training-field of Darkhaven. Hyrgolf brought a squadron of Tungskulder Fjel to watch, forming a loose circle and leaning casually on their spears.

Inside the circle of onlookers, they fought.

Speros saluted him in the old manner; a clenched fist to the heart, then extended with an open palm. *Brother, let us spar. I trust my life unto your hands.* The old traditions died hard in the Midlands. How many times had he and Roscus Altorus saluted each other thusly in their Altorian boyhood?

Too many to count, and the memories were fond enough to hurt.

Tanaros returned the salute and drew his sword. Speros wasted only one glance upon it, briefly disappointed to see that it was not the General's infamous black sword, but merely an ordinary weapon. As well for him, since the black sword could shear through steel like flesh. Afterward, he ignored it, fixing his gaze on Tanaros himself, watching the subtle shifts in his face, in the musculature of his chest, in the set of his shield, that betokened a shift in his attack.

Flick, flick, flick, their blades darted and crossed, rang on the bosses of their shields. It made a prodigious sound on the training-field. Back and forth they went, churning the ground beneath their boots. Such was the swordplay of his youth, drilled into him a thousand years ago by a grizzled master-of-arms, sharp-tongued and relentless, always on the lookout for a pupil of promise.

"Not bad, horse-thief." Tanaros found himself smiling. "Not bad at all!"

"I do better . . . " Speros essayed a thrust and stumbled, wincing, forced to make a desperate parry. "I do better," he gasped, "when I've not been clamped in chains and had hot pokers held to my feet, Lord General."

"You do well enough." Putting an end to it, Tanaros

stepped inside the young man's guard, catching his ill-timed swing on the edge of his shield. The point of his sword came to rest in the hollow of the lad's throat. "I am not displeased."

Speros, with commendable poise, held himself still, although his brown eyes nearly crossed in an effort to look down at Tanaros' sword. "I concede, my lord. You have the better of me."

"Well, then." Tanaros put up his sword. "We have each other's measure."

Deep, booming laughter ensued; Hyrgolf, who stepped forward to clap a massive hand on Speros' shoulder. It rested there, heavy as a stone, talons dangling. "Give the lad a dram of *svartblod,*" he rumbled, beckoning to one of his soldiers with his free hand. "He's earned it."

To his credit, Speros grinned with gap-toothed fearlessness at the Fjel, sheathing his sword and hoisting the skin one of the Tungskulder proffered. It was a foul liquor, black as pitch, fermented from the blood of sheep that drank the tainted waters of the Gorgantus River, and Speros sputtered as he drank, dark liquid running in rivulets from the corners of his mouth. He shook himself like a wet dog, spattering droplets of *svartblod.*

The Fjel, who adored the foul stuff, laughed uproariously.

Tanaros touched the carved *rhios* that hung from his belt. "Take him in hand, Hyrgolf," he said to his field marshal. "Show him what there is to be seen in Darkhaven, and let him have a look at the forges. He may be worth keeping, this one."

"General." Hyrgolf inclined his head. There was a shrewdness in his small boar's eyes. Fjeltroll he might be, Tungskulder Fjel, broadest and strongest of his mighty race, but he was a father, too, and there were things he knew that Tanaros did not. "Aye, General."

"Good." It was a relief, after all, to strip the practice helmet from his head, to raise two fingers to his lips and give

the shrill whistle of command that summoned the black
horse. Tanaros mounted, gazing down at Hyrgolf. "The
Dreamspinner has requested my counsel. We'll resume
drills in two days' time. See that the Midlander's taught the
rudiments of battle formations and the proper commands. I
could use a subordinate on the field."

"Aye, General." The tips of Hyrgolf's eyetusks showed as
he smiled.

Under his thighs, the black's hide rippled. Tanaros raised
his hand. "Speros of Haimhault!" he called. "I'm leaving
you to the untender mercies of Field Marshal Hyrgolf, who
will teach you to be a soldier of Darkhaven. Can you handle
it, lad?"

"Aye, Lord General!" Surrounded by Fjel, the former
prisoner gave his gap-toothed grin and a cheerful salute.
Clearly, Speros found himself at home here, unabashed by
the rough camaraderie of the Fjel. "Can I have one of those
horses to ride if I do?"

Tanaros rode toward the rookery, a lingering smile on his
lips. How long had it been, since one of his countrymen had
served Darkhaven? Too long. Loathe though he was to admit it, he'd missed it.

At the outskirts of the beech wood, he turned his mount
loose and proceeded on foot, boots sinking deep into the
soft mast, his shield slung over his back. Truly, he
thought, the lad had fought well. It was no easy chore, to
spar when one's every step was a waking agony. It must be
so, with the searing wounds Speros had endured. A good
thing Vorax's own physician had attended him. Though it
had done no permanent harm, it had been an ungentle
questioning.

Tanaros' own arrival had differed. He was one of the
Three, and Lord Satoris himself had sensed his broken
heart and his wounded pride, had used the Helm of Shadows to summon him. And in all the wildness of his despair,
Tanaros had answered the summons, had out-faced and out-

shouted the Thunder Voice Fjel, and made his way through the Defile unaided and undeterred.

And presented himself to the Sunderer, who had asked his aid.

Even now, after so long, he shuddered in remembered ecstasy. The knot of scarred flesh that circumscribed his heart constricted at the memory of his branding, of how the hilt of Godslayer, laid against his skin, had *stretched* the chains of his mortality. Even now, when his aching joints remembered their endless sojourn, it moved him.

He had spoken the truth to Speros. In the beginning, there had been only rage. It had driven him to Darkhaven in fury and despair, and he had laid it at the feet of Lord Satoris, willing to serve evil itself if it would purge his furious heart. Since then he had come to understand that the world was not as he had believed it in his youth. He had come to love Lord Satoris, who clung to his defiance in the face of the overwhelming tyranny of Haomane's will, wounded and bereft though he was. Haomane's Wrath had scorched the very earth in pursuit of Satoris. Were it not for Arahila's merciful intervention, the Lord-of-Thought might have destroyed Urulat itself.

Tanaros wondered if Haomane would have reckoned it worth the cost. After all, it would enable him to Shape the world anew, the better to suit his desires. It was the will of Uru-Alat, Haomane claimed, that he should reign supreme among Shapers; and yet, each of them held a different Gift. Was the Gift of thought superior to all others? Once, Tanaros had believed it to be so; until the courage and loyalty of the Fjel humbled him.

It was a pity Haomane First-Born had never known humility. Perhaps he would not be so jealous of his station, so quick to wrath, if he were humbled. Perhaps, after all, it was Lord Satoris' destiny to do so.

He wondered how he could ever have believed in Haomane's benevolence. Surely it must be the power of the

Souma. But as long as Lord Satoris opposed him with God-slayer in his possession, Haomane could not wield its full might. And Tanaros meant to do all in his power to aid his Lordship. Perhaps, one day, he might be healed, and Urulat with him.

O my Lord, he thought, my Lord! Let me be worthy of your choosing.

"Blacksword."

A dry voice, dry as the Unknown Desert. Ushahin Dreamspinner, seated cross-legged under a beech tree, still as the forest. Lids parted, mismatched eyes cracked open. Sticky lashes, parched lips.

"Cousin," Tanaros said. "You wished to see me?"

"Aye." Dry lips withdrew from teeth. "Did you see the ravens?"

"Ravens?" Tanaros glanced about with alarm. The rookery was sparsely populated, but that was not unusual. It was more seldom than not that he espied his tufted friend. "Is it Fetch? Has something happened to him?"

"No." The half-breed rested his head against a beech bole. "Your feathered friend is safe, for the nonce. He keeps watch, with others, on Haomane's Allies as they make ready to depart for Pelmar. But something has happened."

Tanaros seated himself opposite the Dreamspinner, frowning. "What is it?"

"I don't know." Ushahin grimaced, raising crooked fingers to his temples. "Therein lies the problem, cousin. All I can do is put a name to it."

"And the name?" A chill tickled Tanaros' spine.

"Malthus."

One word; no more, and no less. They gazed at one another, knowing as did few on Urulat what it betokened. Malthus the Counselor was Haomane's weapon, and where he went, ill followed for those who opposed him.

"How so?" Tanaros asked softly.

Ushahin gave his hunch-shouldered shrug. "If I knew,

cousin, I would tell you, and his Lordship, too. All I know is
that Malthus' Company entered the Unknown Desert. Some
days past, they emerged. And they brought someone—and
something—with them."

"Bound for Darkhaven?"

"No." Ushahin shook his head. "They went east. That's
what worries me."

"Toward Pelmar?" Tanaros relaxed. "Then Malthus
himself has bought our gambit, and there is no cause for
fear—"

"Not Pelmar." The half-breed tilted his head, the dim,
patterned shadow of beech leaves marking his misshapen
face. "Malthus' Company is bound for Vedasia."

There was a pause, then.

"Send your ravens," Tanaros suggested.

Ushahin spared him a contemptuous glance. "I *did*. Three
I sent, and three are dead, strung by their feet from an Arduan saddlebag. And now, the circle has closed tight around
Malthus' Company, and there is no mind open to me. I cannot find them. I do not like it. Who and what did Malthus
bring out of the Unknown Desert?"

Both of them thought, without saying it, of the Prophecy.

"Does his Lordship know?" Tanaros asked.

Dabbling his fingers in the beech mast, Ushahin frowned.
"What he fears, he does not name. And yet I think some
part of it is unknown to him, for the desert was much
changed by Haomane's Wrath."

"It doesn't matter, does it?" Sitting on the soft ground,
Tanaros squared his shoulders. "We've already thwarted the
first part. The daughter of Elterrion's line is in our keeping,
and the son—" his voice grew hard, "—the son of Altorus'
line is bound for Pelmar at the head of a doomed army."

Crooked lips smiled without humor. "Then why is
Malthus bound for Vedasia?"

"Would that I knew. But I am a military strategist, not a
spymaster, cousin." Tanaros unfolded his legs and stood,

placing a hand in the small of his back, feeling stiff joints pop. Sparring with the young Midlander had taken its toll. "What, then, does his Lordship say?"

"Watch," Ushahin said flatly, "and wait. Report."

"Well, then." Tanaros nodded, half to himself, gazing about the rookery. Haphazard nests rested in the crooks of trees, a dark flurry of twigs protruding. Which one, he wondered, belonged to Fetch? "I can advise you no better, Dreamspinner. Watch, and wait. Learn what you may. In the meantime, I must bring our forces to readiness and plot our course through the Marasoumië. When your knowledge impinges on the disposition of the army, alert me."

Two strides he took; three, four, before Ushahin's voice halted him.

"Tanaros?"

He looked small, seated under a beech tree; small and afraid.

"Aye, cousin?"

"He should kill her, you know." Muscles worked in the half-breed's throat as he swallowed. "Nothing's done, nothing's averted, while she lives."

It was true. True and true and true, and Tanaros knew it. *Cerelinde.*

"He won't," he whispered.

"I know." Unexpected tears shimmered in the mismatched eyes. "There is hope in him; a Shaper's hope, that would recreate the world in his image. If it comes to it . . . could you do it, Tanaros?"

On a branch, a raven perched. Twigs, protruding from a rough-hewn nest. The bird bent low, his head obscured by gaping beaks, coughed up sustenance from his craw. What manner was it? Earthworms, insects, carrion. Even here, life endured; regenerated and endured, life to life, earth to earth, flesh to flesh.

Cerelinde.

"I don't know."

* * *

THE WEATHER WAS BALMY IN Vedasia.

It was the thing, Carfax thought, that one noticed first; at
least, one did if one was Staccian. Summer was a golden
time in Staccia, with the goldenrod blooming around the
shores of inland lakes and coating the harsh countryside in
yellow pollen. It was nothing to this. This, this was sunlight
dripping like honey, drenching field and orchard and olive
grove in a golden glow, coaxing all to surrender their
bounty. Fields of wheat bowed their gold-whiskered heads,
melons ripened on the vine, the silvery-green leaves of
olive trees rustled and boughs bent low with the weight of
swelling globes of apple and pear. This was the demesne of
Yrinna-of-the-Fruits, Sixth-Born among Shapers.

They had gained the Traders' Route shortly after entering
Vedasia proper and Carfax's skin prickled as they rode,
knowing himself deep in enemy territory. It was a wonder,
though, how few folk noted aught awry. Children, mostly.
They stared wide-eyed, peering from behind their mothers'
skirts, from the backboards of passing wagons. They
pointed and whispered; at the Charred Folk, mostly, but
also at the others.

What, he wondered, did they see?

A grey-beard in scholar's robes, whose eyes twinkled beneath his fiercesome brows; Malthus, it seemed, had a kindness for children. A frowning Borderguardsman in a dun
cloak. An Ellyl lordling, whose light step left no trace on
the dusty road. An Arduan woman in men's attire, her longbow unstrung at her side. A young knight sweating in full
Vedasian armor.

A man with nut-brown skin and a rounded belly.

A nut-brown boy with wide dark eyes and a flask about
his neck.

They sang as they traveled, the Charred Folk. Monoto-
nously, incessantly. Thulu, the fat one, sang in a bass rum-

ble. Sometimes Carfax listened, and heard in it the deep tones of water passing through subterranean places, of hidden rivers and aquifers feeding the farthest-reaching roots of the oldest trees. The boy Dani sang too, his voice high and true. It was most audible when running water was near. Then his voice rose, bright and warbling. Like rivers, like streams, bubbling over rocks.

Children noticed.

Malthus the Counselor noticed, too, his keen ears and eyes missing little. He nodded to himself, exchanged glances with Blaise of the Borderguard, with Peldras the Ellyl, nodding with satisfaction and fingering the ruby-red Soumanië hidden beneath his beard. Everything, it seemed, went according to Malthus' plan.

Old man, Carfax thought, I hate you.

And since there was nothing else for him to do, his flesh and his will bound and circumscribed by the Counselor's Soumanië, Carfax rode alongside them, ate and slept and breathed road-dust, keeping the silence that was his only protection, watching and hating, willing them harm. Sometimes, the children stared at him. What did they see? A man, dusty and bedraggled, his tongue cleft to the roof of his mouth. Deaf and dumb, they thought him. Betimes, there were taunts. Carfax endured them as his due.

What folly, to think Malthus would have surrendered his Soumanië!

Sometimes there were couriers, royal couriers, carrying the standard of Port Calibus. They traveled in pairs. One would sound the silvery horn, hoisting the standard high to display a pennant bearing an argent tower on a mist-blue field. Other sojourners cleared the well-kept road in a hurry at the sight of it, including Malthus' Company. The old wizard would stand with his head bowed, one hand clutching beneath his beard, muttering under his breath. Whatever charm it was, it worked. The Vedasian couriers took no notice of them.

Within days of their arrival, they began to see companies

of knights headed east on the Traders' Route. Twenty, forty at a time, riding in orderly formations, baggage trains following. More and more frequently couriers appeared, stitching back and forth the length of the country, horns blowing an urgent warning. Commitments were asked and given, numbers were tallied, supplies were rerouted. The rumors were spoken in a whisper, became news, stated aloud.

Vedasia was committing its knights to war.

Stories were passed from mouth to ear along the Traders' Route. The Sorceress of the East had made an unholy pact with the Sunderer himself, who had promised to make her his Queen in exchange for the head of Malthus the Counselor. She had sent her dragon to abduct the Lady of the Rivenlost and offered a dreadful bargain.

Haomane's Allies had chosen war instead.

Not all of them, no, but already a mighty force was on the march, moving from Seahold to Harrington Bay, where the Free Fishers had agreed to carry them to Port Calibus. There, a fleet of Vedasian ships would ferry them around the lower tip of Dwarfhorn and on to Port Eurus to unite with a Vedasian company under the command of Duke Quentin, the King's nephew. Two of the Five Regents of Pelmar had given pledges of war, and the another was expected to agree soon. It was a force the likes of which had not been seen since the Fourth Age of the Sundered World. The Sorceress of the East, all agreed, had overreached.

These were the stories heard along the Traders' Route, until they turned south onto a lesser road that led unto the heart of the Dwarfhorn.

"Why do you smile?"

It was Blaise of the Borderguard who asked the question one evening, pausing in the process of skinning a rabbit the archer Fianna had shot for the supper-pot. She was some distance away, motionless in the uncultivated field, bow drawn, tracking some unseen movement. Malthus had vanished; communing with Haomane, perhaps. Hobard was gathering firewood, while Peldras knelt in serene concentration, stacking kindling in an intricate structure. Nothing burned hotter and cleaner than an Ellylon-laid campfire, constructed in tiers which collapsed in on themselves with a delicate shower of sparks, laying a bed of immaculate embers. At his side, Dani squatted and watched in fascination, while his fat uncle Thulu went in search of running water.

On alert, Carfax regarded the Borderguardsman in wary silence.

"You smile." Blaise's hands resumed their movement, parting the rabbit's skin from its flesh. His gaze remained fixed on Carfax. In the deepening twilight he looked much akin to General Tanaros, with the same unthinking competence. "Watching the knights pass. I've seen it. Why?"

A thrill of fear shot through him. Had he smiled? Yes, probably. It was the one bitter pleasure left to him, watching Haomane's Allies dance unwitting to a tune of Lord Satoris' piping, marshaling their forces eastward.

"You're afraid," Blaise said softly, plying his knife.

To speak or not to speak? There was no safety in silence, if his face betrayed him. Carfax met the Borderguardsman's gaze. "Afraid, aye." His voice was rusty with disuse. "You want me dead."

"Aye." A brusque nod, brows rising a fraction to hear him speak. "You're a liability, I reckon. You'd do the same if it was your command. But I swore to obey the Counselor's wisdom, and he wants you alive. So why do you smile?"

"Why does Malthus hide from Haomane's Allies?" Carfax asked instead of answering. "Why have we turned south, when the war lies north? What does the boy Dani carry in that flask about his neck?"

"You're stubborn, I'll give you that much." The Borderguardsman set aside the skinned carcass with a speculative look in his eye. "What's your name, Staccian?"

Carfax shook his head.

Blaise wiped his skinning-knife on a tuft of grass. "You know mine."

"Yes." He swallowed.

"Do you serve under his command?" Dark eyes, steady and calm. "You know of whom I speak. He who caused my family name to live in infamy."

Carfax looked away. "General Tanaros Blacksword."

"The Kingslayer." Blaise's voice was flat. "You do, don't you?" He waited, but Carfax kept his silence. "He strangled his wife, Staccian. He put his hands around her neck and he throttled her dead. He walked up to his sovereign lord, a man who was nearly a brother to him, and plunged his sword into his guts. And then he rode to Darkhaven and pledged his life to the Sunderer in exchange for immortality. Are you proud to serve under his command?"

"Who should I serve, then?" He dared a glance. "You?"

"You could do worse."

Carfax laughed in despair.

"What manner of man do you wish to be?" The Border-guardsman watched him keenly. "You have a choice, Staccian. I've heard it said your folk made allegiance with Satoris Banewreaker to preserve peace and prosperity in your country. No one in Urulat would condemn you for deciding the cost was too high."

Peace and prosperity, Carfax thought. Yes. Those were not small things to a people who dwelled in a stony land, to a people whose nation bordered on the territory of the Fjel, who made for ungentle neighbors were there enmity between them. Whatever was said of him, Lord Satoris kept his bargains. And whatever General Tanaros had done a thousand years ago, he treated his Men with honor. Carfax had sworn an oath of loyalty, and they had given him no cause to break it.

Without honor, a Man might as well be dead. Indeed, it was better to die with honor than to live without it. But he hadn't expected it to come so soon.

Across the field, the Arduan archer Fianna stood like a statue in the lowering twilight, longbow drawn in a strained arch, holding the taut string close to her ear. Her figure had an unearthly beauty in the gloaming. Carfax stared at her, thinking of girls he had known, of one he had hoped to wed, long ago. Of how she had laughed and wrinkled her freckled nose when he brushed it with the tip of a goldenrod in full bloom, dusting her skin with pollen. What would he have done, had he known he had so little time? The Archer released her string and her bow hummed. Somewhere unseen, a rabbit squealed, the sound cut short.

Blaise repeated the question, still watching him. "Why do you smile, Staccian?"

"To make a friend of death," Carfax answered.

FIFTEEN

"THEY'RE COMING."

Lilias frowned at her Ward Commander. "How soon?"

"Thirty days." He paused. "Less, if the winds blow fair from Port Eurus."

The weight of the Soumanië made her head ache. Strange, how something so light could weigh so heavy! And yet, how not, when she had had been shifting a mountain with it. Lilias grimaced, pressing her fingertips to her temples. The Beshtanagi sunlight seemed cursedly bright. "And the Pelmarans?"

"Assembling at Kranac, to await the Allies' arrival." Gergon cleared his throat. "Regent Heurich has agreed to send a force."

"How long can we hold them?"

"It depends upon their numbers, among other things." He nodded at the southernmost passage, where workers piled boulders on either side of the opening. "How fast can you seal that breach, my lady?"

Lilias considered the gap in the high granite wall that enfolded the base of Beshtanag Mountain. Beyond lay the forest, spreading its dense apron of dark green. It was through those trees that her enemies would come, in greater numbers than she had reckoned. "Can we not seal it now and be done with it?"

"No." Gergon looked regretful. "We've too many men to feed and water, and too few resources on the mountain. Our stores would not last. After ten days' time, we would begin to starve. If the . . . " He cleared his throat again. " . . . if the Were give ample warning, you will have a day's notice."

"They will," Lilias said, pacing a length of the Soumanië-erected wall, her fingertips trailing along its smooth surface. "And I will. What the Were do not tell me, Calandor will. We are prepared, Ward Commander. If the raw materials are there, the breaches will be sealed, the gaps closed. In the space of a day, no less. So how long, Gergon, will this wall hold off Haomane's Allies?"

He squinted at the fortress, perched atop the mountain. "Three days."

"Three *days?*" She stared at him.

"My lady." Gergon shrugged, spreading his hands. "You have always demanded truth. So my father said, and his father's father before him. We are speaking of the concerted might of over half of Pelmar, augmented by Vedasian knights, the Host of the Ellylon and Midlander troops under the command of the last scion of Altorus. If we cannot hold the forest—and we cannot, without the Were—they will come against the wall. And they will ransack the forest and build ladders and siege engines, and they *will* breach the wall."

"No." Lilias set her jaw, ignoring the ache in her head. "They will *not* breach it, Ward Commander. I have Shaped this wall myself from the raw stone of Beshtanag, and it will hold against their siege engines. I shall will it so."

Gergon sighed. "Then they'll come over the top, my lady. They've no shortage of men, nor of wood for ladders and towers, unless you can close the very forest itself to them."

"No." She shook her head, gazing at the dark carpet of pines. "Not for so many. It is harder to shift forest than stone, and we must leave an avenue open for Lord Satoris' troops. Order more stone brought, and I will raise the wall higher. A foot or more."

"As you wish." He bowed, his eyes wary. "It will delay them, by a few hours. Our enemies will still have ample resources if it comes to it."

"All right. Three days," she repeated, gesturing at the grey expanse of loose scree at the mountain's base. "Let us say it is so, Gergon. And then, if it came to it, we would engage them here?"

"Will it come to it, my lady?"

She met his honest gaze. "No. But we must plan as if it would. So what happens, if we engage them here?"

"It's poor footing." Gergon sucked his teeth, considering. "Knights a-horse would be at a disadvantage, here. They'll come in with infantry. I'd place archers there," he said, pointing to overhangs, "there and there, to cover our retreat."

"Retreat?" Lilias raised her brows.

"Aye." Her Ward Commander nodded his grizzled head. "Once the wall is surmounted, my lady, we've nothing to fall back upon but Beshtanag itself."

"They *will* come, Gergon." Lilias held his gaze. "It won't come to it."

"As you say, my lady." He glanced at the Soumanië on her brow, and some of the tension left his stocky frame. He nodded again, smiling. "As you say! I'll have the lads in the quarry work overtime. You'll have as much stone as you need, and more."

"I *will* hold the wall, Gergon."

"You will." He nodded at her brow, smiled. "Yes, you will, my lady."

Lilias sighed as he left on his errand, her skin itching beneath her clothes in the heat. Where was Pietre with the cool sponge to soothe her temples? He should have been here by now. There he was, hurrying down the pathway from the fortress and lugging a bucket of well-water, Sarika behind him struggling with a half-opened parasol. The collars of their servitude glinted in the Beshtanagi sunlight, evoking an echoing throb from the Soumanië. Her mouth curved in a tender smile. So sweet, her pretty ones!

She wondered if they understood what was at stake.

She wondered if she did.

Calandor?

Yes, Lilias?

Satoris will *keep his word, won't he?*

There was a silence, then, a longer pause than she cared to endure.

Yes, Lilias, the dragon said, and there was sorrow in it. *He will.*

Why sorrow? She did not know, and her blood ran cold at it. Teams of grunting men moved boulders into place. Granite, the grey granite of Beshtanag, mica flecked and solid. The raw bones of the mountain; her home for so many long years, the bulwark that sheltered her people. Now that events had been set irrevocably in motion, the thought of risking Beshtanag made her want to weep for the folly of it.

Beshtanag was her haven, and she was responsible for preserving it, and for the safety of her people. All she could do was pledge everything to its defense. Lilias closed her eyes, entered the raw stone and *Shaped* it, feeling granite flow like water. Upward, upward it flowed, melding with its kinstone. A handspan of wall—two handspans, five—rose another foot, settled into smoothness.

Doubling over, Lilias panted. Despite the patting sponge, the Soumanië was like a boulder on her brow, and there was so much, so much to be done!

And where were Lord Satoris' messengers?

* * *

THE TRACKER WAS RIGHT, TURIN discovered when he relented. The mud *did* help. It itched as it dried, though, forming a crackling veneer on his face and arms. Best to keep it wet, easily enough done as they slogged through water ankle-deep at the best of times, and waist-deep more often than not. Easiest to strip to the skin to do it, and more comfortable in the Delta's heat. Turin kept his short-breeches for modesty's sake. Little else, save the pack on his back and his waterlogged boots. At night, whether they perched in mangrove branches or found a dry hummock of land, he had to peel the soft, slick leather from his calves and feet, fearful of what rot festered inside.

It stank, of mud and sweat and rotting vegetation.

And the worst of it . . . the worst of it was the *desire*.

It made no sense, no sense at all. Why here, amid the muck and squalor? And yet, there it was. Desire, fecund and insistent. It beat in his pulse like a drum, it swelled and hardened his flesh, it made the hair at the back of his neck tingle.

"This is *his* birthing-place." Hunric turned back to him and grinned, his teeth very white in the mud-smeared mask of his face. He spread his arms wide. "Do you feel it, Turin? His Gift lingers, here!"

"You've swamp-fever, man." Turin shoved his hair back from his brow, streaking it with muck. "Lord Satoris' Gift was lost when Oronin Last-Born plunged Godslayer into his thigh."

"Was it?" The tracker turned slowly, arms outspread. "This was the place, Turin. It all began here! Look." His voice dropped to a whisper and he reached for his crude spear with the tip hardened by fire. "A slow-lizard."

Turin watched, fighting despair and desire as Hunric the tracker stalked and killed one of the meaty, slow-moving denizens of the Delta. They were good eating, the slow-lizards. Mantuas, whooping and shouting in the chase, had been the first to suggest it, roasting the white meat over a fire that had taken ages to kindle. It was all different, now.

"What?" Hunric, gnawing at his prey, stared at him.

"Beshtanag," Turin whispered. "Hunric, we have to get to Beshtanag!"

"Do we?" For a moment, the tracker looked confused. "Oh, right!" The febrile light in his eyes cleared and he lowered the slow-lizard's carcass, blinking. "Beshtanag. It lies east, northward and east. We're on the route, Turin."

"Good." Turin nodded. "We have a message to deliver. Remember, Hunric?"

"A message, right." Hunric grinned, showing blood-stained teeth. "We won, didn't we? Got the princess, the Lady of the Ellylon. Did you see her, Turin? You're a poor substitute! Limbs like alabaster, throat like a swan. I could swallow her whole!"

"Don't say that." Turin shook himself. "The other message, Hunric! About Malthus' Company?"

"Malthus." It settled the tracker, and he pointed. "We need to go that way."

"Good." Turin sloshed alongside him. "Hunric," he said, grasping the tracker's forearm. "It's important. We need to deliver this news to the Sorceress of the East. You do remember, don't you?"

"Of course." The tracker blinked. "It's that way."

He hoped so. He fervently hoped so. Because it was obvious, now, that no one had entered the Delta after them. No doubt lingered. They'd been here too long for it.

They'd been here altogether too long.

Turin was no tracker, to hold a place in his mind and chart a path through it unerring, but he'd seen a map of the Delta in Lord Satoris' Warchamber. It wasn't that large. Even on foot, even at this pace, they should have reached the far edge. Following Hunric, he counted on his fingers.

How many days had it been? At least eight since Mantuas
had died.

That was too many.

Had they been walking in circles? It was hard to tell,
here. One had to follow the waterways, winding around
mangroves. It was impossible to keep in a fixed location
relative to the sun's course, and there were no landmarks by
which to chart one's progress, only endless swamp. Hunric
was the best, of course. But Hunric . . . Hunric was
changed, and Turin was afraid. Reaching behind him, he
groped at his pack, feeling for the pouch containing Lord
Vorax's gold coins. Still there, solid and real. It was enough
to buy them lodging in Pelmar, enough to purchase a pair of
swift horses, enough to bribe their way to Beshtanag if need
be.

All they had to do was make their way out of this cursed
swamp.

A bright-green snake looped along a branch lifted its
head to stare at him with lidless eyes. Turin fought down a
rush of fear, splashing doggedly past it. By all the Shapers,
it stank here! Ahead of him, Hunric hummed, deep and
tuneless. The sound worked on his nerves. There was a
leech clinging to his thigh and his sodden short-breeches
chafed. Why this desire? If he'd had a woman, any woman,
he would have coupled in the muck with her. Even the
thought of it filled his mouth with a salty rush of taste. Any
woman. One of Vorax's handmaids or the withered flesh of
the Dreamspinner's oldest madling, it didn't matter.

Or his own sister, Turin thought, remembering how he
had seen her last, yellow braids pinned in a coronet, bidding
him farewell. Or—oh, Haomane help him!—the Lady of
the Ellylon. Ah, Shapers! Slung over the General's pommel, her pale hair trailing. Sprawled on the greensward,
helpless and unaware, her white limbs stirring as the General removed her cloak. He had worn that cloak himself,
still warm and scented by her body.

Unable to suppress himself, Turin groaned aloud.

"You feel it." Hunric glanced over his shoulder, eyes shining. "We're near the heart of it, Turin. The heart of the Delta! I told you Lord Satoris' Gift lived in this place."

"No." He swallowed with an effort. His tongue felt thick. "This isn't right. It's *tainted*. It shouldn't be like this."

The tracker shrugged. "Oh, there's death in it, all right. What do you expect? Godslayer struck him to the quick. Nothing could be the same. But it's still *here*."

"Hunric." Turin, itching and aching and scared, tightened his throat at the sudden sting of tears. "I don't care, do you understand? If there were power in this place that Lord Satoris could use, he would be here, not in Darkhaven. I'm tired, sodden and miserable. All I want to do is find a dry place to make camp, and press on to Pelmar."

All around them, the lowering sun washed the Delta with ruddy gold, glimmering on the standing water. Hunric watched it with awe, fingering his handmade spear. Where was his sword? "Beautiful, isn't it?" he asked softly.

"Hunric!" It was all he could do not to cry.

"All right." The tracker smiled at him. "But you're wrong, you know. There *is* power here. Rebirth, generation. It's all here, Turin. Here, at the beginning. Lord Satoris thinks too much on his brother Haomane, and not enough on his own origin. The Souma is not the only power on Uru-lat, you know."

Shadows lengthened, cast eastward across the swamp. Turin let out his breath in a final plea. "Hunric . . ."

"There." The tracker turned, pointing north. Through the dense mangroves, something was visible in the distance; a vast hummock rising above the stagnant waters under the spreading shelter of a tall palodus tree. "Do you see it? Dry land, Turin, here at the heart of the Delta. We'll camp there tonight, and make for the border in the morning. Does that please you?"

Dry land, a chance to build a fire, eat roasted slow-lizard, nibble the last crumbs of bannock-cake, to remove his rotting footwear and pluck the leeches from his legs. Turin

gauged the distance as no more than an hour's slog and
sighed.

"Yes."

"MY LADY?" TANAROS PAUSED, HIS fist poised to knock
again, when the door was flung open. Meara.

The madling tossed her tangled hair and sized him up
and down. "What brings *you* here, Lord General?"

"Meara," he said politely. "I'm glad to see you well. I've
come to invite the Lady Cerelinde to view the moon-
garden."

Her mouth stretched into a grimace. "Oh, you *have*, have
you?"

"Meara?" A voice from another room, silvery and clear.
"What is it? Does Lord Satoris summon me again?"

Tanaros shifted uncomfortably, tugging at his collar as
Cerelinde entered the foyer. "My lady. Arahila's moon
shines full this evening. I thought it might please you to
view the garden of Darkhaven."

"At night?" Her fine brows rose a fraction.

"It is a moon-garden, my lady." A slight flush warmed his
face.

"Ah." She regarded him, grave and beautiful, clad in a
robe of pale blue. "So you would permit me a glimpse of
sky."

"I would."

"Thank you." Cerelinde inclined her head. "I would like
that."

Meara hissed through her teeth, stamping into the quarters beyond and returning with a pearl-white shawl, woven
fine as gossamer. "Here," she muttered, thrusting it at Cerelinde. "You'll take a chill, Lady."

"Thank you, Meara." The Lady of the Ellylon smiled at
the madling.

"Don't." She bit her lip, drawing a bead of blood, then
whirled on Tanaros. "I told you it was a mistake to bring

her, with all her beauty and kindness! Did you not think it
would make it that much harder for the rest of us to endure
ourselves?"

He blinked in perplexity, watching her storm away, doors
slamming in her wake. "I thought she had taken kindly to
you, my lady."

"You don't understand, do you?" Cerelinde glanced at
him with pity.

"No." Tanaros shook his head, extending his arm. "I
don't."

He led her through the gleaming halls of Darkhaven,
acutely aware of her white fingers resting on his forearm, of
the hem of her silk robe sweeping along the black marble
floors. There were shadows beneath her luminous eyes, but
captivity had only refined her beauty, leavening it with sorrow. Haomane's Child. The Havenguard on duty saluted as
they passed, faces impassive, keeping their thoughts to
themselves.

"Here, my lady." A narrow hallway, ending in a wooden
door polished smooth as silk, with hinges and locks of tarnished silver. Tanaros unlocked the door and pushed it ajar,
admitting a waft of subtle fragrances. He stepped back,
bowing. "The garden."

Cerelinde passed him.

"Oh, *Haomane!*"

The mingled joy and grief in her tone made a knot in his
belly. Tanaros entered the garden, closing the door carefully behind him. Only then did he dare look at her. The
Lady of the Ellylon stood very still, and there were no
words in the common tongue to describe her expression.
The air was warm and balmy, rich with the scent of strange
blossoms. Overhead, Arahila's moon hung full and bright
off the left side of the Tower of Ravens, drenching the garden in silvery light.

It was very beautiful.

She hadn't expected that, Tanaros thought.

Tainted water, feeding tainted earth, saturated with the

seeping ichor of Lord Satoris' wound. Such was the garden of Darkhaven, and such flowers as grew here grew nowhere else on Urulat. By daylight, they shrank. Only at night did they bloom, stretching tendrils and leaves toward the kindly light of Arahila's moon and stars, extending pale blossoms.

Cerelinde wandered, the hem of her robe leaving a dark trail where it disturbed the dewy grass. "What is this called?" She paused beneath the graceful, drooping branches of a flowering tree, its delicate blossoms, pale-pink as a bloodshot eye, weeping clear drops upon the ground.

"A mourning-tree." Tanaros watched her. "It grieves for the slain."

"And these?" She examined a vine twining round the trunk, bearing waxy, trumpet-shaped flowers that emitted a pallid glow.

"Corpse-flowers, my lady." He saw her lift her head, startled. "At the dark of the moon, they utter the cries of the dead, or so it is said."

Cerelinde shuddered, stepping back from the vines. "This is a dire beauty, General Tanaros."

"Yes," Tanaros said simply, taking her arm. Stars winked overhead like a thousand eyes as he led her to another bed, where blossoms opened like eyes underfoot, five-pointed petals streaked with pale violet. "Have you seen these?" A faint, sweet fragrance hung in the air, tantalizing. His eyes, unbidden, filled with tears.

. . . her face, his wife Calista, her eyes huge and fearful as she lay upon the birthing-bed, watching him hold the infant in his arms . . .

"No!" Cerelinde struggled out of his grip, eyeing him and breathing hard. "What manner of flower is this, Tanaros?"

"Vulnus-blossom." His smile was taut. "What did you see?"

"You," she said softly. "I saw you, in Lindanen Dale, your sword stained with my kinsmen's blood."

Tanaros nodded, once. "Their scent evokes memory. Painful memory."

Cerelinde closed her eyes. "What do you see, Tanaros?"

"I see my wife." The words came harsher than he intended. He watched her eyelids, raising like shutters, the sweep of lashes lifting to reveal the luminous grey.

"Poor Tanaros," she murmured.

"Come." He dragged at her arm, hauled her to another flowerbed, where bell-shaped blossoms bent on slender stalks, shivering in the moonlight with a pale, fretful sound. "Do you know what these are?"

She shook her head.

"Clamitus atroxis," Tanaros said shortly. "Sorrow-bells. They sound for every senseless act of cruelty that takes place in the Sundered World. Do you wonder that they are seldom silent?"

"No." Tears clung to her lashes. "Why, Tanaros?"

"Look." He fell to his knees, parting the dense, green leaves of the clamitus. Another flower blossomed there, low to the ground, pure white and starry, shimmering in its bed of shadows. "Touch it."

She did, kneeling beside him, stroking the petals with one fingertip.

The flower shuddered, its petals folding into limpness.

"What have I done?" Cerelinde's expression was perturbed.

"Nothing." Tanaros shook his head. "It is the mortexigus, Lady; the little-death flower. That is its nature, to mimic death at a touch. Thus does it loose its pollen."

Cerelinde knelt, head bowed, watching the plant stir. "Why do you show this to me, Tanaros?" she asked quietly.

A soft breeze blew in the garden, redolent with the odor of memory, making the clamitus sound their fitful chimes. Tanaros stood, his knees popping. He walked some distance from her. "Lord Satoris has summoned you to speak with him."

"Yes." She did not move.

"What does he say?"

"Many things." Cerelinde watched him. "He says that the Prophecy is a lie."

"Do you believe him?" Tanaros turned back to her.

"No." A simple truth, simply spoken.

"You should." A harsh note entered his voice. "He speaks the truth, you know."

Her face was calm. "Then why do you fear it, Tanaros? Why am I here, if the Prophecy is a lie? Why not let me wed Aracus Altorus in peace?"

"Is that what you would bring us here in Darkhaven?" he asked her. "Peace?"

At that, she looked away. "The Lord-of-Thought knows the will of Uru-Alat."

"No!" Tanaros clenched his fist against his thigh, forced himself to breathe evenly. "No, he doesn't. Haomane knows the power of thought, that's all. The leap of water in the stream, of blood in the vein, of seed in the loins . . . these things are Uru-Alat too, and these things Haomane First-Born knows not. That is the core of truth he has Shaped into the lie of the Prophecy."

Cerelinde composed herself. "The other Shapers disagree, General."

"Do they?" Tanaros caught a bitter laugh in his throat and pointed to the moon. "See there, my lady. Arahila's moon sheds its blessing on Lord Satoris' garden."

Her gaze was filled with compassion. "What would you have me say? Arahila the Fair is a Shaper, Tanaros. Not even the Sunderer is beyond redemption in her eyes."

"No." He shook his head. "Oh, Cerelinde! Don't you understand? Any of the Shapers, any of the Six, could leave Torath and cross the Sundered divide. They will not." He raised his chin, gazing at the stars. "They will not," he said, "because they fear. They fear Haomane's wrath, and they fear their own mortality. Even Shapers can die, Cerelinde. And they fear to tread the same earth where Godslayer abides."

"Is that the lesson of the garden?" Her grey eyes were cool, disbelieving.

"No." Tanaros pointed to the mortexigus flower. "That is, Lady, any Son of Man would do to serve your need. In our very mortality, we hold the keys to life. We hold the Gift Lord Satoris can no longer bestow, the key to the survival of the Rivenlost. Your people and mine conjoined. That is the truth of the Prophecy, the deeper truth."

She frowned and it was as though a cloud passed over the moon's bright face. "I do not understand."

"Do the numbers of the Ellylon not dwindle while those of Men increase?" he asked her. "So it has been since the world was Shaped. Without Lord Satoris' Gift, in time the Ellylon will vanish from the face of Urulat."

"Now it is you who lies," Cerelinde said softly. "For the Lord-of-Thought would not allow his Children to be subsumed, not even by fair Arahila's."

Tanaros held her gaze. "Why, then, does Haomane's Prophecy bid you to wed one?"

Her winged brows rose. "To unite our people in peace, Tanaros. Aracus Altorus is no ordinary Man."

"Aye, Cerelinde, he is. As I am." Tanaros sighed, and the sorrow-bells murmured in mournful reply. "The difference is that the House of Altorus has never faltered in its loyalty to Haomane First-Born."

She stood and touched his face with light fingertips, a touch that burned like cool fire. "A vast difference, Tanaros. And yet it is not too late for you."

He shuddered, removing her hand. "Believe as you will, Lady, but the sons of Altorus Farseer were chosen to fulfill Haomane's Prophecy that in their loyalty they might bring down Lord Satoris. The truth is otherwise. It need not be a daughter of Elterrion, nor a son of Altorus. You and I would serve. Our seed holds the key to your perpetuation."

"You!" She recoiled, a little.

"Our people. Any two of us. We hold within ourselves the Gifts of all the Seven Shapers and the ability to Shape a world of our choosing." He spread his hands. "That's all, Cerelinde, no more."

"No." She was silent a moment. "No, it is another of the Sunderer's lies, Tanaros. If it were so simple, why would Haomane not so bid us?"

"Because he requires the Prophecy to destroy Lord Satoris," he said. "We are all pawns in the Shapers' War, Cerelinde. The difference is that some of us know it, and some do not." Something in his heart ached at the naked disbelief on her face. "Forgive me, Lady. I had no intent of troubling you. I thought you would like the garden."

"I do. And I am grateful for a glimpse of sky." She drew Meara's shawl tighter around her shoulders. "Tanaros. I am sorry for your pain, and I do not doubt that you have taken the Sunderer's lies for truths. But Haomane First-Born is chief among Shapers, and I am his child. Your Lord need only bow to His will, and the Sundered World will be made whole. Can you ask me to believe aught else?"

"Yes," Tanaros said helplessly.

Her voice was gentle. "I cannot."

SIXTEEN

❖

DWARFS CAME OUT OF THE gloaming.

It happened a few leagues west of Malumdoorn, the young knight Hobard's ancestral estate. As twilight fell over their kindling campfire, the shadows moved, twining like roots. Four figures, waist-high to a tall man, with gnarled faces and knotted muscles, spatulate hands engrained with soil.

"Yrinna's Children." Malthus the Counselor stood to

greet them, bowing in his scholar's robes. "Hail and well met."

"Haomane's Counselor." One of the dwarfs acknowledged him in a deep, calm voice, then turned to Hobard. "Son of Malumdoorn. You have broken Yrinna's Peace, bringing them here."

"I had cause, Earth-Tender."

The Vedasian's voice was strung tight, Carfax noted. He sat quiet with his arms wrapped around his knees, watching with wonder. Dwarfs! Yrinna's Children had not been seen west of Vedasia for long ages.

"It must be a mighty cause to break Yrinna's Peace."

"It is." Malthus took a step forward, touching the Soumanië on his breast. "You have an item in your possession that does not belong to you."

There was a pause then, a long one.

"It may be," the Dwarf leader allowed, his deep-set gaze scanning the small company. "Haomane's Child. Do the Rivenlost venture in search of this thing?"

"We do, Earth-Tender." Peldras the Ellyl bowed, light and graceful. "Will you not hear our plea?"

A hushed conference, then, among the four visitors. Carfax strained his hearing to no avail. "*Uru-Alat!*" A soft whisper sounded at his ear. "They're so *small!* Are they Men, or children?" It was the boy, Dani, squatting fearless at his side, his dark eyes wide in the firelight. They tell him no more than they do me, Carfax thought, pitying the boy. What was Malthus thinking, to venture into the Unknown and drag the boy from his home, keeping him in ignorance? At least in Darkhaven, one knew the price of one's bargain.

"No," he said. "They are Dwarfs, Dani. A long time ago, they withdrew from the affairs of Men."

One dark hand rose to clasp the flask at his throat, dark eyes bewildered. "What is it Malthus thinks they have?"

"I don't know." He wished he did.

A decision was made, and the Dwarf leader stepped forward. "There will be a hearing on the morrow," he said. "In the orchards of Malumdoorn. Come in peace, or not at all."

"It will be so," Malthus said with dignity.

NIGHT.

It fell hard and fast in the swamps of the Delta. Turin hurried after the fleeting form of Hunric the tracker, falling and splashing and cursing his speed. Before them, the hummock of dry land loomed, elusive and retreating in the fading light. A last, dying spear of light lit the palodus tree that stood sentry over it.

"Come on!" Hunric shouted, scrambling up the hummock ahead of him, the slow-lizard's carcass tied to a string about his waist. "Come *on!*"

Waist-deep in water at the foot of the hummock, Turin set his teeth and grabbed for a handhold. Shale rock, plates as broad as both his hands, slick and overgrown with moss. There would be nothing edible growing on this island. By main force he hauled himself, hand over hand, up the steep incline, his breath searing his lungs.

At the top, he bent double, panting.

"Look!" Hunric was grinning, arms open wide. "The heart of the Delta. Is it not a glorious thing?"

Turin could have wept.

There was nothing, nothing atop the hummock, only moss-covered black shale in articulated ridges that hurt his sodden feet, and a few fallen branches of palodus wood. He was tired and soaked and footsore, and his loins ached with gnawing desire.

"A freshwater spring would have been nice," he said wearily, sitting down and removing his pack, beginning the tiresome process of peeling off his boots. "You're sure this is the way *out?*"

"The way in is the way out." The tracker eyed him, then began gathering branches. "You're done in. Sit, then. I'll do it."

He sat, rubbing his aching feet. No need for a fire, really.

The shale was warm, retaining the sun's heat like a forge. He could almost smell the sulfur. It would be nice, though, to have fresh-roasted meat, even if the kill was a day old. Meat went off fast in the heat; no wonder Hunric was minded to eat it raw.

So warm, here. So warm.

It made his aching flesh prickle.

"This is his place." At the crest of the hummock, Hunric had stacked branches into a neat structure and knelt reverently over them. "*His* place!" he repeated fervently, striking a spark and blowing. An ember kindled, tiny flames flickering.

"His place," Turin echoed dully. In the dark swamp beyond, an ember of yellow-green kindled. "And tomorrow, we head straight for Pelmar, yes?"

"Pelmar." Hunric, kneeling, grinned at him. "Oh, yes."

Something in the air throbbed, echoing the throbbing in his loins. He thought again of the white limbs of the Lady of the Ellylon, gritted his teeth and thrust the thought from his mind. In the air? No. It was the very rock beneath him that throbbed, slow and steady, warm as a pulsing heart.

An ember of yellow-green, lifting.

"Hunric." His voice was frozen in his throat. "Hunric!" A shape, moving, impossibly large. Roots ripped, dripping, from the swamp itself. Slow, so slow! An ember of yellow-green. A lidded eye, a dripping chin. "Hunric . . ." he whispered.

"What?" The tracker sounded almost friendly as he gauged the coals, skewering the slow-lizard and thrusting it into the flames. "Pelmar, yes. I remember. We'll leave on the morrow. Is that what troubles you?"

Unable to speak, Turin pointed.

"*What?*" The tracker squinted into the swamp.

When it struck, it moved fast. A wedge of darkness blotting out the emerging stars, swinging on a sinuous neck. Its hinged jaws opened wide, rows of teeth glistening like ivory daggers. The ground beneath Turin *lurched,* surging with the motion of the strike as, somewhere in the swamp, anchored talons gripped and heaved. He saw the lidded eye as it swung past him, the open maw snapping.

A strangled sound cut short, and the embers of the campfire scattered.

Hunric.

Turin gibbered with fear, scuttling backward crab-wise. Plates of shale beneath his hands and feet, the edges cutting his flesh. Not shale, no; *scales,* ancient and encrusted, dark as iron. Before him, the long neck stretched high, lifting the massive head to the top of the palodus tree while the throat worked in gulps.

It didn't take long. Not long enough.

"Please," Turin whispered as the terrible head swung back his way, arching over its own back, bearded and dripping with moss. "Oh, *please!*"

A nictitating lid blinked over the yellow-green eye. "Who asssskss?"

"Turin of Staccia." His voice emerged in a squeak. "I am here in the service of Lord Satoris."

"Sssatorisss . . ."

"Third-Born among Shapers." Summoning a reserve of courage he hadn't known he possessed, Turin found his feet, confronting the hovering head, fighting his chattering teeth. "This is his place, Lord Dragon, and he sent me here!"

"Yessss." The yellow-green eye blinked. "Your companion was . . . tasssssty."

"Lord Dragon!" Terror threatened to loosen his bowels. "My Lord was a friend to your kind!"

"A friend," the dragon mused. "Yesss, onssse."

"Once, and always." Breathing hard, Turin wrestled his sword free of his pack and held it aloft. Its steel length glinted greenish in the light of the dragon's eye. "I carry a message for the Sorceress of the East and the Dragon of Beshtanag. Will you not let me pass?"

"I grieve for my brother." There was something resembling sorrow in the dragon's fearful mien. "He has chosen his path. There is power in thissss plassse, Sson of Man. It might even have healed Sssatoriss the Ssssower, onssse, but Haomane's Wrath ssscorched his thoughtss to madnesss, and he fled north to the cooling sssnows. It is too late for the Sssower. Now this is *my* plassse, and I mussst abide."

"Who are you?" Turin whispered.

"Calanthrag," the answer was hissed. "The Eldessst."

Swift came the attack, the massive head darting. Turin dodged once, striking with his sword, aiming for the glinting eye. He missed, his blade clattering against impervious scales. This, he thought in an ecstasy of terror, is the end. The dragon's head reared back and swayed atop its sinuous neck, blocking out the sky. Turin's hand loosened on his sword-hilt. He stood on a dragon back, feeling the warmth under his bare, lacerated soles, and thought of the vows he had taken, the women he had known. A smell of rot hung in the air. The dragon's eye roiled, yellow-green. Old, so old!

Older than the Delta.

There were things he knew before the end, Turin of Staccia, things he read in the dragon's roiling eye. Of a knowledge older than Time itself, older than the Chain of Being. Of the birth of dragons, born of the bones of Uru-Alat; firstborn, Eldest. Of warring Shapers, and how they had Sundered the earth. Of their Children and their wars, their endless hierarchies and vengeances. Of Lord Satoris, who spoke to dragons; of dragons, who aided him. Of dragons dying by steel borne by Haomane's Children, by Arahila's. Of Calanthrag the Eldest, hidden in the Delta.

All these things, and the whole more than the sum of its parts. This was the knowledge vouchsafed to Turin of Staccia, whose yellow hair was caked with mud, who stood barefooted on a dragon's back, with a useless sword in his limp hand, bannock-crumbs and gold coins at the bottom of his pack.

He was a long way from home.

Oh mother! he thought at the last.

It was fast, the dragon's head striking like a snake, low and sure and swift. Massive jaws stretched wide, breathing sulfur fumes. A snap! A gulp and a swallow, the impossibly long gullet working, neck stretched skyward. In the swamp of the Delta, the tall palodus tree stood unmoving, while small creatures keened in distress.

Inch by inch, Calanthrag the Eldest settled.

An insect chirruped.

Stillness settled over the Delta, ordinary stillness. Lizards crept, and snakes stirred their coils. Gnats whined, protesting the fall of darkness. A dragon's talons relaxed their purchase in the mire. Straining wings eased their vanes. A long neck settled, chin sinking into muck. Membranes closed over glowing eyes to the lullaby of the Delta. In the moonlight, a hummock, black as slate, encrusted with moss, loomed above the swamp.

Calanthrag the Eldest slept.

GREEN. GREEN AND GREEN AND green.

It whirled in the Ravensmirror, reflected in the sheen of glimmering feathers. Green leaves, palodus and mangrove, a dense canopy. Dark green, pine green, the forests of Pelmar. Softer green, new vines and cedars, wings veering in fear from Vedasia, where death lurked, arrow-tipped.

"ENOUGH!"

Ushahin Dreamspinner pressed his fingertips to his crooked temples, his head aching at Lord Satoris' roar.

The Ravensmirror shattered, bursting into feathered bits, heads tucked under wings in fearful disarray.

Back and forth he stormed, red eyes glowing like coals. The tower trembled beneath his tread. A smell in the air like blood, only sweeter. "What," Lord Satoris asked with deceptive gentleness, "is Malthus *doing?*"

"I don't know, my Lord," Ushahin whispered.

"My Lord." Tanaros executed a crisp bow. "Whatever the Counselor attempts, it matters naught. Our plans proceed apace, and your army stands in readiness. Our course through the Marasoumië is plotted, and Lord Vorax has seen to our lines of supply. Haomane's Allies walk into a trap unwitting. We are prepared."

The glowing red gaze slewed his way. "I mislike it."

"My Lord." Ushahin cleared his throat. "There is one way."

"What?"

He flinched under the Shaper's regard. "Ask the Ellyl. Put her to questioning. I cannot breach Malthus' defenses, my Lord. I have tried. It may be she knows his plans."

Tanaros shifted, disturbed.

"No." The Shaper shook his head. Deep in their throats, ravens muttered. "I am a Shaper, one of the Seven. Let my Elder Brother name me what he will; I will not play into his hands by accepting the role he has allotted me. He holds his pride dearer than I, yet I am not without honor. Would you see it stripped from me? My Elder Brother has made a move, and I have countered it. I will not become the monster he has named me."

Frustration surfaced in Ushahin's crooked gaze. "It is better to live a monster than to die with honor, my Lord!"

"No." There was finality in Lord Satoris' deep voice. "She is a guest, Dreamspinner, and to be treated as such. I will not allow aught else."

"My Lord . . ."

"I said no."

SEVENTEEN

❖

SUNLIGHT SLANTED THROUGH THE APPLE trees in the orchards of Malumdoorn.

It was an unlikely setting for a meeting of such moment. Carfax only wished he knew what it was about. The Dwarfs had assembled en masse, awaiting them, standing in wary ranks amid the gnarled apple trees.

Hobard, they greeted with respect, giving evidence of a long-standing agreement between their folk and the scions of Malumdoorn. The surly young knight glowed at the attention, in his element.

Yrinna's Peace, Carfax thought. It was the bargain the Dwarfs had made, taking no part in the battles that divided the Lesser Shapers. Eschewing Lord Satoris' Gift, they were parsimonious with carnal pleasure, and bore only enough children to ensure their own continuance. In turn, they asked only the freedom to tend the land, making it fruitful as Yrinna Sixth-Born had willed it.

This was the bargain old Vedasian families such as Hobard's had struck, offering protection and noninterference for the goodwill of Yrinna's Children, who made their orchards fruitful.

What now threatened it?

"Earth-Tenders." Malthus' voice was soft and soothing: he spread his arms, indicating he held naught but his staff. "You know who I am. And you know what I have come for."

The Dwarfs murmured, a low sound like the wind through apple leaves.

"We know." A Dwarf elder stumped forward, thrusting out his stubborn chin. Tangled beard, aggressive eyes, honest dirt ingrained in his hands. "You bring war, Counselor. You breach Yrinna's Peace. Why? Why should we heed you?"

"Because Satoris Banewreaker will hold sway over the whole of Urulat if you do not," Malthus said steadily. "Is that your wish, Earth-Tender Haldol? To see the soil of Yrinna's bosom poisoned with his dripping venom? It shall come to pass, and no seed may grow untainted, no blossom bear fruit."

It was not true. In the long years that Staccia had held an allegiance with Lord Satoris, its lands had come to no harm. His Lordship sought only to live unmolested by Haomane's

Wrath. Carfax opened his mouth in protest, found his tongue hopelessly stilled, useless as a dried root. Bright sparks burned in the Elder Haldol's eyes, doubt nurtured by the Counselor.

"We do not take part in the Shapers' War," the Dwarf said.

"Oh, but you do." Malthus the Counselor's voice was soft, sweet and cunning. "Yrinna's Children deny it, yes. But you have withheld that which is not yours, and so doing, you aid the Enemy. Our greatest Enemy, he who would scorch the earth."

"So you say." The Dwarf Elder rubbed his chin. "So you say. We have a test, Counselor, for those who would claim Yrinna's favor. Is your Company willing to attempt the Greening?"

"It is," Malthus said steadily.

There was a stirring among the Dwarfs, a parting of the ranks. From the rear of the gathering, two approached, bearing an object with reverence. Male and female, they were, gnarled as roots, with eyes that shone at the sanctity of their office. Carfax craned his head to see what they carried.

A staff, like unto Malthus' own, but untrimmed—a dead branch wrenched whole from the tree. Twigs it sprouted, and a few desiccated leaves, shriveled and brown. Haldol the Elder received it with both hands, raised it to touch his lips to the rough bark before planting it like a spear in the orchard soil of Malumdoorn, driving the butt-end into the earth.

It stood like a standard, brittle and ash-grey.

"The challenge of the Greening is begun," said Haldol.

"So mote it be." Malthus bowed his head and grasped the Soumanië.

"*No.*" The Dwarf's voice was sharp. "You are Haomane's weapon, Counselor, and bear his tools. What the Souma may accomplish, we know too well. It is Yrinna's will the Greening seeks to divine. We shall choose among your Company who

shall attempt it." His deepset gaze roamed over the Company.
"You," he said abruptly, pointing a thick finger at Dani. "The
least among them. Let us see if Yrinna favors *you.*"

"Earth-Tender—" Malthus glowered, the Soumanië
flickering.

"It is as it shall be." The Dwarf Haldol crossed his arms,
backed by his people. "Do you gainsay it, Counselor? Son
of Malumdoorn, what say you, who brought them here?"

Hobard of Malumdoorn cast a bitter sidelong glance at
the young Yarru-yami. "Malthus, I came in faith to Meronil
to bring you these tidings, but as I am Vedasian, my sworn
oaths are to Yrinna's Children. I abide by their demands.
You drove us into the Unknown to secure the Charred lad,
risking all our lives to find him. Let him answer for it, if it is
their will."

Ranked behind the dead branch thrust like a challenge
into the earth, the Dwarfs waited. Malthus' Company
shifted, awaiting the Counselor's decision. Carfax watched
them all. Blaise Caveros was tense, small muscles moving
along his clenched jaw. The Ellyl, Peldras, was at once
watchful and tranquil. There was hunger in the eyes of Fianna the Archer, desperate and keen.

Why, Carfax wondered?

As for the Yarru, they whispered together, fat uncle Thulu
bending his head to the boy's ear, lips moving. What was he
saying? Why was the boy smiling? Did he not realize, Carfax thought in frustration, he was naught but a pawn?

"*So be it!*" Malthus' voice cracked like thunder, then
softened. "Dani. Try. You can but try, lad."

That he did, Dani of the Yarru, earnest of face, approaching the dead branch in all seriousness. He reminded
Carfax, unexpectedly, of Turin, the young Staccian in his
command. He'd taken his duties thus seriously, Turin had,
given the difficult task of impersonating an Ellyl maiden. It
had galled him to be left out of their ill-fated attack on the
Company of Malthus. Remembering the barrows of grass
where his comrades had fallen, Carfax was glad he'd

spared the lad. He wondered if the young Staccian and his two companions had made it safely to Beshtanag, and hoped they had. In the silence of his locked tongue Carfax hoped, very much, that Lord Satoris' plans were uncompromised.

Dani squatted before the branch, laying hands upon it.

Pale and weathered and grey, the dead wood; the boy's palms were pale too, lined and weathered. He cupped them together, and the radiating lines met to form a star in the hollow of his palms. He bowed his ragged head as if listening, and his uncle, his fat uncle, chanted low under his breath, grinning. Blaise raised an eyebrow. The Archer bit her lip. In the orchard, with the sweet smell of sun-warmed apples in the air, the Dwarfs gathered close, watching.

Dani uncorked the vial at his neck.

One drop; one drop of water he let gather at the lip of the vial. One drop. And it smelled—*oh, Shapers!* Carfax inhaled deeply, unable to help himself. It smelled . . . like water. Like life, dense and condensed, mineral-rich. It swelled, gathering roundness, shining bright as steel. Swelled, rounded . . .

. . . dropped.

Greenness, dizzying and sudden, as the earth rang like a struck bell. Urgent leaves burst from the dead wood, a riot of green. Twigs sprouted and grew buds, blossoms opened, releasing sweet fragrance. Pierced by plunging roots, the very soil buckled, even as the branch thickened into a sapling's trunk.

"Aiee!" Dani leapt back, wide-eyed, clutching his flask. "I did that?"

"You did." Malthus smiled, laying a hand on the little Yarru-yami's shoulder. There was approval in his grave features, and at his breast, the Soumanië lay quiescent and dark; a red gem, nothing more. "You did, Dani."

Gazing at the tree, the assembled Dwarfs murmured in awe.

"The Water of Life," the Elder Haldol said. "That is what he carries."

"Yes." Malthus inclined his head, one hand still resting

on Dani's shoulder. "The lifeblood of Uru-Alat. He is the Bearer. Has he met your challenge, Earth-Tender?"

In the silence that followed, Haldol of the Dwarfs sighed, and the weight of the world was in that sigh, his broad, sturdy shoulders slumping. "Yrinna's Peace is ended," he whispered, then straightened, a terrible dignity in his features. "So be it. Counselor, that which you sought shall be yours."

"It was not yours to keep, Elder," Malthus said gently.

"No." The Dwarf lifted his chin and met his gaze. "But we kept it well, Wise Counselor. It has never been used, for unlike other of Haomane's weapons, it may be used only once, and the Counselor Dergail held his hand. I pray you use it well."

A bright spark wove its way through the ranks of Dwarfs, who shrank at its passage. One more came, wizened and old, eyes closed against the brightness he bore. Even in daylight, it trailed flame. Fianna the Archer stepped forward, her mouth forming a soundless O, hands reaching unthinking.

"Behold," Haldol said. "Oronin's Bow, and the Arrow of Fire."

"They are yours," Malthus said to the Archer.

Her hand closed on the haft of the bow; black horn, with an immense draw. Kneeling, she set the bottom tip, fingers curling, seeking the string unthinking and drawing it to her cheek. A shaft of white fire tinged with gold, the Arrow flamed, illuminating her cheek, the tendrils of hair curling at her temple. "Oh," she said, her tone amazed. "Oh!"

Carfax, watching, shivered to the bone.

When the unknown is made known, when the lost weapon is found . . .

The Prophecy was being fulfilled.

BESIDE THE SWELTERING FURNACE, THE flow of the Gorgantus River, diverted by Lord Satoris himself, powered a wooden waterwheel. From it led a welter of rods and cranks, turning and clanking. Levered weights rose and fell, pressing down on the spring-boards that powered the bellows, which opened and closed on their leather hinges, blowing strong drafts. Teams of Fjeltroll worked steadily, feeding coal and ore into the endless maw of the furnace.

It was hotter than before, so hot Tanaros could feel the skin of his face tightening. And the metal that emerged was glowing and molten, pure iron, collected in molds to cool. No longer did the Fjel need to beat the impurities from it before it was fit for the forge.

"You see?" Speros, soot-darkened, was grinning. He shouted above the clamor of the smelting furnace. "We use the force of the river to drive the bellows, providing more heat than even the Fjel can muster!"

"I see." Tanaros had to raise his own voice to be heard. "A commendable innovation! Is it done thus in the Midlands now?"

"No." Speros shrugged, his restless gaze surveying his efforts. "Only to grind grain, but I thought it might serve. No one ever gave me the means to try it, before. I reckon it will help. No small task, to equip such an army." He settled his gaze on Tanaros. "We *are* going to war, are we not, Lord General?"

"Yes." Tanaros beckoned, leading him a distance from the furnace. Outside, the grass was parched and a reeking cloud of smoke and sulfurous gases hung heavy under the lowering sky, but at least the air did not sear his lungs. "Some of us are, Midlander."

"I want to ride with you," Speros of Haimhault said, direct and sure. "You promised me a horse; one such as *you* ride, General. Have I not done all I promised, and more?"

Of a surety, the lad had done so. His innovations had increased productivity. With the aid of his waterwheel, the forges of Darkhaven smelted iron at twice their usual rate. This was the first chance Tanaros had had to inspect them, but it was said Lord Satoris himself was pleased.

"Aye." Tanaros ignored his own misgivings, clapping a hand to the young man's shoulder. "You have. You'll have your mount, boy, and your place in the ranks."

Speros smiled with fierce, unadulterated joy.

It was not that his trust had proved ill-placed, for it had not. In a short time, Speros of Haimhault had proven himself in Darkhaven. The Fjel trusted him. Hyrgolf spoke well of him, and Tanaros valued his field marshal's opinion above all others. The young man's energies and ambitions, that had found too narrow an outlet in the Midlands, flourished in Darkhaven. He bore no resentment for the harsh treatment he had received at the outset, reckoning it worth the price. Against his better judgement, Tanaros liked the young man.

That was the problem.

How long had it been since Tanaros had donned the Helm of Shadows and led the forces that destroyed Altoria? Eight hundred years, perhaps. Even so, he had not forgotten how, beneath the blaze of hatred in his heart, there had been a twinge of sorrow. For as much as he had been wounded and betrayed, hated and hounded, they had been his people. And he had destroyed them, bringing down a realm and reducing a dynasty to a shade of its former self.

"You may have kin among the enemy, you know," he told Speros. "It may be a cousin or a brother you face in battle. And this war will not be one such as the poets sing. We fall upon them from behind, and allow no quarter until the threat is eliminated. There is no glory in it."

Regarding his furnace with pride, the Midlander shrugged. "You have outwitted them, General. Is that not glory enough?"

"We do not do this for glory. Only for victory."

"Victory." Speros ran a hand through his brown hair, sooty and disheveled. "A Sundered World in which Lord Satoris reigns victorious. What will happen then?"

"Then," Tanaros said slowly, fingering the *rhios* in his pocket, "it may be that the Six Shapers will capitulate and make peace. Or it may be that they will not. Either way, Urulat will be in Lord Satoris' possession, as will Godslayer and two of the three Soumanië. And it may be that the third, Dergail's Soumanië, is not beyond reach."

Speros' eager, indrawn breath hissed between his teeth, and his eyes glowed at the possibilities. "With those things, he could challenge Haomane himself!"

"Yes," Tanaros said. "He could."

"And if he won?" Speros asked. "Would he slay the Six?"

"No." Tanaros shook his head. "I think not. He loved his sister Arahila well, once; I believe he loves her still. Though she sided with Haomane against him, it was she who stayed the Lord-of-Thought's hand when his Wrath scorched the earth, and she who raised the red star in warning. Lord Satoris cares for his honor. It may be that she would persuade him to mercy."

Speros glanced westward. "What manner of world do you suppose his Lordship would Shape?"

"Only his Lordship knows for certain," Tanaros said. "Yet I imagine a world in which the tyranny of one Shaper's will did not hold sway over all. And that," he added, "is enough for me."

"It's a beginning," Speros agreed. He looked curiously at Tanaros. "What would you do in such a world, Lord General?"

Unaccountably, Tanaros pictured Cerelinde's face. "It don't know," he murmured. "Yet I would like to find out. Perhaps I would become a better Man than I have been in this one." He gathered himself with a shake, ignoring the Midlander's quizzical expression. "Come on, lad. Let's choose a horse for you."

Perplexity gave way to a grin. "Aye, General!"

IN THE CHAMBER OF THE FONT, the marrow-fire burned unceasing, a column of blue-white flame rising from its pit, so bright it hurt the eye. And in the center the shard of Godslayer hung, pulsing like a heart to an unseen rhythm.

"My Lord." Cerelinde of the Ellylon clasped her hands in front of her to hide their trembling. Valiant as she was, the fear came upon her every time the tapestry in her quarters twitched at the opening of the secret door, a wary madling emerging to beckon her through the winding passages behind the walls to the three-fold door and the spiral stair, to answer the summons of the Lord of Darkhaven. "You sent for me?"

"Yes." The Shaper's voice was gentle. He moved in the shadows at the outskirts of the room, his massive figure blending into darkness. Only the red, glowing eyes showed clearly. "Be at your ease, Lady."

Cerelinde sat in the chair he indicated, stiff-backed and fearful.

His deep laugh rumbled. "You have been my guest these weeks now. Do you still think I mean you harm?"

"You hold me against my will." She fixed her gaze on the beating heart of Godslayer within the marrow-fire. "Is that not harm, my Lord?"

"Will," Satoris mused, and the stones of Darkhaven shivered under his mighty, soundless tread. A reek of ichor in the air grew stronger at his approach, sweet and coppery. "What do you know of will, little Ellyl?"

"I know it is mine to defy you." The words came hard, harder than she could have imagined. It was hard, in this place, to cling to all that she knew was true.

Fingers brushed her hair. "What if I offered you a kingdom?"

Closing her eyes, Cerelinde shuddered at the touch of a Shaper's power. With Godslayer to hand, he could remake her very flesh if he willed it. "You would not, my Lord Sunderer," she said. "While I live, I am a threat to you, and I do not believe that you will let me live for long, let alone offer me power. I am not a fool, my Lord. I have made my peace with it. I am not afraid to die."

"No." The Shaper withdrew, his voice contemptuous. "Only to *live*. Will you cling to this Prophecy with which my brother Haomane Shapes the world? I tell you this: You are not the only one, you know, daughter of Erilonde."

"What?" Cerelinde opened her eyes. "*What* do you say?"

"Oh, yes." Lord Satoris smiled, a fearful thing. "Elterrion the Bold had a second daughter, gotten of an illicit union. Somewhere among the Rivenlost, your line continues. Do you suppose such things never happen among the Ellylon?"

"They do not." Cerelinde drew herself up taut.

"They do upon very rare occasion." The Shaper's eyes glittered with red malice. "It is a pity your people dare not acknowledge it, Lady. The weight of the world might not rest upon your shoulders if they did."

"You lie," Cerelinde whispered.

Lord Satoris shrugged, the movement disturbing the shadows. "More seldom than you might imagine, Lady," he said, regret in his tone. "These things lie within the purview of the Gift that was mine, and they are mine alone to know. Although the Ellylon themselves do not know it, I tell you: There is another."

"Who?" Cerelinde leaned forward, forgetting herself. "*Who,* my Lord?"

He eyed her, slow and thoughtful. "I will tell you, in exchange for knowledge freely given. The Three would see you put to questioning. I, I merely ask, Lady. What is the purpose of Malthus the Counselor?"

He would ask that; he *would.* Cerelinde hid her face in her hands, wishing she knew the answer. Whether she gave it or not, at least it would be a bargaining chip. With a bitter sense of irony, she remembered Aracus' words in Lindanen Dale. *It is for a short time only, my lady. Malthus knows what he is about.* She wondered if the Wise Counselor had known what would befall her, and prayed it were not so. It was too cruel to contemplate.

Surely, Aracus had not.

"I don't know," she murmured through her fingers. "I don't."

Satoris waited until she raised her head to look at him. Reading the truth written in her face, he nodded once. "I told them as much. Very well, you may go. We will speak anon, Lady."

"All three?" Cerelinde swallowed. "All of the Three would see me questioned?"

For a long time, he did not answer. The marrow-fire burned soundless, shedding brightness throughout the Chamber of the Font; in its midst, Godslayer hung like a suspended wail, pulsing. Darkness gathered around the Shaper like stormclouds and his eyes sparked a slow, inexorable red.

"No," he said at last. "Not all. Not Tanaros."

It gladdened her heart to hear it in a manner that filled her with uneasiness. How far had she fallen, how deeply had this touched her, that the kindness of Tanaros Kingslayer could make her glad? The Sunderer's lies undermined the foundation of her certainty. Could there be another capable of bringing the Prophecy to fruition, another daughter of the House of Elterrion? Malthus kept his counsel close . . .

No. No. To believe as much was to open a door onto despair. Satoris Banewreaker was the Prince of Lies, and behind the courtly courtesies General Tanaros extended was a man who had throttled his wife and slain his sovereign. There were no other truths that mattered.

In the garden, a mortexigus flower shivered untouched and loosed its pollen.

Oh, Aracus! Cerelinde thought in despair. *I need you!*

EIGHTEEN

❖

THANKS TO MERONIN FIFTH-BORN, Lord of the Seas, the winds blew fair from Port Eurus and Haomane's Allies arrived safe on Pelmaran soil, where they were met by a deposition from Regent Martinek. Borderguard, Seaholders,

Midlanders and Vedasians, not to mention the Host of the Ellylon—it was a difficult thing, establishing preeminence among them.

Out of necessity, all bowed to the Pelmaran regent.

"We need him," shrewd Duke Bornin murmured to Aracus Altorus. "We need all of them, else we will not prevail against the Sorceress."

So it was that Aracus, the last scion of House Altorus and king-in-exile of the West, bent his red-gold head in courteous acknowledgment, and all who followed him followed suit save only the Rivenlost, those of the Host of the Ellylon, who held themselves second in stature to none of the Lesser Shapers.

"Right." Martinek's captain, whose name was Rikard, rode up and down the lists, surveying them with a keen eye. "We're bound for Kranac, then. Is there anyone among you who has trouble acknowledging his honor's sovereignty in the third district of Pelmar?"

He halted his mount before Aracus Altorus, raising dark brows.

"Captain." Aracus' voice was steady. "I am here for one reason only: To assure the safe return of my Lady Cerelinde. All else is naught to me."

"And you?" Rikard paused before Lorenlasse of Valmaré, who commanded the Host of the Ellylon. "What of you, my fine Ellyl lord?"

Now the Ellyl did bow, and the gesture was smooth and dismissive, the gilded bee of his House gleaming at the closure of his cloak, its wings wrought of purest crystal. His arms were immaculate, his face beautiful and impassive. Only his luminous eyes gave evidence of his passion, keen and glittering. "We follow Aracus Altorus, Captain. Our kinswoman and his bride has been lost. All else is as naught."

Rikard grunted. "See that it is so." Raising one arm, he summoned the Regent Martinek's forces, scores of Pelmarans in leather armor augmented with steel rings, keen and ready. "You hear it, lads! We ride to Kranac! The Sorceress' days are numbered!"

Out of port they rode, and into the dark forests of Pelmar.

IT WAS A SWIFT SHIP.

If he'd had to guess, Carfax would not have supposed the Dwarfs would make good seafarers. He would have been wrong. It was choice, and not necessity, that kept them primarily land-bound.

Their ship sailed from Dwarfhorn, making good time under a steady wind. The crew was polite and competent, unapologetic for the inconveniences of tall folk on a Dwarf ship. Whatever it was that had transpired with the Greening of the branch in the orchards of Malumdoorn, it had won the aid of Yrinna's Children, if not their goodwill.

Most of Malthus' Company spent their time belowdecks, closeted in close council. For the nonce, Carfax was forgotten, reckoned harmless. Only Malthus' binding held him, circumferencing his mind even as it loosened his tongue.

Fat Thulu stood in the prow, holding his digging-stick and keening exuberant songs. It got on Carfax's nerves.

"What does he *do?*" he snapped at Dani.

"He charts the ways." The young Yarru was surprised. "The ways of water, fresh water, as it flows beneath the sea's floor. Do your people not do the same?"

"No, they don't." Carfax thought of home, of Staccia, where the leaping rivers of Neheris ran silver-bright and a thousand blue lakes reflected the summer sky. No need, there, to chart abundance. "Dani, why are you here?"

"To save the world." Gravely, Dani touched the flask at his throat. "It is necessary. Malthus said so."

"He said so." Carfax regarded him. "Then why does he not invite you belowdecks, to take part in his counsel? Why does he withhold his plan from you?"

There was doubt in the boy's eyes, a faint shadow of it. "He says there are things it is better I do not know. That a choice comes I must make untainted. Malthus is one of the Wise, Carfax. Even my elders said so. He would not lie to me. I must trust him."

"Oh, Dani!" He laughed; he couldn't help it. Bitter laughter, bitter tears. Carfax wiped his stinging eyes. "Oh, Dani, do you think so? Malthus uses you, boy; uses you unwitting. This water—" Reaching out, he grasped the flask threaded around the boy's neck and found it heavy, impossibly heavy, wrenching his wrist and driving him to his knees on the planked deck. "Dani!"

"Let it go!" Hobard of Malumdoorn strode across the deck to strike his hand away, lip curling. "Have you learned nothing, Staccian?"

"Oh, but I have." Cradling his aching hand, Carfax looked from one to the other. "It's the Water of Life the boy bears, isn't it? And no one else can carry it." Laughing and hiccoughing, he fought to catch his breath. "Why else would you bring him?" he gasped. "What virtues does it have, I wonder? No, no, let me guess!"

A dark shadow loomed over the deck.

"Staccian," a deep, accented voice rumbled.

Craning his neck, Carfax saw fat Thulu's face blotting out the sun, his broad belly casting shade. One large hand clasped his digging-stick, and sweat glistened oily on his wide nose. "You." Carfax pointed at him. "You're just here on sufferance, aren't you? A package deal, your presence endured for the boy's cooperation. You're a laughingstock, fat one! The Wise would sooner invite a donkey into their counsels than you!"

"It may be," Thulu said calmly, squatting on his massive hams.

Carfax stared at him. Throwing up his hands in disgust, Hobard of Malumdoorn stalked away. The Dwarf crew whispered and shrugged among themselves, going about their business with disinterested competence. Dani hovered behind his uncle's shoulder, a frown of concentration on his brow. "And you don't care?" Carfax said at last. "You don't *care* that they disdain you? You don't care, in all their wisdom, that they may be *wrong?*"

"Does it matter?" Propping chin on fist, Thulu regarded him. "There is wisdom, and there is wisdom. Dani is the Bearer, and his choice is his own. I am here to safeguard it. That is all."

Sunlight glinted dully on the clay flask that hung about the boy's neck.

Water.

It was the Water of Life, and it could make a dead branch burst into green leaf like a sapling. What else could it do?

When the unknown is made known, when the lost weapon is found, when the marrow-fire is quenched . . .

Ushahin! Dreamspinner! Alone and untutored in the ways of magic, Carfax flung his desperate thoughts out onto the wind. Encountering the circumference of Malthus' will, his call rebounded, echoing in his aching skull like thunder in an empty gorge, only the seagulls answering with raucous, hollow cries.

Huddled on the deck, he clutched his head and wept.

SORCERESS.

A whisper of thought along the ancient Ways of the Marasoumië.

Lilias waited in the cavern, composed and steady, watching the node-light surge, fitful and red, answering pulses traveling eastward along the branching Ways. One was coming, one of the Branded.

This time, she was ready.

Beshtanag was ready.

A wall of stone encompassed the mountain's base; granite, seamless and polished. And though she was exhausted in limb and spirit, the wall stood. Only the narrowest gap remained, and the raw stone was heaped in piles, awaiting her mind's touch to close the gap. The cisterns were full, the storerooms stocked.

There came a figure, blurred—lurching, uneven, an impression of limbs frozen in motion, too swift across Time to register; of pale, shining hair and mismatched eyes. A crooked grimace, caught redly in the node-light's sudden flare.

"Dreamer." Lilias inclined her head.

"Sorceress." For all his body was damaged, he emerged from the Ways with an odd, hunch-shouldered grace, inclining his head. When all was said and done, although he spoke Pelmaran with an accent undistinguishable from her own, he was still half-Ellyl. "I bring you greetings from Darkhaven."

"Is there news?" Raising her brows, she felt the weight of the Soumanië.

"Yes, and no." Ushahin drew a deep breath. "Lady, let us confer."

He followed her through the tunnels into the fasthold of Beshtanag, into the rose-and-amber luxury of her drawing-room, where Sarika knelt waiting to serve them. He spared one glance at the girl, and took sparingly of the offered refreshments.

"The Ways do not tax you as they do the General," Lilias observed.

"No." Ushahin took a sip of water, cool from the cistern. "Tanaros wields a mighty sword, and a mighty command of battle. I have . . . other skills. It is why I am here. Lady Sorceress, what news of Haomane's Allies?"

"They converge upon Kranac." Nervous, Lilias ran a finger underneath Sarika's collar of Beshtanagi silver, wrought in fine links, felt the girl lean adoringly against her knee, offering her soft throat. Calandor had showed her how to bind them to the Soumanië, to her will. "Is that not in accordance with your Lordship's plan?"

"Yes." The half-breed's eyes uneven pupils shone. "What of *Malthus?*"

"Malthus the Counselor?" Lilias blinked. "There is no news. Why?"

The Dreamer turned his head, considering the unused spinning-wheel collecting dust in the corner. "Because I have no news of him either," he said softly. "Sorceress, is Beshtanag ready for assault?"

"It is," Lilias said grimly, straightening. "Do you say the plan has changed?"

"No." After a pause, Ushahin shook his head with a susurrus of shimmering hair. "No," he said, strongly. "I leave you to travel the Ways to Jakar, on the outskirts of Pelmar. There, where the forest of Pelmar abuts the Unknown Desert, is a node, a portal of the Marasoumië. There, two units of mounted Rukhari tribesmen await the arrival of our troops. Lord Vorax has sworn it is so. Do you doubt?"

"No," Lilias whispered, asking silently, *Calandor?*

It is so, Lilias, the dragon affirmed.

"Good," Ushahin said. "There, in Jakar, I will open the portal of the Marasoumië—open it, and hold it. In Darkhaven, Lord Vorax will hold open the other end, and General Tanaros will bring the army through the Ways."

"Can this be done?" she asked him.

"Yes." He gave her a twisted smile. "Not without strain. But with Lord Satoris' aid, Vorax and I will bear the cost of it. Tanaros and his army will be untouched by it. In Jakar, they will rally and prepare to fall on the rearguard of Haomane's Allies."

Lilias looked away. "Jakar is far from Beshtanag, Dreamer. Too far."

The half-breed shrugged. "It is far enough to be safe, Lady. There is nowhere within the boundaries of Pelmar that the army of Darkhaven can assemble unseen, and it is the element of surprise that assures our victory."

"It seems to me it would be a considerable surprise for Haomane's Allies to find them *here*," Lilias said in a dry tone. "There is, after all, a node of the Marasoumië here in Beshtanag."

"Yes." Ushahin looked at her with something like regret.

"There is. And there is a wall to pen us in Beshtanag, and the forest of Pelmar dense around it. A trap must close at both ends, Lady. If we awaited them here, we would have no means of surrounding them, nor of sealing the avenue of their retreat. Do not fear. Jakar is near enough, and General Tanaros' army is capable of traveling at great speed. The path they follow will already have been blazed by the enemy. It will take three days, no more."

She bit her lip. Yesterday, one of the Were Brethren had come—a grey shadow of a yearling, thin-shanked and wary, making his report as the Grey Dam Vashuka had pledged. "Haomane's Allies assemble at Kranac. In five days, they will be here, mounting a siege on Beshtanag." She looked directly at him. "Where will your army be then, Dreamer?"

"On their heels." He returned her gaze unblinking. "One day, or two. Such was the nature of your bargain, Sorceress. Can you hold?"

"What do you think?" Lilias asked grimly. Rising from her cushioned couch, she strode past the kneeling Sarika to the balcony doors, thrusting back the heavy silk curtains that veiled them. "Look and see."

He stepped through the doors and onto the balcony. His crippled fingers rested on the marble railing as he looked down at the mighty wall that encircled Beshtanag Mountain. Gauging by the figures that moved in its shadow, the wall stood three times as high as a tall man. There were no hewn blocks, no mortar—only smooth and polished granite, flecks of mica glinting in the sun.

"Such is the power of the Soumanië?" Ushahin glanced at her.

"Yes."

In daylight, the ravages wrought on his body were more evident. Whatever other gifts the Were possessed, healing was not one. How many bones, Lilias wondered, had been broken? There was a Pelmaran children's counting rhyme that gave the litany, all the way from one left eye-socket to each of his ten fingers. It was told as a heroic act in Pelmar, that beating, a blow struck against the Misbegotten, minion of the Sunderer himself. The stories failed to take into account the fact that it was a child beaten, a child's bones broken. Ill-knit, all of them, from his knotted cheekbone to his skewed torso.

On her brow, the Soumanië flickered into life.

Birds rode the currents of wind above Beshtanag, calling out inconsequential news. Lilias touched the half-breed's arm with her fingertips, watching his knuckles whiten on the railing. It would be easy, so *easy,* to Shape his bones, to straighten what was crooked, smooth what was rough. Easier than Shaping granite, to mold flesh and bone like clay. And he would be beautiful, oh! Prettier than her pretty ones, were he healed.

"Sorceress." Ushahin's mismatched eyes glittered. "Do not think it."

And then he was there, in her thoughts, peeling away her defenses to lay bare her deepest fear—there, alone and defeated, the Soumanië stripped from her brow, leaving her naked and defenseless, *alone.* The Chain of Being reclaimed her, mortality, age sinking its claws into her, withering flesh, wrinkling skin, and at the end of it Oronin the Glad Hunter sounding his horn, for her, for her . . .

"Stop it!" Lilias cried aloud.

"So be it." He turned away, watching the birds soaring on the air. "Leave me my pain, Sorceress, and I will leave you your vanity."

"Is it vanity to cling to life?" she whispered.

The half-breed ignored her and closed his eyes. His long, pale lashes curled like waves against the uneven shoals of his sockets. One of the soaring birds broke loose from its broad spiral, a sturdy-winged raven with a rakish tuft of feathers protruding from his gleaming head. Circling tight, he cawed and chattered at the Dreamer. Frown lines appeared between Ushahin's brows.

"Gulls carry rumors," he said, opening his eyes. "And ravens hear them. Lady, what do you know of a ship sailing from Dwarfhorn?"

Lilias stared at him. *"Dwarfhorn?"*

"I am uneasy." Ushahin made a gesture at the raven, which made a sharp sound and winged off southward, in the direction of the southern coast of Pelmar. "Lady Sorceress, I would speak with the Dragon of Beshtanag."

Calandor? she asked.

Bring him.

She escorted him to the guarded exit at the rear of the fortress, where a doubled guard of ward-soldiers saluted her, eyeing the Dreamer askance with unconcealed fear. Outside, he did not wait for her lead, but climbed steadily up the winding mountain path. Lilias followed, a shadow of fear lying over her thoughts. Ushahin the Misbegotten, who could walk in the darkest places of the mortal mind. It was said he could drive Men mad with a glance. And she had thought, in her folly, that he would be less dangerous, less strange, than Tanaros Kingslayer.

Lilias, little sister.

Ahead on the ledge, a massive brightness shone, bronze scales gleaming in the sun. Calandor awaited them. At the sight of him, her heart lifted, the darkness clearing. "Calandor!"

"Liliasss." The dragon bent his sinuous neck so she could press her cheek to the scale-plated warmth of his. Lifting his head, he fixed his slitted green stare on the half-breed. "Child of three rassses, ssson of none. What is it you ssseek?"

Ushahin stood unflinching. "Knowledge, Lord Calandor."

A nictitating blink, the dragon's slow smile. "You sssseek the Counsselor."

"Yes."

"He chasses the Prophesssy, Dreamsspinner."

"I know that." A muscle twitched along Ushahin's jaw. "*Where?*"

"I do not know, Dreamsssspinner." Raising his head to its full height, Calandor gazed out over the dark green forests of Pelmar. "Uru-Alat is Sssundered, and Malthus the Counssselor was Shaped on the far ssside of that ssschism. Him, I cannot sssee, nor any weapon Shaped there. Only the effectss of their actions."

"What actions?" His voice was taut. "Where?"

"In the desert of Haomane's Wrath." The dragon sounded amused and regretful. "Sssuch a sssmall choissse, on which to hinge ssso much. A boy and a bucket of water. Is that what you sssseek to know, ssson of no one?"

Ushahin, pale as death, nodded. "Yes."

NINETEEN

❖

DARKHAVEN SHOOK WITH LORD SATORIS' fury.

The very foundations trembled at the Shaper's roar. Torches rattled in their sconces, flames casting wavering shadows against the black, marble walls. Overhead, storm clouds gathered and roiled, shot through with smoldering bolts of lightning. In the Chamber of the Font, the marrow-fire surged in blinding gouts and Godslayer pulsed, quick and erratic.

"Where?" the Shaper raged. "*Where are they?*"

Tanaros closed his eyes and touched the *rhios* in his pocket. "I do not know, my Lord Satoris," he whispered.

"The Dreamspinner didn't know, Lordship. Said the dragon couldn't say." Vorax tugged at one ear and scratched his beard. "Only it wasn't heading here, like you'd think.

Vedasia, he thought." The Staccian shrugged. "Something about birds and Dwarfs."

"It's what the ravens saw, those who were shot." Tanaros cleared his throat, summoning the will to meet the Shaper's furious red stare. "Did Ushahin not speak to you of it, my Lord?"

"Yes." It was a low growl, rising as he continued. "Of Malthus and deserts and ravens and Vedasia. *Not* of the *Water of Life!*"

Tanaros winced at the volume. "He didn't know, my Lord."

"So this Water of Life, it can put out the marrow-fire itself?" Vorax cast a dubious glance at the surging blue-white column of the Font, which was the merest manifestation of the Source below. "Take a river's worth, I reckon. No need to fear, my Lord, unless Neheris Fourth-Born herself plans to cross the divide and Shape the rivers."

"No." The Shaper sounded weary. "You misunderstand, Staccian. The Water of Life is the very essence of water, drawn from the navel of Uru-Alat itself. It would take no more than a mouthful to extinguish the marrow-fire. And I . . . I did not know any lived who could draw it forth from the earth."

There was a profound silence.

"Well," Vorax said. "Why would sodding Malthus take it to Vedasia?"

Lord Satoris glared at him, raising his voice to rattle the rafters. "*I don't know!*"

"My Lord," Tanaros said carefully, pressing his fingertips to his temples to still the echoes. "Whatever else is true, it seems certain that he did. Malthus' Company was seen in the marshes, and Carfax's men vanished there. Ushahin said . . . " He cleared his throat again " . . . Ushahin said seagulls bore rumors of a ship, sailing from Dwarfhorn. If it is so, then they are bound for Pelmar to unite with Haomane's Allies."

"Seagulls." The Shaper's glare turned his way. "*Seagulls!*"

"My Lord Satoris." Tanaros spread his hands helplessly. "It is what he said."

The Shaper brooded, pacing the Chamber of the Font. Shadows swirled in his wake, and his eyes were like two red embers. "Ushahin Dreamspinner waits in Jakar," he growled. "Haomane's Allies march toward Beshtanag. The trap lies baited and ready. If my brother Haomane thinks I will fold my hand at this new threat, he is very much mistaken." He halted, pointing at Vorax. "Lord Vorax. With two things, I charge you. You will use the Marasoumië to communicate my will to Ushahin. He is to summon the Grey Dam of the Were. Oronin's Children do not wish to be drawn into war; very well. But this thing, they will do." He smiled, and his smile was grim. "On pain of my wrath, they will hunt Malthus' Company, and slay them. All of them, and most especially this . . . *boy* . . . from the Unknown Desert. The Water of Life, they will spill where they find it."

"My Lord." Vorax bowed, his rings glittering. "And the second thing?"

"I charge you with the defense of Darkhaven. To that end, I lend the Helm of Shadows into your usage." Lord Satoris glanced at Tanaros, and his voice softened. "Forgive me, my general. You have born it nobly in my service. But I dare not leave Darkhaven without a safeguard."

"My Lord Satoris." Tanaros touched the hilt of the black sword at his waist. "This is all I need. This is all I have ever needed."

OVERHEAD, THE STARS CONTINUED THEIR slow, inevitable movement.

In the desert, Ngurra raised his voice. "I hear you, old woman!"

She made an irritated noise, emerging from the spindly shadows of the thorn-brush to join him on the cooling rock. "You've ears like a bat, old man!"

He worked a wad of *gamal* into his cheek, smiling into his beard. "Bats hear much that is hidden from other ears."

The red star had risen on the western horizon, riding higher than before. Warabi settled herself beside him, joints creaking. Together, they watched the stars revolve around the basin of Birru-Uru-Alat and the cleft rock-pile in its center. Alone among the old ones gathered at the Stone Grove, they kept the watch. As for the rest of the Yarru-yami, they were dispersed among the Six Clans. At Dry Gulch and Owl Springs, at Blacksnake Bore, Ant Plains and Lizard Rock, the Yarru had gone to earth.

"So it comes," she said with sorrow.

"It comes." He nodded, shifted the *gamal* wad into his other cheek. It fit neatly into a pocket there alongside his gums, teeth and tongue teasing out the bittersweet juices that sharpened the mind. "They have a choice, old woman. They all have a choice. Even the one who comes with a sword."

"I know." Her voice was muffled, gnarled fingers covering her face. "Ah, Ngurra! It is such a short time we have."

"Old woman!" His hands encircled her wrists, swollen by a lifetime of digging and labor. "Warabi," he said, and his voice was gentle. "An eternity would not be enough time to spend with you. But it has been a *good* time."

Lowering her hands, she looked at him. "It has."

"The children," he said, "are safe."

"But who will teach them if we perish?" Her eyes glimmered in the starlight. "Ah, Ngurra! I know what must be. I know we must offer the choice. Still, I fear."

He patted her hands. "I too, old woman. I too."

She stared at the stars. "The poor boy. Where do you think he is tonight?"

He shook his head. "The Bearer's path is his own, old

woman. I cannot guess. He has chosen, and must choose again and again, until his path finds its end."

THE DWARF SHIP DOCKED AT Port Delian, on the southern coast of Pelmar.

Carfax had the impression that the Dwarfs were glad to be rid of them, for which he did not blame them. Malthus' Company had breached Yrinna's Peace, destroying it irrevocably. As a war-proud Staccian in the service of Lord Satoris, he'd never had much use for peace.

Captivity had begun to change his perspective.

Peace, he thought, did not seem such an undesirable thing. Mayhap it would quench the killing urge he saw in the young knight Hobard's eyes whenever the Vedasian glanced at him, or the cold calculation in the eyes of Blaise Caveros, who still considered him an unwelcome threat.

Mayhap he would know himself deserving of the kindness that Dani and his uncle Thulu extended to him, of the burdensome compassion of Peldras the Ellyl, of the patient regard of Malthus the Counselor. And mayhap, mayhap, Fianna of Arduan would have some tenderness to spare for him, and cast a few of the yearning glances she saved for Blaise in his direction.

Would that be so wrong?

I am confused, Carfax thought as the Company departed Port Delian, I am heartsick and confused. His hands held the reins, directing his newly purchased gelding in a steady line, following on the haunches of Blaise's mount. It was so much easier to follow, to obey unquestioning. What merit was there in fruitless resistance? He had tried and tried and tried, to no avail.

Malthus knew it. He saw it in the Counselor's gaze, gentle and wise.

What if Malthus were a match for Lord Satoris?

It was heresy, the deepest kind of heresy. It froze his

blood to think on it; yet think on it he must. What if it were so? Step by step, the Prophecy was being fulfilled. And they did not seem, after all, so evil. They believed in the *rightness* of what they did, in the quest to render the Sundered World whole.

Was it wrong?

Would Urulat be the worse if they succeeded?

Searching his mind, Carfax found no answers. And so he rode among them as they entered the depths of the Pelmaran forests, his dreams of vengeance giving way to vague thoughts of escape and warning. And he found himself seeking, unwitting, to win their approval, gathering firewood and making himself useful. *Ushahin!* he whimpered in his thoughts from time to time, but there was no answer, for Malthus' binding held, more gentle but no less firm.

And Fianna smiled at him when he gathered pine rosin for her bow, the ordinary Arduan bow she used for shooting game, and her smile echoed the smile of another girl long ago in Staccia. Goldenrod pollen, and freckles on the bridge of her nose.

Oh, my Lord! Carfax prayed. *Forgive me. I know not what I do.*

ALTHOUGH IT HAD STOOD FOR many years, Jakar remained a desert encampment, a few sandstone buildings erected around a scrubby oasis, the rest of it a city of tents. From time out of mind, Rukhari traders had used it as a last stopping-place before entering the trade routes that cut into the forests of Pelmar. Now the traders had fled, making way for fierce warriors with sun-scorched faces and black mustaches, who raced their swift desert ponies between the lines of tents with ululating cries.

It was a good bargain Vorax had offered them.

A half league to the west, a stony ridge sprawled across

the landscape, ruddy and ominous in the light of the setting sun. It was haunted, the Rukhari said; riddled with caverns and haunted by bloodthirsty spirits of the unavenged dead. Small wonder, for it held a node of the Marasoumië, which was death to the unwary traveler.

A half league to the east, the Pelmaran forest began, a dark and ragged fringe looming over the barren plains of Rukhar. Beyond the verge was a darkness even the slanting rays of the sun could not penetrate, where Oronin's Children might lurk in the shadows a stone's throw from the trodden path.

Between the two was Ushahin, cross-legged before his tent. He was Satoris' emissary and one of the Three; he could have had the finest lodging Jakar had to offer, had he wished it. He had chosen otherwise. It was a cruel task his Lord had set him; the cruelest he had known. Still, he understood what was at stake. It was that and that alone that had decided him, that had set his course. Borrowing a pony from Makneen, the Rukhari commander, he had ridden to the verge of the Pelmaran forest and beyond, into the shadows. There, he had given the summons.

Ravens would carry it and Were would answer. The Grey Dam herself would answer. Of that, he had no doubt. It was a rare gift, a rare trust, that Sorash had given her adopted son before she died. Her successor Vashuka had no choice but to honor it.

Oh, Mother!

His eyes stung, remembering. No one's son, the dragon had called him, but he had loved her like a son; loved her enough to know he could not stay among the Were. For the great sacrifice Lord Satoris had asked of her, he had gone as a supplicant. He had asked, praying all the while she would refuse. But she had not, had chosen to find an honorable death in the request, though his heart grieved at it.

In this, there was no honor.

The sun sank below the stony ridge, and shadows crept across the ground. Near the oasis, cooking-fires were lit and the smell of lamb roasted on the grill wafted in the air. Dry, warm air; it made his bones ache less. Lamps were kindled as Ushahin watched, tallow candles lit inside lacquered bladders and hung from the openings of tents. By the shouting and raucous bursts of song, the Rukhari might have been on holiday, awaiting the arrival of the army of Darkhaven. Having walked in their dreams, he knew what a harsh and difficult living there was to be eked out on the skirts of the Unknown Desert, in what fearful contempt the Pelmarans held them, what potential lay in the promise of a Staccian alliance.

Hoofbeats clattered between the tents, and lamplight gleamed on polished horseflesh as a pony rounded the tent, muscles surging as it was drawn up short in a scatter of pebbles. A swarthy face; Zaki, Makneen's second-in-command, peered down at his feet, studiously avoiding eye contact.

"Meat ready, Dream-stalker," the Rukhar offered in broken common. "You eat?"

"No." Sitting straight-backed, Ushahin did not rise. "Thank you, Zaki."

After a moment, the Rukhar shrugged. "Makneen offer. Is good, yes? You are pleased? Not to trouble sleep?"

"It is well done, Zaki. We are allies. I will not trouble your dreams." Ushahin watched as the Rukhar shrugged again, then lashed his pony's rump with trailing reins, startling it into a galloping spurt. The Rukhari feared him. Well and good; they should. He resumed his vigil, watching the darkening verge of the forest.

Time passed.

A half moon rose and the stars emerged, and brightest of them was the red one, high above the horizon.

"Brother."

A grey voice, emerging from darkness. It named him in the tongue of Oronin's Children, which he had spoken seldom since childhood. Ushahin rose, straightening his stiffening joints and inclining his head. "Brother," he replied in kind. "Well met by moonlight."

There was a gleam, as of bared teeth. "I do not think so. Follow."

Follow he did, leaving the illuminated tents behind, traveling on foot over the stony soil. Ahead of him, a grey shadow moved low to the ground, silent but for the occasional click of claw on stone. On and onward they traveled, until the lamps of Jakar were distant sparks and the forest enveloped them.

Into the tall pines his guide led him, leaving behind the beaten paths and treading on soft pine mast, to a glade where moonlight spilled on silvery fur, and one awaited in a circle of many. By this alone, by the honor the pack accorded her, he knew her.

"Old mother." Ushahin bowed low. "I give you honor."

"Son of my self." Ritual words, devoid of affection. Vashuka the Grey Dam stood upright and her amber eyes were narrowed in the moonlight. A score of dim figures crouched around her, hackled and wary. "The Grey Dam Sorash gave you a sacred trust. Why have you used it to summon me here, so near to a place of Men?"

"Honored one, forgive me." He felt sick, the brand on his chest a searing pain. "Oronin's Children are my kin, but I have sworn a deeper oath."

Her lip wrinkled, exposing her canines, still white. "Satoris."

"To my Lord Satoris, yes." Ushahin drew a deep breath, trying to loosen his chest. Where were the ravens? The trees should be full of them; were empty instead. He reached out with his thoughts, and a low, concerted growl came from the crouching circle of Were. "Brethren! Has it come to this?"

Vashuka raised a clenched, clawed hand, and the circle fell silent. Her gaze never left him. "Tell us, Ushahin-who-walks-between-dusk-and-dawn. What *has* it come to?"

"A favor." It was harder than he had imagined to hold his

ground before her. His very flesh was vulnerable. For all that he was one of the Three, he was no warrior like Tanaros or Vorax. His crippled hands could scarce grip a sword, and such powers as he had would avail him little against the Were, who were themselves the stuff of which Men's nightmares were made. "Death."

"War!" she growled, and the pack echoed her.

"No." Ushahin shook his head. "You have refused to commit Oronin's Children to war, honored one, and Satoris Third-Born respects this. It is death he asks of you; a hunt, far from the battlefield. There is a company, a small company, that enters the forests of Pelmar. These, my Lord wishes slain."

"Wishes." The Grey Dam's voice was dry. "Asks. Who are we to slay?"

"Malthus the Counselor," he whispered. "And all who accompany him."

At that, she threw back her head, loosing a howl. It echoed forlorn throughout the forest, and the Were who accompanied her crouched and quivered.

"Old mother," Ushahin said to her. "Has Malthus the Counselor been a friend to our kind? Have the Sons of Men? Have the Ellylon? No! Only Lord Satoris. Seven deaths is not so much to ask."

Closing her jaws with a snap, Vashuka snarled. "Have we not given as much?" She jerked her chin toward the red star above the tree-line of the glade. "There, Ushahin-who-walks-between-dusk-and-dawn! The Counselor Dergail's Soumanië, that we wrested from him! For this, Men and Ellylon name us enemy and hunt us without mercy." She folded her arms across her gaunt bosom. "I am the Grey Dam; I remember. I am the Grey Dam; I say, no more."

"And I say," Ushahin said softly, with infinite regret, "that do you refuse, Lord Satoris will name you his enemy. And there is an army coming, old mother. An army of Fjel-troll with hides like leather and the strength to move mountains, commanded by General Tanaros Blacksword himself. Right now, there is a force—" he pointed, "—of two hundred Rukhari warriors on that plain, and their swords are whetted. Who will you turn to if Lord Satoris turns against you? The Pelmaran Regents, who have sought to stamp out your kind? Aracus Altorus?" He shook his head. "I do not think so. My mother-who-was spent her life's last blood seeking Altorus' throat. He will not be quick to forgive."

She snarled again, and the moonlight glittered on her sharp teeth. "*Ask!* You ask nothing and demand everything!"

Heavy with sorrow, he nodded. "Yes, old mother. Childhood must end, even for immortals. Will you abide or refuse?"

Lifting her muzzle, the Grey Dam gazed at the night sky. "If I refuse," she mused aloud, "who will obey? The Counselor Malthus wields the Soumanië. Who among you can look upon it? Oronin's Children alone can withstand it, we whom the Glad Hunter Shaped, we who can veil our eyes and hunt by scent alone."

"Yes," he said. "It is so. But Oronin's Children are few, and Lord Satoris' armies are many." Thinking of the raging storm of fury emanating from Darkhaven, Ushahin shuddered. In the depths of his shattered bones, it was a madness he understood. "Make no mistake, old mother. One way or another, he will triumph. And if you refuse him, he will have his vengeance."

"*Aaaarrhhhh!*" A raw cry, half howl. Her furred hands rose to cover her face, and the Were Brethren surrounding her keened. "Selves of myself," she whispered to her predecessors' memories, "why did you make an ally of he who Sundered the world?" Lowering clenched hands, she hardened her voice. "So be it." The Grey Dam spun, pointing. "You," she said harshly. "You. You and you, you, you and you! Seven Brethren for seven deaths." Her amber eyes shone hard and cold, and her voice imparted hatred to her words. "Will it suffice, son of my self?"

"Yes, honored one." Ushahin bowed low. "It will."

She turned her back to him, speaking over her shoulder. "Show them."

This he did, opening his mind to them in the ancient tradition of the Were, showing them in pictures the Company as he had witnessed it upon the marshlands of Vedasia: The Counselor, the Ellyl, the Borderguardsman, the Archer, the Vedasian, the Yarru boy and his guardian uncle. He showed them the death that must be, the rent flesh and life's blood seeping into the forest's floor, the red gem of the Soumanië to be kept for Lord Satoris, the clay flask containing the Water of Life that must be broken and spilled. And he showed them the pictures that had filtered through the fractured shards of the Ravensmirror, the rumor of gulls and a ship setting anchor on Pelmaran soil.

"There," he whispered. "Find them and slay them."

In their minds there opened a dry gully of thirst that only red blood could slake. As one, the seven Brethren bowed, obedient to the will of the Grey Dam, and death was their every thought. As one, they crouched low and sprang into motion, seven shadows moving swift and grey through the Pelmaran forests. Only the barest rustle of pine needles marked their passing. Oronin's Children, direst of hunters.

"Go." It was the Were who had guided him who spoke, rising from the shadows to stand upright, his voice harsh and choked. "Go now, no one's son!"

"Old mother . . . " Helpless, Ushahin reached out a hand toward the motionless figure of the Grey Dam, remembering Sorash-who-was, remembering the touch of her rough pelt as she cradled his broken limbs. His boyhood self, and the only mother he had ever known. *The Grey Dam is dead. The Grey Dam lives.* The keen wire of pain that defined him grew tighter, madness pressing in close and a sound rising in his mind, rising and rising, a howl unuttered in his branded chest. "Oh, mother! I am sorry . . . "

"*Go!*"

TWENTY

◆

"LADY." TANAROS CAUGHT HIS BREATH at the sight of her. In the confines of her chambers, clad in the robes of her ancestors, she shone like a candle-flame. It made his heart ache, and he bowed low. "I come to bid you farewell."

Cerelinde's hand rose unbidden to her throat. "You depart?"

"On the morrow." He straightened. "I will return."

"You will kill him," she whispered, eyes wide and fearful. "Aracus."

For a long time he did not answer, remembering the battle in Lindanen Dale and Aracus Altorus struggling with the Grey Dam of the Were on the end of his blade; remembering another, Roscus. His king, his foster-brother. A ready grin, an extended hand. A babe with red-gold hair, and his wife's guilt-ridden gaze. At the end, Roscus had looked surprised. It would end, with Aracus. It would be done.

"Yes," he said. "I am sorry."

She turned her back to him, her pale hair a shining river. "Go," she said, her voice taut and shaking. "*Go!* Go then, and kill, Tanaros Blacksword! It is what you do. It is all you are good for!"

"Lady." He took a step forward, yearning to comfort her and angry at it. "Do you understand so little, even now? Haomane has declared war upon us. We are fighting for our lives here!"

"I understand only grief." Turning, she gazed at him. "Must it be so, Tanaros? Must it truly be so? Is there no room for *compassion* in your understanding of the world? Haomane would forgive, if you relented."

"Would he?" he asked, taking another step. "Would *you?*"

Cerelinde shrank from his approach.

"You see." He felt his lips move in a grim smile. "Limits, always limits. You would forgive us, if we kept to our place. Ah, my Lady. I did keep to my place, once upon a time. I was Tanaros Caveros, Commander of the King's Guard in Altoria. I honored my liege-lord and served him well; I honored my wife and loved her well." He opened his arms. "You see, do you not, what it earned me?"

She did not answer, only looked at his spread hands and trembled.

He had throttled his wife with those hands.

"So be it." Gathering himself, Tanaros executed one last bow, crisp and correct. "Lady, you will be well cared for in my absence. I have sworn it so. I bid you farewell." Spinning on his heel, he took his leave of her. No matter that her luminous eyes haunted him; it was satisfying, hearing the door slam upon his departure.

She did not know.

She did not understand.

Cerelinde was Haomane's Child, Shaped of rational thought. She would never understand the passion with which he had loved his wife and his liege-lord alike, and how deeply their betrayal had wounded him. No more could she comprehend Lord Satoris, who had dared defy his Elder Brother in order that his Gift should not be wrested from Men, that thought should not be forever uncoupled from desire.

Things were not always as simple as they seemed.

But Haomane's Children could not think in shades of grey.

Even now, with the old rage still simmering in his heart,

it grieved Tanaros to think upon all he had lost, all he had cast aside. How much more so, he wondered, must it grieve his Lordship? And yet Cerelinde refused to see it.

Though he wished that she would.

With an effort, he thrust the thought away. A door closed; well and good. Nothing left, then, but what lay ahead. It had come down to it. All the variables, the plans within plans; what were they to him? Nothing. There was a war. War, he understood. At every corner, Tanaros passed sentries standing guard. Hulking shadows, armed to the eyetusks. They saluted him, each and every one, acknowledging the Commander General of Darkhaven.

Yes. These were his people.

"Admit no one," he told the Fjel on guard outside his door. "I will rest."

In his quarters, everything was immaculate. The lamps had been trimmed, the bed-linens were crisp and clean. There were madlings who never left the laundry, taking a remorseless joy in toiling over boiling vats of suds and water, expunging filth. His armor of carbon-blackened steel was arrayed on its stand, each piece polished to a menacing gleam. Buckles and straps had been oiled and replaced. It waited for him to fill it, an empty suit, a warrior of shadows. In the corner, the black sword rested propped in its scabbard. Not even a madling would touch it without permission.

His blood, thought Tanaros, *my Lord's blood.*

There was a tray laid unasked-for on the table, steam seeping beneath the covered dish-domes. Peering under one, he found a pair of quail in a honey glaze; another held wild rice, and yet another a mess of stewed greens. For dessert, a plate of cheeses and grapes sat uncovered. Candlelight danced over the table, illuminating the soft, misty bloom on the purple grapes.

Drawing up a chair, Tanaros sat and ate, and tried not to think how lonely, how terribly lonely, his quarters were. He missed Fetch, but the raven was gone, the half-frozen fledgling grown into a full-fledged bird, another daring scout in Ushahin Dreamspinner's strange army. Digging into his pocket, he found Hyrgolf's *rhios* and set it on the table. The sight of it soothed him, the river sprite's face laughing from its rounded curves.

"Is it to your liking, my Lord General?"

Tanaros started at the soft, unfamiliar voice, rising from his chair and half-drawing his dagger. Seeing Meara, he eased. "How did you get in here?"

The madling sidled toward the table, tangled hair hiding her face as she nodded toward his bathing-chamber. "This is Darkhaven. There are ways and ways, Lord General. Is the meal to your liking?"

"Yes," he said gently, pushing away the plate of picked quail bones. "Meara, you should not be here. Is it not our Lord's wish that you attend the Lady Cerelinde?"

"The Lady Cerelinde." Meara sidled closer, her features contorting in a whimper. "It *hurts* to serve her. She pities us, Lord General. And she grieves, in the manner of the El-lylon. She turns her face to the wall, and orders us away. It was never my wish to leave you, Lord Tanaros. Do you not know it?"

Close, so close! In a paroxysm of courage, she reached him.

Touched him, descended on him.

He could smell the heat of her flesh, of her womanhood. Her hands were on him, beneath the collar of his tunic, sliding against the hard flesh of his chest, the raised ridges of his brand. Tanaros gritted his teeth as her weight straddled him. "Meara . . . "

"Oh, my lord, my lord!" Her face, so close to his, eyes wide.

"Meara, no."

"He was the Sower, once." Wide eyes, pupils fixed. Her breath was warm against his skin, unexpectedly sweet. "Do you not *wonder*, Tanaros, do you not *know*? It was his *Gift*, when he had one!"

Her mouth touched his, her teeth nipping at his underlip, the tip of her tongue probing. Her weight, warm and welcome, encompassing him. Jolted by desire, he stood upright, his hands encircling her waist to dump her unceremoniously onto the floor, her skull jolting at the impact.

"Meara, *no!*"

She laughed, then. Limbs akimbo, she laughed, bitter and shrill. "General Tanaros Blacksword! Some hero, some *man* you are, Tanaros Wifeslayer! Did you offer your wife so little satisfaction? No wonder she found cold comfort in your bed! No wonder she turned to the Altorus to quicken her womb!"

"*ENOUGH!*" Stooping, unthinking, he struck her across the face.

She whimpered.

"Meara, forgive me." Filled with remorse, Tanaros knelt at her side, dabbing with the hem of his overtunic at a trickle of blood in the corner of her mouth. "Forgive me, I am sorry, I did not mean to hurt you."

"Poor General." Her eyes were curiously limpid, as if the blow had cleared her wits. She touched his hand with gentle fingers, cupping it against her bruised cheek, caressing his knuckles. "Poor Tanaros. Does it hurt so much, even still?"

Her skin was warm and soft and the pity in her eyes terrified him. Withdrawing from her, he straightened. "You should go now."

Gathering her skirts around her, she stood. Not beautiful, no. A woman, not yet old, with tangled hair and skin sallow for lack of sunlight. She would have been pretty, once, in an ordinary, mortal way. Pity in her gaze, and a terrible knowledge. "I warned you, my lord," she said softly. "You should have heeded me. She will break your heart. She will break all our hearts."

"My heart." He shook his head, touching his branded

chest. "No, Meara. That lesson, I learned too well. My heart is dedicated to Lord Satoris' service. No other."

"I know," she whispered. "I know."

HAOMANE'S ALLIES ARRIVED EARLY.

Something had happened. The scouting-packs of Were yearlings who were to report on their movements had failed. If not for Calandor's warning, Beshtanag would have been caught unready. As it was, Lilias had closed the last breach in the wall in haste, sealing Beshtanag against invasion, and themselves within it.

Her Ward Commander Gergon brought her bits of gossip, gleaned by soldiers shouting back and forth over the granite expanse of the wall. A siege, after all, was a tiresome thing and some few had friends and cousins on the other side.

It seemed that, against all odds, Martinek, the Southeastern Regent of Pelmar, had taken to Aracus Altorus, the would-be King of the West. The last scion of House Altorus had accorded him the utmost of respect, convincing even the Host of the Ellylon to bend their stiff necks to Pelmaran authority. Deep in their cups, they had established a rapport; so much so that Martinek had allowed himself to be swayed by tales of the Borderguard of Curonan, its small, efficient units able to mobilize and maneuver more swiftly than a full-sized army.

Regent Martinek had taken Altorus' advice, and his fellow Regents had followed suit. Instead of advancing in a united front, they had restructured their troops into winding columns. No need, then, to forge a broad path through the forest. Unchallenged, Haomane's Allies made good time through the dense terrain. The troops of Aracus Altorus were the first to arrive, sizing up the granite wall that surrounded Beshtanag with cool, measuring glances, retreating out of bowshot to set up an encampment that sprawled through the unguarded forest.

Within the space of a day, the others had arrived.

Pelmaran forces from three of the five sitting Regents, a contingent of Vedasian knights, capable Midlanders—and, oh, worst of all was the Host of the Ellylon, the Rivenlost with their piercing beauty and their keen swords. Back and forth they rode, pacing the circumference of the granite wall, needing neither sleep nor nourishment to sustain them in their quest.

Only one thing did they require: The Lady Cerelinde.

"I don't like this, Gergon." On her balcony, Lilias regarded the enemy encampment and shivered in the summer's warmth. "There are so many of them."

"We can hold." Her Ward Commander's face was grim. "As long as you hold the wall, my lady. Our stores will last another seven days, if need be."

"Seven days," she echoed. What a paltry amount!

Gergon glanced at her. "The Banewreaker's army should be here in less. They are coming, my lady, are they not?"

"Yes." She made her voice firmer. "Yes. They will be here."

At the base of the mountain, a distant figure stepped forth, clad in shining armor. He was the herald of the Rivenlost and he bore a staff from which flew the standards of both Ingolin the Wise and Elterrion the Bold—the argent scroll and the Crown-and-Souma. As he did three times a day, he lifted an Ellylon horn to his lips and blew, the silvery tone echoing from the sides of Beshtanag Mountain. His voice rang forth, clear and carrying. *"Sorceress! Surrender the Lady Cerelinde, and your people will be spared!"*

"Ellyl arsehole," Gergon muttered, adding, "your pardon, my lady."

Midway down the mountain, a line of kneeling archers loosed their bows, sending a shower of arrows aloft. Sharp shouts came from sentries posted in the trees, and those of Haomane's Allies in reach crouched low, raising their shields above their heads. Arrows arced above the granite wall and fell, clattered uselessly onto warding shields and the loose scree. The Ellyl herald stood contemptuous, watching them fall, before turning to retreat untouched.

"Too far, too high." Gergon shook his head. "Sorry, my lady."

Lilias sighed. "Tell them not to waste their arrows."

"As you wish." He paused. "If it came to it, my lady, there is one weapon they could not withstand."

"No!" Her reply was sharp. "Not Calandor."

"It seems a folly—"

"Hear me, Ward Commander." Lilias fixed him with a steely stare. "This is Shapers' business, and dragonkind is all but vanished because of it. Calandor will not give battle. Put it out of your thoughts."

"My lady." Gergon bowed, unhappy with her answer. "As you order. I will report again at sundown."

It was a relief to have him gone. Lilias watched a pair of ravens circling in the drafts, hoping they made ready to bear word to Darkhaven on urgent wings. While the wall stood, Beshtanag was safe; but there were so many arrayed against them. She touched the Soumanië at her brow, feeling the Shaping force of it pulsing faintly in her veins, in the stone beneath her feet. Faint, so faint! She was spread too thin. It had taken a great effort to raise the wall, and more to sustain it. Always, it took more effort to create than to destroy. The old linkages were stretched and weak—those incorporating the collars of her pretty ones, binding them to her service; those that bound Beshtanag itself, binding the blood and flesh of her people to loyalty. Even the binding that stretched the great Chain of Being to its limits felt thin and tenuous, and Lilias felt old.

She was old, a thousand years old. Today, she felt it.

Oh, Calandor! she asked silently. *What have we done?*

There was a long pause before the dragon replied, longer than she remembered.

Wait, little sister, and be strong. You must be strong.

There was sorrow in the thought, deeper than she'd known the dragon to evince. Lilias gripped the balustrade with both hands, staring at the mountain's base. There, in the shadow of the forest, a flash of red-gold hair. Aracus Altorus, bare-headed and arrogant, the would-be King of the West. Even at a distance, she saw him pause, his gaze measuring her will and searching the sky for dragon-sign.

And then he turned his back on her, cool and purposeful, ordering his troops as they set about the construction of the implements of war. Ladders of branches, lashed with rope. Siege-towers, capable of holding a dozen men. Entire trunks hewn into battering rams. All of Pelmar's forests provided fodder for his efforts, as if in league with him. Already Haomane's Allies had essayed her wall in a score of places. She could hold it, for now, with the aid of Gergon's wardsmen. What would happen when their stores ran low? What would happen if Malthus arrived to pit himself against her, armed with a Soumanië like her own?

In her deepest self, Lilias knew the answer.

Hurry, she prayed in the direction of Darkhaven; oh, hurry!

TENS OF THOUSANDS OF FJELTROLL were packed into the Chamber of the Marasoumië and the tunnels that underlay Darkhaven. Armor creaked, rough hide jostled hide, horn-calloused feet trod the stony floors. Despite the fact that the ventilation shafts had all been uncovered, the air was stifling with the musky, slightly rank odor of the Fjel. The red node-light was reflected in thousands of eyes, all of them fixed on Tanaros.

Despite it all, they stood patient, adhering to the formations he'd drilled into them and trusting to his leadership. The swift Gulnagel, the ferocious Nåltannen, the dark Mørkhar and the mighty Tungskulder—all his to command, a vast army, divided into dozens of small units, mobile and skilled.

And at his side was Speros of Haimhault, grinning a gap-toothed grin, holding the reins of a pair of the horses of Darkhaven; Tanaros' own black, and a second like enough to be its twin. After much debate, Tanaros had decided to leave the mounted Staccian forces behind. Under Vorax's command, they and the Havenguard would serve to defend Darkhaven. He had made a promise to the young Midlander, let him serve as his equerry.

As for the battle itself; ah! For that, he had his field marshal, and there was no one, Man or Fjel, he trusted more than Hyrgolf. In the suffocating press, their gazes met quietly and Hyrgolf gave a nod, showing his eyetusks in a faint smile.

The Army of Darkhaven was ready.

"My friends." Tanaros raised a hand, and the rustling cavern fell into silence. "Tonight, we go forth to achieve a great good. Tonight, we will travel the ancient Ways of the Marasoumië, that traverse the length and breadth of the Sundered World itself."

There was a murmur; of eagerness, of anxiety.

"Be at ease." He pointed at Vorax, who stood beside the flickering node. "There stands Lord Vorax of Staccia, who will open the entrance. At the other end awaits Ushahin Dreamspinner, who will open the egress. Between them, they will hold open the Way, until the last of us has passed. And I, Tanaros Caveros, the Commander General of Darkhaven, will guide you through it."

They were afraid, these mighty warriors, the feared Fjel. It made him fond, and he smiled upon them. "Do not fear, my brothers. We are the Three, branded by Godslayer itself. We are the chosen of Lord Satoris. We will not fail you."

It braced them like *svartblod*. Tanaros saw it, felt it in his veins. His spirits soared, running high. Within the scarred circle on his chest, his heart beat, strong and steady. This was what he had been born to do. Lord Satoris himself had said it, summoning him to the Chamber of the Font. There, amid the blue-white coruscation of the marrow-fire, Godslayer's pulsing and the sweet reek of ichor, he had spoken words that filled his general's heart to bursting with pride and nameless emotion.

I trust you, Tanaros Blacksword. You will not fail me.

"Brothers!" Tanaros ripped his sword from its sheath, holding it aloft. "Though Haomane First-Born cowers on Torath, for too long his tyranny has held sway over Urulat! In his pride and refusal to relent, he rouses his Children against us, he sends his Counselors to wage war, and looses his Prophecy on us like a hunting dog. Lord Satoris grows weary of being brought to bay like an animal, and I grow weary with him. Have the Fjel not been persecuted by his Wrath, threatened with extinction? I tell you, it need not be so. Our destiny lies within our grasp. Haomane's Allies await us! Shall we make an end to it?"

They roared, then; roared acclaim and battle-readiness, and the sound within the cavern was deafening. Speros dropped the reins he held and clapped his hands over his ears in dismay while the restless horses tossed their heads. Tanaros smiled, letting the sound wash over him in waves, beating against his skin. It was good, this sound. It was a fitting sound to accompany the end of a world; or the beginning of one.

"So be it!" he cried when they had subsided. "By this sword, quenched in the blood of Lord Satoris himself, I do swear it. We will prevail in his name." In a single motion, he sheathed the black sword. "The next blood it tastes will be that of Haomane's Allies, or I am foresworn. We will assemble on the plains of Rukhar. Is all in readiness?"

Hyrgolf turned, repeating the question in the Fjel tongue. Here and there standards rose and dipped, their colors dim in the cavernous light as subcommanders in a sea of Fjel gave answer; yes and yes and yes. The ranks held, the companies were ready. Hyrgolf was smiling broadly as he turned back to his leader, his upper and lower eyetusks gleaming. "They're ready, General," he said in his deep rumble. "For our children and our children's children, shall we make an end to this battle for once and for all?"

"Let's." Tanaros reached out, clasping his field marshal's taloned hand, feeling the stone-roughened hide against his skin. "Let us do that, my brother."

Clearing his throat beside the node-light, Vorax lifted the case that held the Helm of Shadows. "Blacksword," he said softly, red light flickering on the gold inlay of his armor as he summoned Tanaros' attention. "The night is waxing. Are you prepared to depart?"

It was harder than he had reckoned. "You'll keep Darkhaven safe?"

"As immortal fiber can make it." The Staccian smiled into his beard and opened the case, removing the Helm of Shadows. An agony of darkness pulsed between his hands. "Ride forth, cousin. The Dreamspinner is waiting on the other end. Go now, and Lord Satoris' blessings upon you."

So saying, Vorax placed the Helm upon his head and opened the Way. A wash of ruby brilliance filled the Chamber. Squinting against it, Tanaros groped for the reins of his mount, fumbled as Speros handed them to him with tardy alacrity. Swinging himself into the saddle, he set his face toward the open Way and took the first step.

The Army of Darkhaven was on the march.

TWENTY-ONE

❖

DANI SMILED AT HIM IN the twilight. "I'm glad you're staying with us."

Carfax poked at the fire without answering. A knot burst, releasing a crackle of sparks and the fragrance of pine. His muscles ached from the day's hard labor. On the far side of the glade, a dark fissure yawned beneath an overhanging granite shelf, clear at last of the rockfall that had blocked it.

It was there, deep below the earth. A node of the Marasoumië. Alone among Haomane's Allies, Malthus the Counselor knew the secrets of the Ways, and did not fear them.

And he had helped them uncover it.

Wind rustled in the tall pine-tops. Accompanied by the Ellyl, the archer Fianna walked the perimeter of the glade, Oronin's Bow half-drawn. They had seen ravens from afar. At her back, the quiver that held her arrows gleamed with a faint, eldritch light, and one shaft shone a pale silver. It would flame white-gold if she withdrew it.

"Carfax?" Dani prompted him.

"Aye." With an effort, he gathered his thoughts. "Aye, Dani. I'm here."

It had been a near thing. Here, in this glade, their paths would diverge. Malthus the Counselor was leaving them for a time. Alone, he would travel the Ways of the Marasoumië to Beshtanag, where he would confront the Sorceress of the East. Malthus' Company would continue without him, to be reunited in Jakar. Their task—Carfax knew it now—was to shepherd Dani the Bearer and the precious Water of Life to Darkhaven.

To extinguish the marrow-fire and free Godslayer.

There had been quarrels, of course. It had sat ill with the young Vedasian knight Hobard to play nursemaid to a Charred One while his kinsmen gained glory at Beshtanag. Malthus had pointed out the route to the northeast and invited him to depart. In the end, Hobard had elected to stay—but he had argued hard for disposing of Carfax.

The argument had taken hours to resolve.

Dani, soft-hearted Dani, had protested, backed by his uncle. Fat Thulu; not so fat, after their travels. Blaise Caveros stirred, narrowed his eyes, and said nothing. Peldras the Ellyl laced his elegant hands about his knees, thinking ab-

struse Ellylon thoughts. And Fianna . . . Fianna spoke in a
faltering voice on mercy's behalf, her words uncertain.

In the end, of course, it fell to Malthus.

The wizard had fixed him with that keen gaze that
seemed to see right through him, eyes bright beneath his
fierce brows. And Carfax, to his shame, had trembled. Once
upon a time, he had been willing to die for Lord Satoris,
filled with a Staccian warrior's pride. No more. He was
afraid.

"Yes," Malthus had said with finality. "Let him stay."

So it had been decided, and when it was done, Carfax
wished they had killed him after all. It would, at least, be
swift. The itch in Blaise's fingers as they strayed over his
sword-hilt promised as much. It would put an end to his
knowing. Malthus the Counselor traveled the Ways into a
trap, that much he knew. Carfax thought upon it with guilt
and grim satisfaction as he labored to shift rocks on the
wizard's behalf. Oh, Malthus might hope to defeat the Sorceress with her Soumanië—but it would take a mighty effort. When General Tanaros and the Army of Darkhaven
fell upon Haomane's Allies, the wizard would have naught
left to give in their defense.

And yet . . . and yet.

The Company would struggle onward. How doomed
were their efforts, if Darkhaven prevailed? It would become
a game of cat and mouse, with Lord Satoris' paw poised to
strike. He would tell them, if he dared. He would spare
them. Not all, no; not the surly Vedasian, nor Blaise
Caveros—but the others, yes. Dani, at the least. Poor Dani,
who was beginning to feel the weight of his burden, and the
cost of protecting it. He belonged in the Unknown Desert,
he and his uncle, at peace and unaware of the Shapers' War
being waged over Urulat.

Better I should die, Carfax thought, than see this through.
Only I am afraid to die.

And so, alone, he tended the fire and dwelled with his
tongue-locked thoughts, while their stores were shared out

and everyone ate. And then, in the small hours, Peldras the Ellyl stayed awake with him, with his drawn sword over his knees, watching the moon's course. They had become comrades in these small hours. Even the wizard snored. And as before, it was the Ellyl who spoke first, turning his luminous gaze on the Staccian. "You have given thought to Arahila's mercy, have you not?"

"Mayhap." Carfax kept his gaze fixed on the embers. "Does it matter?"

"It does."

"Why?"

There was a long silence.

"Where to begin?" Peldras sighed, a sound like the wind through pine needles. "I am Rivenlost, Carfax of Staccia. I am one of Haomane's Children; Haomane First-Born, who alone knew the will of Uru-Alat. The world as He Shaped it was a bright and shining thing. I am Ellyl, and I remember. I grieve for what was Sundered from me."

Carfax lifted his head. "Lord Satoris did not—"

"Satoris Banewreaker would cover the world in darkness!" The Ellyl cut him off, his tone grim. "A tide is rising, Staccian. In Darkhaven, it rises. The Fjeltroll are seen in numbers, and the Helm of Shadows has been worn once more. What passes in Beshtanag is merely an opening gambit. Look, there." He pointed to the red star, riding high above the horizon. "There is Dergail's Soumanië, that the Sunderer wrested from him. It is a sign, a challenge. And it is one the Six Shapers cannot answer, for they are trapped beyond the shores of the Sundered World, islanded in their might. It falls to us, Son of Man. We are the last, best hope; each one of us. Do you matter?" He softened his voice. "Yes, Staccian. You matter. You are the twig that may turn a flood. If you choose a path of redemption, who is to say how many will follow?"

"No." Carfax stared aghast at the Ellyl, shaking his head in denial. "No! You don't understand! Lord Satoris didn't raise the red star; it was a warning sent by Arahila herself that Haomane First-Born—" Over the Ellyl's shoulder, he glimpsed movement, half-seen shadows moving in the forest's verges, and fear strangled his unspoken words.

Reading his expression, Peldras went motionless. "What is it?"

"There," he whispered, pointing. "Oh, Peldras!"

"The Were are upon us!"

The Ellyl's shout rang clarion in the glade. Already he was on his feet, a naked blade in his hand, his bright gaze piercing the shadows. Already Malthus' Company sprang awake, leaping to the defense. Already it was too late.

From everywhere and nowhere came the attack, for Oronin's Hunters had encircled the glade. Seven hunters for the seven Allies, coming low and fast as they surged from the surrounding darkness. Firecast shadows rippled along their pelts. Oronin Last-Born had Shaped them, and Death rode in his train. Grey and dire, they closed in for the kill with lean ferocity, snarling a song of blood-thirst. Seven throats they sought, and the eighth they ignored, leaving him a helpless witness.

"No," Carfax said dumbly. "Oh, no."

There was Malthus the Counselor in his tattered scholar's robes, the Soumanië blazing in his hand. It lit the glade in a piercing wash of scarlet light; to no avail, for the eyes of the Were were bound with grey cloth. Oronin's Children hunted blind. Their muzzles were raised, nostrils twitching, following scent as keen as sight.

There were the tethered horses, screaming in awful terror. There were the fighters; Peldras, Blaise, Hobard. Back to back to back they fought, forced into a tight knot. They fought better together than Carfax would have guessed, fending off four circling Were. Even the Vedasian proved himself worthy, wielding his father's sword with a ferocity and skill beyond his years.

Still, they were not enough to resist the Were.

Fianna knelt in an archer's stance at the Counselor's feet, drawing the Arrow of Fire with trembling fingers, sighting

on shadows as it illuminated her vulnerable face. The black
horn of Oronin's Bow seemed to buck in her hands, reluctant to strike against its Shaper's children.

And Dani; oh, Dani!

His eyes were wide, reflecting firelight, his slender fingers closed around the clay flask at his throat. Dani, who
had offered him water when he was thirsty. Before him
stood Thulu of the Yarru-yami, a bulky figure wielding his
digging-stick with grim determination. Already, he was
panting and weary, his skin glistening with sweat and the
darker sheen of blood where teeth had scored him.

Two of the Were hunters circled him with cunning,
twitching nostrils guiding them. One feinted; the other
launched past him, a deadly missile, jaws parting to seek
Dani's throat.

"*No!*"

Carfax was not conscious of moving, not conscious of
grasping the butt-end of a sturdy branch from the fire.
Sparks arced through the air as he swung it, interposing
himself between the Were and its quarry. There was a thud,
the impact jarring his shoulders; a keen whine and the smell
of scorched wolf-pelt.

Oh, Brethren, forgive me!

"Dani!" Malthus' voice, strident and urgent. "The cavern! Now! *Now!*"

And the earth . . . *surged.*

Carfax, choking, was flung to the ground. There, scant
feet away, was Dani, his face filled with fear and dawning
knowledge. Outside the circle of churning earth, the blind
hunters gathered to regroup, muzzles raised to quest the air.

"Go," Carfax whispered. "Go!"

He hauled himself to one knee, dimly aware of Thulu
grabbing Dani by the collar and racing toward the cavern of
the Marasoumië, their retreat warded by Malthus, who
caused the very earth to ripple in surging waves, throwing
back the attack of the Were.

The Yarru vanished into the cavern.

"Malthus!" Blaise shouted.

At the cavern's mouth, the wizard turned to face the pursuing Were and planted his staff with a sound like thunder. His lips were moving, his ancient face illuminated by the Soumanië that blazed crimson at his breast. Earth roiled, stones cracking like bones. Oronin's Hunters were tossed like jackstraws, howling in anger. Amid the chaos, Malthus shaped words lost in the avalanche of noise, his urgent gaze striving to communicate. ". . . protect . . . Bearer! Beshtanag . . . Jakar . . ."

"What?" Blaise cried. "*What?*"

Taking a step backward, Malthus the Counselor raised his hand. On his breast, the Soumanië surged with brilliance and deep in the cavern, the node-light of the Marasoumië blazed in answer, washing the glade in crimson light and momentarily blinding the onlookers.

When it faded, they were gone.

Unguarded, unprotected, Carfax stood with a smoldering branch in his hand and fought back an awful laugh as he watched his dumbstruck companions stare at the cavern's empty mouth.

Again, yet again, the Were regrouped. One rose onto his rear legs, clawed hands snatching away his blindfold to reveal amber eyes glowing with all the rage of a thwarted hunt. "You rest," the Were leader growled, "die."

A bow spoke in answer; not Oronin's, but an Arduan longbow made of ashwood and sinew, its string singing as shafts buzzed like hornets in the air. Three of the Were fell, silent and stricken, before their Brethren raced for the shadows, howling in wounded anger. "Not yet," Fianna vowed, tears staining her cheeks. "Not yet!"

Then it was Hobard defending her as the surviving Were renewed their attack with doubled stealth and speed, scattering the fire and spoiling the Archer's aim. The young Vedasian fought with all the pride and skill of his knight's upbringing. He swung his sword with a valiant effort, grimacing as one of the Were passed close, fierce teeth scoring his side.

"Blaise!" A silver shout in the smoke-streaked darkness; Peldras had reached the horses. With an Ellyl charm he bound them, horseflesh shivering in fearful obedience, four sets of equine eyes rolling in terror, four sets of reins tangled in his hands. "'Tis our only chance!"

Blaise of the Borderguard swore, forging a path toward the Ellyl.

Why is it, Carfax wondered, that I am so alone here? What am I doing here? He took a step forward, interposing himself between Fianna and one of the Were, raising his smoldering branch in foolish opposition. A stick, a silly weapon; a few embers and a length of wood. Still, he had done damage with it. The Were halted, dropping to all fours and showing its teeth in uncertainty.

"You were not shown us," it said in guttural common. "You are not prey."

"Yes." Gritting his teeth, Carfax swung the branch at the Were's head. "I am."

The branch connected with a horrible crunch.

There was confusion, then, in the milling darkness; shouts and curses, the high-pitched keen of injured Were. Sparks emblazoned the night and steel flashed, four-legged death dodged and darted with impossible speed, while sharp teeth tore and muzzles were stained with blood. This was battle, and did not need to be understood. Somewhere, Blaise was shouting commands, and Fianna was no longer there. Instead, there were the Were, howling with the fury of betrayal and lunging for his blood, maddened and forgetful of their greater quest. Without thinking, Carfax set his back to Hobard's as to a battle-comrade's and fought, heedless of aught else, until the branch he wielded snapped in two, and he knew his death was upon him.

"Staccian!" The Vedasian gripped his arm. "Go."

Carfax gaped at him.

"Go!" With a curse, Hobard pointed across the glade at the dim figures of mounted riders, horses pitching in barely contained terror. "Go now, and you have a chance! The horses are fresh and the Ellyl can see in the dark."

"Give me your sword!" Carfax thrust out his hand. "Don't be a fool, Vedasian. I've betrayed my loyalties. Either way, I'm a dead man. Let me buy you time. Give me your sword."

"Staccian, if I hadn't argued for killing you, we would not have wasted a day in this place." Hobard jabbed at one of the circling Were. "This is my sword, and my father's before me. I'll not surrender it to the likes of you." In the faint ember-light he gave a grim smile. One cheek was streaming with blood and he no longer looked young. "This is my death. Go."

Carfax hesitated.

"Go!"

He went, racing at full pelt across the darkened glade. Behind him, the three surviving members of Oronin's Hunters gathered, flinging themselves after him like a cast spear. They were swift and deadly, armed with fang and claw, and they could have dropped him like a yearling deer.

But Hobard the Vedasian stood between them.

Once, only once, Carfax glanced behind him, as a terrified Fianna helped him scramble onto horseback. He could scarce make out the figure of Hobard, still on his feet, staggering under the onslaught. Even as Carfax watched, the Vedasian dropped to one knee and the Were closed upon him, a roiling wave of coarse pelts.

It was the last thing he saw as they fled.

He did not know for whom to weep.

SARIKA WAS CARELESS BRAIDING HER hair.

"Let it be!" Lilias slapped the girl's hand in irritation, then sighed as the grey-blue eyes welled with tears, relenting. "Never mind, sweetling. Just don't *pull* so."

"My lady!" she breathed in gratitude. "I will be careful."

After that the girl was careful, her fingers deft and skilled. Lilias watched her in the mirror, winding her braids into an elegant coronet. Her pretty face was a study in concentration. What must it be like to have no greater concern? Even here, in the privacy of her dressing-chamber, the sounds of the siege penetrated, a distant clamor of men and arms, challenges uttered, refuted in jeers. Lilias held the fillet in which the Soumanië was set in both hands. "Sarika?"

"My lady?" The girl met her gaze in the mirror.

"Are you not frightened?"

"No, my lady." Sarika gave her a small, private smile. Around her neck, the silver links of her collar of servitude shone. "You will protect Beshtanag."

Who of us is bound here, Lilias wondered? I thought my pretty ones were bound to my service; now, it seems, I am bound to their protection. She regarded the Soumanië held in her lap. For a thousand years, waking or sleeping, it had never left her touch. Light flickered in its ruby depths, seemingly inexhaustible and endless. Her own energies, like Beshtanag's stores, were nearing their limits. It would be so simple, she thought, to put it down and walk away.

"There!" Sarika tucked a final braid into its coil and beamed.

So simple, so easy.

Instead, Lilias raised the fillet, settling it on her brow. The gold circle gleamed against her dark hair and the Soumanië was crimson against her pale skin. She looked majestic and beautiful. That had seemed important, once.

"My lady." Pietre paused in the doorway, his face frank with adoration above his collar of servitude. "My lady, the Ward Commander is asking for your aid."

A pang of alarm shot through her. "What is it, Pietre?"

He shook his head. "I do not know, my lady."

With their assistance, Lilias robed herself and hurried through the halls, passing servants and wardsmen half-awake in the grey hour that preceded dawn. Everywhere, Beshtanag was feeling the pinch of the siege. Rations had been halved and working shifts had been doubled. An unseasonal chill had caught them unprepared, with a shortage of firewood laid in against the siege and a hard rainfall rendering the fortress dank and cold. The folk of Beshtanag gazed at her with banked resentment as she made her way to her reception hall.

"My lady." Gergon bowed at her arrival.

"Is there a problem, Gergon?" Lilias asked him.

"It's the rain." He looked bleary-eyed and tired, and there were droplets of rain dampening the grey hairs of his brows and beard. "Haomane's Allies have built siege-towers to assail the wall, and moved them into position overnight. We've been firing pots of pitch to keep them at bay, but now the rain aids their cause and the wood will not ignite. They're clearing the wall by the score, and I'm losing men. If it keeps up, they'll wear us down in a day. Can you help?"

"Show me," she said.

Outside, it was hard to see in the dim light, and rain fell in cold, miserable sheets, soaking her hooded woolen cloak in a matter of minutes. Clinging to Gergon's arm, Lilias picked her way down the cobbled mountainside road. Her wall stood, a smooth, rain-darkened expanse of granite, but here and there the framework of siege-towers scaled it. There were four all told, and Men and Ellylon stood atop the rain-slick platforms, archers armed with shortbows defending ladders thrust downward into Beshtanag's fasthold. On the ground, Gergon's archers shot at them, making a poor job of it firing upward in the pouring rain.

One by one, the ladders descended, and Haomane's Allies trickled into Beshtanag. All along the wall there were skirmishes fought in the gloaming.

There, a lone Borderguardsman challenged Gergon's wardsmen.

There, a trio of Midlanders put up a stout defense.

And they fell, fell and died, but for every one that died, two more waited to follow. There were so many of them, and so few Beshtanagi. If it became a war of attrition, Beshtanag would lose.

"Short work for a dragon," Gergon said quietly, surveying the siege-towers.

"*No.*" Lilias drew back her hood, blinking against the rain. "Ready the catapults with their pitch-pots," she said grimly, watching the wall. "And your archers, Ward Commander. We do not need a *dragon* to set fire to these vile towers."

He regarded her for a moment before bowing. "As you order."

Lilias watched him stride away and vanish in the dimness, shouting orders to his wardsmen as he descended the steep incline. Around the base of the wall they obeyed, falling back to regroup around the roofed huts where the warming-fires burned and pitch was kept bubbling in cauldrons. From the fortress, Pietre picked his way out to join her, carrying a waxed parasol, which he raised over her head. Rain dripped off it like silver beads on a string.

"Are you well, my lady?" he asked anxiously. "You will take a chill in this rain!"

"Well enough." Lilias smiled humorlessly. "Let us pray a chill is the worst of it." And so saying, she pressed her fingertips to her temples, concentrating on the siege-towers and drawing on the power of the Soumanië, exerting its influence in an effort to *know* the towers and command their substance.

Wood.

Pinewood.

It was fresh-cut, hewn by the axes of Haomane's Allies. Stout trunks formed the supports and slender ones the platforms. Sap oozed from the shorn, splintered ends. At its heart, where new growth was generated, the wood was pink. Pale wood encircled it, layer upon layer, still springy with moisture. Outside was the encompassing bark, dark and tough, shaggy with flakes and boles. Rain, that should have fallen on rich mast to nurture its roots, fell instead on dead bark, rendering it sodden and slippery, penetrating layer upon layer into the green wood.

Water.

Too much water.

Drawing on the Soumanië, Lilias gathered it.

It was an intricate thing Haomane's Allies had wrought; four intricate things. Branch by branch, trunk by trunk, she desiccated the siege-towers. Heartwood died, its pink core turning grey. Outward and outward, pale layers growing ashen. A cloud of fog surrounded the towers as the bark weathered and dried, wrapping their assailants in a veiling mist. The soldiers of Aracus Altorus' army scrambled, disoriented and disorganized. Where booted feet had struggled for purchase on rain-slick wood, brittle bits of bark flaked and fell.

Holding the thought of water in her mind, Lilias *moved* it, until the air roiled with mist and there was none left in the wooden structures. Sharp, cracking sounds emanated beneath enemy boots as branches cracked and splintered under their weight.

The siege-towers had become tinderboxes.

"Now!" Gergon shouted, waving his arm.

Pitch-pots were ignited and catapults thumped, loosing volley after volley. Some missed; most found their targets. Gergon's archers followed with a volley of arrows, trailing fire from oil-soaked rags. Where it struck, the pitch spread its flames, igniting dead-dry wood. Heedless of the pouring rain, the towers burned fiercely, wooden skeletons alight. Here and there, cries of agony arose from those too slow to escape. Gouts of fire towered into the sky as Haomane's Allies retreated, abandoning their siege-engines for the forest's safety. The Beshtanagi defenders shouted at the victory.

Drained, Lilias swayed on her feet.

"This way," Pietre whispered, taking her elbow. "My lady."

Step by stumbling step, she let him lead her back up the

mountainside. In the entryway of Beshtanag fortress, another of her pretty ones was on hand to remove her sodden cloak. Radovan, who had pleased her once with his smouldering eyes, rebelling now against the force of her binding, eroding her sapped will. He was one she should have released. Too late, now, to contemplate such niceties.

"Lady." His hands were solicitous, his voice skirted courtesy. There was contempt in his hot gaze. "Yet again, you *protect* us."

Pietre stepped forward, bristling. "Leave her alone, Radovan!"

"No." She laid a hand on Pietre's chest, wearied by their antagonism. The Soumanië was like an iron weight on her brow. Her neck ached at it, and she wanted only to rest, though dawn was scarce breaking. "Let it be, Pietre."

Lilias? They come, little sister. Darkhaven's army travels the Ways.

It was the dragon's voice. Her head rose as a fierce surge of joy sent new strength through her veins. Hope, blessed and welcome. The plan was intact, and all was not lost. "Calandor?" she asked aloud, too tired to scry the Ways. "Where are they?"

ETERNITY BEFORE, ETERNITY BEHIND.

Only the *here* was real, and with each step it was elsewhere.

It was a strange thing, to travel the Ways of the Marasoumië without effort, on horseback. Ahead of him, a tunnel of red light pulsed; behind him, the same. Where he had been, he no longer *was*. Tanaros clamped his thighs hard around the black's barrel, aware of its solid warmth, its hide damp with sweat. No ordinary mount could have endured the strangeness of this journey. Here, and here, and here it placed its hooves, and there were no echoes in the Ways. There became here, here no longer was. How many leagues passed with the fall of each hoof?

He dared not think upon it.

The Way was anchored at either end. In Darkhaven, Vorax held it open; in Jakar, Ushahin Dreamspinner did the same. Lead, Tanaros thought to himself, aware of the press of Fjel at his back, a long, winding horde chary of tunnels they could not delve, of a journey they could not end, of leagues passing between each tramping stride. Of their own accord they would never have attempted such madness. It is enough, he thought. It is your task, General. Lead them, and show no fear.

So he did, step by step, concentrating on the passage, his hands steady on the reins, reassured by the scents of horseflesh and leather. Somewhere, above ground, the stars continued to reel and time passed. In the Ways, there was no time. Only one step further, leading them onward.

It had a taste, this journey, a taste of Vorax, holding open the passage. Gluttony and avarice, aye, but oh! There was the pride, the Staccian pride, that had forged its own path in making this fierce alliance. Tanaros felt the strength that poured forth from the Staccian, the courage and costly dedication, amplified by the Helm of Shadows. He could have wept, for undervaluing his cousin Vorax, whose branding echoed his own.

Staccia has weighed the cost and chosen this.

Lord Satoris had kept his bargain. For a thousand years Staccia had prospered in peace, while elsewhere the nations of Men struggled beneath the absent auspices of Haomane First-Born.

A night's passage, no more. Glancing to his left, Tanaros saw the young Midlander a half pace behind him. In the pulsing red light of the Marasoumië, Speros' face was set and eager, unaware of the dangers that threatened. He was someone's son, someone's brother. Did he even know what he risked?

The power that held open their Way shifted, growing more complex as Jakar drew nigh. There was the taste of Ushahin Dreamspinner, a subtle flavor of terrible power and

remorse, of broken things healed awry. *Oh, mother!* It grew
stronger as Darkhaven faded behind them. Somewhere, on
the desert's edge, the Marasoumië flared into life, the node-
points alive and open, rife with regret, loosing it into the
open air.

Somewhere, grey dawn beckoned.

One more step, Tanaros thought, urging the black horse,
conscious of the weight of the world above them. One
more, and one more, and we will be done. And beside him
was Speros and behind him was stalwart Hyrgolf and the
whole of the Fjel army, and ahead of him lay the end, where
all the throbbing crimson lines converged, and there amid
the rocks they would emerge, assembling in force . . .

Something happened.

It happened fast, so fast.

There was a flare of scarlet lightning, an impact like a
meteor's blow, and the Way . . . *changed.* Another sought to
travel them, one with sufficient power to compel the Marasoumië itself. Sundered from its anchors, the Way was
strained beyond bearing as the incoming presence sought to
occupy the same space as Darkhaven's army. Reality buckled, the very stone warping around them. Amid disembod-
ied cries of dismay, Tanaros fought for control of his
now-terrified mount. With a sound like a taut wire snapping,
Ushahin Dreamspinner's presence vanished and the Way
ahead was severed and gone. There was only *here,* and another inhabited it.

There, stark in the wash of ruddy light, was Malthus the
Counselor, with two figures cast in shadow behind him.

Tanaros gaped at him, uncomprehending.

For an instant, the wizard's astonishment was equal to his
own.

And then an awful knowledge dawned in Malthus' eyes,
quicker to grasp what was happening. He was Haomane's
weapon, Shaped for the purpose of defeating Satoris himself, and the might he veiled from mortal sight was formi-

dable indeed. In the dark of underearth, there was a brightness upon him it hurt to behold. The wizard's lips began
working, speaking a spell. His beard trailed into his
scholar's robes, and on his breast the Soumanië, drawing on
Haomane's power, the power of the Souma. Even Sundered,
it was enough to command the Ways.

"Turn back!" Tanaros wrenched at the reins left-handed,
shouting over his shoulder. "Turn back!"

It was too late. Even as his black mount squealed in fear
and ducked its head, sunfishing violently, the Way was collapsing. Terror erupted on every side. Tanaros swore, lurching in the saddle and fighting the black. Behind him there
was only chaos as the Fjel broke ranks, milling in an awful
press. Speros of Haimhault was caught in the crush, his
mount borne along by terrified Fjel.

"General!" Hyrgolf's roar rose above the fray. "Your orders!"

Somewhere, in Darkhaven, Vorax kept a thin, desperate
thread of the Way open to retreat, pitting the Helm of Shadows against the awful might of Malthus. Tanaros could feel
it, taste it. The Ways shuddered and strained beneath their
struggle, threatening to splinter into an infinity of passages,
but there was still a chance, an alley. "Retreat!" he shouted,
willing the Fjel to hear him. "Field marshal, *retreat!*"

And then the black horse convulsed beneath him, and
Tanaros was flung from the saddle. The stony ground
rushed up to meet him, striking hard. He covered his head,
fearful of stamping hooves. Knowing that the Ways could
not destroy him, Tanaros curled around his aching, Souma-
branded heart and held himself *here,* knowing there was
naught else he could do. Somewhere, Hyrgolf was roaring,
trying to organize his troops, trying to follow the thin thread
of hope back to Darkhaven and safety even as the Ways collapsed, flinging them backward in time, sundering their
company.

A good general protects his troops.

Everything seemed very quiet, the shouting receding into echoless silence as Tanaros climbed to his feet to face the Counselor, and drew the black sword. "Malthus," he said, testing the weight of his sword, that was quenched in a Shaper's blood. His circumscribed heart was unexpectedly light. "Your path ends here."

"Dani," Malthus said, ignoring him. "Trust me."

It was a boy who stepped forth from the Counselor's fearsome shadow and nodded; a boy, dark-skinned and unobtrusive, accompanied by a wary protector. There was a clay vial at his throat, tied by a crude thong. With a shock, Tanaros recognized it, knew what it must hold. Here, then, was the true enemy, the one who mattered. Here was the Bearer of prophecy, who carried the Water of Life, who could extinguish the marrow-fire itself. And it was a boy, a mere boy, a pawn in Haomane's game. Their gazes met, and the boy's was questioning, uncertain.

"No," Tanaros whispered. "*Listen . . .* "

Malthus the Counselor lifted his staff, and light shone between his fingers.

Red light pulsed and the Ways opened.

Light flexed, coruscating.

TWENTY-TWO

IT HAPPENED AS SHE CROSSED the threshold of her reception hall.

One moment she was walking, grateful for Pietre at her elbow, concentrating on keeping her head proudly erect for the watching servants. Relief at the dragon's news made it easier. It didn't matter, now, that the circlet felt too tight around her brow, that the Soumanië lay hot against her flesh, that an unnatural awareness stirred at the base of her skull—those were the harbingers of salvation, signs that the Ways had been opened. Tired as she was, Lilias bore them with gladness.

Between one step and the next, everything changed.

She had been a child, once; a mortal child playing children's games of hide-and-chase in her father's estate in Pelmar. Her younger brother had darted from the ice-house, slamming the heavy stone door in her face. A thousand years later she remembered it; the sound like a thunderclap, the unexpected impact and sudden darkness, and how the air was too tight to breathe.

It was like that, only worse, a hundred times worse. A red light burst behind her eyes as a Way was slammed closed, exploding open elsewhere, splintering into a myriad dwindling passages. By the stinging of her palms, she understood that she had fallen onto the flagstones. Her eyes were open and blind. Somewhere, Pietre was tugging at her arm, begging her to get up. There were tears in his voice. Her brother Tomik had sounded that way, once, when he begged her to abandon the Soumanië after she had descended Beshtanag Mountain to show him. "It's a dragon's gift, Lilias! Put it back!"

Lilias.

"Calandor," she whispered.

I am sorry.

With an effort she dragged herself to kneel in a puddle of her velvet robes, running her hands blindly over her face. There were murmurs all around; of anxiety, of sympathy, of mutiny. None of them mattered. Her little brother was centuries in the grave and her choice had been made a long time ago. "Calandor, what happened in the Marasoumië?"

Malthus.

Lilias blinked. Her vision was clearing. Sarika's face swam before her gaze, tear-stained as she knelt before her mistress, fumbling with a goblet of mulled wine as she sought to press it into her mistress' hands. This was her home, after all. For a thousand years, Beshtanag had been hers. "Calandor." Lilias swallowed, tasting fear. "Is Satoris' army coming?"

No.

SOMEWHERE IN THE NIGHT IT had ceased to matter that they had not begun their journey as comrades. In the head-long flight through the forest there were neither prisoners nor captors, only allies seeking a common cause: Survival.

Hobard had given his life for them. For *him,* Carfax thought, numb and awed. Over and over he saw it; the Vedasian knight going down, the dark wave of fur closing over him. It had bought them time. Not much, but enough. By the time the Were pursued, they were in flight.

Trees, trees and more trees; an endless labyrinth of forest, dampened by skeins of rain. A storm broke, driving their flight with increasing urgency. It lashed their faces, rendering them water-blind. Trunks loomed out of the darkness and branches reached, slashing at unprotected skin, lashing the horses' flanks. They shouldn't have been able to outrun the Were, if not for the Ellyl.

Peldras drew deep on the ancient lore of Haomane's Children, using the Shaper's Gifts to master the horses' fear, mastering all their fear. Such was the skill of the Rivenlost, first among the Lesser Shapers. It lent courage to their hearts, speed to their mounts' heels. Onward and onward they followed him, a slender figure on horseback, lit with a faint silvery luminosity, forging a path through the impossible tangle.

Pursuit came, of course; the Were bounding at their sides, leaping and snapping. Not as many, no; only three. A deadly three. And they came with muzzles red with blood, howling for their slain Brethren, a keening sorrow tinged with the rage of betrayal.

Carfax, unarmed, could only follow blindly in the Ellyl's wake, trying to protect Fianna with the simple bulk of his presence, turning his mount broadside and flailing in the saddle in a vain effort to fend off their attackers. It was Blaise who defended them, who brought up the rear; Blaise of the Borderguard. And he fought with a deadly, tireless efficiency, whirling time and time again to face the onslaught, his sodden hair lashing his cheeks. There was bitterness there, and fury; oh, yes! He was the appointed Protector of Malthus' Company, now shattered. If he had to spend his last breath protecting what remained of it, he would do it. Again and again his sword rose and fell, rain-washed and running with dark fluids, until the clouds broke and the grey light of dawn showed it ruddy, and the four of them alive.

When had Blaise slain the last of the Were?

Carfax could not say. Only that dawn had found them alone.

He sat quiet in the saddle, dripping, marveling at the steady throb of blood in his veins, at his hands on the reins, only his knuckles scratched, listening to their quarreling voices mingle with the rising birdsong while his exhausted mount hung its head low, too weary to lip at the undergrowth.

"But where should we *go?*" Fianna's voice, tired and plaintive. "Blaise?"

"Beshtanag . . . Jakar . . ." The Borderguardsman gave a grim smile. "I cannot guess, Lady Archer. You heard him as well as I did, and as poorly. Peldras?"

Troubled, the Ellyl shook his head. "What I can do, I have done. The ways of the Counselor are the ways of Haomane, cousin, and even I cannot guess at them. It is for you to decide."

"So be it." Blaise drew a harsh breath, laying his sword across his pommel. Red blood dripped from its tip onto the forest floor. "We have lost Malthus—and the Bearer. The Company is broken, and we must go where we will best serve. Staccian?"

Startled, Carfax lifted his head. "My lord?" The words came unbidden.

"Where should we go?"

He averted his face from the Borderguardsman's steady gaze, which said all his words did not. Hobard had given his life. A debt was owed. On a nearby tree a lone raven sat, cocking its head. Carfax swallowed hard and looked back at Blaise. "Beshtanag is a trap."

Was that his voice that had spoken? The words sounded so flat, lacking emotion, nothing to do with his tongue, thick in his mouth. But Blaise Caveros only nodded, as if hearing confirmation of a long-held suspicion.

"Do we have time to warn them?"

"I . . . don't know." Carfax said the words and something in him eased as he met the Borderguardsman's level gaze. "It may be. I don't know."

Blaise nodded again, surveying the remnants of their Company. Fianna straightened in the saddle, one hand reaching to check for Oronin's Bow and the Arrow of Fire. "So be it, then," he said. "To Beshtanag."

On a nearby tree, a raven took wing.

So be it, Carfax thought.

He felt numb. Better to die with honor than to live without it. It was too late, now. It was done. In the space of a few heartbeats, in a few spoken words, he had irrevocably betrayed his oath of loyalty. The words he had exchanged with Blaise long ago rang in his memory. If he could have smiled, he would have, but the corners of his mouth refused to lift. He wanted to weep instead.

There was only one end awaiting him.

Why do you smile, Staccian?

To make a friend of death.

*   *   *

IT WAS A COLD DAWN over the plains of Rukhar.

Ushahin lay curled among the rocks where he had dragged himself, his ill-knit bones aching and his teeth chattering. Behind him, in the cavern of the Marasoumië, the node-lights were as dead and grey as yesterday's ashes. Unable to raise his head, he stared at the pocked face of a sandstone boulder until the rising light made his head ache beyond bearing and he closed his eyes.

He had failed to hold the Way open.

Footsteps sounded, and he squinted through swollen lids. A pair of booted feet came into view; Rukhari work, with soft leather soles and embroidered laces. The toe of one boot prodded his ribs. Childhood memories, half-forgotten, returned in a flood and filled his mouth with a bitter taste.

"Dream-stalker." Above him was Makneen, the Rukhari commander. The rising sun silhouetted his head. "Where is your army?"

"Gone," Ushahin croaked, squinting upward and wincing at the brightness.

The Rukhari nodded in understanding. Somewhere, near, horses stamped and men muttered in their own tongue. Yesterday, they had feared him. Today, they wanted to see him dead. Makneen's hand shifted to the hilt of his curved sword, wrapped in bright copper wire. "So our bargain is broken."

"No." He spat, clearing his mouth of bile. "Wait . . ."

"It is broken." Watching him like a wary hawk, the Rukhari raised one hand, then turned away, speaking over his shoulder with careless aplomb. "Tell the Glutton we kept faith. It is you who failed. Now, we go."

They did, even as he struggled to sit upright, lifting the aching burden of his head. Horseflesh surged on either side of him, urged on with jeering cries. Hooves pounded, sending chips of sandstone flying. Ushahin lifted a hand to shield his face from laceration. Whatever Vorax had promised them, it was all gone, all lost. And there was no satisfaction, none at all, in knowing he had been right.

This was Malthus' doing.

He had felt it, had known the instant the Counselor had entered the Ways, seizing control of the Marasoumië and wresting it to his own ends, severing all of Ushahin's influence in one surge of the Soumanië. And he had known, in that instant, utter helplessness.

It should not have happened.

Something had gone terribly wrong.

Weary and defeated, Ushahin buried his face in his hands, taking solace in the familiar darkness, the misshapen bones beneath his fingertips. *My Lord,* he thought, *I have failed you!* In a moment, in a few moments, he would make the effort that was needful, freeing his mind from the bonds of what Men called sanity to sift through their dreams. Now—

Now was the sound of claws on sandstone.

Seated on barren rock, Ushahin lifted his weary head from his sheltering hands. A grey shadow shifted on the rocks, poking his head into view, muzzle twitching. He was young, this one, sent to bear an unwelcome message. Aching and bone-weary as he was, Ushahin observed the old courtesies, asking in his visitor's tongue, "How fares Oronin's Hunt?"

The young Were howled.

It bounded, clearing the ridge with a single leap to land before him. There was pain in its amber eyes, luminous in the sunlight. One forelimb lashed out, and Ushahin reeled backward as taloned claws raked his misshapen cheek. Groping blindly for power, he drew on the brand that circumscribed his heart, remembering Godslayer and the marrow-fire, and his Lord's long torment. "*Enough!*" he cried harshly, feeling Lord Satoris' strength in his bones. "What of your quest?"

The Were cowered, ears flat against its skull. "Eight," it whimpered in angry protest. "There were eight!"

Eight?

"No," Ushahin whispered. "Malthus' Company . . . Malthus' Company numbered seven."

Baring teeth, the young Brother showed him, putting the pictures in his mind, as the Were had done since Oronin Shaped them. There were eight, and the eighth a Staccian, tall and stricken-faced, a burning brand in his hands. A blow struck when the Brethren expected it not. Sparks against the darkness. A branch, a twig to turn a flood.

"Why?" Ushahin groped for a thread of mortal thought. *"Why?"*

"We have *done*." Emboldened, the young Were reared on its haunches, spat its words, red tongue working in its muzzle. "This says the Grey Dam! No more debts, no one's son. There were eight! We will Hunt for us, only, and fight no more!"

Done.

A slash of talons, a bounding leap. Claws scrabbled on sandstone, and the Were was gone, leaving Ushahin bereft, aching in the cold light of dawn, at last and truly alone.

"Mother." He whispered the word, remembering her scent, her sharp, oily musk. How she let him seek comfort in her form, burying his aching, broken face in her fur. How her hackles raised at any threat, menacing all enemies and affording him safety, a safety he had never known. He had healed in her shadow.

The Grey Dam is dead, the Grey Dam lives.

Not his.

His shoulders shook as he wept. The Ellylon could only weep for the sorrows of others, but Ushahin the Misbegotten was the child of three races and none, and he wept for his own bereavement.

When he was done he gathered himself and stood, and began to make his long way toward Darkhaven, to the only home left to him.

* * *

THERE HAD BEEN A CRY, filled with rage and defeat, when the path was severed. A single cry, echoing in Vorax's head, filling his skull like a sounding drum. Through the Helm of Shadows he heard it, filled with an eternity of anguish.

Ah, my Lord Satoris, he thought, forgive us!

It anchored him, that cry, kept his feet solid on the rocky floor of the cavern. It gave him a strength he had not known he possessed and kept him tethered to the Marasoumië. He felt it happen, all of it, as Malthus wielded the Soumanië and wrested control of the Ways from them. And there was only one thing he could do.

Through the eyeslits of the Helm, the node-lights twitched in fitful pain and he saw what he could not see with his naked eyes, the truth no one dared voice. The whole, vast network was dying, aeon by aeon, inch by inch. The Sundering of the world was the slow death of the Marasoumië. Not now, not yet, but over ages, it would happen.

Vorax could not prevent it, any more than he could prevent Malthus from seizing control of the Ways, from closing their egress and sending the army of Darkhaven into flailing chaos. All he could do was hold open his end of the path.

He did.

And he gathered them, scattered like wind-blown leaves through the Ways. It was not his strength, this kind of work, but he made it so. He was one of the Three, and he had sworn to protect his Lord's fortress. What did it matter that his belly rumbled, that the long hours ground him to the bone? He was Vorax of Staccia, he was a colossus. A battle may be lost, but not the war, no. Not on his watch. The army of Darkhaven would endure to fight another day. Like a beacon of darkness, he anchored their retreat, bringing them home.

They surged into the Chamber of the Marasoumië—Fjel, thousand upon thousand of them, stumbling and disoriented, filled with battle-fury and helpless terror. Elsewhere, a struggle continued and he felt the Ways flex and twist under a Soumanië's influence. Malthus remained at large. It didn't matter, that. Only this, only securing the retreat for the tens of thousands of Fjel. Node-points flickered out of his control, slipping from his grasp. It didn't matter. He was the anchor. Wrestling with the portal, he held it open, seeing through the Helm's eyes the fearful incomprehension of the Fjel. So many! It had been easier with Ushahin anchoring the other end.

On and on it went, Fjel streaming past him, until he saw the last, the hulking Tungskulder who was Tanaros' field marshal, who had brought them home to Darkhaven intact. And in Hyrgolf's countenance lay not incomprehension, but a commander's sorrowful understanding of defeat. No Fjel tramped behind him. He was the last.

With relief, Vorax relinquished the last vestiges of his hold and let the Way close. His thick fingers shook with exhaustion as he lifted the Helm from his head, feeling it like an ache between his palms. He needed sleep, needed sustenance—needed to pour an ocean of ale down his gullet, to cram himself full of roasted fowl, slabs of mutton, crackling pork, of handfuls of bread torn from the loaf and stuffed into his mouth, of glazed carrots and sweet crisp peas, of baked tubers and honeyed pastries, of puddings and confits and pears, of anything that would fill the terrible void inside him where Satoris' cry still echoed.

"Marshal Hyrgolf." Was that his voice, that frail husk? He cleared his throat, making the sound resonate in the depths of his barrel chest. "Report."

"We failed," the Fjel rumbled. "Malthus closed the Way."

Vorax nodded. It was what he had known, no more and no less. He wished there was someone else to bear the details of it to Lord Satoris. "And General Tanaros?"

The Fjeltroll shook his massive head. "He stayed to safeguard our retreat from the Counselor. Neheris spare him and grant him a safe path homeward."

Ah, cousin! Vorax spared a pitying thought for him, and another for himself. He was weary to the bone, and starved lean. Sustenance and bed, bed and sustenance. But there would be no rest for him, not this day. Lord Satoris would demand a full accounting, and he was owed it; pray that he did not lash out in rage. Their plans were in ruins, the Three had been riven. Malthus seizing control of the Marasoumië, and Tanaros lost in the Ways, with no telling whether either lived or died, and the Dreamspinner stranded in Rukhar. A vile day, this, and vilest of all for the Sorceress of the East. Beshtanag would pay the price of this day's failure.

At least the army had survived it intact, and there had been no Staccian lives at stake. He ran a practiced eye over the milling ranks of Fjel and frowned, remembering how the army had scattered like wind-blown leaves throughout the Ways, how he had tried to gather them all.

Something was wrong.

Vorax's frown deepened. "Where's the Midlander?"

"WHERE ARE WE?" THERE HAD been a cavern, and an old man with a staff; a terrified crush of flesh. That was when the world had gone away, carried by the General's shouting voice. He remembered the rushing force, the terrible sense of dislocation, and then the fearsome impact. Blinded by the throbbing Marasoumië, jostled and swept away, thrown down and unhorsed, Speros of Haimhault had landed . . . somewhere. He found his feet and staggered, flinging out both arms, hearing his own voice rise in sharp demand. *"Where are we?"*

"Underearth, boss," a Fjel voice rumbled.

There was an arm thrust beneath his own, offering support. Speros grabbed at it, feeling it rocklike beneath bristling hide, as he swayed on his feet. "Where?"

"Don't know."

"Where's the General?"

"Don't know!"

"All right, be quiet." Speros squinted, trying to clear his gaze. They were in a vast space. He could tell that much by the echoes of their voices. Somewhere, water was dripping. Drop by drop, slow and steady, heavy as a falling stone. The mere scent of it made him ache to taste it. "How deep?"

There was a shuffling of horny feet. "Deep," one of the Fjel offered.

It was a pool. Blinking hard, he could see it. A pool of water, deep below the earth. And above it—oh, so far above it!—was open sky. It must be, for there was blue reflected in its depths. Kneeling over it, he made out a dim reflection of his own face; pale, with dilated eyes. "Water," he murmured, dipping a cupped hand into the pool.

The water didn't even ripple. As if he had grasped an ingot of solid lead, his weighted hand sank, tipping him forward. He gasped, his lips breaking the surface of that unnatural water, and he understood death had found him all unlooked-for. How stupid, he thought, trying in vain to draw back from the pool.

One breath and his lungs would fill.

A wet death on dry land.

Then, pressure; a coarse, taloned hand tangled in his hair, yanking his head back and away from the deadly pool. He came up sputtering, his neck wrenched, mouth heavy with water.

"Careful, boss."

They were Gulnagel Fjel; lowlanders, the swift runners, with their grey-brown hides, lean haunches and yellowing talons. They could take down a deer at a dead run, leaping from hill to hill. There were four, and they watched him. Having saved his life, they waited for guidance. Among the races of Lesser Shapers, only Men and Ellylon had received Haomane's Gift, the gift of thought. Speros crouched by the pool, fervently wiping his numb lips, careful to make sure that not a single drop got into his mouth. Thirsting or not, what it might do inside him, he didn't dare guess. One thing was sure, he wouldn't touch that water again.

"All right." He stared at the reflected blue in its depths, then craned his head, squinting. It hurt to look at the sky, even a tiny disk of it. The shaft stretched above him to dizzying heights, and at the top of it lay open skies and freedom. "Up. We need to go up."

It was a despairing thought, here at the bottom of the world. To his surprise, one of the Gulnagel grinned and flexed his yellow talons.

"Not a problem, boss," he said cheerfully. "Up it is."

EVERYWHERE.

Nowhere.

It was dark where he was, and he was not dead. At least he didn't think so. In the darkness, Tanaros flexed his hands. He had hands; he felt them. The fingers of his right hand closed around something hard.

A sword-hilt, he thought.

And, I am lost in the Marasoumië.

What happened to people who got lost in the Ways? Sometimes the Ways spat them out, in some unknowable location, deep beneath the earth. Sometimes the Ways did not. And then they died, of course.

Unless they were immortal.

It was Malthus' doing, may he be cursed with the same fate. In the darkness, Tanaros gave a bitter smile. It had been a near thing at the end. He had hesitated when he saw the boy. He shouldn't have done that. It had given the Counselor time, an instant's time to invoke the Marasoumië's power and send them hurtling away, the boy and his protector, flinging them desperately across the warp and weft of the Ways, enfolded in his enchantments.

A pity, that. But it was all, nearly all, the old wizard had left in him. Tanaros *had* struck, then; had let the rage course

through his veins, had swung his sword with all his might at
his enemy's neck. Ah, it had felt good! The black blade had
bitten deep into the wood of the wizard's staff when
Malthus had parried; bitten deep and stuck fast in the spell-
bound wood.

He had welcomed the struggle, moving in close to see the
fear in the other's eyes, wondering, *do you bleed, old one?
Of what did Haomane Shape you? Do you breathe, does the
blood course warm in your veins? Haomane's Weapon, with
my blade so near your throat, do you understand the
fragility of your flesh?*

And then the Soumanië had flashed, one last time.

The Counselor, it seemed, did not welcome death.

It had cast them both into the oblivion of the Ways. That
was his consolation. He had felt it, sensed Malthus spinning
adrift, unrooted. Tanaros flexed his hand again, feeling the
sword-hilt against his palm, and thought, *I am not ready to
die either.*

There was light, somewhere; a ruddy light, pulsing. So it
must seem to a babe in the womb, afloat in blood and darkness. He remembered a birth, his son's birth, the babe he
thought his son. How Calista had cried aloud in her travail,
her hands closing on his with crushing force as she had ex-
pelled the child.

He had been proud, then, terrified and proud. Awe. That
was the word. It had filled him with awe, that she would endure this thing; that she could produce such a thing from the
depths of her mortal flesh. Life, new life. An infant wholly
formed, perfect in every detail, thrust squalling into the
light of day. He had cradled the babe, cupping the still-soft
skull in his hands, his capable hands, marveling at the
shrunken face, the closed eyes. There had been no telling,
then, that the eyes behind those rounded lids were blue,
blue as a cloudless sky. No telling that the downy hair plastered slick and dark with birthing was the color of ruddy
gold.

Oh, my son!

In the darkness, Tanaros groaned. It bit deep, the old betrayal, as deep as his black blade. He remembered the first time he had seen Calista. She had graced Roscus' court with her fresh-faced beauty, her sparkling wit. Their courtship had been filled with passionate banter. Who now would believe Tanaros Blacksword capable of such a thing? Yet he had been, once. He had shouted for joy the day she accepted his marriage proposal. And he had loved her with all the ardor in his heart; as a lover, as a husband, as the father of the child she bore. How had she dared to look at him so? Hollow-eyed and weary, with that deep contentment. Her head on the pillow, the hair arrayed about her shoulders, watching him hold another man's babe.

Once, he had been born again in hatred.

Why not twice?

A node-point was near, very near. Such was the light he perceived behind his lids, the beating red light. His circumscribed heart thumped, responding to its erratic pulse. If he could reach it . . . one, just one. If he could birth himself into the Marasoumië, he would be alive in the world. And where there was one, there was another, in a trail that led him all the way to Darkhaven.

Home.

Tanaros *reached*.

TWENTY-THREE

Beshtanag endured, half-starved and weary.

From her balcony, Lilias watched her enemies, wondering if they knew. Would it matter? Would they act differently? She thought not. They had never known it for a trap.

They went about the siege as they had begun it, with determined patience. By late afternoon the skies had cleared,
though rain still dripped from the pines. Here and there
Aracus Altorus strode, a tiny figure, recognizable by his
hair. He wasted no time, ordering construction to begin
anew on their siege-engines.

Three days.

That was how long they would have had to wait, if Darkhaven's army had arrived at Jakar as planned. Even now, the
Fjeltroll would be on the march, trampling the undergrowth
beneath their broad feet, commanded by General Tanaros.

Only they were not coming, would never arrive. Lilias
knew. She had gone, alone, to the cavern of the Marasoumië, deep beneath Beshtanag. Had gone and stood, wondering if she dared to flee. The node-lights flickered
erratically. Something was wrong, very wrong, in the Ways.

Probing, she had found it. There were not one, but two
souls trapped within the Marasoumië; no mere mortals, but
beings of power, under whose influence the Ways buckled
and flexed. One bore a power equal to her own, a very
Soumanië, and only the complete exhaustion of his energies
kept him from wielding it. The other was one of the
Branded, and the mark of Godslayer and a Shaper's power
upon his flesh kept the Marasoumië from devouring him
entire. For the rest, it was sheer stubbornness that kept him
alive, forcing the Ways to bend to his will.

Either way, it was unsafe to enter.

She had stared at the node-point for a long time. Once,
she might have dared it, when she was young enough to be
fearless in her abilities. Not now, when she had spent so
much of herself, pouring it into the stone and wood of this
place. In the end, did it matter? Beshtanag was her home.
She didn't know where she would go if she fled it.

So she had stayed.

A hunting-party emerged from the fringe of the forest,
whooping in triumph. They carried long poles over their
shoulders, a pair of deer between them. Regent Martinek's

men, clad in his leather armor overlaid with steel rings. Lilias ground her teeth. Already, they had scoured her smallholders' estates, laying claim to their flocks. Where the armies of Men were camped, the ground was strewn with mutton-bones. Now, they took the bounty of the forest itself while her people went hungry.

"My lady."

It was Gergon, his helmet under his arm. He looked unspeakably tired.

"Ward Commander." Lilias made room for him upon the balcony. "What is it?"

"It is said . . . " He paused, surveying Haomane's Allies. In the waning sunlight, the Ellyl herald was stepping forth to give his third utterance of the day, demanding in a clarion voice the surrender of the Lady Cerelinde. Gergon met her gaze, his features blunt and honest. "You were heard, in the reception hall, where you took ill, my lady. It is said Darkhaven's army is not coming. Is it true?"

Lilias did not answer, watching the Ellyl herald. How could armor shine thusly? It flamed in the slanted rays of sunlight as he turned on his heel, marching back to rejoin the Rivenlost. They held themselves apart from the armies of Men, from the Pelmaran encampment and their feast of bones. Only Aracus Altorus strode between them, stitching together their alliance, Haomane's Children and Arahila's, keeping them united for the sake of the woman he loved; the woman he believed she held captive.

"Is it true?" Gergon's voice was soft and insistent.

What folly, what amazing folly! To think that they had come so far and fought so hard for naught. "No," she said. "It is a lie."

Her Ward Commander gave a sigh from the depths of his being. "Shapers be blessed! Where are they, my lady? How long will it be?"

She met his eyes unflinching. "Three days. They travel from Jakar."

Gergon gave a grim nod and bowed to her. "Then we will hold."

"Good." Lilias bit her lip and swallowed hard. The lie, spoken, seemed to lodge in her throat. And yet what else was there to do? Haomane's Allies might grant merciful terms if she surrendered, but they would take no pity on her. Beshtanag would be dismantled, the Soumanië stripped from her. And Calandor . . . they would slay him if they could. She wanted to weep; for herself, for Gergon, for all of Beshtanag. But it would not do to let Gergon see her weak. Gathering her skirts, Lilias brushed past him. "Carry on, commander."

In her quarters, Sarika startled to her feet, but she shook her head at the girl. Let her get some rest. All her people were hollow-eyed for lack of sleep and hunger. Haomane's Allies had come early; the siege had already endured longer than anticipated. Unattended, Lilias made her way through the fortress, the lie churning in her belly. It would give them hope, for a little while. How long, she could not say.

Her feet trod a familiar path along the stone hallways of Beshtanag, taking her to the tiny egress hidden at the rear of the fortress. For once, it was unguarded; every man who could be spared was on the siege-lines. This too did not matter. No one went this way save her except under duress. Lilias slipped through the door and started up the winding path, heedful of sharp rocks beneath her slippers. After the claustrophobic atmosphere of the fortress, it was good to be outdoors.

The mountain stretched down below her, ringed around with the great wall she had raised. She allowed herself a moment to contemplate it with satisfaction. Even viewed from above, it was a formidable obstacle and, for all their numbers, Haomane's Allies had not breached it yet.

They were trying, though. There, on the eastern side, a group of Altorus' Borderguardsmen had built a roaring fire, seeking to weaken the bindings that held the granite together. Lilias paused, frowning down at them. Tiny figures clustered around a mighty log, a battering ram with its prow sheathed in bronze. Closing her eyes, she probed the section of wall they assailed.

There . . . yes, there. A breach-point, where the smooth stone, annealed by fire, threatened to crack, remembering the composite rocks from which it had been rendered. Faint lines showed on its surface. Drawing on the Soumanië, she Shaped it, restoring it to a seamless whole.

The effort left her weak.

It didn't matter. At the top of the mountain, Calandor was waiting. Gorse bushes caught at her skirts, dragging her back. Lilias tore free, forcing her way upward. Step by weary step, she made her way to the crest of Beshtanag Mountain. When she reached the mouth of the cavern, she was breathless.

He was there, waiting.

"You knew," she panted, the tears coming unbidden. "You *knew!*"

For a long time, the dragon was silent; then he moved, one clawed foot scraping the cavern floor as his mighty head lowered until one green-gold eye was level with hers. "No, Liliasss." A deep voice, laden with sorrow and sulfur fumes. "Only what mussst be. Not when, nor how."

"Why?" Her voice cracked. "*Why?*"

He let her strike him then, her soft fists thudding against his bronze-plated cheeks and jaw. His sinuous neck bent to gather her in a protective coil. "All things musst be as they mussst, little sssisster," Calandor murmured, his voice rumbling in his furnace-chest beneath her ear. "All things."

Defeated, she slumped against him. "Must it be *now?*"

The dragon moved, his vanes stirring. "Is it your wish that I carry you, Liliasss? Far away? To Sstaccia, with itss ice and sssnow?"

Uncertain, she drew back. "Is there such a place, where no one could find us?"

"Yesss." The dragon's eyes glowed with regret. "And no. For a time, Liliasss. Only that. In the end, they will always find usss. Is it your wish?"

Walking away, she stood with her back to him, gazing down the mountain. There were dozens of campfires burning at its base. The evening breeze carried the faint strains of revelry and shouting. Inside the wall, Gergon's warders paced the perimeter, or hunkered around braziers and gnawed half-rations, keeping a watchful eye out for assaults. How many, she wondered, would live to see the end of this? They were her people. For generation upon generation, Lilias had bound them to her service. Her actions had brought this fate upon them. It was too late to undo what was done, and yet, if she could do nothing else, at least she would not abandon them.

She would stand or fall with Beshtanag.

It was not much, but it was all she had to offer.

"No," she said. "I will stay."

EVEN FOR THE GULNAGEL, IT was difficult.

Throughout the day, Speros watched them with wide-eyed astonishment. Fjel were meant to delve, not to climb.

Still, they managed it. They worked in shifts, shucking the straps of leather armor that held their weapons. One would crouch low beside the pool, bending his back to make a broad surface, boosting up his fellow. And up the other would go, plunging his yellowed talons into the smooth surface of the rocky cistern, forging hand- and footholds by dint of brute strength, stone giving way beneath their blows.

None of them could last more than a few minutes, that was the problem. Their own body weight was too great, threatening to crack their talons the longer they hung suspended. It was Speros who got them to form the base of a pyramid around the pool, arms outstretched to catch their fellows as they made the precarious descent. And they did it. Working without complaint, hour upon hour, they scaled the cistern.

Foot by torturous foot, the Gulnagel forged a ladder.

"Oof!" The last volunteer descended, helped onto solid ground amid the jests of his companions. He rested his hands on his bulging thighs, fighting to catch his breath. "Reckon that's about done it, boss," he said cheerfully, regaining his voice. "Few feet from the lip, any mind. You want to go on up?"

Grabbing a handy shoulder, Speros leaned over the deadly pool and craned his neck, gazing upward. Faint stars twinkled in the distant circle of sky, emerging on a background of twilight. "What's up top?"

Exchanging glances, the Gulnagel shrugged.

"Hot," one said helpfully. "Gets hotter the higher you go."

"Nothing living, don't think," another added. "Quiet, if it is."

"All right." Speros gnawed at thumbnail, thinking. The Gulnagel waited patiently and watched him. In General Tanaros' absence, he was their commander; he was one of Arahila's Children, endowed with Haomane's Gift. A piece of irony, that. He'd been raised on tales of Fjel horrors. In Haimhault, parents threatened to feed misbehaving children to the Fjeltroll; at least his own Ma had done, often enough. Now here he was, with four Fjel patiently awaiting his orders. Well, he'd cast his lot, and he had to live with it. Still, it wasn't so bad, was it? Few mortal men could say they'd had Fjeltroll jump at their command. "Yes, let's try it. Better by night than by day, when we'd be sitting targets emerging. Odrald, will you take the lead?"

"Aye, boss!" The smallest of the Fjel saluted him.

"Good." Speros flexed his muscles, anticipating the climb. "You, give me a boost. The rest of you, follow me."

* * *

HE DID NOT SPEAK AFTER he summoned her, not for a long time.

Cerelinde sat in the chair he provided, staring with a fixed gaze at the throbbing image of Godslayer. How could something immersed in the marrow-fire itself retain such a crimson glow? It seemed impossible.

He stalked the outskirts of the chamber.

He was angry, no, he was furious. She felt it on her skin, tasted it in her mouth. A prickling like needles, like an impending storm. A taste of copper, only *sweet*.

"You know what has happened." His voice was a husk, but resonant.

"No." She shook her head, willing her denial to be true. It was true, for the most part. A plan had been made; a plan had failed. That much she knew, and no more. The Fjeltroll had returned. And when she spoke of Tanaros, her maidservant Meara had wailed and fled the room. "I know nothing, Lord Satoris."

"*Malthus was waiting!*"

Unseen rafters rattled at the Shaper's raised voice. Cerelinde winced, and laced her hands together. The light of the marrow-fire cast her raised knuckles in sharp shadow. "Does his Lordship hold me to blame?"

There was a sigh then.

It came from every corner of the room, and it came from him; *him*. And he was before her, then, stooping as a thundercloud might stoop, humbling himself in front of her. The swell of his shoulders blotted out the marrow-fire. His eyes, crimson as Godslayer's beating heart. "No, Cerelinde. I do not blame the blameless. That is my Elder Brother's job."

She shrank back as far as the chair would allow. At close range, the odor was overwhelming; a sweet charnel reek, burned flesh and an undertone of rotting vegetation. It stirred terror in her; mindless terror, and something else, a dark and awful quickening. Trapped and fearful, she lashed out with words. "Your jealousy speaks, Sunderer! What do you *want* of me?"

The Shaper laughed.

It was a hollow sound, filled with bitterness and despair. He bent his head, mighty hands lifting to cover his face. A Shaper's hands, immaculately articulated, for all they were burned black as pitch by Haomane's Wrath. His fingertips dug into the flesh of his brow, pitting the blackened skin.

Somehow, that was the most terrible thing of all.

"Want?" His head snapped upright, crimson eyes glaring between his fingers. "Oh, I *want,* Haomane's Child! I want my innocence back, and the happy, happy ignorance that has served your race for so long! I want my Gift back! I want to see my sister Arahila's smile! I want to see my brother Haomane grovel, and his Wise Counselor's head on a pike!"

"I didn't—" she breathed.

"Who are you to ask me what I want?"

The Shaper's words ricocheted and echoed in the cavern. The marrow-fire surged in answer, a fierce blue-white light, casting shadows knife-edged and blinding. Cerelinde held herself taut, frozen with terror, fighting the awful tendrils of pity that probed at her heart. "Forgive me," she said softly. "My Lord Satoris."

He rose and turned away from her.

The marrow-fire dwindled. The Shaper's massive shoulders twitched; or was it a trick of the flickering shadows? "You did not know." His voice was rough-edged, pitched to an ordinary tone. "Cerelinde."

She fought back another wave of pity. "I have not lied to you, my Lord."

"No." Again he sighed, filling the chamber, and turned to face her. "Do not take too much hope from this, little Ellyl. What has happened, has happened. If my plans have gone awry, no less have my brother's. And if Tanaros Blacksword is trapped in the Marasoumië, so is the Wise Counselor."

"Tanaros?" The word escaped her unwittingly.

Something that might have been a smile shifted the

Shaper's ebony features. "My Commander General is re-
sourceful, Cerelinde. Let us hope together, you and I, for
his safe return."

She gripped the arms of her chair and steeled her
thoughts, willing them to fix where they belonged. Blue
eyes, at once demanding and questioning, met hers in memory. A promise given, a promise made. It lent a sting to her
words. "The Kingslayer has wrought his own fate, my Lord.
What of Aracus Altorus? What of my betrothed?"

"Your betrothed." The Shaper turned away from her, re-
suming his pacing, his shoulders slumping as if beneath a
heavy burden. "Ah, Cerelinde! He may fail, you know. Even
in Beshtanag, he may yet fail."

Her chin rose. "And if he does not?"

From a far corner of the chamber, he regarded her with
crimson eyes. "He will destroy something precious," he
said softly. "And the fault will be mine."

She stared at him, uncomprehending.

Satoris Third-Born laughed his awful, hollow laugh. "Ah,
Cerelinde! You want me to say he will pursue you in all
haste; that he will come here, seeking you. That Aracus Altorus will lay siege to Darkhaven itself. Shall I say it? It is
true, after all."

Hope and fear warred in her breast. "And what will become of me, if he does?"

"Do you care so little for what he will destroy?" The
Shaper's voice was wistful. "Will you not even ask what it
is?"

"My Lord—!"

"Never mind." He turned away from her again, a dark
shape in a dark corner. One hand moved, dismissing her.
"Begone from me, daughter of Erilonde. Your presence
does not ease my grief this night."

She took her leave, then, rising and gathering her skirts.
Beyond her the stairwell beckoned, the three-fold door at
the top opening onto the shadowy, twisted passages that led
back to her chambers, to the hidden door behind the tapes-

try. Hesitating on the first step, she glanced over her shoulder. He stood yet, motionless, a column of darkness, hands laced behind his back. "My Lord Satoris . . . "

"Go!"

His voice echoed like thunder.

Cerelinde fled. Behind her, the three-fold door closed with a mighty crash. On the far side, she found herself shaking.

In the thousands of years she had lived, she had never doubted the nature of truth. Now, uncertainty assailed her; doubt and insidious pity. A thing she had never before grasped had grown clear: the Sunderer believed his own lies. And in the irregular glimmer of the marrow-fire, a worm of doubt whispered a thought.

What if they were not lies?

"No." Cerelinde said aloud. "It is madness that speaks, not truth."

The words brought a measure of comfort; but only a measure. She made her way slowly through the walls of her prison, the sound of Satoris Banewreaker's terrible, despairing laughter still echoing in her ears.

THREE RAVENS CIRCLED OVERHEAD.

Ushahin watched them, shading his eyes with one hand. The skies above the plains of Rukhar were a merciless blue and the sun's bright light drove a spike of pain through his left eye. It didn't matter. He was used to such pain, and his awareness rode upon it as if borne upward on a warm draught, rising skyward.

Come, little brothers, he thought. What have you seen?

A flurry of images filled his mind in reply; stone, grey and barren. Straggling weeds, bitter ants crawling. There was a paucity of life on the plains, and the ravens did not want to land.

His mouth twisted in a wry smile. For that, he did not blame them.

With Tanaros and Malthus both trapped within them and struggling for mastery, the Ways of the Marasoumië were too dangerous to enter. He had walked out of Jakar; walked a day and a night across the plains, sifting through the dreams of Men as he went, until his ill-knit bones protested at every step. That didn't matter to him either. The only pain that mattered was the one that circumscribed his heart, Godslayer's branding beckoning him *home*, to the only home left to him. But without the Ways, his path was uncertain. To the west lay the Unknown Desert, its blazing sands forbidding. To the north lay the encampments of the Rukhari tribesmen and their scorn. To the east . . . ah, to the east lay Pelmar, where once the Grey Dam had called him her son, and there he did not dare go.

So he had gone south.

You need not land, Ushahin told the ravens. *Only tell me what you have seen.*

The ravens dipped lower, sunlight glinting violet and green on the edges of their wings as they circled in a narrowing gyre. Flickering images flitted from mind to mind; of the tops of pines like a dark green ocean; of columns of Men and Ellylon winding through the dense forest, amassing at the base of a mountain; of a fortress hunkered on the mountain's swell; of a seamless wall of granite. Of the explosion of sunlight refracting on bronze scales and a sinuous neck lifting a vast-jawed head, amusement in one slitted green eye.

Yes, little brothers, he thought; *I know. What of the south?*

Their vision skirted the edges of Arduan, where men and women gathered in the marketplaces and exchanged news, waiting; waiting, with longbows close at hand. There the ravens dared not go, remembering the arrows that had felled their brethren. But beyond, the marshes of the Delta unfurled like a rich, grey-green carpet, fecund and plentiful. There, they landed and fed. The shiny carapaces of beetles loomed large in memory, crunching with satisfaction under beaks; small snails, sweet and tasty.

At that, Ushahin smiled.

And further . . . one had flown, only one, following the sluggish path of the Verdine River as it emerged from the marshes. There, where the sharp-toothed sedge grass grew in abundance, three horses grazed. They were tall and strong and clean of limb, with dark, glossy hides and ill-kept manes and tails, tangled from the remnants of a long-abandoned disguise. Whatever had become of the Staccians who had entered the Delta, they had left their mounts be-hind and no one had succeeded in laying possessive hands on the horses of Darkhaven. One tossed its head as the raven swooped low, nostrils flaring and sharp teeth bared, a preternatural gleam of intelligence in its eyes.

Yes.

Ushahin Dreamspinner laughed. "So, my Lord Satoris," he said aloud. "It seems my path lies through the place of your birth."

Free of his mind's hold, the ravens broke from their tight spiral and soared, winging higher, rising to become specks in the blue sky.

Go, he sent a final thought after them. *Go, little brothers, and I will meet you anon!*

TWENTY-FOUR

EVEN IN SUMMER, IT WAS cold in the mountains.

It had not seemed so bad when they emerged, though he reckoned that was due to the relief at finding themselves alive. Frightened, yes. He was frightened. One moment, they had been in the Ways of the Marasoumië, under Malthus' protection. He hadn't been afraid, then, after they escaped the Were. Not for himself, only for those they left behind. The Ways were fearful and strange, but Malthus was there.

And then they had encountered the others, with a jolt he still felt in his bones. Thousands and thousands of them, huge and hulking, like creatures from a nightmare. The red light of the Marasoumië illuminated their jutting tusks, their massive talons, the heavy armor that encased their hide-covered bodies. A column of Fjeltroll, an army of Fjeltroll, winding back into the Ways as far as the eye could see.

It was a man on a black horse who led them, and he did not have to be told to know it was one of the Three. The Slayer, who had throttled love with his bare hands. And the sword he bore, the black blade, was forged in the marrow-fire itself and quenched in the blood of Satoris the Sun-derer.

Everything the Counselor had said was true.

Whatever Malthus had done with the Soumanië had swept them into the Ways, driving them backward—but not the Slayer. Though he had been unhorsed, the Soumanië's power could not touch him. There was a circle of burning shadow that surrounded and protected him.

He had drawn his black sword, preparing to slay the Counselor.

Trust me, Malthus had said.

And then the world had exploded in a rush of crimson light, and stone had swallowed them whole, sending them hurtling. Away, away, farther than he had dreamed possible. Swallowed them and digested them and spat them out in the cavern in the mountains, so far north that pockets of snow lay in the gulches. And here they had to fight for their survival.

"Dani, you need to eat."

Uncle Thulu's face was worried. He extended a roasted haunch of hare on a spit. It had taken him the better part of a day to catch it.

"Yes, Uncle."

The meat was hot and greasy. Dani picked at it, burning

his fingers. It felt slick on his tongue and juices filled his mouth as he chewed. He swallowed, feeling the meat slide down his throat. His belly growled and contracted around it, and he took another bite, suddenly voracious.

Uncle Thulu's dark face creased in a grin. "The Bearer is hungry!"

"Yes." He smiled back around a mouthful of meat. "I am."

"Good."

For a long time, neither of them spoke. There was only the sound of teeth rending meat, the murmurs of gladdened bellies. Between them they picked the bones clean and sucked them. Their little fire crackled merrily. Dani had lit it himself, twirling a sharpened stick between his palms until the pine mast he had gathered caught and glowed, sending a tendril of smoke into the clean air. A good thing, as cold as they were.

When they had done, Uncle Thulu leaned back and patted his belly. "Ah," he sighed. "That's good."

"Uncle." Dani hunched forward, wrapping his arms about his knees, staring at their fire. Afternoon shadows played over his features and the clay vial strung about his neck bumped his bare, bony kneecaps. "Where are we? What has become of us? What has become of Malthus?" He rested his chin on his knees, his expression miserable. "What do I do now, Uncle?"

"I don't know, lad." Uncle Thulu's voice was brusque. Leaning forward he placed another deadfall on the fire. "We're in Staccia, I think. Or Fjeltroll country. North."

"It's cold." Dani shivered.

"Aye." Uncle Thulu watched a shower of sparks rise. "A good job that Blaise bought cloaks for us. Wish I'd taken him up on the boots. Might have, if they'd fit."

Dani regarded his own feet, bare and calloused, broadened by a lifetime of walking on the desert floor. He did not mind the stones, but the beds of his toenails were faintly blue. "It's cold here."

"Aye." Uncle Thulu nodded. "We're in the north, all right."

He lifted his head. "He must have had a plan."

"Malthus?"

Dani nodded.

"I don't know, Dani." His uncle picked at his teeth with a splintered bone, thoughtful and frowning. "I don't think he reckoned on the Sunderer's army being in the tunnels. I think he did his best to protect us, that's all. Sent us as far away as he could. As to what happens next, that's up to you."

"I don't *want* to decide!"

His voice sounded childish. Uncle Thulu gazed at him silently. He sighed and bowed his head, cupping his hands in front of him. The radiating lines that marred his palms conjoined, forming a perfect star. What a simple, silly thing! Why should it mean he, and he alone, could draw the bucket from the well? But it did, and he had. The proof of it was bound on a cord around his neck. Dani swallowed, remembering the words that had first stirred him, spoken by Malthus. *Yet in the end, the fate of Urulat rests in your hands, Bearer.* He had heeded the Counselor's words. He had drawn the Water of Life. He had borne it. In Malumdoorn, it had drawn life out of death. He remembered that, the green leaves springing from dead wood, the surge of joy he had felt at the sight.

"The choice is yours, Dani." Uncle Thulu's voice was gentle. "Always and forever. That is the trust Uru-Alat bequeathed to the Yarru-yami, revealed to us by Haomane's Wrath. We ward the Well of the World. You are the Bearer."

Dani hunched his shoulders. "What if I refuse?"

"Then that is your choice. Do you want to go home?" With the tip of his bone-splinter toothpick, Uncle Thulu pointed southward, to the left of the lowering sun. "It lies that way, Dani. The rivers of Neheris run south. We have but to follow them until they sink beneath the earth and the desert begins."

It was heavy, the vial. It hung about his neck like a stone. The water in it—the Water of Life—could extinguish the very marrow-fire. It had seemed like a glorious destiny at Birru-Uru-Alat. To think he held the power, cupped in his hands, to heal the world! The danger had seemed very far away. Even on the marsh-plains, when they had been attacked, it seemed there was no danger from which Malthus could not protect them. Not any more. Not since the Were had come out of the forest, silent and deadly. Not since he had seen the army of Darkhaven in the Ways in its incomprehensible numbers, led by one of the Three. All that Malthus said; it was true. Satoris the Sunderer had raised a vast legion and he meant to conquer the world.

And the Company that had sworn to protect the Bearer . . .

"Do you think any of them are left alive?" he asked.

"I don't know, Dani," Uncle Thulu said. "It didn't look good."

He turned his head and gazed in the direction of the setting sun, thinking about their companions. Malthus, whom he had believed could do anything. Blaise, steady and competent. The Haomane-gaali, Peldras, so gentle and wise. Proud Hobard, whose anger was not really anger, but a thing driven by fear. Fianna, who was kind and beautiful. And Carfax—oh, Carfax! The Staccian had saved him in the end. Tears stung Dani's eyes. A golden wash of light lay over the mountain peaks, casting the valleys in shadow. Already the sun's warmth was fading. He dashed away his tears with the back of one hand and took a deep breath. "How far is it to Darkhaven?"

Uncle Thulu shook his head. "I cannot be sure. A long way."

"Can you find it?"

There was a pause. "Are you sure that's what you want?"

"Yes." Dani laced his fingers about his knees to hide their trembling and met his uncle's somber gaze. "If they died, they died trying to protect me. And if they did not . . . " He swallowed. "I would be ashamed to have them know I failed without trying."

Picking up his digging-stick, his uncle hummed deep in his chest, a reassuring and resonant sound. "Then we will find it, Dani. You are the Bearer, and I have promised the Yarru-yami to remain at your side, to guide your steps no matter how you choose." He turned the stick in his hands, humming absently. "Where water flows beneath the earth, I will chart the ways. When we find the taint of the Shaper's blood, we will follow it to Darkhaven."

"Good." His burden felt lighter for having decided. He edged closer to his uncle. They sat in companionable silence, sharing the warmth of their cloaks, watching blue twilight descend over the mountains. "Uncle?"

"Aye, lad?"

"We're not likely to live through this, are we?"

The deep humming faltered. He looked up to meet his uncle's gaze. "No," Uncle Thulu said quietly. "Venturing into the bowels of Darkhaven? Not likely, lad."

He nodded, remembering the gleam of moonlight on the pelts of the Were, the companions they had abandoned. "That's what I thought."

"I'm sorry, Dani."

"It's all right." Beneath his cloak, Dani fumbled for the vial at his throat, closing his fingers about its strange weight, obscurely comforted by his burden. "Uncle, what do you think he meant?"

"Who?"

He shivered. "The Slayer. The man with the black sword. 'Listen,' he said."

Uncle Thulu gazed at the fire, his hands gone still on his digging-stick. It was dark now, and the flickering light cast shadows in the hollows of his eyes and the crease beside his broad nose. "I don't know, Dani," he murmured. "I am only the guide. You are the Bearer."

"He sought to kill Malthus."

"Aye." His uncle nodded. "Aye, that I believe he did."

He held the vial, pondering its heft. "Well," he said at length. "It is a long way to Darkhaven. We will see."

"Aye," his uncle said softly. "That we will."

THE MARASOUMIË WAS LOOSENING ITS grip on Tanaros.

The terrible will he exerted was only part of it. In truth, he should not have been able to prevail against Malthus; not with the wizard wielding the Soumanië. Once he regained a measure of his depleted strength, Malthus should have been able to wrest himself into the Ways, sealing Tanaros in the Marasoumië.

He hadn't, though. Foolish wizard. It seemed his priorities lay with his Companions. Even now he struggled like a fly caught in amber, sending his strength *elsewhere* to shore up a fading spell, using the dregs of his exhausted power to cast a pall of protection over those who had none. Sensing it, Tanaros grinned without knowing it, the memory of his face shaping a rictus. With his right hand clenched on his sword-hilt, feeling the annealing power of a Shaper's blood temper his will, he fought for mastery of the Ways.

Fought, and won.

It came all of a rush, a node-point opening to his command. Gathering himself and his will, Tanaros scrambled for selfhood, wresting his shape out of the molten *nowhere* of the Marasoumië, reclaiming the mortal form he had worn for more than a thousand years. If there was a hand to grip a sword-hilt, there must be an arm to wield it. If there was a mouth to grin, there must be a face to wear it. If there was a heart to beat, there must be a breast to contain it. Bit by bit, Tanaros gathered himself until he was a man, standing, his feet beneath him.

There.

His lungs opened, drawing in a sobbing breath. Without a

second thought, he hurled himself into the Ways, into the constricting passage. One step, two, three; my Lord, I am *coming,* he thought, an ecstatic rush surging into his palm, fueling his veins. The black blade trembled, keening its own song. Stone rushed past him, disorienting.

Crimson light pulsed.

Tanaros stumbled, staggering, into open air.

It was a cavern. That much he saw, as his mastery of the Marasoumië faded. He set his feet and turned slowly in a circle, his sword extended. The sound of his breathing filled the empty space. The node-light went grey and lifeless, and darkness reclaimed the cavern. Somewhere in the Marasoumië, Malthus the Counselor had realized his error and managed to close the Ways at last.

Wherever Tanaros was, he was trapped.

He gave a short laugh at the irony of it. The cavern lay within the Ways, so there must be tunnels—but he was deep, deep below the surface, with no idea in which direction an egress might lie. No food, no water. There was air, for the moment. How long could he endure without them? What would become of his immortal flesh? Tanaros closed his eyes, remembering another journey beneath the earth, and beauty and terror commingled. "Cerelinde," he mused aloud. "Have I found the death you feared?"

His voice echoed in the vaulted space, punctuated by the sound of a drop of water falling; amplified, louder than any drip should be.

Tanaros opened his eyes.

It was dark in the cavern, but not wholly so. And it smelled of water; of the essence of water, of something that was to water as the Shaper's ichor was to mortal blood. Like water, only *sweeter.*

With dark-adjusted eyes he saw it—there, on the far side, a pool of water and a tiny point of light upon it, refracting a distant glitter of sun. Putting up his sword, Tanaros approached it. Deep, that cistern; unknowably deep. A single stalactite overhung it, glistening with gathering moisture. Leaning over the pool and craning his neck, he saw fresh marks gouged into the wall of the cistern. He knew those gouges. Deep and plunging, taking bites from stone as if from a hunk of stale bread; that was the work of a Fjeltroll's talons. A man could climb using those handholds, if he were strong enough to hoist himself up there.

Far, far above was sky, a blue disk no larger than a teacup.

Sheathing his sword, Tanaros reached out into the air above the cistern. The narrow shaft of sunlight illuminated his hand. It was warm on his skin; hot and dry. He rotated his hand. Sunlight lay cupped in his calloused palm. On the underside, the air that kissed his knuckles was cooler and moist, rising from the pool below. He could almost taste it.

"The Well of the World," he whispered.

It seemed impossible . . . and yet. What other water was so still, so motionless? Surely this must be the very navel of Urulat. He crouched beside the pool and watched the motionless water. It was folly to be here, and folly to linger. Still, he could not leave. If it was true, this water was old. It had been old when the world was Sundered; it had been old when the world was Shaped. With the utmost care he extended his arm and dipped the tip of one finger into the water, which didn't even ripple.

It was cool.

It was wet.

It was water, and it was the lifeblood of Urulat; of Uru-Alat, the World-God that was. It was the essence of water, all water, everywhere. Of the snow that fell in the mountains of Staccia, of Meronin's seas that circumscribed dry land. Of rain that fell like mercy on the plains of Curonan, and springs that bubbled in the forests of Pelmar. Of stagnant water standing in the Delta, and swift rivers flowing fresh through the Midlands.

With an effort, Tanaros withdrew his hand.

A single drop of water gathered on the tip of his finger. It was heavy, so heavy! With his free hand, he braced his forearm, watching the drop swell and gather, hanging round and full on his fingertip. It gleamed in the narrow sunbeam, refracting an entire world in its globular walls. Sun and sky, water and stone. As he watched, the drop of water changed shape, its rounded base broadening. Where it touched the pad of his fingertip, there where his skin whorled in tiny ridges, the connection narrowed, becoming a taut band of water, stretching, impossibly thin, until it snapped.

It fell.

A drop of water, falling into the pool. At close range, it rang like a gong in the enclosed space. Slow concentric ripples spread from the center of the pool, measured and perfect. Watching them lap against the edges of the pool and rebound with infinite precision, Tanaros stuck his finger into his mouth and sucked it.

Moisture, the essence of moisture, penetrated his parched tissues.

He hadn't know, until then, how deeply he thirsted. But there was enough life, enough *water*, in the thin film that clung to his skin to revitalize the flesh he had reclaimed from the Marasoumië. Strength, green and young, surged in him; he felt made anew. Every fiber of his being sang with vitality. He had not known such hope and urgency since his wedding night.

That, too, had been a kind of rebirth. A celebration of a mystery, of two becoming one. Of the quickening of desire, the joining of the flesh. A shared breath passed from one mouth to another, hearts beating in rhythm. Calista had laughed aloud in wonder at the discovery; the memory of it still cut like a blade. Tanaros could never have believed, that night, that she would betray their marriage bed.

But she had, and something in him had died. Yet here he was, born anew.

And he had his Lordship's trust, aye, and the loyalty of

the Fjel. These things alone sufficed to render life worth the living. Who was to say what else his future held in store? Desire, perhaps; or even love. Not even the Seven Shapers knew the whole of what-might-be.

Tanaros bounded to his feet and laughed. With a standing leap, he caught the lowest tier of holes gouged into the cistern wall, digging his fingers into them. He hung suspended. With an effort he hauled his body upward until his gaze was level with his own knuckles. His armor dragged at him, threatening to dislodge him. Too late to remove it now.

This would be the hard part.

Taking a deep breath, he let go with one hand, reaching upward without hesitation. If he'd swung on Malthus with the same speed at their first encounter, the wizard might have died in the Ways. He shouldn't have hesitated when he saw the boy. Blind and questing, his fingertips found the second tier of handholds; found, and held. Trusting for an instant to his grip, he dangled from one arm. Then he found the second hold with his left hand. His arms strained in their sockets as he hoisted his body upward.

Once more.

In a strange way, it felt good. His muscles quivered in agony at the strain, but it was a simple pain and one he understood. The Water of Life, the lifeblood of Urulat, coursed in his veins and he had never felt more hale or alive. There was no mystery here, only the body's strength, pitted against the sheer rockface. At the third tier of gouges his scrambling feet found purchase. Wedging his booted toes into the lowest holes, Tanaros clung to the cistern wall and caught his breath, letting his legs take his weight.

After that, it was simply a matter of climbing.

It took long hours, and there were times when his fingers ached and his muscles quivered and he could do nothing but press his face to the rock and wait for the trembling to pass, longing only to let go, to let himself fall, plunging into the deep cistern below. Easy, so easy! But he was Tanaros Blacksword, one of the Three, and he would not give up that easily. Inch by inch, he climbed, tenacious as any spider to scale the Defile's walls. Above him, the disk of sunlight broadened, the quality of the light slanting and changing as the sun moved in its circuit westward.

At length his searching hand found no gouge where it reached, only a lip of rough-hewn stone. His fingertips scrabbled, catching a grip. Remembering the taste of the Water of Life in his mouth, Tanaros drew his right leg up beneath him, finding a foothold. Pushing hard and heaving with both arms, he cleared the lip of the well. His head emerged in open air and he shoved hard against the foothold, the rest of his body following as he tumbled over the edge, armor clattering against rock.

"Lord General!" A relieved shout in an unmistakable Midlander accent greeted his arrival. "Am I glad to see *you!*"

Tanaros found his feet and stood.

The setting sun was as red as blood, flooding the desert with a sanguine hue. He stood atop a promontory of rock situated in the center of a dry basin. Arrayed around its perimeter were standing stones, two and three times the height of a man, casting stark shadows on the sand. Within the circle were other figures, human and Fjel alike, set in a strange tableau.

"Speros!" Tanaros shaded his eyes, unreasoningly glad to see the Midlander alive. "How did you come here? Who *are* these people?"

"As to how we got here, I can't say, my lord." Speros picked a path across the basin, carrying his sword unsheathed in one hand and ignoring the motionless figures who sat on their haunches on the cooling sands. A squadron of four Gulnagel Fjel shifted position as he moved, maces at the ready, keeping a watchful eye on the still figures. "The five of us were caught in the Marasoumië, when the wizard came, and here we found ourselves; or underearth, rather. I'm not one of the Three, to understand the workings of the Ways. But these—" arriving at the base of the rocks, he nodded backward at the squatting humans, "—are the Charred Ones, those whom Haomane's Wrath drove under-earth. And unless I miss my guess, Lord General, these are the ones plotting to extinguish the marrow-fire."

Tanaros stared at him.

Behind the Midlander, one of the squatting humans rose to his feet in a painstaking effort, joints creaking. He was old, his dark, wrinkled face bearing a map of his years. They were all old, all of them. An elderly woman beside him hissed in disapproval and tugged at his kneecap, though he paid her no heed. The Gulnagel moved in a step closer, their hided muscles flexing.

Tanaros held up one hand, halting their movement. "You would speak, old one?"

"Slayer!" The old man returned his greeting in the common tongue. Shifting an unseen wad into one cheek, he hawked and spat onto the sands. "Welcome to Birru-Uru-Alat. We have been expecting you."

"You DID A GOOD THING back there, Staccian."

The Borderguardsman's voice was quiet, but it spoke volumes in praise. Kneeling over the fire, Carfax felt the back of his neck flush. He concentrated on the fire, feeding it bit by bit, laying branches in such a way as would build a solid blaze. The silence lingered between them, growing heavy. "Don't know about that," he muttered at length. "I couldn't watch the boy slaughtered, is all."

"Or Fianna," Blaise said softly, so softly the Archer could not hear.

Carfax looked up sharply, rubbing his palms on his thighs. "What of her?"

"Nothing." The Borderguardsman shook his head. By firelight his resemblance to General Tanaros was more apparent; the same spare, handsome features, the same errant lock of dark hair across his brow. "You have a good heart, Staccian. Why is it so hard for you to hear?"

On the far side of the fire, the Ellyl stirred as if to speak, then thought better of it, rising instead to check on the horses. The gentle whickering sound of their greeting carried in the night air. Carfax watched as Peldras touched them, laying pale hands on their hides, soothing aching knees, strained hocks. The Ellyl spoke inaudibly to Fianna, who rummaged through their stores. He could hear her soft laugh of delight at whatever the Ellyl said, and wondered what it must be like to move through the world with such grace that all must acknowledge it. Even so, it was the Borderguardsman she loved. The Ellyl was beyond her reach, a Lesser Shaper of a higher order. It had taken Haomane's Prophecy and a thousand years of refusal before the Lady of the Ellylon would consider a mortal lover. An ordinary woman like Fianna would never dare to dream of such a liaison. What the Ellyl thought, only Haomane knew.

"Staccian?" Blaise prompted him.

"I don't know." Carfax mumbled the words. Shifting, he sat on the pine mast, hiding his face against his knees. "Don't be so quick to speak kindly to me," he said without looking up. "If I had thought deeper, my lord Blaise, I might not have acted. Because of me, the Bearer's quest continues."

"Aye," Blaise said. "Haomane's Allies are in your debt."

Carfax gave a strangled laugh. "I have betrayed my loyalties and all I hold dear."

"No. Only those false loyalties you were taught. It is not the same." Removing a whetstone from a pouch at his belt, Blaise began honing his sword, smoothing away the nicks it had gotten battling the Were. It was a homely sound, stone grinding on metal. "I asked you once what manner of man you wanted to be, Staccian. You have shown me through your actions. A man of honor, willing to risk his life to protect the innocent. I tell you tonight, Aracus Altorus would welcome one such as you into his service."

"Why?" he whispered.

"Because he understands what it means to be King of the

West." Fianna had approached him from behind, her steps inaudible on the pine mast. Her hands lit on his shoulders, her face bending down beside his. "Oh, Carfax! You have proved a true companion in this venture when all but the Wise Counselor would have doubted you. Do you think Aracus Altorus will not see it?"

It was hard to think, with her soft breath brushing his cheek. Exhaling hard, he lifted his head and focused on the Borderguardsman. "Why *him*, Blaise? What has he done to win *your* loyalty?"

"Can you not guess?" Blaise Caveros laid his sword across his knees. His dark eyes held Carfax's in a steady gaze. "You, who have served under the Kingslayer? He trusted me, Staccian. Since we were boys. Always." His mouth twisted in a wry smile. "If the Kingslayer's wife had not betrayed him, his blood would run in Aracus' veins. Instead, Aracus is the last scion of the House of Altorus, while for a thousand years, my family's name has been a byword for betrayal. Aracus Altorus measured me by the contents of my heart and made me his right hand. He gave my family back its honor, Staccian. Is that not enough? Can you say as much of Tanaros Blacksword?"

"No," Carfax whispered.

"And Satoris Banewreaker?" Blaise's voice hardened. "How is it you serve *him?* Has the Sunderer dealt so gently with his Staccian allies?"

"No." He pressed the heels of his hands against his eyes. "Yes! I don't know, my lord!" Carfax drew a long, shuddering breath. "What would you have me say?" he asked miserably, raising his bloodshot gaze. "He played us fair! Battle-glory and generous recompense for the fallen. That's the bargain Lord Vorax has ever offered on Lord Satoris' behalf, and from time out of mind, we've taken it. And he has kept his terms! For a thousand years, no enemy has lifted a blade within our borders, and no child has hungered. This, Lord Satoris has done for us. Can any other nation of Men claim the same? My family dwells in peace and comfort because I serve his Lordship. Is it so wrong?"

"If it keeps the world Sundered, aye." Blaise's tone was surprisingly gentle. "Forgive me, Staccian, but I do believe it."

"You have so much *faith!*" The words burst from his lips. Carfax glared at them; glared at them all, for now the Ellyl had returned and all four were arrayed about the campfire. "How can you *know?* How can you be so *sure?*"

They glanced at one another, and at him, pitying.

It was Peldras who answered, lowering himself gracefully to sit cross-legged beside the fire. "Carfax of Staccia," he said, "let me ask you this: How is it you cannot?"

Carfax shook his head, unable to articulate a reply.

"My people are dying." The Ellyl tilted his head, regarding the distant stars. "We are fading, bit by bit. We are Haomane's Children, and we drew our strength from the Souma. Without it, we are bereft. We are the Rivenlost. The way home is forbidden us." He turned the weight of his luminous gaze on Carfax. "We are Haomane's Children, and while we live, we are an affront to the Sunderer, and one he would destroy. Do you deny it?"

"No," he said, miserable. "But—"

"But tomorrow we will be in Beshtanag," Blaise said brusquely. "Which is a trap. You have said so yourself, Staccian. I mean to give warning to my lord Aracus Altorus. I spoke the truth, before. You acquitted yourself well. Now I need to know: Do you stand with us or against us? Will you pledge your loyalty to me?"

Carfax blinked, his vision streaked by tears. Why was it that the rest of the world seemed so far away? It felt like a lifetime had passed since he set out from Darkhaven. These people had become his companions, the only ones left to him. He had traveled with them, eaten with them, fought with them back-to-back. One had sacrificed himself to save his worthless life. He remembered Hobard, his father's sword in his hand and urgency straining his bloodstained face, the wave of Were that had swallowed him. *This is my death. Go!*

But . . .

He remembered Turin, Hunric; the men he had left behind, obedient to his orders. He remembered the men he had led and how they had trusted him. How he had led them into battle, singing, sure of victory. They had been good comrades, and true. They had trusted his leadership, and General Tanaros had trusted him to lead them. And he had erred in his folly and the earth had risen to engulf them. He was a traitor, aye. He had saved Dani's life. He had admitted that Beshtanag was a trap, and Lord Satoris' raven had watched him do it. Oh, aye, Carfax of Staccia was a traitor of the first order, but he was man enough still not to profit by it. Not while his own men rotted in barrows beneath the sedge grass.

"I can't." The words came harshly, catching in his throat. The tears were flowing freely, coursing his cheeks. "Forgive me, Blaise, but I can't."

The Borderguardsman nodded with regret.

"Carfax, please!" Fianna's face swam in his vision, and there were tears in her own eyes, shining on her cheeks. How not? Archer or no, she was a woman, and women reckoned the cost. Always, women reckoned the cost. Her hands found his, gripping them tightly. "You saved my life! How can you name yourself aught but a friend?"

"I wasn't prey." He blinked at her, clutching her hands. Soft, so soft, save for the bowstring's calluses. "Do you understand? The Were wouldn't attack me. I might as well have struck an unarmed man."

"As *they* did!" Her voice rose. "You defended Dani, too, who never raised his hand to anyone! Where is the wrong in that?"

Carfax shook his head and looked away, withdrawing from her grasp. "Dani raised his hand against Darkhaven

when he drew forth the Water of Life," he murmured.
"Malthus knew it, if the boy did not. And the Were knew it,
too. I'm sorry, Fianna." Gathering himself, he met Blaise's
eyes. "I'll do nothing to thwart your purpose. You have my
word on that, my lord. But I cannot pledge you my loyalty."
He swallowed against the lump in his throat. "I ride into
Beshtanag as your prisoner."

"So be it." The Borderguardsman's gaze was steady. "My
hand is extended in friendship, Staccian. It will be there
should you wish to take it."

Not trusting himself to speak, Carfax nodded.

TWENTY-FIVE

❖

THE WALL WAS FAILING.

It was simply too much to hold. For three days, Haomane's Allies had assailed it without cease. Day and night,
night and day. No one could sleep for the sound of battering
rams thudding mercilessly against granite, seeking cracks
where Lilias' power weakened.

She had held out longer than she had dreamed possible. It
wasn't easy work, Shaping, and she was neither Ellyl nor
Counselor, with Haomane's Gifts in her blood to make it
easier. Rock and stone fought her will, seeking to return to
their original form. Again and again, her bindings loosened.
With grim determination, she held them in place, until exhaustion left her weak and dizzy, forgetful of her surroundings.

"Please, my lady! You *must* drink."

The cool rim of a cup touched her lower lip. Raising her
head with a jerk, Lilias saw Sarika kneeling before her, eyes

pleading. "Sweetling." She steadied the girl's hands with her own, drinking deep. The water forged a cool trail into her empty belly, lending the illusion of fullness. "Our stores endure?"

"Water." Sarika licked her lips involuntarily. "There is water, and quarter-rations of gruel for the wardsmen. As you ordered, my lady."

"Yes." Lilias pressed one hand to her brow, feeling the weight of the Soumanië. "Of course." A hollow boom shook the mountain as a battering ram struck her wall for the hundredth time that morning, and she shuddered. "Where is Gergon?"

"He's coming." It was Radovan's voice that spoke; Radovan, whose smouldering eyes had pleased her once. Now they stared at her with dark hatred, and disdain laced his voice. "My lady." He spat the words like an epithet, running one grimy finger beneath the linked silver collar that bound him to her.

It was folly, of course. She should have freed him before this began; should never have bound them so close. Any of them, her pretty ones. It had never been necessary, not with the good ones. How had it begun? A sop to her mortal vanity; to pride, to desire. What was power good for if not for that? It pleased her to be surrounded by youth in all its fleeting beauty. What was immortality good for without simple pleasures? She was a generous mistress. None of them had ever taken any harm from it, only tales to tell their grandchildren.

Too late, now. As strained as the linkage was, it would take more to sever it than to maintain it. Lilias shoved aside her regrets and shook her head like a fly-stung horse, impatient. "Gergon?"

"There, my lady." Sarika pointed, her voice soothing.

He looked like an ant toiling up the mountainside. They all looked like ants. Her wardsmen, the Warders of Beshtanag, defending the mighty wall. Other ants in bright armor swarmed it, creeping along the top with their

siege-towers and ladders, while the battering ram boomed
without ceasing. Lilias sat back in her chair, surveying her
crumbling empire. She remembered, now. She'd had a
high-backed chair of office placed here, on the terrace of
Beshtanag Fortress itself, to do just that.

Lilias.

Calandor's voice echoed in her skull. "No," she said
aloud. "No."

Her Ward Commander, Gergon, toiled up the mountainside, nodding as he went to archers posted here and there,
the last defenders of Beshtanag. It was warm and he was
sweating, his greying hair damp beneath his helmet. He
took it off to salute her. "My lady Lilias." He tucked his helmet under his arm, regarding her. His face was gaunt and
the flesh beneath his eyes hung in bags. He had served her
since his birth, as had his father and his father's father before him. "I am here in answer to your summons."

"Gergon." Her fingers curved around the arms of the
chair. "How goes the battle?"

He pointed. "As you see, I fear."

Below, the ants scurried, those inside the wall hurrying
away under its shadow.

A loud *crr ackk!* sounded and a web of lines emerged on
a portion of the wall, revealing its component elements.
Rocks shifted, boulders grinding ominously. Lilias stiffened in her chair, closing her eyes, drawing on the power of
the Soumanië. In her mind she saw her wall whole and
gleaming; willed it so, Shaped it so, shifting platelike seg-
ments of mica, re-forming the crystalline bonds of silica
into a tracery of veins running throughout a single, solid
structure. What she saw, she Shaped, and held.

There was a pause, and then the sound of the battering
ram resumed.

Lilias bent over, gasping. "There!"

"Lady." Gergon gazed down at the siege and mopped the
sweat from his brow, breathing a sigh that held no relief.
"Forgive me, but it is the third such breach this morning,

and I perceive you grow weary." His voice was hoarse. "I
am weary. My men are weary. We are hungry, all of us. We
will defend Beshtanag unto the death, only . . . " The cords
in his weathered throat moved as he swallowed, hale flesh
grown slack with privation and exhaustion. "Three days,
you said. Today is the fourth. Where are they?"

Lilias, you must tell him.

"I know." She shuddered. "Ah, Calandor! I know."

Before her, Gergon choked on an indrawn breath, a fearful certainty dawning in his hollow-set eyes. He glanced
down at his men, his shoulders sagging with defeat, then
back at her. "They're not coming," he said. "Are they?"

"No," she said softly. With an effort, Lilias dragged herself upright in her chair and met his gaze, knowing he de-
served that much. "I lied. I'm sorry. Something went awry
in the Marasoumië. I thought . . . " She bowed her head. "I
don't know what I thought. Only that somehow, in the end,
it wouldn't come to this. Gergon, I'm sorry. I'm so sorry."

A sound arose; two sounds. They seemed linked, at
first—the redoubled sound of the battering ram, Radovan's
rising shout. He plunged at her, his smouldering eyes gone
quite mad, the paring-knife held high overhead. Somewhere, Sarika's shrill scream echoed against Gergon's be-
lated cry of protest.

Lilias dealt with it unthinking.

The Soumanië on her brow flared into life, casting its
crimson glow. Abandoning every tendril of her defense of
the wall, she drew upon the Soumanië and hurled every
ounce of her remaining strength at him, Shaping the pulse
of his life-force as surely as she had Shaped the veins of silica. Radovan stiffened mid-strike, his free hand clutching at
his throat; at the silver collar he wore, the token of her will
circumscribing his life. Sunlight shone on the edge of the
paring-knife, casting a bar of brightness across her face.
When had he stolen it? How long had he planned this? She
had known, known she should have freed him! If he had

only asked, only spoken to her of his resentment . . . but, already, it was too late. Panicked and careless, Lilias forgot all else, concentrating the Soumanië's power upon him, until his heartbeat fluttered and failed.

Lifeless knees buckling, Radovan slumped to earth.

At the base of the mountain, a great shout arose.

The crash resounded across the forests of Pelmar as a portion of her wall crumbled; crumbled, resolving itself irrevocably into shards and chips, rough-hewn boulders. There was a price to be paid for her lapse, for the act of will that had saved her life and taken his. A gap wide enough to drive a team of four through stood open, and Haomane's Allies poured through it. For three days, Aracus Altorus had held his troops at the ready, waiting for such an opening. Now he seized it unhesitating, and a trickle of ants grew to a stream, swelled to a flood. A clangor of battle arose and, all along the wall, defense positions were abandoned as the wardsmen of Beshtanag surged to meet the influx. Siege-ladders thumped against undefended granite. Haomane's Allies scrambled over the wall by the dozen, their numbers growing. On the terrace, her Ward Commander Gergon shouted futile orders.

"No," Lilias said, numb with horror. "No!"

How could it all fall apart so swiftly?

They came and they came, erecting battle-standards on Beshtanag Mountain. Regents of Pelmar, lords of Seahold, ancient families of Vedasia, and oh! The banners of the Ellylon, bright and keen, never seen on Beshtanagi soil. And there, inexorable, moved the standard of Aracus Altorus, the dun-grey banner of the Borderguardsmen of Curonan, unadorned and plain.

"No," Lilias whispered.

Now, Lilias.

"No! Wait!" She reached for the power of the Soumanië; *reached.* And for once, found nothing. After all, when all was said and done, she was mortal still, and her power had found its limits. Radovan lay dead, a paring-knife in his open hand, his heart stopped. The earth would not rise at her command and swallow her enemies; the roots of the dense forest would not drink their blood. The Soumanië was a dead ember on her brow. Somewhere, Sarika was weeping with fear, and it seemed unfair, so unfair. "Calandor, *no!*"

It is time, Lilias.

She had fallen to her knees, unaware. In a rising stillness no one else perceived, something bright flickered atop Beshtanag Mountain. Sunlight, glinting on scales, on talons capable of grasping a full-grown sheep, on the outstretched vanes of mighty wings. No one seemed to notice. At the base of the mountain, Haomane's Allies struggled on the loose scree inside the wall, fighting in knots, surging upward, gaining ground by the yard. Assured of her temporary safety, Ward Commander Gergon, striding down the mountain, shouted at his archers to fall back, fall back and defend. All the brightness in the world, and no one noticed.

"Please don't," Lilias whispered. "Oh, Calandor!"

Atop the mountain, Calandor roared.

It was a sound like no other sound on earth.

It held fire, gouts of fire, issuing forth from the furnace of the dragon's heart. It held all the fury of the predator; of every predator, everywhere. It held the deep tones of dark places, of the bones of the earth, of wisdom rent from their very marrow. It held love; oh yes. It held love, in all its self-aware rue; of the strong for the weak, of the burden of strength and true nature of sacrifice. And it was like trumpets, clarion and defiant, brazen in its knowledge.

"*Calandor,*" Lilias whispered on her knees, and wept.

Haomane's Allies went still, and feared.

Roaring, with sunlight glittering on his scales, on his taloned claws, on the vanes of his wings, rendering pale the gouts of flame that issued from his sinuous throat, the Dragon of Beshtanag launched himself. Below the bright-

ness in the sky, a shadow, a vast shadow, darkened the
mountain.

At last, Haomane's Allies knew terror.

LONG BEFORE THEY REACHED BESHTANAG they heard the
clamor of battle, and another, more fearful sound, a roar
that resonated in their very bones and made the blood run
cold in their veins. Among the four of them, only the Ellyl
had heard such a sound before. Blaise looked at him for
confirmation and Peldras nodded, his luminous eyes gone
dark and grave.

"It is the dragon."

Blaise looked grim. "Ride!"

For the last time, they charged headlong through the
dense Pelmaran forests, matted pine needles churned beneath the hooves of their horses. Half-forgotten, Carfax
brought up the rear, wondering and fearing what they would
find upon reaching Beshtanag. From the forest's verge they
saw the encampment of Haomane's Allies. Above the battlefield, at the foot of the great walled mountain, fire searing
the skies.

Blaise Caveros uttered a wordless cry, clapping his heels
to his mount's sides. When they reached the point where the
treetops were smouldering he streaked into the lead, the
other three following as they burst from dense cover. With
his bared sword clutched in one fist, he abandoned his company and charged into battle shouting.

"Curonan! *Curonan!*"

Trailing, Carfax halted and watched in awe.

The wall that surrounded the mountain seemed impreg-
nable; seamless granite four times the height of a tall man.
And yet it had been breached. A vast gap lay open in the
great wall that had surrounded Beshtanag, a gaping hole
where the wall crumbled into its component stones. There,
Men fought in the rubble, Men and Ellylon, and above it all,
a bright shadow circled; circled, and breathed gouts of fire.

His heart caught inexplicably at the sight of it, at the dragon's vaned wings, outstretched to ride the drafts. Such terrible beauty! But where were the others? Where were the Fjel, stalwart and faithful? Where was the company of Rukhari that Lord Vorax had promised? Where was General Tanaros?

Peldras drew rein alongside him. "You did not expect this."

"No." Carfax frowned, following the dragon's flight. "Beshtanag was meant to be a trap. But not like *this*."

"How?" The Ellyl's voice was calm.

Atop her mount, Fianna was trembling. "Oh, Haomane!" The quiver she bore at her back pulsed with light. "Carfax, they are dying. *Dying!*"

It was true. Whatever had transpired before to breach the wall, Haomane's Allies were dying now, by the score. Bodies littered the ground inside the wall, many of them charred beyond recognition. Beshtanag's defenders surged toward the gap, seeking to secure their position and retake the breach, sealing it. And above them all, the dragon circled, casting a vast shadow on the base of the mountain.

"*Curonan!*"

A knot of men answering to the dun-grey standard had forged their way to the forefront. It was to their aid that Blaise had streaked, battling against the tide to reclaim the gap in the wall; where a handful of men held the gap by dint of sheer valor. Above them the dragon circled, then stooped. The prudent Beshtanagi fell back to regroup on the mountainside. The men of Curonan flung themselves to the ground beneath the dragon's shadow. It passed over them, so low that its scaled belly almost scraped the top of the wall. The mighty jaws opened and gouts of white-hot flame issued forth from the gaping furnace.

One of the Borderguardsmen screamed, rolling. Others cried out and beat at smouldering garments. The smell of burning flesh hung in the air.

"Blaise!" Fianna whispered in anguish.

He was clear, wrenching his horse's reins mercilessly, his mount sidling free of the fire's scorching path. The dragon's wings beat hard, creating a powerful downdraft as its gleaming body banked and rolled. Its scaled tail, tipped with deadly spikes, swept like a cudgel. Blaise's mount danced, avoiding it by a narrow margin.

"Retreat, you idiots!" Watching the battle unfold, Carfax clenched his hands, longing for a blade. "For the love of Urulat, retreat!"

Horns echoed, silvery and clear, sounding a charge.

"My kinsmen!" Peldras' voice held a yearning note.

Beneath the banner of the gilded bee of Valmaré, a squadron of Rivenlost archers advanced in a gleaming line, paused and knelt, bows bent in taut arcs. A flurry of Ellylon arrows split the air, grey shafts arcing. In midair, the dragon turned, effortless as a fish in water, presenting a scaled shoulder. Arrows fell like rain, glancing off that scaled flesh and bouncing harmlessly on the stony ground as the dragon launched itself skyward, ascending out of range. Another horn sounded, Man-wrought, calling the retreat in urgent, brassy tones. Under the cover of Ellylon archers, the Borderguardsmen began a methodical retreat to the siege-lines, flanked by Pelmaran and Midlander soldiers. Blaise wheeled his mount, cantering alongside them. On the slope of the mountain, Beshtanagi wardsmen watched and waited.

"It's all right," Fianna breathed. "That's all right, then."

Peldras shook his head, pointing. "I fear not, Lady Archer."

High overhead the dragon halted its ascent, turning and stooping. There it hung, held aloft by the steady beating of its enormous wings, a glittering speck against the vast expanse of blue. Like a noonday star, Carfax thought, and wondered what had gone wrong. Something had. Something had gone terribly, terribly awry. The Army of Darkhaven had not come, and the Sorceress' power had failed. What else could have caused the wall to fall? He hadn't known every detail of Lord Satoris' plan—only the Three had known—but he was certain that the Dragon of Beshtanag had played no part in it. Not like this. The dragons had aided Lord Satoris once, and most of them had been slain for their role, in the days of old when doughty warriors like Altorus Farseer strode the earth and the Lords of the Ellylon wielded terrible power.

This was one of the last. It should not be here. Not like this.

"Oh, my Lord!" Carfax whispered, numb with horror.

Haomane's Allies halted in their retreat, turning and regrouping, wary of the dragon. They were bunched together; too tight, the ranks too close. Gathering their ragtag forces, the Beshtanagi wardsmen advanced, reclaiming the gap and surging through it, re-forming their line in front of the wall.

I should have been there, Carfax thought, among those men. If all had gone as planned, I would be among them. If not for Malthus, I would be. And if the rest had gone as planned, Turin, Mantuas and Hunric *should* be among them, even now. They should have won through to Beshtanag. Have matters gone so terribly wrong that even their mission failed?

He strained his eyes for a glimpse of a familiar Staccian face, and did not know whether to be glad or anxious to see none.

I have no people here, he thought, despite all of Darkhaven's cunning.

Amid the army of Haomane's Allies, Blaise Caveros leaned down from the saddle, clasping hands with one of the Borderguardsman. There were discussion, protest, insistence. Dismounting, Blaise cupped his hands to boost the other into the saddle. Carfax watched as the last living descendent of the first King of Altoria removed his steel helmet, throwing back his head to address his army, words lost in the distance. The sunlight glinted on his red-gold hair.

Aracus Altorus, who did not fear to lead men into battle, drew his sword, pointing it at the fortress of Beshtanag. Overhead, the dragon's wings beat steadily, holding it in position, patient as a hawk before it stoops. Aracus Altorus raised his sword aloft like a pennant. A single word tore loose over the din, shouted like a paean, echoed by a thousand throats, Men and Ellylon.

" . . . *Cerellnde!*"

"They're going to stand," Peldras said somberly. "For the Lady of the Ellylon, they're going to stand their ground."

Something that might have been a laugh or a sob caught in Carfax's throat. He rocked back and forth in the saddle, digging the heels of his hands into his eyes, unable to express the futility of it all. So many assembled, so many dying! And to what purpose? None. There was nothing here but a failed gambit. The agonizing cries of the wounded and dying on both sides of the battlefield scourged his soul. In anguish, Carfax of Staccia committed his final betrayal. "She's not there," he gasped. "She's not even *there!*"

The Ellyl touched his forearm, frowning. "What are you saying?"

"Oh, Haomane!" Fianna cried. "No!"

Too late, too late for everything. Far, far above them all, the dragon folded its wings and dove, dropping like a falling star. Its jaws stretched wide, opening onto an impossible gullet. Smoke trailed from its nostrils. Plated armor covered its breast, a nictitating membrane protected its eyes and its foreclaws were outstretched, each talon like an iron spike, driving earthward.

Whatever resolve Aracus Altorus had instilled in Haomane's Allies shattered.

Crying out in fear, vast numbers of the Pelmaran soldiery fled like leaves blown before a gale, carrying ill-prepared Midlander forces with them. Here and there, pockets of Vedasian knights gathered, seeking to rally around their standards, and the archers of the Rivenlost kept their line intact.

But it was the Borderguard of Curonan that held steadfast in the center.

At the last possible moment, the dragon's wings snapped open, membranes spreading like sails to brake its dive. Arrows and spears clattered from its impervious hide. Its neck wove back and forth like an immense serpent's, fire belching from its open maw as it swept low over the field, cutting a swathe through Haomane's Allies, not discriminating between nations and races. Everywhere, Men and Ellylon gibbered and wept, cowered under shields, died screaming and scorched. The dragon's claws flexed and gathered, and bodies dangled from the clutch of its gleaming talons as it soared upward; dangled, and fell like broken dolls as the talons released.

Somewhere, Aracus Altorus was shouting, and the surviving Borderguard answered with grim determination, gathering tight around him. In the smoke and chaos left in the dragon's wake, the Beshtanagi forces spread out and advanced, closing in on the far-flung edges of their attackers' forces, driving toward the center with desperate urgency.

Their numbers were few—but they outnumbered the Borderguard.

A lone figure stepped forth beneath the dun standard to meet the onslaught.

"Blaise!" Fianna spurred her mount unthinking, guiding it with her legs, her Archer's hands reaching as she sped across the battlefield, dodging around unmounted Beshtanagi wardsmen. Oronin's Bow was in her hand, her hand reaching over her shoulder. Light spilled from her quiver as she grasped an arrow, an ordinary arrow, fitting it to the string. The black horn bow sang a single, deadly note as she loosed it, and a wardsman fell, clutching his chest where an arrow sprouted. *"Blaise!"*

"Fianna!" Starting after her, Carfax felt the Ellyl's grip tighten on his forearm. "Peldras, let me go," he said, trying to pull away. "She's like to get slaughtered out there without armor or a guard!"

"Peace, Arahila's Child. I seek only the truth." The Ellyl's grip was gentle, but surprisingly firm. His deep gaze searched Carfax's face. "Will you withhold it while people die in vain?"

Above the battlefield, the Dragon of Beshtanag circled low, harrying fleeing soldiers and driving them back onto the battlefield as it came in for another pass. Fire roared, and cries of agony rose; a din of chaos and anguish. Somewhere, Oronin's Bow was sounding its single note, over and over. On the outskirts of it all, Carfax met Peldras' gaze. "Can you stop the fighting if I tell you?"

"I don't know, Carfax of Staccia." The Ellyl did not flinch. "I fear it may be too late to sue for a truce. But if the Lady Cerelinde is not here, I will do my best to carry word. Perhaps some lives may be saved, and Fianna the Archer's among them."

It was too late, after all. Too late for everything.

"She's in Darkhaven," Carfax said simply. With those few words, he surrendered the long burden of his loyalty and knew, in doing so, he accepted his death. When all was said and done, it was a relief, an unspeakable relief. He should have died with his men. He wished that he had. There was no honor in a life foresworn. It would be good to have it done. "Your Lady Cerelinde is in Darkhaven. She was never here. It was a trick, all a trick. General Tanaros was supposed to lead the army through the Ways and fall upon you from behind. Something went wrong. I don't know what."

Peldras nodded. "Thank you."

"May I go now?"

The Ellyl removed his hand from the Staccian's arm and drew his sword. Grasping it by the blade, he presented the hilt. "Take my blade, and my blessing. May Arahila the Fair have mercy upon you, Carfax of Staccia."

He grasped the hilt. It felt good in his palm. Firm. He hoisted it. The blade was light in his grip, its edge keen and silver-bright, its balance immaculate. Ellylon craftsmanship. "Thank you, Peldras."

Once more, the Ellyl nodded. "Farewell, my friend."

ON THE BATTLEFIELD, ALL WAS madness.

The Pelmaran forces had been routed to a man. Last to commit, first to flee. Carfax had to dodge them as he rode, his mount's hooves scrabbling on the loose scree at the base of Beshtanag Mountain. Here and there Beshtanagi wardsmen pursued them. It was hard to tell one from the other, clad alike in leather armor with steel rings, colors obscured by veils of smoke.

No matter. He wasn't here to fight anyone's war.

A pall of smoke hung over the battlefield, which reeked of smoke and sulfur, of charred flesh and spilled gore, of the inevitable stench of bowels voided in death. Carfax ignored it, guiding his horse with an expert hand past the dead and the dying, deserters and their pursuers, avoiding them and thinking of other times.

There had been a girl, once, in Staccia. He had brushed her skin with goldenrod pollen, gilding her freckles. And he had thought, oh, he had thought! He had thought to return home a hero, to wipe away the tears his mother had shed when he left, to smile into his girl's eyes and see her a woman grown, and wipe away the remembered traces of pollen from her soft skin.

Blaise had asked him: *Why do you smile, Staccian?*

To make a friend of death.

Thickening smoke made his eyes sting. He squinted, and persevered.

Fianna had smiled at him when he brought her pine rosin for her bow. Her Arduan bow, wrought of ordinary wood and mortal sinew. Not this one, that was made of black horn and strung with . . . strung with what? Hairs from the head of Oronin Last-Born, perhaps, or sinew from the Glad Hunter's first kill, sounding a Shaper's battlecry. It had twisted in her hands when she fought against the Were, refusing to slay its maker's Children.

Not so, here. Oronin's Bow sang in her hands, uttering its single note, naming its victims one by one. She had smiled at him, and he . . . he had made a friend of death. Here, at the end, there was a hand extended in friendship, and it was one he could take at last. A traitor, yes. He was that. Carfax of Staccia would die a traitor.

Still, there was honor of a kind in dying for a woman's smile. If nothing else, there was that.

He found himself singing a Staccian paean as he rode, and the Ellyl's sword was light in his grip as he swung it, forging a path toward the song of Oronin's Bow. Toward the center, the battle was in progress and it was necessary to fight his way through it. With expertise born of long hours on the drill-field, Carfax wielded the Ellylon blade. Left side, right side! On either side of his mount's lathered neck, the silver-bright blade dipped and rose dripping. A man's snarling face appeared at his stirrup and a spearhead gouged a burning path along his right thigh. Carfax bared his teeth in response and made a slashing cut, shearing away a portion of his opponent's face. Friend or foe? Which was which?

No matter.

Peering through the dense smoke, he won through to where the fighting was fiercest. A tight knot of men, hard to see in their dun-grey cloaks. The kneeling line of Ellylon, pausing in their retreat to fire and fire again, the points of their arrows clattering uselessly off their prey. The fine-wrought faces of the Rivenlost were grim. The dragon's body was vast and gleaming, churning the smoke-filled air. Only portions of it were visible at such close range, too vast for the mortal eye to encompass. Despite the whispered in-

cantations of the Ellylon, the terrible courage of the Borderguardsmen, their weapons clattered harmlessly off its
hide. Swords shattered, arrows fell to earth.

After all, what could penetrate those scales? This was no
mere dragonling, but one of the ancient ones, one of the
last. Even Elterrion the Bold would have hesitated to engage the Dragon of Beshtanag in the fullness of its wrath.
Under cover of the devastation it wreaked, a desperate
wedge of Beshtanagi wardsmen fell upon the enemy. Hand
to hand, blade to blade, hollow-eyed and starving, ready to
claim victory at the price of death. Some of the outnumbered Borderguard were standing, many were down. A
charnel reek hung over them all. It didn't matter. There was
only one person for whom Carfax searched. There was only
one whose weapon mattered here.

And amidst all the chaos, she stood, calm and ready.

A smoke-wreathed statue, limned in pure light. Her
quiver was empty. The Archer of Arduan had drawn her last
arrow, *the* arrow, tracking the dragon with it, as calmly as
though she were hunting rabbit. Oronin's Bow was in her
left hand, the fingers of her right hand curled about the
string, drawing it taut to her ear. A shaft of white fire, tinged
with gold, illuminated the soft tendrils of hair that curled on
her cheek.

The Arrow of Fire, Dergail's lost weapon, was ready to
be loosed.

When, Carfax wondered, did she lose her horse?

A vaned pinion passed near overhead, a gout of fire was
loosed elsewhere, and his mount squealed in terror, half-
rearing and bucking. All unwitting, it took him closer to
her, shaking him half-loose in the process. Carfax slid down
its back, clutching at its mane with his free hand. He saw
her shift at the sound, then gather herself, refusing to relinquish her focus. He saw the body she straddled, protecting
it. Blood seeped from a wound on Blaise Caveros' brow, the
Borderguardsman's face pale and drawn. He saw the vast,
scaled expanse of the dragon's flank sliding past him. He

saw a determined squadron of Beshtanagi making for the Archer. Before his thrashing, terrified mount threw him, he heard, somewhere, a voice he knew belonged to Aracus Altorus, shouting futile exhortations.

He saw the stony ground rushing up to meet him and felt it strike him hard.

"Here, dragon! Here, damn you! I'm waiting!"

It was Fianna's voice, rough-edged with despair, strung taut with defiance. Lying on his back, Carfax blinked and lifted his head. He saw tears making clean tracks on Fianna's soot-smudged cheeks. The bow was steady in her hands and the Arrow of Fire trailed flames of white-gold glory as the scaled underbelly of the dragon passed overhead. He groped for the Ellyl's sword and found he held it still, though his knuckles were scraped and raw. He felt at his body and found it intact. Completing its pass, the dragon climbed in the air, gaining altitude. Still alive and standing, Fianna tracked its progress, the Arrow's point blazing like a star. Carfax levered himself to his feet, lurching upright. Wet blood ran down his wounded right thigh, soaking his breeches, squelching in his boot. A reminder of another wound, one that never healed.

Forgive me, my Lord . . .

"The Arrow! The Arrow of Fire!"

It was an Ellyl voice that raised the cry, silvery and unmistakable. It was Men's voices that echoed it, harsh and ragged, forced through throats seared by smoke and fire. They had seen Fianna, seen what she held. With their diminished numbers, the Borderguard of Curonan sought to rally. But no one had expected to find the Archer of Arduan and the lost weapon on the battlefield, and she stood alone, isolated in a tightening circle of Beshtanagi wardsmen, her steady gaze and the Arrow's blazing point tracking the dragon's ascent.

He alone could protect her.

"Time to die," Carfax said aloud.

He took the closest man first. A thrust to the gut, no time

wasted. The tip of the Ellyl blade pierced cured leather like butter. His wounded right leg quivered as he withdrew the sword, threatening to give way beneath him. No time for that. He ignored the weakness and made his feet move over the harsh terrain, picking another target, swinging two-handed. Another wardsman fell, and another, clearing a path around Fianna, who hadn't even registered his presence. No matter. It felt good to have a sword in his hands. Better if he had been wearing armor, good Staccian armor. It might have kept him from enduring the myriad strokes that scored his flesh until he bled from a dozen places or more. It might have turned aside the cold blade that ran him through from behind, penetrating something vital. Blood soaked his clothing, mingling with sweat, running down his skin.

Panting, Carfax pivoted on his numb leg and cut down his foremost attacker, and another who followed, and two more after, three more. They came and they came, and he struck and he struck, weaving a circle around her, until his blood-slickened arms had no more feeling in them. Again and again, until he could no longer raise his sword and the battlefield seemed to darken in his vision.

Death is a coin to be spent wisely.

Falling to his knees, he tried to remember who had spoken those words. It sounded like Lord Vorax. It might have been his mother. Oh, there was brightness in the world, for all that it was slipping from his grasp. He thought about blue lakes under a blue summer sky and goldenrod in bloom, a dusting of pollen. A Beshtanagi wardsman loomed out of the smoke, grimacing, a hand-axe held above his head, prepared to deliver the final blow. On his knees, Carfax blinked and thrust upward with both hands, taking the man under the chin. The point of his borrowed sword stuck in the man's brain-pan. "Staccians," he whispered, "die hard."

There was shouting, then, and the clashing of steel. Somewhere, the Borderguard of Curonan claimed ground,

driving back the Beshtanagi. Horns were blowing an order
to stand, and straining above them were the clarion sounds
of the horns of the Rivenlost in the encampment, pleading a
retreat no one heeded. With an effort, Carfax tried to rise.
Instead, the world keeled sideways. He blinked, realizing
his cheek was pillowed on the loose scree of rocks, and he
could no longer feel his body.

So must his men have felt, when they died.

He lay prone, lacking the strength to move. All he could
do, he had done, whether she knew it or not. No matter. He
had not done it for her, but for her smile, and a memory of
what might have been. She was close; so near, so far. The
heels of her boots were inches from his open eyes, cracked
and downtrodden. How many leagues had they traveled together? He could see every shiny crease worn in the
leather. He might have loved her if she had let him. It
would have spread balm on the aching wound of his betrayal. But it was not to be, and all he could do was die for
her sake. It would have to be enough, for there was nothing else left to him. Between them lay the man she loved
and protected. Blaise's calloused hand was outflung, open,
as if to reach in friendship. His closed lids fluttered and
his fingertips twitched.

There was another sound. The dragon's roar.

It hurt Carfax to move his head, but he did. Enough to see
the black horn of Oronin's Bow silhouetted against the sky
and the blazing shaft of the Arrow it held taut. Enough to
see the tension in her body as the stooping dragon began its
last dive, growing from a dwindling speck of brightness to a
massive comet. Fianna's legs were trembling, though she
had her feet firmly planted. He saw the strong muscles of
her calves quivering in fear. But she was the Archer of Arduan and her arms held steady. In the midst of chaos and battle, she held. Even in the face of the dragon's dive, as its
wings shadowed the sky and its gleaming talons threatened
to gouge the earth.

Even when its jaws gaped wide, revealing the depths of

its impossible gullet, and fire spewed from the furnace of its belly. With tears on her face, she held her ground, shoulders braced, a shaft of white-gold fire blazing in the arc of horn and hair circumscribed by her hands. As he watched, her lips shaped a single, desperate prayer and her fingers released the string.

The Archer of Arduan shot the Arrow of Fire.

Trailing white-gold glory, it flew true between the dragon's jaws; flew true and pierced the gullet, pierced the mighty furnace of its belly. There was an explosion, then; a column of fire that seared the skies, while Men and Ellylon flung themselves to earth, and from somewhere, a cry, a terrible descant like the sound of a heart breaking asunder.

Dying, the dragon fell.

The impact made the mountain shudder.

Once the tremors faded there was a great deal of activity. Crushed Men screaming, defeated Men surrendering. Hailing shouts, and orders given crisply. Ellylon voices like a choir, intermingled with the sound of horns. A name uttered in a futile paean. None of it had anything to do with him. Carfax closed his eyes, and did not open them for a long time. It would have been better not to know. Still, he looked. Near him, so near him, a massive jaw lay quiescent on the scree, attached to a sinuous neck. Twin spirals of smoke trickled from bronze nostrils, wisping into nothingness in the empty air. The massive body lay beyond the bounds of his vision, broken-winged. Life was fading from a green-gilt eye. "I'm sorry," Carfax said; or tried to say, mouthing the words. There was no strength in his lungs to voice them, and his eardrums were broken. "I'm sorry."

Distant shouting; victory cries.

In a green-gilt eye, a dying light flickered, and a faint voice spoke in his mind. *This battle is not of your making, Arahila's Child. You played your part. Be forgiven.* And then words, three words, wrested forth in an agonizing wrench, one final throe before the end. *Lilias! Forgive me!*

Not for him. No matter. It was enough.

Carfax sighed, and died.

TWENTY-SIX

❖

THE CRASH SHOOK THE VERY foundations of Beshtanag.

Brightness, fading. All the brightness in the world. Kneeling on the terrace, Lilias bent double and clutched at her belly, feeling Calandor's death go through her like a spear. Her throat was raw from the cry his fall had torn from her and her heart ached within her, broken shards grinding one another into dust.

Whatever scant hope remained, his final agonized words destroyed.

Lilias! Forgive me!

Calandor! No!

She clung to the fading contact until his mighty heart-beat slowed and stopped forever. Gone. No more would the sun gleam on his scales, no more would he spread his wings to ride the drafts. Never again would she see a smile in the blink of a green-slitted eye. Her heart was filled with bitter ashes and the Soumanië was a dead ember on her brow, scraping the flagstones as she rocked in her grief, pressing her forehead to the grey stones. For a thousand years he had been her mentor, her friend, her soul's companion. More than she knew. More than she had ever known. "Calandor," she whispered. "Oh, Calandor! Please, no!"

In her mind, only silence answered.

Huddled over the flagstones, the Sorceress of the East grieved.

"My lady." At length a hand touched her shoulder. Lilias raised her tear-streaked face to meet Pietre's worried gaze. He nodded toward the base of the mountain, the linked chains of silver that bound him to her will gleaming around his throat. "They are coming."

They were coming.

Calandor was dead.

On stiff limbs she rose, staggering under the weight of her robes. Pietre's hand beneath her elbow assisted her; nearby, Sarika hovered, her pretty face a study in anguish. At the base of Beshtanag Mountain, her wall lay in ruins. Beyond—no. She could not look beyond the wall, where Calandor's corpse rose like a hillock. Inside the gap, Haomane's Allies were accepting the surrender of her Chief Warder. Even as she looked, Gergon lay his sword at Aracus Altorus' feet and pointed toward the terrace.

"Our archers—" Pietre hissed.

"No." With a weary gesture, Lilias cut him short, touching his cheek. There was courage of a kind in resolve. "Sweetling, it is over. We are defeated. Escort me to my throne room. I will hear their terms there."

They did, one on either side of her, and she was grateful for their assistance, for the necessity their presence imposed. Without it, she could gladly have laid down and died. Step by step, they led her into the grey halls of Beshtanag, past the silent censure of her people, hollow-eyed and hungry. They had trusted her, and she had failed them. Now they awaited salvation from another quarter. Her liveried servants, who wore no collars of servitude, had vanished. Her throne room seemed empty and echoing, and the summer sunlight that slanted through the high, narrow windows felt a mockery.

"How is it, my lady?" Sarika asked anxiously, helping her settle into the throne. It was wrought of a single block of Beshtanagi granite, the curve of the high back set with emeralds from Calandor's hoard. "Are you comfortable? Do you wish water? Wine? There is a keg set aside for your usage. We saw to it, Pietre and I."

"It's fine, sweetling." The effort it took to raise the corners of her mouth in something resembling a smile was considerable. Closing her eyes, Lilias gathered the remnants of her inner resources, the thin trickle of strength restored since Radovan's death. A faint spark lit the Soumanië. It was not much, but enough for what was necessary. She opened her eyes. "Do me a favor, will you? Summon my attendants. All of them, all my pretty ones."

Pietre frowned; Sarika fluttered. In the end, they did her bidding. Marija, Stepan, Anna—all of them stood arrayed before her, their silver collars gleaming. All save Radovan, whose lifeless body lay unmoving on the terrace. So young, all of them! How many had she bent to her will in the course of a thousand years? They were countless.

And now it was over. All over.

"Come here." Lilias beckoned. "I mean to set you free."

"No!" Sarika gasped, both hands rising to clutch her collar.

Sullen Marija ignored her, stepping promptly to the base of the throne. A pretty girl, with the high, broad cheekbones of a Beshtanagi peasant. She should have been freed long ago; Radovan had been a friend of hers. Lilias gazed at her with rue and leaned forward, touching the silver collar with two fingers. Holding a pattern in her mind, she whispered three words that Calandor had taught her and *undid* the pattern the way the dragon had shown her, so many centuries ago.

Silver links parted and slithered to the floor. Eyeing the fallen collar warily, Marija touched her bare throat. With a harsh laugh she turned and fled, her footsteps echoing in the empty hall. Lilias sighed, pressing her temples. "Come," she said wearily. "Who is next?"

No one moved.

"Why?" Pietre whispered. "Why, my lady? Have we not served you well?"

She was a thousand years old, and she wanted to weep. Oh, Uru-Alat, the time had gone quickly! "Yes, sweetling," Lilias said, as gently as she could. "You have. But you see, we are defeated here. And as you are innocent, Haomane's Allies will show mercy, do you submit to it. It is their way."

They protested, of course. It was in their nature, the best of her pretty ones. In the end, she freed them all. Pietre was the hardest. There were tears in his eyes as he knelt before her, blinking. He cried aloud when the collar slipped from his neck.

"Be free of it." Lilias finished the gesture, the *unbinding,* resting the back of her head against her throne. The last connection slid from her grasp, the final severing complete. It was done. On her brow, the Soumanië guttered, and failed for the last time.

She was done.

"Lady." Though his throat was bare, Pietre's hands grasped hers, hard. His throat was bare, and nothing had changed in his steadfast gaze. "A delegation is at the door. Shall I admit them?"

"Yes." Relying on the unyielding granite to keep her upright, Lilias swallowed against the aching lump in her throat. "Thank you, Pietre," she said, her voice hoarse. "I am done here. If you would do me one final service, let them in."

THEY WERE FIVE WHO ENTERED the hall.

The foremost, she knew. She had seen him from afar for too long not to recognize him. His dun-grey cloak swirled about him as he strode and sunlight glinted on his red-gold hair. Mortal, yes; Arahila's Child, with the breath of Oronin's Horn blowing hot on his neck. Still, there was

something more in his fierce, wide-set gaze, an awareness
vouchsafed few of his kind.

Of their kind.

Lilias sat unmoving and watched them come. Over her
head, emeralds winked against the back of her granite
throne, ordinary gems sunk into the very stone. She had
wrought it herself when Calandor first taught her to use the
Soumanië to *Shape* elements, almost a thousand years ago.
For that long, for ill or for good, had she ruled Beshtanag
from this seat.

The delegation halted before her.

No one bowed, least of all their leader. "Sorceress." His
voice was curt. "I am Aracus Altorus of the Borderguard of
Curonan, and I speak for Haomane's Allies. You know what
we have come for. Is she here?"

Lilias looked past him to the other four. Two of them
were mortal, and one she knew; Martinek, Regent of Southeastern Pelmar, whose face bore a cruel, gloating expression. The other, a Borderguardsman, seemed unsteady on
his feet. There was something vaguely familiar about him;
his dark, sombre eyes and the shock of hair falling over his
pale and bandaged brow. The remaining two were Ellylon,
their fine-wrought features startling in her stone halls. One
of these too she knew, having seen his standard oft enough;
Lorenlasse of Valmaré, gleaming in his armor. The other
Ellyl, in travel-worn garb, she did not recognize. He looked
at her with sorrow.

"No," she said at last; to him, to all of them, letting the
word fall like a stone. Her fingers clutched the throne's
arms; there was a bitter satisfaction in the message. "You
have assailed us in vain, would-be King of the West. Beshtanag has committed no crime. The Lady Cerelinde of the
Rivenlost is not here."

Aracus Altorus' sword rasped free of its scabbard. The
point of it came to rest in the hollow of her throat. Lilias sat
unflinching. Calandor was dead, Beshtanag had fallen, and

she did not care if she lived or died. He leaned forward, one foot on the throne's base, pressing hard enough to draw a trickle of blood.

"*Where is she?*"

His breath was hot on her face; well-fed, smelling of heat and battle-rage, his strength fueled by mutton and deer purloined from the pastures and forests of Beshtanag. "Aracus," the wounded Man murmured, cautioning. One of the Ellylon spoke to the other in their melodious language. Lilias ignored them and smiled with all the bleak emptiness in her heart.

"Darkhaven," she said, relishing his reaction. "She is in Darkhaven, in the Sunderer's keeping. It is where she has been all along, my lord of the Borderguard. Your people were misled."

He swore, Aracus Altorus did, turning away from her. His shoulders shook, and cords stood out in his neck, taut with anguish. Lilias was glad of it. Let him suffer, then, as she did. Let him know the taste of failure. He had destroyed everything she held dear. And for what? For nothing.

"Son of Altorus." Lorenlasse of Valmaré addressed him in the common tongue, his voice gentle. "Believe me when I tell you that this news is as grievous to the Rivenlost as to you, if not more so. And yet there is another matter at hand."

"Yes." He went still, then turned back to her. "There is."

Despite everything, Lilias found herself shrinking back against the throne. He should have been afraid. He wasn't. His grief, this defeat in the midst of victory, had granted him that much. There was no anger in his face, nor mercy, only a weary nobility for which she despised him. Why should he be appointed to this victory? What accident of birth, what vagary of Haomane's will, vouchsafed him this prize?

Two steps toward her, then three.

He reached out one hand, palm open. "The Soumanië."

It was a dead weight on her brow and it shouldn't have hurt to face its loss. It did. Especially to him, to this one. Lilias gripped the granite arms of her throne until her nails bent and bled. "Will you take it from me, then?" she asked him. "How then, when you have not won it? Do you claim a victory here? I think not, Altorus. This prize belonged to the Dragon of Beshtanag." She laughed, the sound of her laughter high and unstrung. "Do you think Calandor did not see his end, and I with him? Do you think I did not see who wielded Oronin's Bow and the Arrow of Fire? Where is the Archer, son of Altorus? I see no women in your train. Do you fear to give such a prize unto a woman's hand?"

"Sorceress," he said patiently. "The Soumanië."

"No," she whispered. "Martinek! You are Pelmaran. Think what this means. Will you let him claim sovereignty over my lands and yours?"

The Southeastern Regent shifted, adjusting his sword-hilt, setting his mouth in a hard, thin line. He had the decency not to meet her gaze. "I've sworn my allegiance."

"What of you, my lord Valmaré?" In despair, Lilias forced her tone to one of sweet reason, addressing Lorenlasse of Valmaré. "Have matters changed so in Urulat? Do Haomane's Children cede the spoils of victory to Arahila's? This is not a prize for mortal hands to sully. Am I not living proof?"

The Rivenlost Lord frowned, hesitating.

"Lorenlasse." The travel-worn Ellyl spoke the common tongue with soft regret. "Ingolin the Wise himself dared not take on such a burden. Will you gainsay his wisdom, that Malthus the Counselor informed? Let the Son of Aracus claim it. He is the betrothed of the Lady Cerelinde, granddaughter of Elterrion the Bold. Our time ends, and this is his victory. It is his right."

Lorenlasse of Valmaré stepped back, nodding, sorrow and a grave acceptance in his countenance. "So be it," he said. "As I am Haomane's Child, I fulfill his Prophecy. Son of Altorus, the Soumanië is yours."

"Sorceress," Aracus Altorus said simply, extending his hand.

He did not threaten. With a conquering army at his back, he didn't need to.

"Take it, then!" With trembling fingers, Lilias lifted the fillet from her brow. The Soumanië was a dull red stone in its center. For a thousand years it had maintained contact with her unaging flesh. Even now, when she was spent beyond telling, when its power lay beyond her grasp, the Soumanië sustained her, maintaining the bond that stretched the Chain of Being to its uttermost limit. So it had done for a thousand years, since the Dragon of Beshtanag had divulged its secrets to a headstrong Pelmaran girl. Tears burning in her eyes, Lilias placed the fillet in Aracus Altorus' outstretched palm and relinquished it. "Let the Shapers themselves bear witness, I do this against my will."

He closed his hand upon the Soumanië and claimed it.

It was done. The bond was severed, a shock as sudden as icy water, and Lilias dwindled back toward mortality. The confines of her flesh closed in upon her, unexpected and suffocating. Her thoughts, that had extended to the boundaries of Beshtanag, became circumscribed by skin and bone. The dense forests, the harsh mountain crags; lost, all lost. Never again would she *reach* into the world beyond her fingers' touch, not even toward the emptiness of Calandor's absence. It was gone, all gone, and the sands of time that the Soumanië had held at bay began to trickle through the hourglass of her fate. Even now, she felt the slow decay of age creeping. Flesh would wither, bone would grow brittle.

The Sorceress of the East was no more.

In her place sat a mortal woman, a Pelmaran earl's daughter, a vain and foolish woman who had lived beyond her allotted years and brought ruin upon herself and her people. In the face of her conquerors' contempt, Lilias bowed her head, no longer able to meet their eyes. "Calan-

dor," she whispered to the empty space inside her. "Oh Calandor, I miss you!"

Somewhere in the distance, Oronin's Horn was blowing.

STORMCLOUDS GATHERED OVER THE VALE of Gorgantum.

Seated in his deep-cantled saddle atop one of the horses
of Darkhaven, Vorax frowned, watching the roiling skies
blot out the faint red disk of the sun. The terminal half-light
of the Vale grew ominous. Beneath his resplendent armor,
the scar that branded his sturdy chest itched and burned.
Over plain and forest and rising hills, from the cleft of the
Defile to the outermost boundaries of the walls, clouds
gathered, dense and heavy. On the training-field, the Fjel
broke ranks to glance uneasily at the skies.

"A storm, do you reckon, sir?" Beside him, Hyrgolf
squinted at the clouds.

Vorax scratched at his armored chest with absentminded
futility. His mount shifted restlessly, stamping a hoof. "I'm
not sure." His brand was beginning to sting as if there were
a hornet's nest lodged under his armor and there was a dis-
tinct *tugging* in the direction of the fortress. "No." He shook
his head. "No ordinary storm, anyway. Field marshal, can-
cel the exercise. Dismiss the troops."

Hyrgolf roared a command in the Fjel tongue, a signal relayed by his bannerman. Pennants dipped and waved under
the glowering skies, and a rumble of thunder answered.
Thousands of Fjeltroll began to disperse in semi-orderly
fashion, forming into winding columns and setting off at a
slow, steady jog for their barracks.

Above the looming edifice, clouds built. Layer upon
layer they gathered, dark and billowing, echoing the towering structure below. Angry lightning flickered, illuminating
the underbellies of the bruise-colored swells. Whatever
they contained, it didn't bode well for anyone caught on the
field.

"It's his Lordship," Hyrgolf observed. "He's wroth."

"I think you're right." Vorax grimaced and bent over his pommel as pain clutched at his heart like a fist and the tugging sensation intensified. "Field marshal!" The words emerged in a grunt. "Help me. I have to get back there. *Now*."

"Aye, sir!" Hyrgolf gave a crisp salute and stooped to grasp the reins of Vorax's mount a half a foot below the bit. "Make way!" he bellowed at the retreating backs of his army as he forged a path. "Way for Lord Vorax!"

The columns wavered at his order and parted to create an alley. Through his pain, Vorax was dimly aware of being impressed at the discipline Tanaros had drilled into his troops and at the steady competence of the Tungskulder Fjel who commanded them. Then a bolt of lightning cracked the skies and thunder pealed. His mount, unwontedly skittish, sought to rear, tugging at the reins the Fjeltroll held in an iron grip. With his chest ablaze, it was all Vorax could do to stay upright in the saddle.

Thunder pealed again, sharp and incisive, and the clouds split open to unleash their burden. The rain that spat down was greasy and unclean, reeking of sulfur. Worse, Vorax realized with a shudder, it *burned* like sulfur. It was an unnatural rain, carrying the taint of a Shaper's fury. His flesh prickled beneath his armor, fearful of its touch on his skin, and he was glad his Staccian company wasn't on the field.

"Sir!" Hyrgolf was bawling in his ear, his hideous face looming close. Water dripped from his brow-ridges, carving steaming runnels in his obdurate hide. "Sir, I've called for a Gulnagel escort! It's the fastest way!"

Another seizure clutched at his chest, and his mount trumpeted with pain and fear, flaring its nostrils at the rain's stench. "My thanks!" Vorax managed to gasp; and then the others were there, one on either side, a pair of Gulnagel baring their eyetusks as they leapt to secure his reins.

They set out at a run, ignoring the deluge. The reins stretched taut and his horse followed anxiously in their wake, moving from a trot into a canter, settling into a gallop as the Gulnagel lengthened their strides into swift bounds. Their taloned feet scored deep gouges in the earth as they passed their hurrying brethren. Vorax clutched his deep pommel with both hands, concentrating on keeping his seat. The field was a blur. Corrosive rain sheeted from his Staccian armor and he tucked his chin tight against his chest, letting the visor of his helmet deflect the rain from his face; otill, burning droplets pelted his cheeks. His mount squealed, steam arising from its sleek hide. The Fjel yelped and ran onward, leading him at breakneck speed.

At the outermost postern gates, one of Ushahin's madlings was dancing from foot to foot. He held out his hand for the reins in a pleading gesture, heedless of the bleeding scores the rain etched on his face. Still ducking his chin, Vorax struggled to free his feet from the stirrups as the Gulnagel helped him dismount. The madling crooned to his mount, shoulders hunched against the punishing rain.

And then Vorax was on solid ground, screwing his eyes shut as burning moisture seeped under his visor, trickling down his brow. He heard hoofbeats echo on the flagstones as Ushahin's madling led his horse at a run for the shelter of the stables. The obedient Gulnagel gripped his arms, hustling him through the rain toward the inner gate, where the Mørkhar Fjel of the Havenguard granted them passage.

Beneath the tall, heavy ceilings they were safe from the rain. One of the Gulnagel spoke in their guttural tongue, and the Havenguard replied in the same. With deft care, Fjeltroll talons unbuckled straps, removing his armor piece by piece, lifting the helmet from his head. Rainwater dripped and sizzled harmlessly on the stone floor, making the entryway reek of rotten eggs. The Fjel wiped his sword-belt dry, settling it around his waist. Vorax braced his hands on his thighs and took a deep breath against the dizzying pain in his chest. Straightening, he wiped his brow with his sleeve. The fumes made his eyes sting as he opened them and a patch of blisters was rising on his forehead, but he was whole.

"The army?" It was important to ask.

"On their way, boss." One of the Gulnagel pointed past the open door toward the outer gates, where the columns were making their way toward their deep-hewn barracks. He shook himself like a dog, shedding water. Slow, dark blood oozed from pockmarks in his yellowish hide. "This is no good, though, even for Fjel."

"No," Vorax said, wincing at the sight. "It's not." Outside, angry thunder pealed. One of the Mørkhar fingered a carved talisman, leathery lips moving in a whispered prayer. "You, lad," Vorax said to him. Tanaros would have known his name; he didn't. For the first time, he felt bad about the fact. "Take me to his Lordship."

"Aye, Lord Vorax." The Mørkhar stowed his figurine. "This way, sir."

It felt like a long walk, longer than usual. Ushahin's madlings were in hiding, and there were only the empty halls of Darkhaven, veins of marrow-fire pulsing with agitation in the gleaming black walls. Vorax felt his own pulse quicken in accord, his heart constricting. Ah, Neheris-of-the-Leaping-Waters, he thought. Have pity on your Children, and those who have dwelled alongside them! We mean no harm, no, not to you. This is your brother Haomane's quarrel.

There was no answer, of course. For ages beyond counting, no Shaper had ever answered the prayers of mortal kind save Lord Satoris. Distant and remote on Torath, they bent their wills to Haomane's pride, while on the face of Urulat, Lord Satoris fought against a dark tide of pain, and kept his promises to all who honored him.

There was only the journey, and its ending, where the towering iron doors of the Throne Hall had been flung apart, standing open as if onto a vast furnace. The diorama of the Shapers' War was split wide open, separating Lord Satoris from the Six Shapers. Beyond lay a maelstrom of darkness and a throbbing red light, source of the infernal *pull*, beckoning to him like a lodestone.

Godslayer, Vorax thought, his mouth going dry. He's taken it from the Font.

The Havenguard on duty saluted, hands clutched firm on the hafts of their battle-axes. Fjel seldom looked nervous, but these two did. "Lord Vorax," one acknowledged him, deep-set eyes glittering in the light of the marrow-fire. "Be wary. He is wroth."

"I know." Vorax wiped his sweating, blistered brow and sighed. "My thanks, lads," he said, and crossed the threshold. Inside, torches sprang alight with the marrow-fire. He squinted at the blue-white effluence, the shadows of his own body looming in the corners. Fair Arahila, he thought, you've a name for mercy, even his Lordship said so. What wouldn't I give, now, for all that I've taken for granted? A meal fit for a king, a hungry king. A warm bath and a sweet lass to rub oil into my aching shoulders. Is it so much to ask? The red light of Godslayer flared, disrupting his thoughts. Pain seized his chest and hammered him to his knees.

"*Kill them!*" Lord Satoris' voice cracked like thunder, until the very walls creaked and trembled in protest. "*Do you understand? I am giving this order. Kill them. Kill them ALL!*"

"My Lord!" Vorax gasped, floundering on the carpet. His eardrums ached with the pressure and his heart was beating so fast it threatened to burst his chest. I am too old for this, he thought, and too fat. "As you will, it shall be done!"

There was silence, and the pressure abated. "Vorax. My words were meant for another. Tanaros Blacksword lives. He has won free of the Marasoumië."

"Good news, my Lord." Gratefully, he struggled to his feet. He could see, now. The black carpet stretching in front of him and the figure on the Throne, illumed in darkness. Vorax made his feet move. It was not hard, after all. That which compelled him was held in his Lord's hands, a shard of red light pulsing like lifeblood. It reeled him onward as surely as a hook in his heart, and he placed one foot in front of the other until he stood before the Throne and gazed at Satoris' face, hidden behind the aching void of the Helm of Shadows. "You summoned me?"

"My Staccian." The Shaper bent his head. "Yes. Matters have . . . transpired."

"Aye, my Lord." It was hot within the Throne Hall, cursedly hot. The news about Tanaros was welcome. He did not think the rest would be. Vorax watched the dagger throbbing between the Shaper's palms, held like a prayer-offering. The beat of his own scarred heart matched its rhythm. "What matters?"

The shard flared in Satoris' hands. "One of the Eldest has fallen."

Vorax swallowed, hard. "The Dragon of Beshtanag?"

"Yes." Through the eyeslits of the Helm of Shadows, the Shaper stared at him without blinking. "His name was Calandor, and he was old when I first walked the earth; oldest of all, save one. He was my friend, many ages ago."

Dire news, indeed. The Ellylon of old had slain dragons, but never one of the most ancient, the Eldest. Only in the Shapers' War had that come to pass. In the face of the Helm's hollow-eyed stare, Vorax had to look away. "How was it done?" he asked.

Lord Satoris gave a mirthless laugh. "With the Arrow of Fire."

In the sweltering heat of the Throne Hall, his skin turned cold and clammy. Haomane's Prophecy pounded like a litany in his skull. "They did it," Vorax said, forcing the words past a lump of fear in his throat. "Found the lost weapon."

"Yes." The Shaper contemplated the dagger in his hands. Godslayer's flames caressed his fingers, shadows writhing in the Helm's eyeslits. "They did. And they will be coming for us, my Staccian, these Allies of my Brother." His head lifted and his eyes blazed to life. "But what they plan, I have *seen!* I dare what they did not think I would dare! I am not my Brother, to quail in mortality's shadow! I dare to don the Helm, I dare to pluck Godslayer from the marrow-fire and *see!*"

"Right." With a prodigious effort, Vorax filled his lungs, then exhaled. He was tired, his blistered skin stung and his knees ached, but he was one of the Three, and he had sworn his oath a long, long time ago. "What now, my Lord?"

"Vengeance," Satoris said softly, "for one who was a friend, once. Protection, for us. There is something I must do, a grave and dire thing. It is for this, and this alone, that I have taken Godslayer from the marrow-fire. And I have a task for you, Vorax, that will put an end this talk of my Elder Brother's Prophecy."

"Aye, my Lord!" Relief outweighed remorse as Vorax reached for his sword-hilt. To slay a defenseless woman was no welcome chore, but such was the nature of the bargain he had made. Immortality and plenitude for him; peace and prosperity for Staccia. It was the only sensible course, and he was glad his Lordship had seen it at last. One stroke, and the Prophecy would be undone. She would not suffer, he would see to that. It would be swift and merciful, and done in time for supper. "Elterrion's granddaughter will be dead ere dawn, I promise you."

"No!"

Vorax winced at the thunderous word, relinquishing his hilt.

"No," the Shaper repeated, leaning forward on the throne. The sweet reek of blood mingled with the distant stench of sulfur, and his eyes burned like red embers through the Helm's dark slits. "I am not my Brother, Staccian. I will play this game with honor, in my own way. I will not let Haomane strip that from me, and force me to become all that he has named me." His voice dripped contempt. "I will not become the thing that I *despise*. I will assail my enemies as they assail me. The Lady Cerelinde—" he lifted one admonishing finger from Godslayer, "—is my guest. She is not to be harmed."

"As you will." Vorax licked his lips. Had his Lordship gone mad? He pushed the thought away, trying not to remember stormclouds piling high over Darkhaven, a foul rain falling, seething flesh. What did it matter if he had? After all, Satoris Third-Born had reason enough for anger. And he, Vorax of Staccia, had sworn an oath, was bound and branded by it, upon a shard of the Souma itself. There was no gainsaying it. To be foresworn was to die. "What, then?"

"Your work lies in the north." Satoris smiled with grim satisfaction. "Malthus erred. He spent his strength shielding his Bearer from my sight, but he cannot conceal the lad's path through the Marasoumië. I know where he lit. The one who would extinguish the marrow-fire is in the north, Vorax. Send a company; Men you trust, and Fjel to aid them. Find the Bearer, and kill him. Let the vial he carries be shattered, and the Water of Life spilled harmless upon the barren earth."

"My Lord." A simple task, after all. Relieved, he bowed. "It will be done."

"Good." Satoris regarded Godslayer, turning the shard in his fingers. "Ushahin comes apace," he mused, forgetting the Staccian's presence, "and Tanaros has his orders, though he likes them not. You must be consigned to the marrow-fire, my bitter friend, for you are too dangerous to be kept elsewhere. But first; ah, first! We have a task to accomplish, you and I."

"My Lord?" Vorax waited, then inquired, uncertain if his services were needed.

The eye slits of the Helm turned his way, filled with all the darkness and agony of a dying world. "It is time to close the Marasoumië," Lord Satoris said. "Now, while Malthus is trapped within it, before he regains his strength."

"Now? Then how will Tanaros and—"

"*Now!*" The Shaper pounded a clenched fist on the arm of the throne. Behind the Helm, his teeth were bared in a rictus. "Understand, Vorax! Aracus Altorus has seized one of the Soumanië! Does he gain mastery over it, with two Soumanië to hand, he and my Elder Brother's Counselor could control the Ways. If I do this thing *now,* then Malthus remains trapped, and the son of Altorus remains ignorant of his counsel. Is that not worth any price?"

There was only one answer, and Vorax gave it. "Aye, my Lord."

"So be it," Satoris said, taking hold of the dagger with both hands. "And you shall bear witness." In his grip, Godslayer's light intensified, bright as a rising sun. "Ah! It burns! Uru-Alat, how it burns!" Rubescent light exploded in the Chamber, and Vorax's branded chest contracted. Struggling for breath, he dropped back to his knees. There he saw Satoris rising triumphant, a vast figure of darkness. Held aloft, Godslayer pulsed in his fist, bleeding light. It was a shard of the Souma itself, filled with the power of the world's birth. Light seemed to illume the Shaper's bones beneath his obdurate flesh, streamed from the wound in his thigh.

"My Lord!" Vorax gasped, wheezing. "Please!"

"Death and death and death," the Shaper whispered, ignoring him. "Oh, Malthus! Haomane's Weapon, my Brother's pawn! Do you think I do not know my true enemy? Do you know what you bring to this world? Do you know how the story ends? Ah, no! So be it, Counselor. I bind you in the web you spun." He tightened his grip on Godslayer and cried aloud, summoning his will in the form of a Shaper's skills, and pouring his strength into the effort. *"Let the Marasoumië be sealed!"*

Attuned to the shard's power, Vorax felt it, and closed his eyes in pain. What he had seen begin through the eyes of the Helm of Shadows came to pass. Deep below the surface of the earth across the vast nation of Urulat, node-points flickered and died, going ashen-grey.

A part of the world, dying, went dead.

"So," Satoris said with vicious satisfaction. "Free yourself from *that,* Counselor!"

TWENTY-SEVEN

TANAROS' BOOTS CRUNCHED IN THE sand as he walked
away from the Stone Grove encampment. With every step
his scabbard brushed his thigh in reminder, unwanted and
unneeded. His Lord's words echoed over and over in his
head, and the sun blazing in his face made his ringing head
ache.

Kill them. Kill them ALL!

"Lord General?"

"Go away, Speros," he said without looking.

"It's just . . . did Lord Satoris give us orders? Is he going
to open the Ways and bring us home? Because I could have
the lads back at the node—"

"Go *away*, Speros!"

There was a pause. "Aye, General. We'll be at the camp-
site when you're ready."

When he was ready; there was a bitter jest! Lifting his
head, Tanaros stared at the blinding face of the sun. He remembered how good it had felt in Beshtanag to see the
sun's rays gilding the forest after long years of Darkhaven's
eternal gloom. Did the sun still shine in Beshtanag? He supposed it did, despite what had befallen there. It seemed
closer, here, where Haomane's wrath had scorched the
earth in pursuit of Satoris. What was it like, living with this
surfeit of light?

Bare feet made no sound on the desert floor. "Slayer."

"Ngurra." Tanaros regarded the sun. "What do you
want?"

"Truth." One simple word, spoken in the common
tongue. Tanaros sighed and turned. Ngurra squatted on the

desert floor, squinting up at him, his brown face a map of
wrinkles in the sun's unforgiving light. "It's your choosing-
time, isn't it?"

After a day in the Yarru's company, Tanaros didn't bother
lying to the old man. "Why?" he asked instead, resting one
hand on the black sword's hilt. "Why did you do it? Why
did you send this boy, this Bearer—"

"Dani."

"—this *Dani* to extinguish the marrow-fire?" Tanaros'
voice rose. "*Why,* Ngurra? Has Haomane been so good to
your people? Did he have a care for your welfare when he
scorched the earth? Look at this place!" He gestured at the
desert. "It's barely enough to sustain life! We would have
perished here if you'd not shown us how to survive! For
this, you seek to thank Haomane First-Born by destroying
my Lord?"

"No, Slayer." Ngurra shook his head. "This is Birru-Uru-
Alat. Here, where the Well of the World abides, is the center, the choosing-place. We are the Yarru-yami, and that is
the trust we preserve."

"*Haomane's* trust," Tanaros said bitterly.

The old man gave a weary chuckle. "When did the
Lord-of-Thought ever hold choice to be a sacred trust?
No, Slayer. He gave us no choice when he brought the
sun's wrath upon us, no more than your Lord Satoris did
when he fled to this place. Together, they drove us into
hiding. This wisdom comes from the deep places in Uru-
Alat, from a time when the world was newly Sundered."
He held up his empty hands, palms marked with ordinary,
mortal lines. "Such is the burden we carry. That, and the
promise that one among us would be born to Bear a
greater one."

"Aye." The words came hard, sticking in his throat. "To
extinguish the marrow-fire, freeing Godslayer. To fulfill
Haomane's Prophecy and destroy my Lord."

Ngurra nodded. "That is one choice."

"It's the choice he *made!*" With an effort, Tanaros controlled his anger. It would do no good to shout at the old man. If nothing else, a day among the Yarru had taught him that much. "Why, Ngurra? Why *that* choice?"

Tilting his head, the old Yarru regarded the sky. "Where were you, to offer another? There are things I could say, Slayer, and the simplest one of all is that it is the choice he was offered. Was Dani's choice right?" He shook his head again. "I do not know. I only know he is the Bearer, and it was his to choose."

Tanaros gritted his teeth. "That's not good enough, old one."

"Isn't it?" Ngurra's eyes shone with sympathy in his wrinkled face. "And yet here you are at the choosing-place." With a grunt he straightened his legs and rose, turning back toward the camp. "Think on it, Slayer," he said over his shoulder. "We are ready. We have been waiting for you. You have a choice to make."

He watched the old man's steady progress across the sand. At the encampment, the Yarru elders hailed his return under the benign gaze of the Gulnagel Fjel on guard. He could hear white-haired Warabi, the old man's wife, scolding him for his folly.

We have been expecting you.

If Ngurra had not greeted him with those words, he might have ordered them slain. Why not? It was true, they were the ones who had sent forth the Bearer to extinguish the marrow-fire. But instead, he had stayed his hand out of curiosity. He had ordered Speros and the Fjel to accept the Yarru's hospitality. And a good thing, too. They would be half dead of thirst if the Yarru hadn't shown them how to find water-holes in the Unknown Desert, how to catch basking lizards, how chewing *gamal* heightened the senses and moistened parched tissues. The Yarru had shown them kindness. Whatever they were, whatever strange beliefs they held, these Charred Ones were not foes.

Old men. Old women.

"I don't want to kill them," Tanaros whispered. Unaccountable tears stung his eyes, and he covered his face with both hands. "Oh, my Lord! Must it be so?"

Distant power flickered as if in answer, and pain seared his scarred breast, so acute it was almost unbearable. So. It had begun as his Lordship had said it would. In the west, in Darkhaven, Satoris was wielding Godslayer with the full might of a Shaper's power, a thing he had not dared since Darkhaven was raised. Tanaros felt his teeth begin to chatter. He dropped to his knees in the sand and pressed his fingertips hard against his temples, willing his flesh to obedience. All across the world, it was as though a thousand doors had been slammed at once. Everywhere, light flared and died, a vast network of connections turning to ash.

The Marasoumië was closed.

That was that, then. The thing was done. His Lordship had no intention of changing his orders. Tanaros waited for his pounding heartbeat to subside, then climbed heavily to his feet and brushed the sand off his knees.

You have a choice to make.

There was no point in waiting. The task was onerous; the journey afterward would be grueling. Trudging across the desert toward the encampment, he drew his sword. It glinted dully in the sun, a length of black steel laying a black bar of shadow on the desert floor. Where would he go if he disobeyed Satoris' orders? What would he do? He was General Tanaros Blacksword, one of the Three, and he had made his choice a long, long time ago.

Speros sprang alert at his approach, whistling for the attention of the Gulnagel. "Lord General! What was that happened just now? Is it time to—" He stopped, eyeing the drawn sword. "What are you doing?"

"They know." Tanaros gestured wearily at the Yarru, who had gathered in a circle. Old men and old women, linked by age-knotted hands clasped tight together. There were tears in the creases of Warabi's dark cheeks as she clung to Ngurra's hand.

"You mean to kill them all?" Speros swallowed, turning

pale. "Ah, but Lord General, they're harmless. They're—"

"—old," Tanaros finished for him. "I know." He rubbed his brow with his free hand. "Listen, lads. Beshtanag has fallen, and Lord Satoris has closed the Ways. We're going home the hard way. But we've got business to attend to here first. We're going to bury that cursed well, that no one else may find it. And . . . " he drew a deep breath, pointing his sword at the Yarru, " . . . we leave no survivors to tell of it."

With stoic shrugs, the Gulnagel took up positions around the ring of Yarru elders, who shrank closer together, murmuring in their tongue. Ngurra gently freed his hand from his wife's and stepped forward. There was fear in his face; and courage, too.

"Slayer," he said. "You do not have to choose this."

"Give me a reason, Ngurra." Rage and bleak despair stirred in Tanaros' heart, and he tightened his grip on his sword-hilt, raising it with both hands to strike. "*Give me a reason!* Tell me you're wrong, tell me you're sorry, tell me the Bearer made a bad choice! Send a delegation to bring him back! Can you do that, old man? Is that so much to ask? I didn't ask for this choice! *Give me a reason not to make it!*"

The Yarru elder shook his head, profound regret in his eyes. "I can give you only the choice, Slayer," he said sadly. "Choose."

"So be it," Tanaros whispered. Sick at heart, he swung the blade.

His sword cut clean, cleaving the old man's scrawny chest in a mortal blow. Dark flesh, cleaved by a black blade. There was a single agonized cry from Ngurra's wife, a collective whimper from the other Yarru. The old man went down without a sound, bleeding onto the desert floor as silently as he'd walked upon it. Turning away, Tanaros nodded to Speros and the four Gulnagel Fjel. "See it finished."

Meaty thuds filled the air as the Gulnagel went to work with their maces. There were cries of fear and pain; though not many, no. Hunting Fjel preferred to kill with one blow, and the Gulnagel were swift. Tanaros sat on an outcropping of rock, wiping Ngurra's blood from the black blade. He didn't glance up from his labors until he heard footsteps approaching. "Is it done?"

"Aye, Lord General." It was Speros, looking ill and abashed. "The Fjel have finished." He glanced at the ground, then blurted, "I'm sorry, sir, I couldn't do it. I've got a grandmam at home."

"A grandmam." Tanaros laid his sword across his knees and rubbed his aching temples, not sure whether to laugh or weep. He'd had a grandmother, once. She was long-dead bones, and had died cursing his name. "Ah, Speros of Haimhault! What are you doing here? Why in the name of the Seven Shapers did you come here?"

"Sir?" The Midlander gave him a quizzical look.

"Never mind." He rose to his feet, sheathing his sword. There was a taste of bile in his throat and he knew, with utter and horrible certitude, that he would never remember this day's work without cringing in his soul. "Gather the Fjel, we've got a lot of work to do."

USHAHIN DREAMSPINNER WAS IN ARDUAN when the Marasoumië was sealed.

He was grateful for Lord Satoris' warning. It had been unexpected; the reaching tendrils of Godslayer's power making his scar itch and burn, and suddenly Satoris was *there*, touching his mind, sifting through his thoughts. So it must feel to mortals when he used his Were-taught skills to walk in their dreams.

"I understand, my Lord," he said when the Shaper had finished, bowing to the empty air. A pair of Arduans strolling in the marketplace gave him a wide berth. "I will come as I may."

There was a banyan tree growing on the eastern side of

the square. Ushahin found space amid its roots and sat cross-legged in its shade, waiting. He bowed his head, drawing the hood of a cloak he had stolen from a sleeping hunter down to hide his features. It was hot and humid here along the fringe of the Delta; still, better to be uncomfortable than to be recognized.

Arduans were a polite folk, their tiny nation founded on respect for individual rights, including that to privacy. No one would disturb him if he claimed it; no, not unless he showed his face. That, he suspected, would invoke the other great passion of Arduan. There was only one misshapen Ellyl half-breed in Urulat. Even Arduans would require no further justification than his face to nock an arrow and fire.

Ushahin waited.

A part of the world died.

It hurt. He felt the passing of each node-point as it flared and died. Little deaths, each and every one, a shock to his flesh where a shard of the Souma had branded it. He made himself breathe slowly, enduring it. He wondered if it took Vorax and Tanaros the same way. He thought about Malthus the Counselor trapped in the Ways, and smiled through his pain.

It was done.

"Are you all right, mister? Something funny happened just now."

A high voice; a child's voice. Ushahin opened his eyes to see a young girl stooping under the banyan tree to peer at him. She had a spray of freckles across the bridge of her nose, and a child's bow clutched in one grimy hand. The children who had set upon him so long ago in Pelmar, breaking his bones and rending his flesh, had been scarce older. Neither had he, then.

"Aye, lass," he said, slipping behind her eyes and into her thoughts without an effort, *twisting* them to his own ends. "I'm fine, and so are you. I need to purchase a boat; a skiff, such as fishermen use in the Delta. Surely a clever girl like you would know where I might find such a thing."

"Oh, aye, you need to see Caitlin's Da!" She beamed with pride, happy to have an answer. Whatever she had sensed of the death of the Marasoumië was forgotten. "He's a boatwright, mister. He'll sell you a skiff!"

"Well done, lass." Ushahin unfolded his legs, rising. He adjusted the hood of his cloak, then extended a hand, suppressing a smile as she took his crooked fingers into her trusting, grubby grip. "Take me to him."

SHE HAD NO PRIVACY LEFT.

That was one of the worst aspects of the occupation of Beshtanag. It had been hard to watch when Gergon was led through the fortress in chains, shooting her an agonized glance of apology and regret. It had been painful to behold the gratitude with which her Beshtanagi people welcomed the intervention of Haomane's Allies, the alacrity with which they surrendered, eager for a handful of grain, a plate of mutton. Blaise Caveros, Aracus Altorus' second-in-command, took quiet control of the situation. Despite the injury he had sustained on the battlefield, he was calm and competent, seeing to the housing of their troops, ordering supply-trains into the fortress.

Only her Ward Commander and his lieutenants were taken into custody; the rest of her wardsmen were confined to barracks under the eye of Regent Martinek's forces. Members of her household staff were pardoned in exchange for a pledge of loyalty to the Southeastern Pelmaran Regent. A few wept, but what of it? It was only a few. Most helped them search the fortress, scouring it from top to bottom, lest it transpire that the Lady Cerelinde was housed there after all. Haomane's Allies were thorough.

These things, Lilias had expected. The vast numbness that filled her, the void in her heart left by Calandor's death and the Soumanië's loss, insulated her. And in truth, she could not blame her people. She had lied. She had erred. She had failed to protect them. Left to her own devices, she would have begged leave to retire to her chambers, to turn her back upon the world and eschew all sustenance, letting her newly mortal flesh dwindle until Oronin's Horn made good its claim on her spirit. What else was left for her? At least on the far side of death, she might find Calandor's spirit awaiting her.

But Aracus Altorus did not leave her to her own devices.

He didn't know how to use the Soumanië, and there was no one else to tell him. Even the Ellylon shook their heads, saying it was a thing only Ingolin the Wise might know. It afforded her a grim amusement. They were fools to think the Soumanië would be so easily claimed. And so, far from letting her retire in solitude and turn her face to the wall, Aracus kept her at his side, and Lilias kept her silence. He sought to woo her with sweet reason, he bullied her, he chivvied her, he offered her bargains she refused. He would not stoop to torture—there was that much, at least, to be said for Haomane's Allies—but neither would he let her out of his sight. He dragged her into the Cavern of the Marasoumië beneath Beshtanag Mountain, where he made an ill-guided attempt to use the gem to summon Malthus the Counselor.

Even if he had known its secret, he would have failed that day.

Lilias had laughed, close to hysteria, as the foundations of the world shifted and the node-point of the Marasoumië turned dull and inert, a dead hunk of grey granite. The bundled fibers of light that had traced the Ways went dead, leaving empty tunnels through solid rock. Aracus had cried aloud in pain, scrabbling at his forehead, removing the fillet from his brow and clutching it in his hand. As the Soumanië shone like a red star in his grasp, answering to the distant power of Godslayer, she knew what it was that the Sunderer had done, and that the Counselor was trapped within the Ways.

"Tell me how to reach him!" Aracus had raged. "Tell me how to *use* this!"

Lilias had shrugged. "Give me the Soumanië."

He didn't, of course; he wasn't a fool. He had merely glared at her, while the Ellylon spoke to him in hushed tones of what had transpired, explaining that not even one of the Soumanië could undo Godslayer's work. If they could not tap the Soumanië's power themselves, still, there were things they knew; things they *understood*, Haomane's Children. A death at the heart of Urulat was one such. They explained it to the would-be King of the West, their perfect faces strained and bone-white. The Ellylon did not love the deep places of the earth.

In the end, they trooped back to her warchamber, where Lilias was not allowed to leave. She was a piece of excess baggage, but one too valuable to discard. Dignity, along with privacy, was a thing from another life. She sat in the corner, covering her face with both hands, while Haomane's Allies spoke in portentous tones of assailing Darkhaven. They let her hear their plans, so little did they fear her. A bitter irony, that.

"My lady," a voice whispered. "Is there aught I can bring you?"

Lilias gazed upward through the lank curtain of her hair. "Pietre!" It was appalling, the gratitude in her acknowledgment. Tears welled in her eyes. "Are you well? Have they treated you kindly?"

"Aye, my lady, well enough. It is as you said, they show us mercy." Stooping on one knee, Pietre offered the tray he held; a silver salver from her own cupboards, laden with cheese and dark Pelmaran bread. There was concern in his gaze. "Will you not eat? A bit of bread, at least? I can ask the cooks to sop it in wine, make a posset . . ."

"No," Lilias began, then paused. "Would you do this for me?"

"Anything."

She told him, whispering, her lips close to his ear. Pietre shook his head vehemently, his brown hair brushing her cheek. Only when one of the Ellylon glanced over in idle curiosity did he relent. Even then, his willingness was fitful. "Are you *sure*?" he asked, begging her with his eyes to say no.

"Yes." Lilias almost smiled. "I am sure."

It gave her reason to live, at least for a little while longer, and that, too, was a bitter irony. She huddled in her corner, arms wrapped around her knees, half-listening to the council of Haomane's Allies while awaiting Pietre's return. In time he came, carrying the silver platter. It made her proud to see the straight line of his back, the pride with which he performed his duties. Aracus Altorus and his peers accepted his service without thinking, reaching for a bite of bread and cheese, a cup of wine. Only Blaise remained on guard, distrustful, making certain Pietre was willing to taste aught he served to Haomane's Allies.

And he was, of course. All save the posset; that was reserved for her.

Pietre knelt to serve it to her, steadying the tray with one hand. There were tears in his eyes now, liquid and shining. "It is what you asked for," he murmured. "Sarika knew where it was kept. But, oh, please my lady! Both of us beg you . . ."

"You have my thanks, Pietre. And my blessing, for what it is worth." Lilias reached eagerly for the cup. Cradling it between her hands, she inhaled deeply of its aroma. Wine and hoarded spices, and an underlying bitterness. It was a fit drink for the occasion. "Both of you," she added. "Are you sure there is enough?"

"Yes, my lady." Swallowing tears, he nodded. "Enough for a whole colony of rats. It will suffice."

Lilias did smile, then, lifting the cup in toast. "You've done a noble deed. Farewell, Pietre."

Bowing his head, he turned away without answering, unable to watch. Still, it gladdened her heart to have him there, loyal to the end. It hadn't all been the Soumanië's power, not all of it. She had loved them well, her pretty ones; as she had loved Beshtanag. Its grey crags, its green forests; hers, all hers. From the sheep grazing in mountain pastures to the Were skulking in the shadow of the pines, she had *known* it, more truly and deeply than anyone else ever would.

And now it was lost to her, all lost. Would it have been different if she had refused Satoris' emissary? A war to prevent a war, she thought, gazing at the cup's contents. So Tanaros Blacksword called it. He had been wrong; but he had been right, too. Ever since Dergail's Soumanië had risen in the West, she had known it; for what Calandor had known, she had shared.

All things must be as they are, little sssisster.

It was a glorious haven they had made in Beshtanag, but the dragon's wisdom held true. Sooner or later, they would have come for her. Better, perhaps, that it was Haomane's Allies than the Lord-of-Thought himself. If Haomane First-Born was coming, Lilias did not intend to wait for him.

"Farewell," she whispered, raising the cup to her lips.

A man's hand dashed it away, hard and swift.

Crockery shattered, and Lilias shrank backward into her corner beneath a sudden shadow. Blaise Caveros stood over her, having shoved Pietre out of his way. "Sorceress." He sighed, rumpling his dark hair. The bandage was gone from his brow and the gash on his temple was knitting cleanly, but he still looked tired and drawn. "Please don't make this difficult."

A wine-sodden piece of bread sat on the stone floor, while dark liquid pooled in the cracks between the flagstones. A pair of flies buzzed, sampling the dregs. As Lilias watched, one twitched in midair and fell. Its wings beat feebly, then went still. "You deny me a clean death," she said in a low voice. "Would you do so if I were a man?"

Blaise nodded at the spilled wine. "Poison? You call that a clean death?"

"It is what is allotted to me!" Lilias shouted, lifting her head. Tears of frustration stung her eyes. "Must I meet you on the battlefield? I'm no warrior, Borderguardsman! I don't *want* to wield a sword! You have won; why can you not let me die?"

Her words rang in a warchamber gone abruptly silent. They were staring, now; all of them, Aracus Altorus and the others, leaving off their poring over maps and plans. She hated them for it. The Ellylon were the worst, with their smug compassion, their eternal condescension toward all things mortal.

No; worst was the Archer, the Arduan woman, who stared aghast and uncomprehending. *She* wouldn't mind dying on a battlefield.

"You," Lilias said to her. "Do you think *you* would be here if you hadn't proved yourself with a sharp, pointy weapon?" Her voice broke as grief rose up to overwhelm her. "Ah, by all the Shapers! Do you even *know* what you destroyed?"

"Sorceress." Blaise moved wearily to block her view, interposing his tall figure between her and the rest of the room. Behind him, the Arduan Archer's voice rose in anxious query, swiftly hushed by others. Haomane's Allies resumed their council in more subdued tones. "We are sorry for your grief. Believe me, we are all of us well acquainted with the emotion. But we cannot allow you to take your life."

Defeated, Lilias let the back of her head rest against the stone wall, gazing up at him. "I have lived too long already, Borderguardsman. If you were truly an honorable man, you'd let me die." A short laugh escaped her. "And if you were a wise one, you'd do the same. I promise you, this is an action you will regret."

"If you were an honorable woman," Blaise said quietly, "you would not have conspired with the Sunderer to deceive and destroy us."

"All I wanted was to be left in peace," Lilias murmured. "To live, unmolested, in Beshtanag, as I have done for so long. Satoris himself in his fortress of Darkhaven desires nothing more. Is it so much to ask? We require so little space upon the face of Urulat. And yet it seems even that is too much for Haomane's pride to endure. Lord Satoris afforded an opportunity, and I seized it. In the end, it is still Haomane's Allies who raised the specter of war. Did you not seek to fulfill his Prophecy?"

Blaise frowned at her, uncomprehending. "We are neither cruel nor unreasonable, Lilias of Beshtanag. If you give us a chance, you may come to see it. If that is not your will . . . You know full well, lady, that you may have your freedom—to do whatever you wish with your life, including end it—for one simple price. Tell us how the powers of the Soumanië may be wielded. Give us the dragon's lore."

Lilias shook her head, aware of the solid wall behind her. Her home, her fortress. Her prison, now. Still, it stood, a testament to what she had achieved. A monument to Calandor's death. The irony in what had passed seemed no longer bitter, but fitting. "No, Borderguardsman. Whatever else you may accuse me of, that is one trust I will never betray, and one death I will never forgive."

He sighed. "Then you remain with us."

TWENTY-EIGHT

❖

"RIGHT HERE, LADS." VORAX TAPPED the map with one thick forefinger. "In the Northern Harrow. There's a node-point in the middle of the range; or was, at any rate. That's where Lord Satoris suspects they landed, based on their trajectory through the Ways."

He glanced up to make sure they were following. Osric

and the other Staccians were no worry, but one was never certain with Fjeltroll. A few of them had a look of cheerful incomprehension, or at least one he'd come to recognize as such. For someone unacquainted with their features, it was hard to tell. Still, the one Hyrgolf had recommended to lead their contingent—Skragdal, the young Tungskulder— seemed alert and attentive.

"Now, these are desert folk," Vorax continued. "And bear in mind, they've never been out of their desert before; or at least not that we know of. So they're likely to stick with what they know, which is lowlands. See here, where the Harrow dips." He traced a line on the map. "If they're coming for us, and we have every reason to think they are, they're like to take the valleys, follow the riverbeds."

"Lord Vorax." Osric, bending over the map, met his eyes. The Staccian lieutenant was a man of middle years, solid and reliable. Not the best or boldest of his lads—that had been Carfax, entrusted to lead the decoys—but sensible, a man one could trust. "What if they're *not* coming for us?"

"Well, then we've nothing to worry about, have we?" Vorax grinned through his beard, clapping Osric's shoulder. "Let's say they are, lad. If we're wrong, you retrace your steps. Pick up their trail at the node-point, or what's left of it, and follow them south. Do you see?"

Osric nodded. "Aye, my lord."

"General." Skragdal frowned at the map. "I know the Northern Harrow, though I do not understand how this shape on paper shows it. This I know to be true. Even if we hurry, we will be many days behind their departure. There are valleys and valleys, routes and routes. How do we know which these smallfolk will take?"

"We don't," Vorax said bluntly. "That's why his Lordship wanted Fjel on this mission. See, here." He pointed. "This line is where Fjel territory ends, and Staccia proper begins. That's what it means."

"Neherinach." The Tungskulder's deep voice was sombre. It was a place the Fjel knew well, the ancient battle-ground where Haomane's Allies had fallen upon them in the First Age of the Sundered World. Their fate had been sealed at Neherinach, for it was there that they had retrieved Godslayer from the hands of the Rivenlost and brought it to Lord Satoris.

"Aye," Vorax said. "Neherinach. If these ... smallfolk ... travel southward, Staccians will note their passage. But if they stay to the north, it will be Fjeltroll who track their progress. Either way, they should be easy to mark. They are the Charred Ones, desert folk, dark of skin and unskilled in the ways of mountains." He splayed his hands on the map, gazing at Skragdal. "You may need to divide your forces. That is why I asked both contingents to be present. Hyrgolf said the tribes would give you aid if needed. Is it true, Tungskulder? Does the old oath still stand?"

"Aye, General," the Fjel rumbled. Skragdal's small eyes were grave under the bulging ridge of his brow, the thick hide scarred where Lord Satoris' sulfuric rain had fallen. "We are not like you. Neheris' Children do not forget."

It stung him, though it shouldn't have. "Then you will find aid along the way!" Vorax snapped. "Let the tribes be your guide. I don't care how you find them, Tungskulder, just *find them*. Find them, and kill them, and spill the Water upon barren ground. Do you understand?"

"Aye," the Fjel said softly. "I do."

"General?" Osric cleared his throat. "Lord Vorax, sir? I told my lads there would be hazard pay in this for them."

"Hazard pay." Vorax eyed him wryly. "We're preparing for the whole of Urulat to descend on us, and you want hazard pay for tracking a pair of desert rats through the mountains? This ought to be a pleasure jaunt, my boy."

Osric shrugged. "And we ought to have taken Haomane's Allies at Beshtanag, sir, but we didn't. Instead we lost General Tanaros, and Shapers only know what's become of

Carfax and his lot. You say it's just a pair of Charred Folk, but that's just guesswork. What if the Altorian king sent an army to guard them? What if the wizard is with them?"

"It's not *guesswork!*" Vorax brought one fist down hard on the map-table, making his lieutenant jump. "Listen to me, lads. His Lordship took up Godslayer itself, do you hear? What he knows, he *knows*. Haomane's damnable wizard is trapped in the Ways, and like to stay there. The Charred Folk are alone, and as for Tanaros Blacksword, he's about his Lordship's business." He glared at Osric. "Do you think the Three are that easy to kill?"

"No, sir." Osric held his ground. "But mortal men are, Lord Vorax. And we hear the rumors, same as anyone. They say the lost weapon's been found." There was no guile in his grey eyes, only steady honesty and a measure of fear. "A son of Altorus looking to wed a daughter of Elterrion. The lost weapon. Now this Bearer, and you say he's carrying water could put out the marrow-fire. I'm a Staccian, sir, and I'm as true to my word as any lug-headed, leather-hided Fjel. But if I'm going into the teeth of Haomane's Prophecy, I want what I was promised. Battle-glory, and fair recompense for the fallen."

The other Staccians murmured agreement. Vorax blew out his cheeks in a huge sigh, calculating sums in his head. He would be glad beyond words when Tanaros returned. Vorax didn't mind leading a good skirmish, but this business of serving as General was wearying. Bargaining was his strength, not overseeing morale. How could he do one while worrying about the other? Blacksword might be dour company, still mooning over his dead wife's betrayal a thousand years later, but he had the knack of commanding an army. "Fine," he said. "Triple pay. How does that sound, Lieutenant Osric?"

"In advance, sir?"

Vorax stared at the ceiling. "In advance." Lowering his gaze, he fixed it on Skragdal. "What about you, Tungskulder? Are the Fjeltroll afraid of Haomane's Prophecy?"

"Aye, General," Skragdal said simply. "That's why we go."

"Good lad." He clapped a hand on the Fjel's hulking arm, his shoulder being too high to reach. It was like slapping a boulder; ye Shapers, but the lad was huge! "There's nothing wrong with being afraid. His Lordship has powerful enemies, and they'll stop at naught to see him destroyed. They've waited a long time for this. But we haven't exactly been sitting idle, have we, lads? We're ready for them. That's the important thing to remember. Beshtanag may have gone awry, but we *did* succeed at Lindanen Dale, and we'll succeed in this, too." He grinned at them, showing his eyeteeth like a Fjel. "You want to know where our General Tanaros Blacksword is this very moment? His Lordship knows. Our Tanaros is in the heart of the Unknown Desert itself, putting the Charred Folk who sent the Bearer to the sword and silting that cursed well they guard! How do you like *that* news?"

They liked it, well enough to cheer.

"Haomane's Prophecy might be fulfilled someday, lads." Vorax shook his head. "But not today," he said with satisfaction. "Not on *my* watch! And not on yours, damn your eyes. Mark my words, Darkhaven will prevail!"

It braced them like strong drink, and the cheering continued. Vorax grinned some more, slapped a few more sturdy shoulders, ordered a keg of *svartblod* breached and raised a cup to the success of their mission. The Fjeltroll drank deep, roaring toasts in their guttural tongue. Nåltannen, most of them; a few Kaldjager for scouting work, and a pair of Gulnagel from the lowlands. Skragdal was the only Tungskulder, save one. The other Staccians drank the *svartblod* too, gasping and sputtering. It was a matter of pride with them to keep it down.

"Right," Vorax said, gauging the moment. "You have your orders, lads. Report to field marshal Hyrgolf for weapons and supplies, and head out at dawn."

* * *

THE DELTA'S WARMTH WAS A GLORIOUS thing.

Against all likelihood, Ushahin found himself humming as he poled the skiff along the waterways. Dip and push; dip and push. It was a soothing motion. The flat-bottomed skiff he'd purchased in Arduan glided effortlessly over the still water. Caitlin's Da, he reflected, was a fine craftsman.

Passing beneath a stand of mangroves there was a green snake, unlooping itself lazily from a limb. Its blunt head quested in the air beside his face, forked tongue flickering.

"Hello, little cousin." Leaning on his pole, Ushahin smiled at the snake. "Good hunting to you, though you may wish to seek smaller prey."

The questing head withdrew and he pushed onward. Dip and push; dip and push. The hot, humid environs of the Delta were kind to his aching, ill-knit bones. For once, his joints felt oiled and smooth. He had not felt such ease in his flesh since he had been a child; indeed, had forgotten it existed. Out of sight of Arduan, he had shed the concealing cloak with its itchy hood. It was good to be unveiled in the open air. Sunlight usually made his head ache, but the dense foliage filtered it to a green dimness gentle to his eyes. That terrible awakening on the plains of Rukhar seemed distant, here.

"*Kaugh!*" Atop the highest branches of a further mangrove, a raven landed and perched there, swaying, its claws clenched on a too-slim branch. It clung there a moment, then launched itself in a flurry of wings, finding a similar perch a few yards to the south. "*Kaugh!*"

"I see you, little brother," Ushahin called to the raven, one of those serving to guide him through the swamp. He thrust strongly on his pole and the skiff turned, edging southward. "I am coming."

Satisfied, the raven pecked at something unseen.

In truth, it would be easy for a man to lose his way in the Delta. And would that be such an ill fate? Pausing to swig from his waterskin, Ushahin pondered the matter. There was something . . . pleasant . . . about the swamp. He felt *good* here. It wasn't merely a question of the moist air being kind to his bones, no. Something else was at work, something *deeper*. There was a pulse beating in his veins that hadn't surged since . . . since when?

Never, perhaps. One half of his blood, after all, was Ellylon. Haomane's Children did not know desire of the flesh, not in the same way other races among the Lesser Shapers did. The Lord-of-Thought had Shaped them, and the Lord-of-Thought had refused Satoris' Gift, that which was freely bestowed on other Shapers' Children.

The other half . . . ah.

Arahila Second-Born, Arahila the Fair. She had accepted his Lordship's Gift for her Children; and Haomane's, too, that which he had withheld from all but his beloved Sister's Children. Thus the race of Men, gifted with thought, quick with desire.

Ushahin had never reveled in the mortal parentage of his father, in his possession of Lord Satoris' Gift. Here, in the Delta, it was different. The songs he crooned under his breath were cradle-songs, sung to him by his mother aeons ago, before his body was beaten, broken and twisted.

"So, Haomane!" Ushahin addressed his words to a cloud of midges that hung in the air before him, standing in lieu of the First-Born among Shapers. "You're afraid, eh? What's the matter? Was Lord Satoris' Gift more powerful than you reckoned?" Pushing hard on his pole, he hummed, watching the midges dance. "Seems to me mayhap it was, Lord-of-Thought. At least in this place."

"*Kaugh, kaugh!*"

Ravens burst from the tops of the mangroves; one, two; half a dozen. They circled in the dank air above the center of the swamp, and sunlight glinted purple on their wings. Ushahin paused and rested on his pole, gazing upward. Images of a hillock, vast and mossy, flickered through his mind.

"What's this?" he mused aloud. "What do you wish me to see? All right, all right, little brothers! I come apace."

He shoved hard on the pole, anchoring its butt in the sludge beneath the waterways. The skiff answered, gliding over still waters made ruddy by the afternoon sun. In the center of a watery glade stood a single palodus tree, tall and solitary. In the shadow of its spreading canopy arose the mossy hillock he had glimpsed. For no reason he could name, Ushahin's mouth grew dry, and his pulse beat in his loins. It was a strange sensation; so strange it took him long minutes to recognize it as carnal desire.

Such desire! He was tumescent with it. The image, all unbidden, of the Lady of the Ellylon, slid into his mind. Cerelinde, bent over the saddle, the tips of her fair hair brushing the earth.

"Oh," Ushahin said, grinding his teeth, "I think *not*."

Sluggish bubbles rose in the murky water before him; rose, and burst, carrying the sound of laughter, slow and deep. In the branches, ravens arose in a clatter, yammering. Beneath the surface of the water, a pair of greenish eyes opened, slit with a vertical pupil and covered by the thin film of an inner lid.

Gripped by sudden fear, Ushahin propelled the skiff backward.

Iron-grey and slick with moss, the dragon's head emerged from the water. It was twice the size of the skiff, dripping with muck. Droplets slid down its bearded jaw, plunking into the water, creating circular ripples. It stirred one unseen foreleg, then another, and Ushahin struggled to steady his craft as the swamp surged in response. The dragon's inner lids blinked with slow amusement as it regarded him, waiting until the waters had quieted and he had regained control of the skiff. Only then did the massive jaws, hung on either side with strands of rotting greenery, part to speak.

"Is thisss desire sso disstasssteful to you, little brother?"

Ushahin laid the pole across the prow of the skiff and made a careful bow. "Eldest," he said. "Forgive me, Lord Dragon. I did not know you were here."

Overhead, ravens circled and yammered.

The dragon's gaze held, this time unblinking. "You bear Sssatoriss' mark. You are one of his. You have ssseen my brother and know his fate."

"Yes," Ushahin said quietly. "Calandor of Beshtanag is no more."

Turning its head, the dragon sighed. A gout of bluish flame jetted from its dripping nostrils, dancing eerily over the oily waters to set a stand of mangrove alight. A single tree flamed, black and skeletal within a cocoon of fire. The circling ravens squawked and regrouped at a distance. In the skiff, Ushahin scrambled for his pole.

"Peasssse, little brother." The dragon eyed him with sorrow. "I mean you no harm, not yet. Calandor chose his path long ago, thisss I know. We know. We always know." It shuddered, and ripples emanated across the swamp, setting the skiff to rocking upon the waters. "Ssso why come you here?"

"Seeking passage." Emboldened, Ushahin rode out the waves, planting the pole in the mire and gripping it tight in both hands. "Will you grant it, Elder Brother?"

"Brother." Beneath yellow-green eyes, twin spumes of smoke issued forth in a contemptuous snort. "What makesss you think I am your *brother?*"

Ushahin frowned, shifted his grip on his pole. "Did you not name me as much?"

"I named *you*." The dragon snorted. "Brother!"

"What, then?"

"Would you know?" The nictitating lids flickered. "Guesssss."

A mad courage seized him. What was there to lose, here in the Delta? Whether he would continue onward or die in this place was the dragon's to choose. Craning his neck, Ushahin gazed at the dragon's nearest eye. The yellow-green iris roiled in the immense orb, colors shifting like oily waters. The vertical pupil contracted like a cat's, but vaster, far vaster. Blacker than the Ravensmirror, blacker than a moonless night, it reflected no light, only darkness.

If he hesitated, he would falter; so he didn't. Using the skills taught him long ago by the Grey Dam, Ushahin slid his thoughts into the mind behind that black, black pupil.

It was like stepping into a bottomless pit.

There was nothing *there;* or if there was, it was a thing so huge, so distant, he could not compass it. The way back was gone, the filament that connected him to himself might never have existed. There was only an encompassing, lightless vastness. Deeper and deeper he fell, a tiny star in an immense universe of darkness. There were no boundaries. There would be no end, only an endless falling.

Sundered from himself, Ushahin shaped a soundless cry . . .

. . . and fell . . .

. . . and fell . . .

. . . and fell . . .

Something flickered in the incomprehensible verges of the dragon's mind; something, many somethings. Tiny and urgent and defiant, they came for him like a cloud of midges, a storm of claws. Feathered, frantic thoughts, scrabbling for his. Yellow beech leaves, shiny black beetles, an updraught beneath the wings and the patchwork of the tilting earth glimpsed below.

The ravens of Darkhaven had come for him.

Such were the thoughts they cast out like lifelines to Ushahin Dreamspinner; for they were, after all, ravens. It was enough. Clinging to the filaments of their awareness, Ushahin braked his endless fall and wove of the ravens' thoughts a net, a ladder, and fled the darkness, back to whence he'd come.

Behind him, the dragon's laughter echoed.

The world returned, and he returned to it.

Ushahin opened his eyes and found himself lying on his back in the skiff, half-soaked with bilge water. Hung upon the sinuous length of an arching neck, the dragon's head hovered above him, blotting out a large portion of the sky. Beyond it, he caught sight of the ravens exiting from their frantic ellipse, landing in the high branches of the palodus tree. Though his head ached like a beaten drum, Ushahin sent thoughts of gratitude winging after them. Satisfied, the ravens preened their feathers.

"The wise man," the dragon rumbled, "does not play games with dragons."

With an effort, Ushahin levered himself upward to sit on the bench in the skiff's stern and rested, arms braced on his knees. A strange exhilaration filled him at finding himself alive and whole. He took an experimental breath, conscious of the air filling his lungs, of having lungs to fill with air. "True," he said, finding the experiment a success. "But I am not a man, and I have been accused of being mad, but never wise. Elder Sister . . . " he bowed from the waist, " . . . forgive my folly."

"Ssso." The dragon eyed him with amusement. "It has gained sssome wisdom."

"Some." Ushahin wrapped his arms around his knees and returned the dragon's gaze. "Calanthrag the Eldest, Mother of Dragons. I am a fool, indeed. But tell me, why here, in the heart of the Delta?"

Sulfurous fumes engulfed him as the dragon snorted. "Child of three rasses, ssson of none. Not a Man, yet ssstill a man. You deny your own desire. Do you deny the power here, where Sssatorisss Third-Born arose?"

"No, Mother." Ushahin coughed once, waving away fumes. He shook his head gravely, feeling his lank silvergilt hair brush his cheeks. "Not the power. Only the desire."

"Why?" The dragon's voice was tender with cunning. "Anssswer."

She had let him call her mother, had not denied it! No one had done as much since the Grey Dam Sorash, whose heir had castigated him. Ushahin hugged the thought to him and tried to answer honestly. "Because I despise Haomane's Children above all else, for their cowardice in forsaking me and my begetting," he said. "And I will not allow my flesh to become the vehicle by which they receive Lord Satoris' Gift."

"Ssso." The sinuous neck flattened, its spikes lying low as the iron-grey head hovered above him. "You glimpssse the Great Pattern?"

"It may be," Ushahin said humbly. "I do not know."

Smoke puffed from the dragon's nostrils as Calanthrag the Eldest, Mother of Dragons, laughed. "Then tie up your boat," she said, "and I will tell you."

The bark of the palodus tree was silver-grey, smooth as skin. Ushahin poled the skiff underneath its vast canopy. There was a rope knotted through an iron ring in its prow. He laid down his pole and knelt on the forward bench to loop the rope around the trunk of the palodus, securing the skiff. Mud-crabs scuttled among the thrusting roots of the palodus, and waterbugs skittered here and there on the surface of the water. The setting sun gilded the swamp, lending a fiery glory to the murky waters. Some yards away, the charred skeleton of a mangrove shed quiet flakes of ash, long past the smouldering stage. How many hours had he lost, falling through the dragon's mind?

It didn't matter.

Overhead, the first pale stars of twilight began to emerge and the ravens of Darkhaven fluffed their feathers, settling on their perches and calling to one another with sleepy squawks. All was quiet in the Delta, and at its heart, a pair of yellow-green eyes hung like lanterns in the dimness, hinting at the enormous bulk beyond. Ushahin gave one last tug on the bilge-sodden rope, and smiled. "Mother of Dragons." He bowed to her, then sat, feeling the skiff rock a little beneath his shifting weight. "I am listening."

"In the beginning," said Calanthrag the Eldest, "there was Urulat . . ."

* * *

"PULL!" SPEROS SHOUTED.

The Gulnagel groaned, hauling on the ropes. They were heroic figures in the red light of the setting sun, broad backs and shoulders straining, the muscles in their bulging haunches a-quiver. The chunk of rock they labored to haul moved a few paces on its improvised skid, built of a dented Fjel buckler and rope salvaged from the Well. It hadn't been on a pulley, either; just a straight length of it, impossible to draw. He'd had to send one of the Fjel back down the Well to sever it and retrieve as much as was possible.

"Pull!" Speros chanted. "Pull, pull, *pull!*"

With grunts and groans, they did. It moved, inch by inch, grinding across the hard-packed sand. He joined his efforts to theirs at the end, rolling it manually to the lip of the Well. It wasn't easy. The standing monoliths of Stone Grove had shattered when toppled, but even the pieces into which they had broken were massive. Atop the mound of the Well, Speros stood shoulder to shoulder with the Gulnagel, heaving.

"All right, lads," he panted, loosening the rope with dirty fingers. "Now *push.*"

It fell with a satisfying crash, landing only a few yards below. Their long labors showed results at last; the shaft of the Well was well and truly clogged. Speros flopped onto the cooling sand, giving his aching muscles a chance to recover.

"More, boss?" One of the Gulnagel hovered over him.

"A few more, aye." With difficulty, Speros rose, gathering the rope. It was vine-wrought, but sturdy beyond belief. Those poor old Yarru had woven it well. "*One* more," he amended, weaving toward a distant boulder. "Bring the skid."

Stout hearts that they were, they did. He helped them lever the next rock onto the concave buckler and wrapped the rope around it, securing the boulder in place, lashing it to the handles. "Once more, lads," he said encouragingly, helping the Gulnagel into harness. "Remember, push with the legs!"

One grinned at him, lowering his shoulders and preparing to haul. Freg was his name; Speros knew him by the chipped eyetusks that gleamed ruddily in the sunset. There were marks on his shoulders where the rope's chafing had worn the rough hide as smooth as polished leather. "You drive a team hard, boss."

"Aye, Freg." Speros laid a hand on the Fjel's arm, humbled by his strength and endurance. Never once, since the Marasoumië had spat them out, had he heard one complain. "And you're the team for it. Pull, lads, *pull!*"

Groaning and straining, they obeyed him once more. Taloned feet splayed, seeking purchase on the churned sand. Yellowed nails dug furrows on top of furrows, strong legs driving as the Fjel bent to the harness, and the buckler moved, iron grating and squealing as it was dragged across the desert.

How many times had they done this? Speros had lost count. It had seemed impossible on the first day. Boulders were like pebbles, dropped into the Well of the World. On the first day they had merely fallen an impossible distance, shattering, dispersing fragments into the cavern of the dead Marasoumië. He had been uncertain that the Well could be blocked. It had taken all his cunning to achieve it; rigging the skid, utilizing the full strength of the Fjel, moving the largest pieces first.

Even then, he had been unsure.

And yet . . . and yet. In time, it had happened.

The last boulder crashed like thunder as they rolled it over the lip. Speros straightened, putting his hands at the small of his back. His lower back ached, and his nails were torn and bloodied. "Good job, lads," he gasped. "Fill in the rest with loose rock and sand, make it look natural. That ought to do it."

The Gulnagel surrounded the shallow mouth of the Well, backing up to it and squatting low. Sand and shale flew as they dug dog-wise, shoveling a flurry of debris betwixt their rear legs, braced and solid. The remaining feet of the Well's open throat dwindled to inches.

"Good job, lads," Speros repeated, eyeing the rising level and trying to remain steady on his feet. "Remember to make it look natural."

One of them grunted; Freg, perhaps. It was hard to tell from the rear. Speros clapped a hand on the nearest Fjel appendage and let his staggering steps take him down the mound. The earth was churned and torn. He had to tread with exhausted care to avoid turning an ankle. All around the desert floor, the jagged stumps of the monoliths remained, raw and accusatory.

General Tanaros was seated on one, sharpening his sword and gazing westward.

Speros wove toward him. "Lord General!" He drew himself up in a weary salute. "The Well is filled."

"Thank you, Speros." The General spoke in a deep voice, absentminded. "Look at that, will you?" He pointed with the tip of his sword; to the west, where a red star hung low on the horizon. "Dergail's Soumanië still rises. What do you think it means?"

"War." Speros' quivering legs folded, and he sat abruptly. "Isn't that what they say? It is in the Midlands, anyway." He rubbed his eyes with the heels of his hands, trying to scrub away the exhaustion. "The red star, reminder of Dergail's defeat. It's the Sunderer's challenge, a declaration of war."

"So they do," the General mused. "And yet, Lord Satoris did not raise the star. He thought it a warning. A sister's kindness."

"Does it matter?" Speros fumbled for the waterskin lashed to his belt and managed to loosen the stopper. It sloshed, half-empty, as he raised it to his lips and took a sparing mouthful.

"Betimes, I wonder." General Tanaros drew his whetstone down the length of his sword. "I fear we have not chosen our battlefield wisely, Speros."

Speros glanced up at him. "Beshtanag, sir? Or Darkhaven?"

"No." The General shook his head. "Neither. I mean the hearts and minds of Men, Speros." He examined one edge of his ebony blade, testing it with his thumb. "Do you suppose it would have made a difference?"

"Sir?"

"The Bearer." Sheathing his sword, General Tanaros turned his attention to the Midlander. "He made the only choice he was offered. Would it have made a difference, do you think, if we had offered another one?"

"I don't know, Lord General."

"I wonder." Tanaros frowned. "But what would we have offered him, after all? Wealth? Power? Immortality? Those are merely bribes. In the end, it all comes down to the same choice."

Speros shrugged. "A reason to say no, I suppose."

"Yes." General Tanaros glanced across the Stone Glade. The smaller mound that had been erected outside the circle of broken monoliths was barely visible in the deepening twilight. It had taken the Gulnagel less than an hour to dig a grave large enough to contain the corpses of the slaughtered Yarru elders. "I suppose so."

"Sir." Speros cleared his throat. "Will there be a lot of . . . that sort of thing?"

Tanaros smiled bleakly. "You told me you'd shed innocent blood before, Midlander."

"Aye." He held the General's gaze, though it wasn't easy. "But not gladly." A creeping sense of alarm stirred in his heart. Was the General thinking of dismissing him? Speros ran his tongue over his teeth, feeling the gap where one had been lost in the dungeons of Darkhaven. He had gambled everything on this. He thought about the Midlands and the disdain his name evoked, the disappointment in his mother's eyes. He thought about how General Tanaros had deigned to meet him as an equal on the sparring-field. He thought of the camaraderie of the Fjel, and their unfailing admiration and loyalty, and knew he didn't want to lose it. Not for this, not for anything. What did the death of a few old Charred Folk matter? They'd brought it on themselves, after all. The Lord General had asked them to give him a reason to spare them. A reason to say no. It wasn't that much to ask. His hands clenched involuntarily into fists, and he pressed one to his heart in salute. "I failed you, I know. It won't happen again."

It was the General who looked away first. "I almost would that I'd failed myself in this," he murmured, half to himself. "All right." He sighed, placing his hands flat on his thighs. "You say the Well is filled?"

"Aye, sir!" Speros sprang to his feet, light-headed with relief. "It would take a team of Fjel a lifetime to unblock it!"

"Good." General Tanaros stood and gazed at the twilit sky. It seemed larger, here in the desert, and the red star of Dergail's Soumanië pulsed brighter. "We'll take a few hours' rest, and leave ere dawn." Turning, he poked Speros' half-empty waterskin. "The water-hole here is deep; Ngurra told me it never runs dry. So don't stint yourself, Midlander, because I don't know how lucky we'll be crossing the desert."

"Aye, sir." Speros raised the skin and took an obliging swallow.

"I mean it." The General's eyes were shadowed and his face was hard. What had transpired here in the Unknown Desert had taken its toll on him. For a moment it seemed he might speak of it; then he shuddered, gathering himself. He fixed Speros with a clear gaze. "Drink while you can, and see to it that every waterskin we can salvage is filled to bursting. I mean to get us home alive."

"Aye, sir!" Speros smiled, relishing the word. "Home."

TWENTY-NINE

"Don't look."

Blaise Caveros' voice was low as he attempted to interpose his mount between her and the sight of the fallen dragon. It was a futile courtesy. Calandor's bulk loomed beyond the gap in Beshtanag's wall like a second mountain. There was no way Lilias could avoid seeing him as the train of Haomane's Allies made their way down the slope, passing through the broken wall.

It was true, what the old legends claimed. In death, the dragon had turned to stone. The glittering scales had faded to dull grey, veined with a reddish ore. Already, the clean, sinuous lines of his form had grown weathered and vague. Lilias' hands trembled on the reins as she tried to trace his shape with her gaze.

There, she thought; the smaller ridge is his tail, and those are his haunches. How did he land? Oh Shapers, that crumpled part underneath is a wing! It must have broken in the fall.

Without thinking, Lilias drew rein and dismounted, tugging blindly at robes that caught and tore on the buckle of her mount's girth. "Sorceress!" Blaise's call seemed distant and unimportant. She stumbled across the battlefield into the shadow of Calandor's body, hands outstretched. There. That was his shoulder, that was one of his forelegs against which she had so often leaned, feeling the warmth of his mighty heart radiating against her skin.

"Calandor," she whispered, laying her hands on the harsh grey stone. It was sun-warmed. If she closed her eyes, she could almost pretend. The long ridge of his neck slanted along the ground, ending in the dim outline of his noble head, chin resting on the earth. Only knobs of dead stone remained where his green-gilt eyes had shone. Oblivious to the waiting train, Lilias embraced as much of the fallen dragon as her arms could encompass, and wept.

Hoofbeats rattled on the stony ground behind her, and leather tack creaked. "Sorceress," Blaise said. "It's time to go."

Lilias rested her brow against the sun-warmed rock. If she tried, she could almost imagine the pulse beating in her own veins was the steady throb of the dragon's heart. "Can you not allow me even a moment of grief?"

"No. Not here. Not now."

She turned slowly to face him, squinting through tear-swollen eyes. He sat impassively in the saddle, leading her mount by the reins. Beyond him, Haomane's Allies waited in shining, impatient panoply. At the head of the column, Aracus Altorus was frowning, the Soumanië bright on his brow. A coterie of Ellylon and a handful of Borderguard surrounded him. The woman Archer was watching her with distrust, an arrow loosely nocked in Oronin's Bow. A long line of soldiery—Pelmarans, Midlanders, Vedasians—stretched behind them, mounted and on foot, all regarding her with triumphant contempt.

It was too much to bear.

Averting her head, Lilias left the dragon's side and fumbled for the stirrup. Someone laughed aloud as she struggled to mount without the aid of a block. Blaise reached over and hauled her unceremoniously into the saddle. He kept control of her reins, leading her back toward the train. Aracus gave the signal and progress resumed.

Behind them, a cheer arose as a Pelmaran foot-soldier passing in the ranks jabbed at the ridge of Calandor's tail with the butt-end of his spear. It set a trend. Sick at heart, Lilias twisted in the saddle to watch as each passing man ventured a thrust or a kick, bits of stone crumbling under their blows. One of them spat.

"Darden." Blaise beckoned to one of the dun-cloaked Borderguardsmen. "Tell them to stop."

The man nodded, turning his horse's head and riding back down the line. The order was received with grumbling, but it was obeyed. After the battle, few of Haomane's Allies would venture to disobey one of the Borderguard.

"Thank you." Lilias spoke the words without looking at him.

Blaise shrugged, shifting his grip on the twin sets of reins. "He was one of the Eldest. If nothing else, that is worthy of a measure of respect."

The train continued, passing over the well-trodden ground of its own encampment. The vast city of tents had been struck and folded, but the ravages of their occupation remained. Trees had been clear-cut for siege-engines and battering rams, leaving raw stumps and scattered debris. Ashes and bones littered the sites of a hundred campfires. Gazing at it, Lilias shook her head. "He was only trying to protect his home," she said. "To protect *me*."

Blaise gave her a hard look. "Tell that to the mothers and widows of the men he roasted alive in their armor."

In the forefront of the vanguard, their column narrowed as Aracus Altorus entered the verge of the forest. The pine shadows muted his red-gold hair and gave a watery green tint to the silver armor of the Rivenlost who surrounded him.

"You could have withdrawn," Lilias said quietly. "It would have been enough."

"And you could have surrendered!" A muscle worked in Blaise's jaw. "What do you want from me, Sorceress? Pity? You chose to take part in the Sunderer's scheme. You could have surrendered when it failed, and pleaded for honest clemency."

She laughed mirthlessly. "Would my fate be different, Borderguardsman?"

"Yours?" He raised his brows. "No."

"So." She rubbed her cheeks, stiff with the salt of drying tears. "It doesn't matter, does it? Nothing matters, in the end. Let us leave it at that, Borderguardsman. If you would speak, speak of something else."

He shrugged as they entered the shadow of the pines. "Aracus entrusted me with the task of warding you. I have no need to speak."

The horses' hooves thudded softly on the broad, beaten path, gaining speed as Aracus Altorus stepped up the pace to a slow trot. Soon, the vanguard would pull ahead of the foot-soldiers, leaving them behind. An occupying force of Regent Martinek's men remained to oversee Beshtanag's affairs. The remaining Pelmarans would assemble a council of Regents to determine what aid they could send westward; in the south, the Vedasian knights would seek to rally their own overlords. Duke Bornin of Seahold would gather the forces of the Midlands. As for the rest of them, they were bound for the Rivenlost haven of Meronil and the counsel of Ingolin the Wise; to seek news of Malthus, to attempt to unlock the power of the Soumanië, to plan an assault upon Darkhaven.

And their prisoner, Lilias of Beshtanag, who held the answers to two of these matters, would be carried along with them like a twig in a flood.

Turning in the saddle, Lilias glanced behind her one last time. Already the fortress was invisible from this angle. She caught a glimpse of the dull grey hummock of Calandor's remains before low pine branches swept across her field of vision, closing like a curtain upon Beshtanag.

"Good-bye," she whispered. "Good-bye, my love."

IN HER QUARTERS, CERELINDE BALKED.

"Thank you, Lord Vorax," she said stiffly. "I pray you tell his Lordship I decline his invitation."

The madling Meara hissed with alarm in the corner. Vorax the Glutton grimaced, planting his heavy hands on the gilded belt that encircled his girth; which had, in fairness, grown considerably less than it had been when he greeted her at the gates of Darkhaven. "Do you think I fancy being his errand-boy, Lady? I have more important duties. Nonetheless, his Lordship's invitations are not *optional*."

"Very well." She laid aside the lace-work with which she had been occupying her hours. "As his Lordship *commands*."

Vorax held open the door to her chambers with a sardonic bow, smiling in such a way as showed his sturdy teeth above his beard. Small scabs stippled his brow and cheeks. Cerelinde repressed a shudder at having to pass close enough to feel the heat of his body. "You are too kind, Lady."

"Not at all." She returned his false smile, watching the Staccian's eyes narrow. It was a relief, in some ways, to deal with him instead of Tanaros. Vorax the Glutton did not confuse her senses or her thoughts, and however he had spent the long years of his immortality, it had inured him to the allure of the Ellylon. He would as lief see her dead as alive, and made little effort to disguise the fact.

"To the garden, then." His thick fingers took impersonal possession of her arm, and he steered her down the halls. The pace he set was fast enough to make her stride hurried. Here and there, where tapestries hung, there was a scurrying sound in the walls, and Cerelinde had been in Darkhaven long enough to guess it was Meara, or the other madlings, at work. There seemed no end to their knowledge of the passages that riddled Darkhaven.

She noted, as they passed, that the Mørkhar Fjel of the Havenguard saluted Vorax with less alacrity than they had Tanaros. It filled her with a sense of uneasy pride.

"Here." Vorax led her into the narrow corridor, with the door of polished wood and silver hinges at the end of it. Cerelinde shrank back against the wall as he fumbled at his belt for a ring of keys. He shot her a wry glance. "Don't worry, I'm only fulfilling his Lordship's wishes. I've no interest in aught else."

Cerelinde straightened. "I'm not afraid."

"Oh, aye." He smiled dourly, fitting a small key to the lock. "I can see that."

It stung her pride, enough to make her reach out and lay gentle fingers on the scabbed skin of his brow. If she had possessed the ancient magics Haomane's Children were said to have before the world was Sundered, she might have healed him. She watched his eyes widen at the delicate touch of Ellylon flesh against his rude skin. "Are you injured, Lord Vorax?"

"No," he said shortly, pulling away from her and opening the door. "Go on," he added, giving her an ignominious shove. "His Lordship is waiting."

Lifting her skirts, Cerelinde stepped across the threshold and raised her face to the night sky, breathing deep. Arahila's moon rode high overhead, a silvery half-orb; and yet, it was not the same garden she had visited with Tanaros. There was a sulfuric tang to the moist air that caressed her skin, with an underlying odor of rot. Dead patches pocked the grass, pallid by moonlight.

It hurt to see it, which surprised her.

"My Lord?" Cerelinde called.

"I am here," the deep voice answered. "Come."

There, where a dark form blotted out the stars. Stumbling over the dying grass, she made her way toward him. A faint sound shivered the night; bells, crying out. On slender stalks the bell-shaped blossoms shivered, heedless of the acid rain that had pierced their petals, leaving yellowish holes with seared edges. The sound they emitted was a plangent and sorrowful alarum, sounding without cease.

"Oh!" Cerelinde stooped, reaching for them. "Poor blossoms."

"Clamitus atrox." Lord Satoris gazed at the stars revolving in their slow dance. "Sorrow-bells, sounding for every act of senseless cruelty in Urulat. Were they as loud, when you heard them before?"

"No." She bent her head over the flower bed.

"Nor I." The Shaper sighed. "Though I fear it is I who has set them ringing, I do not relish the sound, Cerelinde."

Cerelinde stroked the seared petals of the sorrow-bells, feeling them shudder under her fingertips. *Aracus.* "What have you done, my Lord?" she murmured, the blood running cold in her veins at the Shaper's words.

"There was time when I did," he mused. "It was sweet to my ears, a gratifying reminder that you Lesser Shapers are more than capable of wounding one another to the quick without my aid. And yet, I find it not so sweet when I am the cause. Vengeance sours quickly upon the palate when it fails to find its rightful target. It was never my wish to be what fate has made me, Lady."

Cerelinde straightened and took a step forward. *"What have you done?"*

"Have no fear." A hint of contempt edged his voice. "The Son of Altorus is safe enough. It was no one you knew, Lady. Victims of Haomane's Wrath, once. Now victims of mine. This time, they brought it upon themselves."

"The Charred Folk." The knowledge brought relief, and a different sorrow. "Ah, my Lord. Why?"

"Will you tell me you do not know?" the Shaper asked.

"My Lord." Cerelinde spread her hands. "I do not."

"Senseless." Reaching down, Lord Satoris wrenched a handful of sorrow-bells from the earth. Throttling them in his grip, he regarded the thin, trailing roots twitching below. The fragile petals drooped against his dark flesh, still emitting a faint peal. "How so?" he asked the shuddering blossoms. "I Shaped you and gave you existence. Why do you sound for *their* deaths? Senseless? How so, when they seek to use the Water of Life to extinguish the marrow-fire? How so, when they seek to destroy me?"

Hope leapt in Cerelinde's breast, warring with unease. "Haomane's Prophecy," she breathed.

"*Haomane's Prophecy.*" He echoed the words with derision, tossing the wilting plants at her feet. "My Elder Brother's Prophecy is the framework of his will, nothing more, and you are the tools with which he builds it. Do not be so quick to hope, Lady. I have a will of my own, and tools at my disposal."

Root tendrils writhed over the toes of her slippers and the dying bells' ringing faded to a whimper, while those left in the bed keened anew in mourning. The Sunderer was in a strange mood, untrustworthy and fey. The copper-sweet tang of his blood mingled with the lingering odor of sulfur. If he were willing to turn upon Darkhaven itself, what hope was there for her? Cerelinde repressed a shudder, mortally tired of living on the knife-edge of fear.

"Why not end it?" she asked, feeling weary and defeated. "If it's the Prophecy you fear, why not simply take my life? Your Vorax would be glad enough to do it."

"No," he said simply. "I will not."

"*Why?* Is it because there is another?" Her pulse beat faster, remembering what he had told her before, the words she had been certain were lies. It would be easier to accept death if they were not. "Is it true? That Elterrion's line continues elsewhere?"

"No, Lady." The Shaper gave a bitter laugh. "Oh yes, that part was true. There are others. There will be others. Other heroes, other heroines. Other prophecies to fulfill, other adversaries to despise. There will be stories told and forgotten, and reinvented anew until one day, perhaps, the oldest are remembered, and the beginning may end, and the ending begin. Ah, Uru-Alat!" He sighed. "Until the sorrowbells fall silent forever, there will be others."

"I do not understand," she said, confused.

"What if I asked you to stay?" His mood shifted, and the red light of malice glinted in his eyes. "You might temper this madness that comes too soon upon me, this anger. There would be no need for war were you to choose it willingly. You have seen, Daughter of Erilonde; there is beauty in this place. There would be more, did you choose to dwell here." He extended a hand to her. "What would you say if I asked it?"

What if they were not lies?

Moonlight cast the shadow of his mighty hand stark on the dead and dying grass. Cerelinde thought of the years of uneasy truce her acquiescence might bring, and measured it against the hope, the eternal hope, of the Rivenlost. Of Urulat, of all the world; but most of all, of her people. It was the ancient dream, the hope bred into their ageless flesh ever since the world was Sundered, of the Souma restored, the land made whole. It was nearer now than ever it had been, and she was willing to die to make it so. She could not allow herself to believe otherwise.

"I would say no," she said softly.

"So." He let his reaching hand fall back to his side. "It is no less than I expected, Lady. No less, and no more."

"Why did you refuse?" The words sprang impulsively from her lips, and Cerelinde wished them unsaid the moment she uttered them. But having been uttered, they could not be taken back. She forged onward. "This . . . rift, the Shapers' War. Haomane First-Born asked you three times to withdraw your Gift from Arahila's Children. Why did you refuse?"

"Why?" Thunder rumbled in the distance and clouds began to gather above the Vale of Gorgantum, obscuring the stars. Lifting his head, the Shaper watched as scudding wisps occluded the sundered disk of the silvery moon. In the dim light that remained his throat was an obsidian column, his breast a shield of night and the slow tide of seeping blood that glimmered on his thigh and trickled down one leg was oily and black. Something in his stance, in his *presence,* reminded her that he was one of the Seven Shapers; reminded her of the unbearable torment glimpsed when he had donned the Helm of Shadows. "Ask my Elder Brother, Lady. It is him you worship."

"He is not here to ask," Cerelinde said humbly, clasping her hands together.

"No." Slowly, Lord Satoris lowered his head to regard her, and his eyes glowed as red as blood, or dying embers. "He is not, is he?"

The *clamitus atroxis* shivered in resonant grief as the Shaper turned away, head held low, the dark bulwark of his shoulders rising like the swell of a wave. Cerelinde struggled against a sense of loss. A loss, but of what? Of a moment lost, an opportunity passing. Something slipped away, slipped between her slender fingers and through the gaps in her keen Ellylon mind as He who had Sundered the world trudged across the garden, leaving droplets of dark blood on the dying grass in his wake.

"My Lord!" she cried aloud in despair. "*Why?*"

A gentle rain began to fall as Satoris walked away from her, his words floating back to reach her. "Whatever stories they tell of me, Cerelinde, they will not say I slew you out of hand. That, at least, I may ensure."

Left standing alone in the garden, she flinched as the first drops struck her, but it was an ordinary rain. Water, no more and no less, leaving damp spots on her silk robes. It fell like a soft balm on the moon-garden, washing away the stench of sulfur, the dark traces of the Shaper's blood. In a nearby bed, pale flowers opened like eyes to welcome the clean rain, and the poignant odor of vulnus-blossom wafted in the air.

Their scent evokes memory. Painful memory.

Tanaros' words.

It was an aroma like nothing else, delicate and haunting. Cerelinde stumbled, backing away from the source, not wishing to see what it had evoked before: Lindanen Dale on her wedding day, Aracus struggling under the deadly onslaught of the Were, her kinsmen and his falling, slaughtered, and Tanaros looming before her on his black horse, reaching for her, blood staining the length of his black blade.

"No," she whispered.

It didn't come. Instead, she saw again the dark silhouette of the Shaper; Satoris Banewreaker, Satoris the Sunderer, with the shadow of his extended hand on the dying grass between them.

"I do not understand!" Turning her face to the night sky, Cerelinde let the rain wash away the gathering tears. "Lord-of-Thought," she pleaded, "I pray you lend me wisdom."

"Lady." A bulky figure trudged across the garden toward her, its path marked by the yellow glow of a bobbing lantern. "The Mørkhar said his Lordship had left you. Come on, I've not got all night." Holding the lantern aloft, Vorax sniffed. "Vulnus-blossom," he said in disgust. "You're better off avoiding the foul stuff. After a thousand years, I can tell you, some things are best forgotten."

"Lord Vorax." Cerelinde laid one hand on his arm. "What do you see?"

He turned his broad face toward her, illuminated by the lantern's glow. It was a Man's face, an ordinary Staccian face, plain and unhandsome. For all that, it was not a mortal face; the eyes that regarded her had watched a thousand years pass, and gazed without blinking at all the long anguish contained within the Helm of Shadows.

"You," he said bluntly. "I see you."

USHAHIN TURNED HIS FORKED STICK, rotating the slow-lizard's gutted carcass.

It was an unlikely breakfast, all the more so for being prepared by virtue of a dragon's courtesy. The lizard was roasting nicely in the outer verges of the searing flame she provided, held under careful control. Its charred hide was beginning to crackle and split, tasty white flesh bulging in the seams. Ushahin brought it in for inspection and scorched his fingers wedging loose a chunk of flaky meat. It had a sweet and mild flavor, with a smoky undertone. "Very pleasant," he said, extending the stick. "And done, I think. Will you not share it, Mother?"

The twin-sourced jet of flame winked into nonexistence as Calanthrag the Elder closed the iron-scaled valves of her nostrils, blinking with slow amusement. "My thanksss, little ssson. As I sssaid, I have eaten."

"Anyone I know?" He picked out another chunk of roasted lizard.

"Perhapsssss." The dragon shifted one submerged claw.

Ushahin paused in the act of raising the piece to his mouth. "Vorax's Staccians."

"Perhapsssss."

He chewed and swallowed the bite, conscious of the fact that he owed its delectation to her hospitality. "And yet you spared me."

"Are you sssorry?"

"No." He thought about it and shook his head. "Of a surety, I regret their deaths. Yet if you had not devoured them, I do not think I would be sitting here. And you would not have told me such mysteries as stagger the mind."

The nictitating lids blinked. "Even ssso."

The morning sun slanted through the mangrove and palodus trees, its warmth dispersing the vapors that rose from the swamp's waters in the cool hours of night. Insects chirred and whined. Overhead, birds flitted, dining on the prodigious swarms. Here and there the raucous *kaugh* of a raven punctuated their calls. Filled with a deep sense of contentment, Ushahin Dreamspinner sat in his skiff and ate roasted slow-lizard, until his belly was as full as his thoughts.

When he was finished, he laid his roasting stick carefully in the skiff beside his pole and the makeshift spear with which he had slain the lizard. The restless ravens settled in the trees, watching and waiting. The dragon was watching too, endless patience in her inhuman eyes. Ushahin touched his chest, feeling the scar's ridges through the fabric of his shirt, remembering the pain and the ecstasy of his branding. The scar throbbed beneath his touch, exerting a westward tug on his flesh. He thought of Lord Satoris, left with only one of his Three at his side, and the urge grew stronger.

Raising his head, he watched the ravens fluff and sidle, catching the tenor of their feathered thoughts. A winding wall encircling a vale, dark towers rearing under an overcast sky, yellow beech leaves and messy nests.

Home, home, home!

Calanthrag's voice hissed softly. "Do you ssstruggle againsst your dessstiny, Sson of No One?"

"No." He shook his head. "What you have told me, I will hold close to my heart, Mother, and ponder for many years. But it is Lord Satoris who gave meaning to my existence. I am his servant. I cannot be otherwise."

"He is the Sssower. Ssso it mussst be. Ssso it is."

There was a tinge of sulfur and sorrow in the dragon's exhalation. Turning away, Ushahin knelt in the skiff and worked at the knot in the rope he had tied around the palodus tree. His crooked fingers were unwontedly nimble. Oh, there was power in this place! It sang in his veins, heating his blood and rendering irrelevant the myriad aches that were his body's legacy. There was a part of him that was reluctant to leave. He sighed, bowing his head and winding the rope, laying it coiled in the prow. Straightening, he grasped the pole and stood, meeting the dragon's gaze. "Do you know how my story will end, Mother?"

"No." Calanthrag did not blink. "Only the Great Ssstory, little ssson."

Whether or not it was true, Ushahin could not say, for he had learned truth and lies were but two sides to the same fabric for dragonkind, inextricably interwoven. He thought of the things the dragon had shown him in the long night he had passed in the Delta; of the Chain of Being looped and looped and looped again, gathering him in its coils. A mighty consciousness, fragmenting, sighed and consigned itself to its fate. A world was born and died, and dying was born anew. Across the vastness of the stars, in the hidden bones of the earth. Nothing was born but that died; nothing died but was born. Fragmented. Striving, all in ignorance, at cross-purposes and folly. Waiting, all unknowing, for magic to pass from the world, for the deep fires to be extinguished, until there was only the hunger, the memory and *wanting*.

Such were the things the Eldest knew; the Eldest remembered.

Only then; only then would the cycle have come full circle, and true sentience reemerge, ready to be reborn.

Ushahin's hands tightened on the pole. "Will it truly come to pass, Mother?"

The dragon's jaws parted in a laugh, a true laugh, punctuated with jets of smoke. "Yesss," Calanthrag the Elder said. "Oh, yesss. Sssome day. Without usss, it shall not passs. Yet may it come later than sssooner for ssuch as I and you."

"So." Ushahin nodded. "I will play such a role as I may."

Plumes of smoke rolled and roiled, dark and oily, coiling around the branches of the palodus tree and obscuring its spatulate leaves. Ushahin coughed and the ravens of Darkhaven rose in a ruckus into the cleaner air above, chattering with annoyance.

When the smoke cleared, the dragon regarded him. "Go, little Ellyl-Man," she said. "It is time. Go, and remember." She moved one foreleg, then another; legs like columns, churning the mire. The vast hummock shuddered, moving. Murky water surged as Calanthrag's plated breast emerged from the swamp, mossy and dripping. Along the dragon's sides, vaned pinions stirred, revealing their sharp angles, hinting at their folded spans. The thick, snaking column of her neck arched, spines jutting erect as her head reared into the sky to brush the uppermost branches of the tall palodus tree. Gilt-green eyes glowed from on high and the massive jaws parted, revealing rows of jagged teeth, darkened with the Delta's corrosion. A forked tongue, red as heart's blood, flickered between them. "Remember the plasse of the Sssower's birth," Calanthrag hissed. Behind those terrible jaws, the opening of the dragon's iron-grey gullet glowed like the glory-hole of a kiln. "Remember *I* am here!"

The skiff rocked under the dragon's shadow. Ushahin Dreamspinner rode it out, legs braced, holding tight to his pole and craning his neck, caught between awe and terror. "I will not forget, Mother!" he shouted. "I will not!"

"Go!" the Eldest roared in a gout of fire.

Ushahin crouched, jamming the pole into the submerged roots of the palodus and shoving hard, launching his skiff into the waterways. A blue-white ball of flame passed low over his head, singeing his pale hair. Above, the ravens gathered in a flock launched themselves like an arrow in a southern trajectory, heading for the outskirts of the Delta.

"GO!"

He went, hard and fast, arms a blur planting and moving the pole. Dip and push; dip and push. The pain that wracked his ill-set bones was never more forgotten. Dip and push; dip and push. The skiff hummed over the waters, Dark-haven's ravens fanned out before it in a flying wedge. They found a path; he followed. How far was far enough? Mangrove and palodus ignited in their wake, bursting into flame in this unlikely, water-sodden place. In moments they had left the heart of the Delta behind them. Ushahin poled the skiff without thinking, winding his way through the narrow waterways, his gaze fixed on the flying wedge before him; small figures, darkly iridescent in the sunlight, beating frantically, tilting the knife-edges of their wings to catch and ride the wind.

He followed.

Stand upon stand of mangrove passed uncounted, measuring the distance they traveled. Two, four, eight . . . how far was far enough? Whatever the distance, they traversed it. Gouts of fire gave way to tendrils of smoke, until its reaching fingers crumbled, fading into nothingness in the bright air.

The glade, with its tall palodus tree and its strange hummock, was behind them.

Stillness settled over the Delta.

Ushahin leaned upon his pole, panting. After a moment, he laughed softly.

Amid the quiet hum of insects, the ravens settled around him, closer than they had dared in the dragon's presence. One spread its wings and dropped, landing neatly on the top of his pole, fine talons clutching the raw wood. He cocked his head, eyeing the half-breed, an effect rendered comical by an irregular tuft of feathers.

"Greetings, Fetch." Ushahin smiled. "I thought it was you I saw among the flock. Have you learned something of the uncertain nature of dragons? So have I, little brother; so have I." He dragged his sleeve across his forehead, smearing the residue of unwonted sweat. "I thank you for guiding me to that place, and I thank you for guiding me out of it. I am glad to leave it alive."

The raven squawked and wiped its beak on the pole, quick and nervous.

"Tanaros?" Ushahin's brows rose. "He travels the Unknown Desert, or so his Lordship says. Would you seek him, Fetch? There is no water there."

The raven bobbed its head, sidling from foot to foot.

"Very well." He shrugged, too weary to argue the matter. "Go, if you will. I have companions enough to guide me home, and much to contemplate along the way."

Fetch squawked once more and launched himself in a flurry of feathers, dark wings beating. Ushahin Dreamspinner watched him go, bemused. "Why?" he asked aloud. "Is it *love?* What a strange conceit, little brother!" There was no answer, only the stares of the other ravens, hunched and waiting, the sheen of their feathers purple in the swamp-filtered sunlight. Ushahin sighed, planting his pole. "Home," he said to them, giving a strong shove. "Home, it is. Onward, brethren!"

The remaining ravens took wing, arrowing for the fringes of the Delta. Somewhere ahead, where the mangrove thinned and the swamp turned to marshy plains, there was a mount awaiting; a steed of Darkhaven, with arched neck and preternatural intelligence in its eyes. Ushahin poled his skiff and followed, navigating the waterways.

Only once did he pause and gaze behind him.

The Great Story that encompassed the world was vaster than he had reckoned; than any had reckoned. Even Lord Satoris, who had listened to the counsel of dragons, could not hold the whole of it in his sight, enwrapped as he was in his Elder Brother's enmity. It was older than time, and it would outlive the Shapers' War, and perhaps Ushahin's role in it had only begun.

"I will not forget, Mother," he whispered.

In the glade at the heart of the Delta, Calanthrag the Eldest chuckled, settling her bulk into the swamp. Twin plumes of smoke trailed above as her sinuous neck stretched, her head lowered. Sulfurous bubbles arose as her nostrils sank below the water's surface, breaking foamy and pungent. Nictitating lids closed, filmy and half-clear, showing the unearthly gleam of gilt-green orbs below until the outer lids shut like doors. The last ripple spent itself atop the waters.

Beneath the tall palodus tree, the hummock in the heart of the Delta grew still, and the bronzed waters reflected sunlight like a mirror.

Calanthrag the Eldest slept, and laughed in her dreams.

THIRTY

◆

For the first time, Skragdal of the Tungskulder Fjel was ill at ease underground.

It was a short journey through the Vesdarlig Passage, one he had made before. All of them had. It was the oldest route through the tunnels to southwestern Staccia. It was a good tunnel, broad and straight. The walls were wide, the ceiling was high. The floor had been worn smooth by the passing tread of countless generations of Fjel. The Kaldjager patrolled it ruthlessly, ensuring that its egresses remained hidden, that its safety remained inviolate, that its ventilation shafts remained clear. It should have been a haven of comfort. It would have been, before.

It was Blågen, one of the Kaldjager who noticed it, loping back from a scouting excursion. His broad nostrils flared and his yellow eyes gave Skragdal an assessing glance. "You have the reek."

Skragdal grunted. "I was in the Marasoumië."

Blågen shrugged. "Ah."

The Men had it too, but Men often reeked of fear, except for General Tanaros. It didn't seem to bother the Nåltannen or the Gulnagel, and the Kaldjager hadn't been there for the terrible moment when the world had gone away in a rush of red light and stone had closed in upon them all. And now all that was gone, too, and the old wizard trapped inside it. The Men were talking about it, had been talking about it since they entered the tunnels, talking without cease, talking over one another, releasing nervous energy.

" . . . tell you, I'd rather be above ground, where you can see what's coming at you. Who knows what's down here *now?*"

"Yah! What, are you afraid the wizard's gonna get you?"

" . . . keep *telling* you, he's not dead, not with a Soumanië on him. He'll be back."

" . . . love of his Lordship's weeping wound, they're not even the same *tunnels,* the Ways aren't the same as our tunnels!"

"Sometimes they are, sometimes they aren't."

" . . . Kaldjager would catch him a mile away!"

" . . . even *hear* what happened? The old bugger's got a *Soumanië,* he can come out of nowhere and turn our arses to stone!"

" . . . Godslayer!"

" . . . back in the marrow-fire, where it belongs."

"And a right lot of good it'll do *us* there."

"Shut it, Einar." Osric, delivering an order. "That's treason you're talking."

"Lieutenant, I'm just *saying*—"

"Shut it!"

Skragdal wished Men wouldn't talk so much. Their restless minds grasped at thoughts like squirrels at nuts, gnawing and stuffing, dashing here and there, burying some and discarding others. And then words. Words! An endless stream, spewing from their lips, wasted with careless ease. It stemmed from Haomane's Gift, he supposed, and he ought to envy it. That's what Men and Ellylon said.

Only Lord Satoris had ever said otherwise.

They made camp in a vast cavern that night, a day's ride away from the Vesdarlig Door. Countless thousands had camped there before; Skragdal had done it himself, as an eager young pup on the way to honor the Fjel oath. The sleeping-places were worn smooth, broad grooves in the cavern floor, with suitable rough spots left untrammeled. He took comfort in seeing his fellows situated, freed from their cumbersome armor, rumbling and grumbling, working backs and shoulders against the stone. There was comfort in the evidence of countless members of the tribes who had done the same, leaving faint traces of their scent. It felt good to scratch itching hides against the rock.

Osric's Men took the southern quadrant, as was tradition.

They scratched the rock, too; only differently. Marks, etched with shards onto the cavern walls. Men lit fires, huddling under the ventilation shafts, sharing their fears and dreams, griping about the journey's hardship. Ruddy flames danced on the walls, showing the marks clearly. Scritching lines, narrow and perplexing. Sometimes they formed characters; sometimes, only shapes. Always, the lines shifted and changed, taunting him with elusive meaning.

Skragdal studied them, blinking.

"You can't read, can you?"

He glanced down at the Staccian commander. "I am Fjel," he said simply. "We do not share Haomane's Gift."

Osric's brow wrinkled. "You've tried, then?"

"No, lieutenant." He did not tell the story. None of the Fjel did; not to Men, not to anyone. Only to their pups. A long time ago they had wanted to learn. Neheris' Children had wanted it badly enough to plead with the wounded Shaper who had fled to their lands. And during the long years of his recuperation from Haomane's Wrath, Lord Satoris had tried to teach his people. In the end, it came to naught. The meaning of scratched lines—on stone, on parchment—was too evasive. How could a handful of symbols, which bore no intrinsic meaning, represent all the myriad things in the world? What relationship did they bear to the thing itself? It was a pointless endeavor.

Osric glanced at the scratchings. "Well, you're not missing much. Lads' folly for the most part, writing their names to let the ones who come after know they were here. That, and empty boasts. You'll have the Kaldjager stand watch again tonight?"

"Aye, lieutenant."

"Good man. Get some sleep."

He tried. Others slept, rumbling and snoring, comforted by stone's solid presence. It did not bother them that they had seen stone turn to an engulfing enemy in the red flash of a Soumanië's power. It should not bother him. Fjel had the gift of living in the present. Only important things were carried in the heart; only sacred memories, passed from generation to generation. All that was not worth carrying—fear, envy, hatred—was left to be washed away and forgotten in the flowing rivers of time.

Do not mourn for the Gift Haomane withheld from you. Did Neheris-of-the-Leaping-Waters not Shape her Children well? This I tell you, for I know: One day Men will covet your gifts. Treasure them, and rejoice.

Lord Satoris' words.

Those were the words that had restored Fjel pride and faith, the ones they passed on to their offspring. Those were the words that had inspired their ancient oath. Skragdal had heard them as a pup. He had carried them in his heart with pride, but he had never understood them as he did now, lying sleepless beneath the earth. Could such gifts be lost? Could the nature of the Fjel change, tainted by long exposure to the ways of Men? Was it the burden of command that weighed upon him, shaping his thoughts into fearful forms? Would he, if he could, scratch his name upon the wall?

No, he thought. No.

Reaching into a pouch that hung from his belt, Skragdal withdrew a half-carved lump of green chalcedony and examined it in the dim light of the cavern. There were flaws in the stone, but the fluid form of the *rhios* was beginning to emerge, a sprite as blithe as water flowing through a river bend. This is a thing that is not the thing itself, he thought. Yet it has a shape. I can hold it in my hands, and I can coax a truer shape from it. It is a stone, a real thing. It is a green stone that looks like water. These things I understand. He cupped the *rhios* in his hands and whispered a prayer to Neheris-of-the-Leaping-Waters. "Mother of us all, wash away my fear!"

There was an ease in saying the words. Words held power when they were spent with care. He felt a measure of fear ebb. The surrounding stone became a kinder companion. The memory of the Marasoumië faded, taking with it the image of the wizard with his terrible, glaring eyes, his lips working in the thicket of his white beard as he spoke the words to command the Ways, the red gem of the Soumanië ablaze on his chest. He would not forget, but neither would he carry it with him.

Skragdal sighed.

It was a gift.

Lord Satoris was right, had always been right. How wise

were the Elders who had seen it! Did the Fjel not slumber in peace while Men whimpered in their dreams?

It was so, it had always been so.

"ARE WE GOING TO DIE here, Lord General?" Speros' voice cracked on the question, and his eyes rolled in his head, showing dry white crescents below the brown iris. The noonday sun stood motionless overhead. His footsteps had begun to stagger, leaving a meandering trail in the sand. Their water supply had been gone since last night, and hours of trekking had taken their toll.

"No." Tanaros gritted his teeth, grabbing the Midlander's arm and hauling it across his shoulders. Lowering his head, he trudged onward, taking up the weight that sagged against him. "Come on, lad. Just a little way further."

Speros' breath was hot and ragged against his ear. "You said that before."

"And I will again," he retorted, still trudging.

"General!" one of the Gulnagel shouted. "Water-hole!"

The staggering cavalcade made its way across the wasteland of the Unknown Desert. They fell to their knees and dug by hand in the scrubby underbrush, marking the signs the Yarru had taught them. There, where thorn-brush grew and the termites built their mounds. There was life, ounce by precious ounce. Moisture darkened the sand and collected, gleaming, where they dug. An inch of water, perhaps more. Sand flew as the Fjel widened the hole, then scooped assiduously at the gathering moisture with Tanaros' helmet, husbanding every drop. They had carried the general's armor on their backs, reckoning it too precious to leave.

A lucky thing, since it made a good bucket.

"Sir?" A Gulnagel held out his helmet. It looked small in his massive hands. An inch of water shone at the bottom. "Drink."

Tanaros licked his dry lips, squinting at the sky. It was

blue and unforgiving, the white sun blazing in it like Haomane's Wrath. "Let him have it," he said, nodding at Speros, whom he had laid gently in what scant shade the thorn-brush afforded. "What is left, take for yourselves."

"All right, boss." The Fjel squatted on the parched earth, cradling Speros' head in his lap and tilting the helmet. "Drink," he said, coaxing.

The Midlander drank, his throat working, then sighed.

What was left, the Gulnagel shared. It amounted to no more than a sip apiece. One of them approached the largest termite mound and thrust a thorny branch into the opening at the top, stirring and teasing. The others gathered around the dry tower as indignant insects emerged in a marching line, pinching with deft talons and popping them into their mouths, crunching antennae and legs and swollen thoraxes with relish.

"Eat, General." Freg, grinning through his chipped eye-tusks, approached him. His horny hands were cupped and filled with squirming bounty. "They're *good*."

Tanaros shook his head. "You have them, Freg. You've earned them."

"You're sure?" The Gulnagel seemed anxious.

"Aye." He nodded.

Better that the Fjel should eat, and imbibe whatever moisture the termites held. It was not that Tanaros disdained the meal. They needed it; as much as Speros, though they reckoned it less. He knew. He knew Fjel. They were Neheris' Children, born to a land of mountains and leaping rivers, not made for desert travel. The hides of the Gulnagel had grown desiccated and stark on this journey; leeched of color, dry and cracking.

Still, they would go and go and go, obedient to his orders, legs churning, never a complaint among them.

They ate until there were no more termites.

"We're ready, General." Freg stooped over the Midlander's supine form. "You want I should carry him? I've strength enough for it."

"Aye." Tanaros drew a deep breath, feeling the arid air burn in his lungs. If his eyes had not been so dry, he might have wept. The lad had followed him out of a sense of belonging. He should never have been allowed to pledge his loyalty; he did not deserve to be left. "Aye, Freg. Carry him while you can."

The Gulnagel did, hoisting Speros onto his own back. The Midlander's limbs dangled, jostled by each wayward step. Onward they staggered, over the parched earth. Tanaros led the way. He knew it; knew it as the migrating swallow knows its way. His branded heart served as compass. *There.* There it was before him. Darkhaven. Home, where Lord Satoris sat on his Throne and Godslayer hung blazing in the marrow-fire. It exerted its own pull, guiding his faltering steps across the shortest route possible, no matter how inhospitable the land.

Alas, in the Unknown Desert, the shortest route was not always the best. The Yarru had known as much. The Unknown was crossed one water-hole at a time, one place of sustenance after another. They knew the way of it. If he had let them live, they might have guided him.

Better not to think about it.

Thus did they sojourn, onward and onward. The sun moved in immeasurably small increments across the sky. If there were shade, they would have traveled by night; but they had found no shade, not enough to shelter them. The Gulnagel panted like dogs, with open mouths and labored breathing. Even so, none would lay down his burden.

Tanaros forced his legs to move. One step, then another and another. After all, what did it cost him? He would not die in this place. It was like the Marasoumië. It might kill him, in time; it would take a long time. He could lie on the desert floor, dying of thirst, for ages. He had time. Let him set an example, instead. The black blade of his sword banged against his hip as he trudged onward through the empty desert, leading his staggering band.

The burning sun sank its leading edge below the horizon.

Night would follow, with no water in sight. No chance of finding it by starlight; the signs were too subtle. He wondered, grimly, how many would live to see the dawn.

"Lord General!" One of the Gulnagel flung out a rough-hewn hand, pointing.

Wings, the shadow of wings, beating. They were cast large upon the parched earth and there was something familiar in the sound. Tanaros lifted a head grown heavy with exhaustion, raising an arm.

"Fetch!" he cried.

A familiar weight, settling. Talons pricked his arm, and a tufted head bobbed, cocking a beady eye at him. *"Kaugh!"*

"Fetch," Tanaros murmured. A feeling in his heart swelled, painful and overlarge. It was foolish. It didn't matter. He stroked the raven's feathers with one forefinger, overwhelmed with gratitude. "How did you find me?"

Something nudged at his thoughts, a scrabbling sensation.

Surprised, he opened his mind.

A patchwork of images flooded his vision; sky, more sky, other ravens. A fecund swamp, leaves and bark and beetles. Ushahin Dreamspinner standing in the prow of a small boat, squinting through mismatched eyes. A dragon's head reared against the sky, ancient and dripping. Darkness; darkness and light. The world seen from on high in all its vastness. Laughter. A dragon's jaws, parting to breathe living fire.

"You saw this?" Tanaros asked.

"Kaugh!"

A green blur of passing swamp, bronze waters gleaming. Wings beating in a flying wedge; a pause, a caesura. Ushahin wiping sweat from his brow. A lofting, the downbeat of wings. Aloneness. Tilting earth, marsh and fertile plains, a shadow cast small below. It wavered, growing larger, then smaller. A blur of night and stars, pauses and launches. Blue, blue sky, and the desert floor.

The shadow held its size, held and held and held.

Greenness.

A drought-eater; no, three! Thick stalks, succulent leaves. Green-rinded fruits hung low, ripe with water. The shadow veered, growing large, then veered away again.

Desert, parched desert, beneath the lowering sun.

Tanaros and his company seen from above.

"Oh, Fetch!" His dry eyes stung. "Have you seen this? Can you show me?"

"*Kaugh!*" Bobbing and chuckling, the raven launched itself from Tanaros' arm, setting a northward trajectory.

"Follow him!" Marshaling his strength, Tanaros forced himself in the direction of the raven's flight, departing from his heart's compass. With mighty groans and dragging steps, the Gulnagel followed. Speros, unconscious, jounced on Freg's back, ungainly as a sack of millet and thrice as heavy.

It was not a long journey, as Men reckon such things. How long does it take for the sun to set once the outermost rim of its disk has touched the horizon? A thousand beats of a straining heart; three thousand, perhaps, here where the desert lay flat and measureless. With the distance half-closed, Tanaros saw the silhouettes of the drought-eaters, stark and black against the burning sky. Hope surged in his heart. He set a steady pace, exhorting the Gulnagel with praise and curses. If they had stuck to their course, they would have passed them by to the south, unseen.

But there was water ahead, *water!* The plants held it in abundance.

For a hundred steps, two hundred, the drought-eaters appeared to recede, taunting, ever out of reach. And then they were there, and Fetch settled atop a thick trunk, making a contented sound. The raven ruffled his feathers. A dwindling sliver of flame lit the western horizon and the scent of moisture seeped into the arid air. With rekindled strength, Tanaros strode ahead, drawing his sword to sever a green-ripe fruit from its fibrous mooring and holding it aloft.

"Here!" he cried in triumph. "Water!"

One by one the Gulnagel staggered into his presence, each burdened with a piece of his armor. Each laid his burden on the sand with reverence; all save the last.

With heavy steps, Freg of the Gulnagel Fjel entered the stand of drought-eaters, a loose-limbed Speros draped over his back like a pelt. Freg's taloned hands held the Midlander's arms in place where they were clasped about his neck. His dragging tread gouged crumbling furrows in the dry earth. One step, then another and another, following Tanaros' example. The drought-eaters cast long shadows across his path. Freg's face split in a proud, weary smile.

"General," he croaked, pitching forward.

"Freg!"

In the dying wash of light, Tanaros crouched beside the Gulnagel and rolled him onto his back. He spread his hands on the broad expanse of the Fjel's torso, feeling for the beat of his sturdy heart. There was nothing. Only dry hide, harsh and rough to the touch. The heart that beat beneath it had failed. Freg's chipped grin and empty eyes stared at the desert sky. Tanaros bowed his head. The other Gulnagel murmured in tones of quiet respect, and Fetch ducked his head to preen, picking at his breast-feathers.

Thrown free by Freg's fall, Speros stirred his limbs and made a faint noise.

"Water," Tanaros murmured, extending one hand without looking. A severed drought-fruit was placed in it. He tipped it and drank; one swallow, two, three. Enough. He placed it to the Midlander's parched lips. "Drink." Water spilled into Speros' mouth, dribbled out of the corners to puddle on the dry earth. Tanaros lifted his head and gazed at the watching Gulnagel. "What are you waiting for?" he asked them, blinking against the inexplicable burn of tears. "It's water. Drink! As you love his Lordship, drink."

Stripping the plants, they hoisted drought-fruit and drank.

It was a mighty stand, and an old one. The plants seldom

grew in pairs, let alone three at once. The Yarru must have
told stories about such a thing. There was enough water
here to quench their thirst, enough water here to carry.
Tanaros fed it in slow sips to Speros until the Midlander's
eyes opened and consciousness returned, and he shivered
and winced at the cramps that gripped his gut. Under
starlight he scanned the remaining Fjel with a fevered gaze,
and asked about Frog. His voice sounded like something
brought up from the bottom of a well.

Tanaros told him.

The Midlander bent over with a dry, retching sob.

Tanaros left him alone, then, and walked under the stars.
This time he did not brood on the red one that rose in the
west, but on the thousands upon thousands that outnumbered it. There were so many visible, here in the Unknown
Desert! Arahila's Gift against the darkness, flung like diamonds across the black canopy of night. Nowhere else was
it so evident. There was a terrible beauty in it.

It made him think of Ngurra's calm voice.

It made him think of Cerelinde, and her terrible, luminous beauty.

It made him think of his wife.

Alone, he pressed the heels of his hands against his
closed lids. Her eyes had shone like that at the babe's birth.
Like stars; like diamonds. Her eyes had shone like that
when he killed her, too, glistening with terror as his hands
closed about her throat. And yet . . . and yet. When he
sought her face in his memory, it was that of the Lady of the
Ellylon he saw instead. And there was no terror in her eyes,
only a bright and deadly compassion.

"My Lord!" he cried aloud. "Guide me!"

Something rustled, and a familiar weight settled on his
shoulder, talons pricking through his undertunic. A horny
beak swiped at his cheek; once, twice. *"Kaugh?"*

"Fetch." It was not the answer he sought, but it was an answer. Tanaros' thoughts calmed as he stroked the raven's

feathers; calmed, and spiraled outward. "How did you know to find me, my friend? How did you penetrate the barrier of my thoughts? Was it the Dreamspinner who taught you thusly?"

"*Kaugh*," the raven said apologetically, shuffling from foot to foot.

An image seeped into Tanaros' mind; a grey, shadowy figure, lunging, jaws open, to avenge an ancient debt. Always, there were her slain cubs, weltering in their blood. A sword upraised between them, and Aracus Altorus' face, weeping with futile rage as her weight bore him down, half-glimpsed as Tanaros wheeled his mount to flee and the Lady Cerelinde's hair spilled like cornsilk over his thighs. The Grey Dam of the Were had died that day, spending her life for a greater gain.

"Ah."

Ushahin's words rang in his memory. *Do you know, cousin, my dam afforded you a gift? You will know it, one day.*

"Yes, cousin," Tanaros whispered. "I know it." And he stroked the raven's feathers until Fetch sidled alongside his neck, sheltering beneath his dark hair, and remembered the broken-winged fledgling he had raised; the mess in his quarters, all the small, bright objects gone missing. And yet, never had he known the raven's thoughts. A small gift, but it had saved lives. On his shoulder, Fetch gave a sleepy chortle. Tanaros clenched his fist and pressed it to his heart in the old manner, saluting the Grey Dam Sorash. "Thank you," he said aloud. "Thank you, old mother."

Vengeance. Loyalty. Sacrifice.

Such were the lodestones by which his existence was charted, and if it was not the answer he sought, it was answer enough. Thrusting away the thoughts that plagued him, Tanaros turned back toward the drought-eaters, walking slowly, the raven huddled on his shoulder.

There were not enough stones to build a cairn, so the Fjel

were digging. Shadows gathered in the mouth of the grave. Dim figures looming in the starlight, the Gulnagel glanced up as he entered the encampment, continuing without cease to shift mounds of dry sand and pebbles. Tanaros nodded acknowledgment. No need for speech; he knew their ways.

The unsteady figure of Speros of Haimhault labored alongside them. "Lord General," he rasped, straightening at Tanaros' approach.

"Speros." He looked at the fever-bright eyes in the gaunt face, the trembling hands with dirt caked under broken nails. "Enough. You need to rest."

The Midlander wavered stubbornly on his feet. "So do they. And he died carrying *me*."

"Aye." Tanaros sighed. The raven roused and shook its feathers, launching itself from its perch to land on the nearest drought-eater. "Aye, he did." Casting about, he spotted his helmet amid the rest of his armor. It would hold sand as well as water, and serve death as well as life. One of the Gulnagel grunted, moving to make room for him. "Come on, then, lads," Tanaros said, scooping at the grave, filling his helmet and tossing a load of sand over his shoulder. "Let's lay poor Freg to rest."

Side by side, Man and Fjeltroll, they labored beneath Arahila's stars.

IT WAS ON THE VERGES of Pelmar, a half day's ride outside Kranac, that the Were was sighted. Until then, the journey had been uneventful.

The forest was scarce less dense near one of the capital cities, but the mounted vanguard had been moving with speed since leaving Martinek's foot-soldiers behind, weaving in single-file columns among the trees. If she had not despised them, Lilias would have been impressed at the woodcraft of the Borderguardsmen. Plains-bred they might be, but they were at ease in the forest. The Ellylon, of course, were at home anywhere; Haomane's Children, Shaped to rule over all Lesser Shapers. Although they acknowledged him as kin-in-waiting and King of the West, even Aracus Altorus treated them with a certain respect. Always, there was an *otherness* to their presence. Grime that worked its way into the clothing and skin of Men seemed not to touch them. The shine on their armor never dimmed and an ever-willing breeze kept their pennants aloft, revealing the delicate devices wrought thereon. Under the command of Lorenlasse of Valmaré, the company of Rivenlost rode without tiring, sat light in the saddle, clad in shining armor, guiding their mounts with gentle touches and gazing about them with fiercely luminous eyes, as if assessing the world of Urulat and finding it lacking.

In some ways, she despised them most of all.

And it was an Ellyl, of course, who spotted the scout.

"Anlaith cysgoddyn!" It was like an Ellylon curse, only sung, in his musical voice. He stood in the stirrups, one finely shaped hand outflung, pointing. *"Were!"*

She saw; they all did. A grey, slinking figure, ears flattened to its head, ducking behind a thick pine trunk. Once sighted, it moved in a blur, dropping low to the earth, fleeing in swift, leaping bounds. Patches of sunlight dappled the fur on its gaunt flanks as it lunged for deeper shadow.

Aracus Altorus gave a single, terse order. "Shoot it!"

"Wait!" Lilias cried out in instinctive protest, too late.

A half dozen bowstrings twanged in chorus. Most were Ellylon; one was not. Oronin's Bow sounded a deep, anguished note, belling like a beast at bay. This time, it shot true against its maker's Children. The same fierce light that suffused the eyes of the Rivenlost lit the Archer's face as she turned sideways in the saddle, following her arrow's flight with her gaze. Its path ended in a howl of pain, cut short in a whimper. The underbrush rustled where its victim writhed.

"Blaise," Aracus said implacably. "See what we have caught."

"Stay here," Blaise muttered to Lilias, relinquishing the reins of her mount and dismounting in haste.

Since there was nowhere to go, she did. With a sick feeling in the pit of her stomach, she watched as he beckoned to other Borderguardsmen, as their dun cloaks faded into the underbrush. And, sitting in the saddle, she watched as they tracked down their prey and brought him back.

He was slung between them like a hunter's quarry, a Borderguardsman attached to each outspread limb. It was a pathetic sight, a Were stripped of all his shifting glamour. The haft of a yellow-fletched arrow protruded from the right side of his narrow, hairy breast. His chest heaved with each shallow breath, the wound burbling. Where they passed, crimson droplets of blood clung to the pine-needles.

"*Phraotes!*" Lilias whispered.

The one-time Were ambassador was panting. He hung in his captors' grip, jaws agape. His amber eyes, meeting hers, rolled. There were foam and blood on his muzzle. "Sorceress," he gasped. "It seems, perhaps, I should not have fled."

Aracus Altorus raised his eyebrows. "You know this creature?"

"Yes." A tide of anger rose in her. "*Yes!*" she spat. "I know him, and I know he has done you no harm! He is the Grey Dam's ambassador to Beshtanag, O King of the West, and he brought to me the news that his folk would do nothing to oppose your passage. *Nothing.*" Lilias drew a breath. "What harm has he done you now, that you would slay him out of hand? Nothing!"

"Lilias," Blaise said. One of four, he maintained a cruel grip on Phraotes' right foreleg, keeping the Were's hairy limbs stretched taut. "Enough."

"What?" she asked sharply. "No, I will speak! For a thousand years the Were dwelled in Beshtanag in peace. What do I care for your old quarrels?" She stared at the faces of her captors, one by one. "What did he care? Is there to be no end to it?" Against her will, her voice broke. "Will Hao-

mane order you to slay everything that lives and does not
obey his command?"

For a moment, they stared back at her. The Ellylon were
expressionless. Blaise's face was grim. Fianna, the Archer
of Arduan, turned away with a choked sound. Aracus Altorus sighed, rumpling his red-gold hair. "Sorceress—" he
began.

"We were attacked," a soft voice interjected; an Ellyl
voice. It was Peldras, of Malthus' Company, who alone
among his kind traveled in worn attire. He gazed at her with
deep sorrow. "I am sorry, Lady of Beshtanag, but it is so.
Blaise and Fianna will attest to it. On the outskirts of Pelmar, in deepest night, the Were fell upon us. Thus was
Malthus lost, and the Bearer, fleeing into the Ways of the
Marasoumië. Thus did one of our number fall, giving his
life so that we might flee."

"Hobard of Malumdoorn," Blaise murmured. "Let his
name not be forgotten."

"Even so." Peldras bowed his head.

"Phraotes?" Lilias asked in a small voice. "Is it true?"

"What is truth?" The Were bared his bloodstained teeth.
"A long time ago, we made a choice. Perhaps it was a bad
one. This time, we were forced into a bad bargain. Yet, what
else was offered us? Perhaps *you* made a bad bargain. I am
only an ambassador. I would be one to this Son of Altorus
did he will it."

Aracus frowned. "Do you gainsay the testimony of my
comrades? Your people attacked Malthus' Company under
cover of night, unprovoked. A valiant companion was slain,
the wisest of our counselors was lost, the greatest of our
hopes has vanished. You have shown no honor here, no remorse. Why should I hear your suit?"

"Why not?" The Were's head lolled, eyes rolling to fix
his gaze on him. "It was a favor extracted by threat, nothing
more. We failed; it is finished. We did not make war upon
you in Beshtanag, Arahila's Child. The Grey Dam fears the
wrath of Satoris Third-Born, but Haomane's is more dire.

We seek only to be exempted from the Shapers' War. Yea, I feared to approach in good faith, and I have paid a price for it. Will you not listen before it is paid in full?"

Angry voices rose in reply; in the saddle, Aracus Altorus held up one hand. "Set him down." He waited while Blaise and the others obeyed. Phraotes curled into a tight ball and lay panting on the pine mast. His ears were flat against his skull and the shaft of the arrow jerked with each breath, slow blood trickling down his grey fur, but his visible eye was watchful. The Were did not die easily. Aracus gazed down at him, his expression somber. "There remain many scores between us, not the least of which is Lindanen Dale. And yet you say you are an ambassador. What terms do you offer, Oronin's Child?"

With a sound that was half laugh, Phraotes coughed blood. His muzzle scraped the loam. "The Grey Dam is dead; the Grey Dam lives. Though she carries her memories, the Grey Dam Vashuka is not the Grey Dam Sorash." One amber eye squinted through his pain. "What terms would you accept, King of the West?"

"Son of Altorus!" There was a stir in the ranks, and the gilded bee of Valmaré fluttered on its pennant as Lorenlasse rode forward, glittering in his armor, to place a peremptory hand on Aracus' arm. "Dergail the Wise Counselor *died* through the treachery of Oronin's Children," he hissed, "and Cerion the Navigator was lost! The Lady Cerelinde would be your bride if they were not faithless. You may forget, but *we* remember. Will you treat with them and be a fool?"

Plain steel sang as Blaise Caveros unsheathed his sword. "Unhand him."

Finely chiseled Ellyl nostrils flared. "What manner of villain do you take me for, traitor-kin?" Lorenlasse asked in contempt. "Our way is not *yours*. We do not slay out of misguided *passion*."

"Enough!" Aracus raised his voice. "Blaise, put up your sword. My lord Lorenlasse, abide." He sighed again and rubbed his temples, aching beneath the Soumanië's weight. "Would that Malthus was here," he muttered. "Sorceress!"

Lilias glanced up, startled. "My lord Altorus?"

"Advise me." He brought his mount alongside hers and looked hard at her. "You know them; you have made pacts with them, and lived. I do not forget anything, but I have erred once in mistaking my true enemy, and innocent folk have died. I do not wish to err twice. Are the Were my enemy?"

"No." She shook her head. "They wish only to be let alone."

"Whence Lindanen Dale?"

He was close, too close. Their horses' flanks were brushing. His presence crowded her, yet there was no room to shrink away on the narrow path. Lilias swallowed. "It was your kinsmen slew her cubs. Do you not remember?"

"I was not born." His face was implacable.

"Faranol," Phraotes rasped. "Prince Faranol."

"Yes." Lilias drew a shallow breath, wishing Aracus would give her space to draw a deeper one. He was close enough that she could smell him, the tang of metal and the sharp odor of human sweat. This urgency, the exigencies of mortal flesh, pressed too close, reminded her too keenly of the limits that circumscribed her own existence, of her own aching, aging body. "Faranol of Altoria slew the offspring of the Grey Dam Sorash. A hunting party in Pelmar. Surely you must know."

"Yes." Because he did not need to, he did not say that Faranol was a hero to the House of Altorus. "I know the story."

"Hence, Lindanen Dale," she said simply.

"So." Aracus' fingertips pressed his temples. "It is a cycle of vengeance, and I am caught up in it by accident of birth." With a final sigh he dropped his hands and cast his gaze upon the Were. "You are dying, Oronin's Child. What power have you to make treaties? Why should I believe you?"

Lying curled upon the ground, Phraotes bared his bloody teeth. "We have walked between life and death since the Glad Hunter Shaped us, blowing his horn all the while. Death walked in his train as it does in yours. We are a pack, son of Altorus, and our Shaper's Gift lies in those dark corridors. Though Oronin's Horn now blows for me, the Grey Dam hears me; I speak with her voice. Ushahin-who-walks-between-dusk-and-dawn is banned from our company. The fetters of old oaths are broken, we are despised in Urulat, and Oronin has raised his hand against us this day. New oaths may be made and honored. What will you, King of the West?"

"Sorceress?"

His eyes were wide, demanding. Demanding, and trusting. For the first time, Lilias understood why they had followed him; Man and Ellyl alike. The knowledge made her inexplicably weary. "For so long as the Grey Dam Vashuka endures," she said, speaking true words to him, "the Were will abide by what bargain you strike. I have no other counsel."

"It is enough." He nodded. "Thank you."

Something in her heart stirred at his thanks. The mere fact of it made bile rise in her throat. Lilias looked away, not watching as Aracus left her side. He dismounted, walking away a small distance. Others followed, raising voices in argument: gilded Ellylon voices, the deeper tones of the Borderguard, the pleading voice of the woman Archer. Lilias glanced across the backs of milling, riderless horses. Aracus listened to the arguments without speaking, his broad shoulders set, his head bowed under the useless weight of the Soumanië. She wondered if they would regret having sworn their fealty to him this day. There was a twisted satisfaction in the thought.

"He'll do it, you know."

Glancing down, she saw Blaise standing beside her mount, gathering its reins in his capable hands. "Do what?"

"Forge a truce." He handed the reins up to her, his fingers

brushing hers. Blaise's eyes were dark and intent. Her chestnut mare snuffled his hair, and he stroked its neck absently, still watching her. "He's big enough for it, Lilias, despite their fears. I ought to know."

Lilias shook her head, unsettled in the pit of her stomach. What did it matter that Aracus Altorus had forgiven Blaise Caveros his immortal ancestor's betrayal? Calandor, her beloved Calandor, was no less dead for it. On the ground, Phraotes coiled tight around a knot of pain and waited. Only the wrinkled, foam-flecked lips of his muzzle gave evidence to his slow death throes. He met her gaze with a glint of irony in his amber eye. He was the only creature here she understood. "It's easy to be magnanimous in victory, Borderguardsman," she said.

"No." Sighing, Blaise straightened. "No, it's not. That's the thing."

In time, the arguments fell silent and Aracus returned, retracing his path with heavy steps. The Rivenlost were amassed behind him, a quiet, glittering threat. A concord had been reached. Aracus Altorus stood above the dying Were, gazing downward, his face in shadow. His voice, when he spoke, sounded weary. "Will you hear my terms, Oronin's Child? They are twofold."

Phraotes' sharp muzzle dipped and lifted. "Speak."

"One." Aracus raised a finger. "You will foreswear violence against all the Shapers' Children, in thought and deed, in property and in person. Only such simple prey as you find in the forest shall be yours. You shall not conspire upon the soil of Urulat in any manner. You will disdain Satoris the Sunderer and all his workings."

The Were ambassador exhaled, crimson blood bubbling through his nostrils. It might have been a bitter laugh; the arrow in his breast jerked at the movement. "The Grey Dam Vashuka accedes. So it shall be. Do you swear us peace, we will retreat unto the deepest forests to trouble the Lesser Shapers no more, and be forgotten."

"Two." Aracus raised a second finger. "You will abjure the Sunderer's Gift."

Behind him, Lorenlasse of the Valmaré smiled.

So, Lilias thought; it comes to this. That offering, which Haomane disdained for his Children, he cannot bear another's to possess. The Shapers' War continues unending, and we are but pawns within it. Silent atop her mount, she thought of the things Calandor had shown her in his cavern atop Beshtanag Mountain, the things that filled her heart with fear. *One day,* he had said, *when his own are gone, Haomane will adopt Arahila's Children as his own. Until then, he will eliminate all others.*

She wondered if Oronin Last-Born would protest, or if he were willing to sacrifice his Children on the altar of Haomane's pride for the sin of having aided Satoris Banewreaker. In the silence that followed Aracus' pronouncement, it seemed that it must be so. Like Neheris-of-the-Leaping-Waters, the Glad Hunter would abide.

"No cubs?" Phraotes rasped. "No offspring?"

Aracus Altorus shook his head. "None."

It took longer to obtain an answer. The Were's eyes rolled back into his head, his body writhing upon the loam. Whatever path his thoughts traveled, it was a difficult one. Phraotes gnashed his teeth, blood and foam sputtering. His body went rigid, then thrashed, the protruding arrow jerking this way and that, his clawed hands digging hard and scoring deep gouges in the pine mast.

"Lord Aracus," Peldras the Ellyl whispered. "Such a request, whether you will it or no, embroils the Were in the Shapers' War . . . "

Aracus raised one hand, intent. "Such are my terms."

Say no, Lilias thought, concentrating her fierce will. *Say no, say no, say NO!*

"Yea!" Phraotes, panting, opened slitted eyes. "The Grey Dam Vashuka accedes. Do you leave us in peace, Oronin's Children will abjure the Gift of Satoris Third-Born, and procreate no more in her lifetime. Like Yrinna's Children, we shall not increase; nor shall we remain. We shall dwindle, and pass into legend. Like—" his amber gaze fell upon Lorenlasse, "—like Haomane's Children, in all their pride." Head lolling, he gave his bloody grin. "Is it a bargain, King of the West? Will you swear to leave us in peace, and guarantee the word of all who are sworn to your allegiance?"

"I will," Aracus said simply. "I do."

There was a moment of silence, broken only by the sound of horses shifting, stamping restless hooves, cropping at foliage. It didn't seem right, Lilias thought. There should have been a vast noise; a shuddering crash such as there had been when Calandor fell, an endless keening wail of Oronin's Horn. Not this simple quietude. She wanted to weep, but there were no tears left in her, only a dry wasteland of grief.

"So be it." Phraotes closed his eyes. "Oronin has wrought this and the Were consent. With my death, it is sealed. Draw out the arrow, King of the West."

Aracus knelt on one knee beside the crumpled figure, placing his left hand on the Were's narrow chest. With his right, he grasped the arrow's shaft. Murmuring a prayer to Haomane, he pulled, tearing out the arrow in one hard yank. Blood flowed, dark and red, from the hole left by the sharp barbs. Phraotes hissed, tried to cough, and failed. His lids flickered once and, with a long shudder, he died.

"All right." Aracus Altorus climbed to his feet, looking weary. He rubbed at his brow with one hand, leaving a smear of blood alongside the Soumanië. "Give him . . . give him a proper burial," he said, nodding at the still figure. "If the Were keep their word, we'll owe him that much, at least."

There was grumbling among the Borderguard; the Ellylon made no complaint, assuming that the order was not intended for them. But it was Lilias who found her voice and said, "No."

Aracus stared at her. "Why?"

"The Were do not bury their dead," she said harshly. "Leave him for the scavengers of the forest if you would do him honor. It is their way."

He stared at her some more. "All right." Turning away, he accepted his reins from a waiting Borderguardsman and swung into the saddle. "Blaise, send a rider to Kranac to notify Marthiek of this bargain. Tell him I mean to keep my word, and do any of the Regents of Pelmar break it, I will consider it an act of enmity. By the same token, do the Were break it, they will be hunted like dogs, until the last is slain. Let it be known."

"Aye, sir." Blaise moved to obey. In a few short minutes a rider was dispatched and the remainder of the company was remounted, preparing to depart. There was barely time for Lilias to take one last glance at Phraotes. It was hard to remember the Were ambassador as he had been; a keen-eyed grey shadow, gliding like smoke into the halls of Beshtanag. Dead, he was diminished, shrunken and hairy. His eyes were half slitted, gazing blankly at the trees. His muzzle was frozen in the rictus of death, wrinkled as if at a bad scent or a bad joke. Phraotes did not look like what he had been, one of the direst hunters ever to touch the soil of Urulat.

We shall dwindle, and pass into legend.

Lilias shuddered. "I'm sorry," she whispered, horribly aware that if she had not given counsel to Aracus, the bargain might never have been struck. "I didn't know what he would ask. Phraotes, I'm sorry!"

There was no answer, only the Were's dead, sharp-toothed grin.

If it were a bad joke, she hoped it was on Haomane's Allies.

THIRTY-ONE

A HALF DOZEN RAVENS PERCHED in the green shadows of the outermost edges of the Delta, drowsy in the midday sun. Beneath them, Ushahin Dreamspinner crouched, watching horses grazing on sedge grass.

He had been raised by the Grey Dam Sorash and, outcast or not, a part him would always be kindred to the Were. He knew the paths the Were trod; the dark paths of the forest, the dark paths of the pack mind. Although his path had diverged, he heard the echoes of their thoughts. When Oronin's Bow was raised against one of his Brethren, he felt it, and shuddered at the killing impact. When a dire bargain was struck, he bowed his head and grieved.

"You are too hasty, Mother," was all he whispered.

It was her right, the Grey Dam Vashuka. And he understood, oh yes, the thought behind it. Oronin's Children had never sought anything but solitude; the right to hunt, the right to be left alone. Still, he thought, she had surrendered too much, too soon. Perhaps it was a trick; yes, perhaps. The bargain held only as long as the Grey Dam lived. And she might live many hundreds of years upon the hoarded years her brethren sacrificed to her. His dam, the Grey Dam Sorash, had done so.

Or she might not. It was yet to see.

Ushahin watched the horses.

They did not care for him, horses. Although he was of the blood of two races, Lesser Shapers whose mastery of the lower orders of being went unquestioned, it was his years among the Were that had shaped him the most. Horses sensed it as if it were an odor on his skin. Ushahin, the predator. They carried him reluctantly at best, and when all was said and done, he preferred to travel on his own two feet. It had been a fine arrangement, until his Lordship had closed the Ways. Now, Ushahin had need of speed. Darkhaven was waiting; and the horses of Darkhaven lay to hand.

They were splendid creatures, there was no denying it. Their inadequate disguises had long since worn off; ill-cropped manes and tails regrown in flowing splendor. They were poorly groomed, aye, but they had shed winter's shaggy coat, and their summer hides gleamed with good health.

He had his eye on the best of the lot, an ill-tempered bay with a coat the color of drying blood, a black mane and tail. It had been Hunric's mount, if his memory served. A long-legged stallion with a fine, wedge-shaped head and snapping teeth to boot. The others bore scars of his temper.

The horses of Darkhaven had sharper teeth than those bred elsewhere.

Ushahin waited until dusk, when his own abilities edged toward their height. It was then that he emerged from the verges of the Delta, a length of rope in his crooked hands. It had served to secure his skiff; it would serve for this.

"Come," he crooned. "Come to me, pretty one."

It didn't, of course. His target stood poised on wary legs, showing the whites of its eyes, aware of his intent. He had to use the glamour, a Were trick, catching its mind in the net of his thoughts. Once it was done, the horse stood still and trembled, its hide shuddering as if flystung. Ushahin limped from his place of concealment, placing the rope around its neck, winding a twist about its soft muzzle and knotting it to create a makeshift hackamore.

"So," he whispered. "Not so bad, is it?"

The blood-bay stallion shuddered. So close, their hair was intertwined; Ushahin, leaning, his fine, pale hair mingling with the horse's black mane. He could smell the sweat, the lather forming on the horse's blood-dark hide. Its defiance would only be held in check so long, unless he wanted to fight it all the way to Darkhaven. He did not. Now, or never. Ignoring the pain in his crooked limbs, he slid one arm over its neck and hauled hard, pulling himself astride, and clamped hard with both thighs.

"Home!" he shouted, casting aside the net of thought that bound it.

The bay exploded beneath him: bucking, sunfishing, limbs akimbo. Ushahin laughed out loud and clung to its back. It hurt, hurt beyond telling, jarring his ill-mended bones. Yet he was one of the Three, and he had breakfasted with a dragon. No mere horse would be his undoing, not even one of the horses of Darkhaven.

It was a long battle nonetheless. Almost, the bay stallion succeeded in unseating him. It plunged toward the Verdine River and planted its forelegs in a halt so abrupt Ushahin was thrown hard against its neck. The other horses watched with prick-eared interest as the bay twisted its head around to snap at him. It charged, splashing, into the fringes of the Delta and sought to jar him loose against the trunk of a palodus tree, bruising and scraping his flesh.

None of it worked.

By the time the bay's efforts slowed, stars were emerging in the deep-blue twilight. The capitulation came all at once; a slump of the withers, the proud head lowering. It blew a heavy breath through flared nostrils and waited.

"Home," Ushahin said softly, winding his thoughts through the stallion's. Leaning forward, he whispered in one backward-twitching ear. "Home, where the Tordenstem guard the Defile as it winds through the gorge. Home, where the towers of Darkhaven beckon. Home, tall brother, where your attendants await you in the stable, with buckets of warm mash and *svartblod,* and silken cloths for your hide."

The blood-bay stallion raised its head. Arahila's gibbous moon was reflected in one liquid-dark eye. It gave a low whicker; the other two horses answered. From verges of the

Delta, a half dozen ravens launched themselves, flying low on silent wings over the moon-silvered sedge grass.

Ushahin laughed, and gave the bay its head. "Go!" he shouted.

With great strides, it did. Bred under the shrouded skies of the Vale of Gorgantum, it ran with ease in the pale-lit darkness, and thundering on either side were two riderless horses. One was a ghostly grey, the color of forge smoke; the other was pitch-black. And before them all, the shadowy figures of the ravens of Darkhaven forged the way.

Homeward.

DANI HAD SLIPPED.

It was as simple as that. He did not know that the terrain he and his uncle traversed was called the Northern Harrow, but he did not need to be told that it was a harsh and forbidding land. He knew that bare feet toughened by the sun-scorched floors of the desert were a poor match for the cruel granite and icy clime of the northern mountains. And he had discovered, too late, that ill-sewn rabbitskin made for clumsy footwear. When the cliff's edge had crumbled under his footing, he slid over the edge with one terrified shout.

Unmindful of the pain of broken and bending nails, he clung to the ledge he had caught on his downward plunge, fingertips biting deep. Below him, there was nothing. It was an overhang that had broken his fall; beneath it, the cliff fell away, cutting deeply back into the mountain's peak. His kicking feet, shod in tattered rabbitskin, encountered no resistance. There was only a vast, endless drop, and the churning white waters of the Spume River below.

"Uncle!" Craning his neck, Dani fought terror. "Help me!"

Uncle Thulu—*lean* Uncle Thulu—peered over the edge of the cliff, and his eyes were stretched wide with fear in his weather-burnt face. "Can you pull yourself up, lad?"

He tried, but something was wrong with the muscles of his arms, his shoulders. There was no strength there. It might, Dani thought, have had to do with the popping sound they'd made when he caught himself. "No."

"Wait." Uncle Thulu's face was grim. "I'm coming."

Since there was nothing else for it, Dani waited, dangling from his fingertips and biting his lip at the pain of it. Overhead, Uncle Thulu scrabbled, finding the braided rope of rabbit-hide he'd made, looking for an anchor rock to secure it.

"Hang on, lad!" Thulu called over his shoulder, letting himself down inch by careful inch, a length of rope wrapped around his waist, his bare feet braced against the mountainside. "I'm coming."

The rope was too short.

Dani's arms trembled.

At home, the rope would be made of thukka-vine. There was an abundance of it. It was one of the earliest skills the Yarru-yami learned; how to braid rope out of thukka. Here, there was only hide, only the scant leavings of one's scant kills, poorly tanned in oak-water. And if Uncle Thulu had not tried to make him shoes, Dani thought, the rope would be longer.

"Here!" Plucking his digging-stick from his waistband, Thulu extended it, blunt end first. "Grab hold, lad. I'll pull you up."

Dani exhaled, hard, clinging to the ledge with the fingers of both star-marked hands. Against his breastbone, the clay flask containing the Water of Life shivered. A fragile vessel, it would shatter on the rocks below, as surely as his body would. What then, if the Water of Life was set loose in Neheris' rivers, where her Children dwelled? It was the Fjeltroll who would profit by it. "Take the flask, Uncle!" he called. "It's more important than I am. Use your stick, pluck it from about my neck!"

"No." Thulu's face was stubborn. "You are the Bearer, and I will not leave you."

Gritting his teeth, Dani glanced down; down and down and down. Far below, a ribbon of white water roared over jagged rocks. It seemed it sang his name, and a wave of dizziness overcame him, draining his remaining strength. "I can't do it," he whispered, closing his eyes. "Uncle, take the flask. As I am the Bearer, I order it."

Without looking, he heard the agonized curse as his uncle reversed the stick. He felt the pointed end of his uncle's digging-stick probe beneath the cord about his neck, catch and *lift*. For an instant, there was a sense of lightness and freedom, so overwhelming that he nearly laughed aloud.

And then; a gasp, a sharp *crack* as the tip of the digging-stick broke under the impossible weight of the Water of Life. The flask thudded gently against his chest, returning home to the Bearer's being, nestling against his flesh.

"Dani." Thulu's voice brought him back, at once calm and urgent. "It has to be you. Grab hold of the stick."

Fear returned as he opened his eyes. Once again, it was the blunt end of the stick extended. The braided leather rope, stretched taut, creaked and groaned. "The rope's not strong enough to hold us both, Uncle."

"It is." Uncle Thulu's face was contorted with effort, his own arms beginning to tremble under the strain. "Damn you, lad, I wove it myself. It has to be! Grab hold, I tell you; grab hold!"

"Uru-Alat," Dani whispered, "preserve us!"

The end of the peeled baari-wood stick was within inches of his right hand. It took all his courage to loose his grip upon the steady ledge, transferring it to the slippery wood. What merit was there in the mark of the Bearer? Dani's palm was slick with terror, slipping on the wood. The vertiginous drop called his name. He struggled to resist its call as Uncle Thulu's digging-stick slid through his grasp, scraping heedlessly past the Bearer's starry markings.

Slid; and halted.

Against all odds, Dani found a grip; there, near the end,

where the slick wood was gnarled. It wasn't much, but it was enough. Clinging to the rope with one arm, Uncle Thulu hauled hard with the other, grunting and panting with the effort. The leather rope thinned and stretched, thwarting their efforts . . . but it held and did not break. The muscles of his arm quivered as, inch by torturous inch, Thulu of the Yarru-yami pulled his nephew from the abyss. When his head reached a level with the overhang, Dani clawed at the rock with his free hand, ignoring the pain in his shoulders and levering himself upward until he got a foot beneath him, toes digging hard against the granite, and drew himself up onto the ledge to stand on wavering legs.

"Oh, lad." Uncle Thulu embraced him with one arm, weeping. "Oh, lad!"

"Truly, Uncle," Dani said, his voice muffled against Thulu's shoulder, "if I am the Bearer, I could ask no better guide."

It took a long time to get from ledge to cliff-top. When it was done, both were trembling with a mix of exertion and the aftermath of fear. Uncle Thulu unwound the rope from his waist and unknotted it from the anchor, a proud jut of granite. He kissed the rope in gratitude, and for good measure, the stone itself. "Uru-Alat be praised," he said fervently, shoving his digging-stick into his waistband.

"Truly," Dani murmured, collapsing onto the chilled stones. His arms ached and his shoulders felt half-pulled from their sockets. "How much farther, Uncle?"

Uncle Thulu paced the edge of the cliff, eyeing the river below. "We'll find another route." His voice was decisive. "A *better* route, Dani. The Spume is a key, I'm sure of it. There are . . . traces, a foulness in the current." He stroked his digging-stick, humming absently for a moment, then stopped. "There is a branch underground that leads to the Defile. That much I sense for, even here, the waters are tainted." Pausing in thought, he tapped his lips. "It must happen some leagues to the west. Perhaps, if we abandon the heights and cut westward . . . yes. Such is the pattern of

Uru-Alat's veins." Thulu glanced at his nephew, who sat huddled in his cloak, cradling his aching limbs. "Have you the strength, lad?" he asked gently.

"Aye." Dani shuddered, and laughed. "At least," he said, "we've not encountered the Fjeltroll."

"WE HAVE RECEIVED NO REPORTS of such travelers."

Their host spoke smoothly; but then, Coenred, Earl of Gerflod, was a smooth man. His auburn hair was smooth, flowing over his shoulders. His beard was groomed and silken, and his ruddy lips were smooth within their tidy bracket of facial hair.

Osric nodded. "Like as not, they've not been spotted yet."

"Like as not," Earl Coenred agreed, hoisting a tankard of ale. His fingers, with their smooth nails, curved about the bejeweled tankard. He nodded to one of the serving-maids. "Gerde, fill our guests' cups. Drink up, lads, the mutton's yet to come!"

Bobbing a nervous curtsey, she obeyed, circulating around the long trestle table. It took a long time to serve the Staccian lord's contingent and Osric and his men. There were a great number of the former, clad in handsome attire. Another servant brought her a fresh jug of ale. As she reached the far end of the table, where the Fjeltroll were seated, her steps began to drag, and her hand trembled visibly as she poured.

Osric and Coenred spoke in murmurs, ignoring both her anxiety and its source. While the earl had extended hospitality to the Fjel in a gesture of allegiance, it did not include taking them into the counsel of Men.

With an attempt at a benign smile, Skragdal extended his tankard. For Lord Satoris' sake, Skragdal was doing his best to honor the earl's hospitality, hunkering on the tiny chair provided him. It was built to Men's scale and he perched awkwardly on it, broad thighs splayed, his rough-hided knees bumping the edge of the table. It was not his fault it was too small, nor that his taloned grip dented the soft metal of his tankard, rendering it lopsided. He tried to convey these things with his smile; easy and apologetic, wrinkling his upper lip and baring his eyetusks in a gesture of goodwill.

The serving-maid squeaked in terror, and the lip of her jug rattled against his tankard. Ale splashed over the rim. Setting the half-empty jug upon the table with a bang, she fled. Earl Coenred glanced up with brief interest, beckoned to another serving-maid to bring another jug, then resumed his conversation, intent on Osric, spinning a web of smooth words.

Skragdal frowned.

"I . . . do not like how this smells."

A deep voice; a Fjel voice, speaking their tongue. He glanced up sharply to see the young Tungskulder Thorun, sitting with shoulders hunched, a posture of uncertainty. "Speak," he said.

Thorun's hunched shoulders shrugged as he peered out from under his heavy brow; his eyes were red-rimmed and miserable. "I do not trust my senses."

"Ah." Skragdal remembered; there was a story, one that mattered. "Bogvar."

Thorun nodded. They remembered it together—Thorun who had lived it, Skragdal who had heard it, left behind to command as field marshal in Hyrgolf's absence. Cuilos Tuillenrad, the City of Long Grass, where the Lady of the Ellylon had awoken the wraiths of the dead. There, confused by the magic she had awakened, Thorun had mistaken his comrade Bogvar for an Ellyl wraith. Death, a foul death, had been the result. Thorun had offered his axe-hand in penance. The Lord General had refused it.

Skragdal flared his nostrils, inhaling deeply. "There is no enchantment here," he said calmly. "Only fear, only greed. Such are the scents of Men. Speak, Tungskulder."

"Lies." Thorun shuddered in his hide. "This earl reeks of lies."

The Nåltannen were squabbling over the fresh ale-jug, laughing as their steely talons clashed in the effort, drinking deep and making toasts. The Gulnagel were little better, hunkering over the table with slitted eyes and rumbling bellies, awaiting platters of mutton. And the Kaldjager ... the Cold Hunters would not commit themselves to any hall built by Men. They remained outdoors and kept a safe distance, scouting the perimeter of Gerflod. Neither the earl nor his Men knew of their existence.

For once, Skragdal was glad for their distrust.

He flared his nostrils again, inhaling softly, letting the delicate odors of Men's emotions play over his palate. There was Osric, dogged and determined, grateful for Earl Coenred's kindness. There were Osric's Men, dreaming of gain and glory, hoping the serving-maids would return. There were Coenred's Men, nervous and wary in their thoughts. And there ...

Skragdal smelled the lie.

It was smoothly spoken. There had been no word—no word—since their company had emerged from the Vesdarlig Passage. No one knew what had transpired in Beshtanag, how badly their plans had gone awry. How not? It was his Lordship's business. His Enemies were slow. And yet ... and yet. Here, mere leagues south of Neherinach, where Osric's Men and Skragdal's Fjel would part ways, word had emerged.

Earl Coenred had heard news, dire enough to undermine his loyalties. All was known. Nothing was said. The lie was there in every smooth denial, every polite inquiry. The Earldom of Gerflod had turned.

Skragdal exhaled with regret. He wondered how it had happened. A traitor among the Staccians? It could be so. Fjel had never trusted them. Men did not remember the way the Fjel did, trusting carelessly to their ink-scratched markings to preserve memory. And what manner of loyalty was it that could be purchased for mere gold? He did not doubt Lord Vorax, no—he was one of the Three, and beyond doubt. Yet his countrymen . . . perhaps.

He dismissed the thought. What mattered was at hand.

"You smell it," Thorun said.

"Aye." Skragdal realized he was staring at the earl; Coenred had noticed it, a nervous sheen of sweat appearing on his brow. His smooth mask was slipping, and the sour tang of ill-hidden fear tainted the air. Skragdal looked away. Relieved, the earl called in a loud voice for more ale, more ale. Once again, fresh jugs were set to circulating, born by a procession of nervous servants. At least they made no pretence of hiding their fear.

"Should we kill them?" Thorun asked simply.

It was a hard decision. Hyrgolf, he thought, would approve it; he would not hesitate to trust a Tungskulder's nose. Would General Tanaros? No, Skragdal thought. He would not hesitate to believe, but nor would he sanction violence against an ally who had not betrayed his hand. So, neither will Osric turn on a fellow Staccian on my word alone. I cannot count on his support.

That left only the Fjel.

As platters of mutton were brought to the table, heaped high and steaming, Skragdal cast his gaze over his comrades. They tore into the meal with tooth and talon, terrifying the earl's staff. The Nåltannen had drunk deep, and continued to heft their tankards, alternating between mutton and ale. The Gulnagel ate with a will, smearing grease on their chops as they lifted slabs of meat with both hands, gnawing and gnawing, eyes half-lidded with pleasure.

Such was the Fjel way; to gorge until replete, to rest upon satiation. Those were the dictates of life for Neheris' Children, raised in a harsh clime where summer's bounty inevitably gave way to barren winter. Survival dictated it.

What was disturbing, Skragdal thought, was that Earl

Coenred knew it. This abundance had been deliberately provided. He watched his comrades gorge and pondered the expression of satisfaction that spread, slow and sleek, over the carl's features. What were the odds? There were sixteen Fjel in the Great Hall of Gerflod Keep, and all of them unarmed. Their arms and armor were stacked in a stable lent them for shelter; a cunning stroke, that. How many Men? Coenred must have two hundred within the walls.

It could be done, of course. Skragdal hunched his shoulders and flexed his talons, feeling his own strength. He had labored in the mines and in the smelting yards. He knew the weaknesses of metal, where armor was willing to bend and break. With his talons, he could peel it from them, piece by piece. Men were soft, as General Tanaros had taught them. Men died easily, once their soft flesh was exposed.

"Boss?" Thorun's red-rimmed eyes were hopeful.

Reluctantly, Skragdal shook his head. "No. Lying comes easily to Men. We have no proof that they mean us harm because of it," he said softly. "General Tanaros would want *proof* in this matter. But I will speak to Osric of it."

It proved harder than he had anticipated. Once the meal was consumed, Earl Coenred rose, tankard in hand. He made an elegant speech in Staccian about Gerflod's loyalty to Darkhaven, the long arrangement by which Staccia prospered and dwelled in peace alongside the Fjel border. He praised Osric's diligence and vowed Gerflod's aid in the quest. He made much of thanking the Fjel for their unflagging bravery and support. " . . . and it is my hope that you have enjoyed my hospitality tonight, as poor token of those thanks," he added.

The Nåltannen roared in approval, banging their tankards.

I should not have let them drink so much, Skragdal thought.

Earl Coenred raised his free hand for silence. "I apologize that Gerflod has no quarters to adequately house you, but Lieutenant Osric assures me that the stable we have provided will suffice," he said. A contingent of Men entered the hall, wearing light armor underneath the livery of Gerflod. "My men will escort you there forthwith," the earl continued, "and with them, a full keg of ale!"

Ah, but it is hard, thought Skragdal. How am I to command their appetites, when it is how Neheris Shaped us? I am not General Tanaros, to preach the joys of discipline. He is one of the Three. On his tongue, it sings with glory; on mine, it would be a lie. Must I betray what I am to command my brethren?

All around him the Fjel roared with goodwill, surging to their feet to follow Coenred's Men. Already, they were halfway out the door, following the promise of more drink and sweet slumber. And why not? They had earned it. And yet, there was Thorun with his hopeful gaze. There was the earl smiling, with his smooth beard and his combed hair, the lie stinking in his teeth.

Skragdal sighed and rose from his chair. Leaning over the table on his knuckles, he took a deep breath and raised his voice. "*Osric!*" He was no Tordenstem, to make his enemies quake to the marrow of their bones with the Thunder-Voice, but the shout of a Tungskulder Fjel could rattle any rafters built by Men. In the fearful silence that followed, Skragdal added, "We must speak."

It was an awkward moment. The smooth mask of the earl's expression slipped, revealing fear and annoyance. He made a covert gesture to his Men, who stepped up their pace in escorting the Fjel from the Great Hall. Skragdal nodded at Thorun, not needing to speak his thoughts. Thorun nodded in return, following the exodus quietly. Skragdal waited. Osric, flushed with embarrassment, made his way around the table. Although his head only came to Skragdal's breastbone, his fingers dug hard into the flesh of his arm, drawing him into the far corner of the hall's entryway. "They're our *hosts*, Tungskulder!" he hissed under his breath. "Have a care for Staccian courtesy, will you?"

"Osric." Ignoring the Staccian's importunate grip, Skrag-dal dropped his voice to its lowest register, a rumble like large rocks grinding. "This earl is lying."

Osric blew out his breath impatiently, smelling of ale. "About what?"

"He knows." How to communicate it? There were no words in Men's tongues to explain what he knew, or why; no words to describe the scent of a lie, of ill-will behind a smooth smile, of danger lying in wait. "More than he is say-ing. Osric, we should leave this place. Now. Tonight."

"Enough." The Staccian lieutenant's voice was sharp. He released his grip on Skragdal's arm, taking a step backward and craning his neck to glare at the Fjel. "We part ways at Neherinach, Tungskulder. Until then, by Lord Vorax's or-ders, you are under my command. Your Fjel have embar-rassed Darkhaven enough for one night. Go with them, and keep them under control. Do not embarrass his Lordship further by insulting our host."

Skragdal flared his nostrils, smelling the lie. "Osric . . . "

"Go!"

He waited.

"Go!"

With a curt bow, Skragdal went. Behind him, he heard one of the earl's Men make a cutting comment, and the wave of laughter that answered; then Osric's voice, at once dismissive and apologetic. *What can you expect? They are little better than brutes, after all. But his Lordship insisted on it. We need the tribes, you know.*

It galled him, prickling his hide all along the ridge of his spine. Skragdal made his way down the halls of Gerflod Keep, past the earl's startled guards, to emerge outdoors. It was quiet in the narrow courtyard. He took deep breaths of night air, filling his lungs and seeking calm. He had thought better of Osric. That was his mistake. Staccia was not Dark-haven. Here, the balance had shifted. Arahila's Children were reminded of their superiority, compelled to exercise it.

"Hey." One of the earl's Men peered tentatively at him

beneath the steel brim of his helmet. With the point of his spear, he gestured toward a stable across the courtyard, where lamplight poured through the crack of the parted door. Faint sounds of Fjel merriment issued from within, muffled by sturdy wood. "Your lodgings are that way, lad."

Skragdal rumbled with annoyance.

"As . . . as you will." The Gerflodian guard's words ended on a rising note of fear.

Shaking his head, Skragdal trudged across the courtyard. A patch of gilded lamplight spilled over the paving-stones. He flung open the stable door and was hailed by shouts. Thorun, who had donned his armor, met his gaze with a shrug; he had done his best. The Gulnagel, having gorged deepest on the meat, were half asleep, bellies distended. Everywhere else, it seemed, Nåltannen lounged on bales of clean straw, their kits strewn about the stable, tankards clutched in their talons. They raised their tankards in salute, shouting for him to join them.

"Shut up!" With an effortless swipe, Skragdal slammed the door closed behind him. In the echoing reverberation, the Fjel fell silent. "Where is the ale-keg?"

One pointed.

"Good." He trudged across the floor, pausing to catch up his axe. Bits of straw stuck between his toes as he approached, hefting the axe over his shoulder. It only took one mighty swing to breach the keg, splintering its wooden slats. Brown ale foamed over the straw, rendering the whole a sodden mess.

"Awww, boss!" someone said sadly.

"Shut up." Skragdal pointed with the head of the axe. "Listen."

They obeyed. For a moment only the hiss of foaming ale broke the silence; then, another sound. A slow scraping as of wood against wood, a gentle thunk.

"That," Skragdal said, "was the sound of the earl's Men barring the stable door." Tramping across the straw, he kicked a dozing Gulnagel in the ribs in passing, then began to rummage in earnest through his pile of arms and armor. "Get up, Rhilmar," he said over his shoulder, donning his breastplate and buckling it. "All of you. Up and armed."

They gaped at him.

"Now!" he roared.

There was a scramble, then; deep Fjel voices surging in dawning anger, metal clattering as armor was slung in place, arms were hefted. It was just as well. To Men's ears, the sounds of Fjel preparing for battle would be indistinguishable from the sounds of Fjel at their leisure. Skragdal smiled grimly.

"What now?" a Nåltannen growled.

"We wait." Watching the barred door fixedly, Skragdal settled the haft of his battle-axe on one armor-plated shoulder. "There's no harm in it. We've waited this long, lads, and the Kaldjager will be keeping watch from the borders. We'll wait until the earl's Men show their hand. And then . . . " He bared his eyetusks in another smile, " . . . we'll see what there is for a Fjeltroll to *learn* here."

They cheered him for it, and Skragdal's heart swelled at the sound. His words had struck them where they lived, speaking to the old unfairness, the old hurt. Although his name might be forgotten in the annals of Men and Ellylon—no one would write down this night's doings, and if they did, they would not record the name of Skragdal of the Tungskulder Fjel—if it was worth the telling, Neheris' Children would remember the story.

It was a long wait, and a dull one. Outside, the stars moved in their slow dance and, in the west, the red star ascended over the horizon. Inside, the lamps burned low, and there were only the slow breathing of the Fjel, and the sound of straw rustling underfoot as this one or that adjusted his stance. Funny, Skragdal thought, that Men were so anxious to bar the door, yet so fearful to attack. If they had waited longer for the former, it might not have tipped their hand.

But it had, and the Fjel were patient. Even drunk, even

sated, the Fjel knew how to be patient. Now they had shaken off their torpor. They were awake, waiting and watching. If it took all night, they would wait all night. One did not survive, hunting in a cold clime, without patience.

In armed silence, they waited.

And in the small hours, there were new sounds.

There were footsteps, and whispering and hissing. Men's voices, tight with fear and urgency. Liquid sounds, splashing. Skragdal's nostrils widened, inhaling the sharp odor of seep oil. It was the same oil used in the lamps, only more, much more.

"Boss . . . " someone murmured.

He hoisted the axe in his right hand and settled his shield on his left arm, General Tanaros' words ringing in his memory. *Keep your shields up!* "Soon," he promised. "Keep your shields high, lads."

They were alert, all of them. The earl was a fool if he reckoned them slaves to their appetites; Skragdal's words had done the trick. Words; Men's tools. He had used them well. In guttering lamplight, Fjel eyes gleamed under heavy brows. It made him proud to see the determination in Thorun's visage; a fellow Tungskulder, here at his side. Broad shoulders for heavy burdens; so Neheris had said when she Shaped them.

Krick . . . krick . . . krick . . .

"A flint-striker," one of the Gulnagel said unnecessarily.

Outside, flames whooshed into the air, licking at the dry, oil-soaked tinder. Inside, there were only slivers of brightness, showing between the planks. Smoke, grey and choking, crept under the door. Someone coughed.

"Now!" Skragdal shouted, hurling his weight at the door.

He remembered, and kept his shield high. It hit the stable door with splintering force, the full might of his charge behind it. The door burst outward in an explosion of sparks, singeing his hide. They were minor wounds; he had endured worse when the acid rain fell over Darkhaven, an understandable expression of Lord Satoris' ire. He kept his head low, letting his charge carry him into the courtyard.

"Who is first?" Skragdal bellowed, axe in hand. *"Who is first to die?"*

There was no shortage of volunteers. It had been a dozen Men, no more, who had undertaken the mission. They died easily at the bite of his axe, dropping empty jugs of lamp-oil, cowering in their armor. Skragdal laughed aloud, feeling blood splash his arms, slick and warm on his hide. It felt good, at last, to do what he did best. He strode sure-footed across the cobblestones, laying about him like a Midlander harvesting hay. The earl's Men poured through the doors of Gerflod Manor, emerging in scores, even as Fjel after Fjel leapt from the burning stable, joining him in the massacre until the narrow courtyard was churning and it was hard to find fighting-space. Over and over he swung his axe, rejoicing in the results. By the leaping flames of the stable he saw the terror in his attackers' faces. It didn't last long. Their swords and spears clattered ineffectually against his shield, against the heavy plates of his armor, glancing blows scratching his tough hide where it was unprotected. Neheris had Shaped her Children well. Meanwhile, the keen blade of his axe, swung by his strong arm, sheared through the thin metal of their armor, until the head was buried deep in soft flesh. Again and again, Skragdal struck, wrenching his axe loose to strike again. As their warm blood spilled, ebbing from their bodies, terror gave way to the calm stare of death.

Men died so easily.

"Sir! That was the last of them!" Someone was grappling with him; one of his own. A shield locked with his; over its rim, he met Thorun's gaze. "You spoke of *learning*," the Tungskulder reminded him.

"Aye." Panting, Skragdal disengaged. "Aye, I did. My thanks." He gave his head a shake, clearing the haze of battle-frenzy, and lowered his axe. The stable was engulfed in flame, blazing toward the heavens, throwing heat like a forge and illuminating a courtyard awash in blood. Everywhere the bodies of the earl's Men lay strewn and discarded, pale flesh gouged with gaping wounds. Here and there, one groaned. The Nåltannen hunted through the dead, dispatching the dying. There were too many to count, but he reckoned a good number of the earl's Men had died in the courtyard. More than the earl had intended to risk. Turning his head, he saw the doors of Gerflod Keep standing open and unbarred. "So," he said. "Let us *learn*."

Once the words were uttered, there was no stopping the Fjel. The Gulnagel, blood-spattered, howled, racing for the doors in great, bounding leaps. Even as they entered the Keep, Nåltannen caught up the cry and streamed after them, weapons clutched in gleaming steel talons, half-forgotten shields held low and dangling.

Skragdal sighed. "Summon the Kaldjager," he said to Thorun. "We'll need to leave this place. *Swiftly.*" Thorun nodded, thrusting his axe through his belt-loop, moving with steady deliberation through the flame-streaked darkness. A good lad, Skragdal thought, watching him go. A good one.

Gerflod Keep lay waiting, its open doors like the mouth of a grave.

Shouldering his axe, Skragdal trudged across the courtyard. He paused in the open door and cocked an eye toward the stable. Its roof sagged as a beam collapsed somewhere inside the burning structure, sending up a huge shower of sparks. Safe enough, he reckoned. Gerflod Keep was stone; stone wouldn't burn.

He entered the Keep, his taloned feet leaving bloody prints on its marble floors, mingling with the tracks of the Fjel who had gone before. He followed their trail, opening his nostrils wide.

The stink of fear and lies had given way to the reek of terror and the stench of death. All along the way, Men lay dying; Gerflod's Men, Earl Coenred's men. Here and there,

where they were unarmored and wore only livery, the Nåltannen had given in to old instincts, slitting their bellies
with the swipe of a steel-taloned paw. Those Men groaned,
dying hard. The Nåltannen had been in a hurry.

Skragdal snorted at the odor of perforated bowels,
bulging and blueish through the rents in soft mortal flesh,
oozing fecal matter. Those Men, clutching at their spilling
entrails, still had terror in their eyes. Murmuring a prayer to
Neheris, he raised his axe to dispatch them, one by one.
Some of them, he thought, were grateful for it.

In the Great Hall, he found Osric and his Men. None of
them were alive. Osric was leaning backward in his chair,
grinning. A half-empty tankard sat in front of him and the
hilt of a belt-knife protruded from his throat. It was a small
knife, made for a Man's hand, with the earl's insignia on the
hilt. A trail of blood lay puddled in his lap.

"Ah, Osric," Skragdal said, with genuine sorrow. "I tried
to tell you."

The Staccian lieutenant continued to grin at the ceiling,
wordless and blind. Near the head of the table there was a
low groan and a scraping sound, a hissed curse. Skragdal
trudged over to investigate.

On the floor, Earl Coenred writhed in his shadow, one
hand clamped to his throat. Blood seeped through his fingers, where the rending marks of Nåltannen talons were
visible. He did not, Skragdal thought, look so smooth with
red blood bubbling on his ruddy lips. Stooping, he leaned in
close enough to grasp a handful of the earl's auburn hair
and ask the question.

"*Why?*"

The earl's eyes rolled up in his head, showing the whites.
"The Galäinridder!" he gasped, catching his breath in a burbling laugh. "The Bright Rider, the Shining Paladin!"
Droplets of blood spewed from his lips in a fine spray. "We
did not welcome him, but he came. Out of nowhere, out of
the mountains, he came, terrible to behold, and he told us,
told us everything. Haomane's Wrath is coming, and those

who oppose him will pay. Even here, even in Staccia. There is nowhere to hide." The earl's face contorted as he summoned the will to spit out his last words. "You are *dead*, Fjeltroll! Dead, and you don't even know it!"

"Not as dead as you," Skragdal said, releasing his grip and straightening. Raising his axe, he brought it down hard, separating the earl's head from his body.

The edge of his axe clove through flesh and bone and clanged on marble, gouging a trough in the floor and making his arms reverberate. Skragdal grunted. The earl's head rolled free, fetching up against a table leg. There, it continued to stare at him under drooping lids.

Dead, and you don't even know it.

"Fjel!" Skragdal roared, straightening, adopting General Tanaros' words without even thinking. "Fall out! *Now!*"

THIRTY-TWO

❖

IT WAS DUE TO THE raven that no one else had yet died in the Unknown Desert.

Tanaros didn't count the days; none of them did. What would be the point? None of them knew how long it would take to cross the desert on their meandering, uncharted course. When they could find shade, they rested by day and traveled by night. When there was no shade, which was most of the time, they marched beneath the white-hot sun. He put his trust in Fetch, in the gift of the Grey Dam Sorash, and led them staggering onward. Better, he reckoned, to walk toward death than let it find them waiting.

It didn't.

Again and again, Fetch guided them to safety; to shade, to water. Hidden water-holes, drought-eaters, rocky ledges that cast deep shade, anthills, basking lizards, nests of mice: all these things the raven found. Tanaros followed his shadow across the parched earth, the raven's squawk echoing in his ears, until they reached the place where the raven alighted. Again and again, Fetch preened with satisfaction upon their arrival, as they found themselves in a place where sustenance was to be had.

"How do you know?" Tanaros mused on one occasion, studying the raven where it perched on his forearm. "No raven ever traveled this desert, nor any Were. How do you *know?*"

The bright eyes gleamed. *"Kaugh!"*

It was a jumbled impression of thoughts that the raven projected; water, beetles and a tall palodus tree, a dragon's head, rearing above the treetop. Over and over, the dragon's head, ancient and iron-grey, dripping with swamp-water and vegetation, its jaws parted to speak or breathe flame.

"I don't understand," Tanaros told him.

Hopping onto a thorn-branch, Fetch settled and rattled his feathers.

"And *why?*" he asked the raven.

One bright eye cracked open a slit, showing him his quarters in Darkhaven, customary order giving way to mess and disarray. An injured nestling. A pair of hands, strong and capable, made to grip a sword-hilt, shaping themselves to cup feather and hollow bone with an unaccustomed tenderness.

"For that?" He swallowed. "It was a whim. A small kindness."

"Kaugh." The raven closed both eyes and slept.

In the end, he supposed, it didn't matter. What mattered was that they survived, step by step, day by day. But it opened a chink in his heart, that might have sealed itself like stone against the thought of love. When the somber faces of Ngurra and the Yarru-yami haunted his dreams, it gave him a tiny brand to hold the darkness at bay.

A small kindness, a confluence of compassion, had saved his life. Was that strength, or a weakness?

Tanaros could not say. If there had been compassion in his heart the day he learned Calista and Roscus had betrayed him, perhaps he would have found the strength to walk away. What brought them together? Passion? Compassion? They had lacked the strength to resist desire. And yet that thought, too, was anathema. In their hearts, they had already made a cuckold of him. Had they been stronger, he would have spent his life living an unwitting lie, and the world would be a different place.

He did not know if it would be a better one.

Nothing was simple.

"Lord General?" Another day without shade, another day's trek. If there were a chink in the wall of his heart, it was Speros who thrust a wedge into it. Recovered from the ravages of dehydration, the Midlander had shown surprising and stubborn resilience, regaining sufficient strength to place one foot in front of the other, day after day, refusing the aid of the Gulnagel. Now he turned a sunburnt face in Tanaros' direction, his voice wistful. "What's the Lady of the Ellylon like?"

"Like a woman," he said shortly. "An Ellyl woman."

"Oh." Speros returned his gaze to the desert floor, watching his feet trudge across the sand. It crunched rhythmically under their boots, under the taloned feet of the Gulnagel, who traded glances over their heads. "I've never seen an Ellyl," he said eventually. "I just wondered . . . "

"Yes." Tanaros took a deep breath, the desert's heat searing his lungs. "They're very beautiful. *She* is very beautiful. Do you want to know how much?" He remembered Cerelinde in her chamber, the night he had bade her farewell, and how she had shone like a candle-flame, pale hair shining like a river against her jeweled robes as she turned away from him. *Go then, and kill, Tanaros Blacksword! It is what you do.* "So much that it hurts," he said harshly. "So much it makes you pity Arahila for the poor job she made of Shaping us. We're rough-hewn clay, Speros, a poor second next to her Elder Brother's creation. So much it makes you despise Arahila for trying and falling so short, yet giving us the wit to know it. Is that what you wanted to hear?"

Speros glanced wryly at him. "Not exactly, my lord."

"Well." Despite himself, Tanaros smiled. The unfamiliar movement made the skin of his dry lips split. "You've seen Ushahin Dreamspinner."

"No." Speros shook his head. "I've only heard tales."

"Ah." Tanaros licked his split lip, tasting blood. "Well, he is a paltry, cracked mirror through which to behold the beauty of the Ellylon, but I imagine you'll see him in time. And if the Dreamspinner isn't Ellyl enough for you, unless I am much mistaken, you'll encounter Ellylon aplenty on the battlefield, and be sorry you did, for they're doughty fighters beneath their pretty hides."

"Aye, Lord General." For a few moments, the Midlander was silent. "I would like to see the Lady, though," he mused. "Just to see her."

Tanaros made no reply.

Speros glanced at him again. "Will Lord Satoris kill her, do you think?"

"No." The word leapt too quickly from his cracked lips. Tanaros halted, rubbing his hands over his face. It felt gritty with sand and grime. His head ached from the effort of walking, from Speros' questions, from too little food, and too much light. Once, in Beshtanag, he had welcomed the sight of it. Now he yearned for the dim, soothing light of Darkhaven, for the familiarity of its gleaming black walls and corridors. After the endless sunlight of the Unknown Desert, he wouldn't be sorry if he never left the cloud-shrouded Vale of Gorgantum for another mortal lifespan. "Speros, save your breath. We've a long way to go yet today."

"Aye, Lord General."

This time the Midlander was properly subdued, and his silence lasted what Tanaros gauged to be the better part of a league. He set as brisk a pace as he dared, rendering further speech impossible. He wished he could outpace his own thoughts. There were too many words etched into his memory, chasing themselves around and around in his mind. Cerelinde's voice, his Lordship's, Ngurra's . . . and now Speros', his voice with its broad Midlands accent, asking a question in innocent curiosity.

Will Lord Satoris kill her, do you think?

The thought of it made his palms itch and bile rise in his throat. He remembered altogether too well how his wife's face had looked in death; blind eyes staring, all her lively beauty turned to cold clay. Even in his fury it had sickened him. The thought of seeing Cerelinde thusly was unbearable.

He was glad when the landscape made one of its dull, inhospitable shifts from rippled sand to barren red earth, dotted here and there with thorn-brush. Loose rocks and scattered boulders made the footing tricky, and it was a relief to have to concentrate on the task of walking. Fetch's shadow wavered on the uneven ground, then vanished as the raven veered westward, becoming a tiny black dot in the unbroken blue sky, then disappearing altogether. Tanaros led his company in the direction the raven had taken, keeping its flight-path fixed in his mind and placing his feet with care. There was little else to relieve the tedium. Once, a hopping-mouse broke cover under a thorn-brush, bounding into the open in unexpected panic.

With a grunt, one of the three remaining Gulnagel dropped his burden and gave chase, returning triumphant with a furry morsel clutched in his talons. Despite the fact that he was panting with the effort, he offered it to his general.

"No, Krolgun," Tanaros said, remembering Freg, and how he had offered him a handful of termites. "It's yours."

He looked away as the Fjel devoured it whole, hoping the scant nourishment was worth the effort.

Another hour, and another. Tanaros slowed their pace, scanning the skies with growing concern. He forgot to watch his steps, fixing his gaze on the sky. Had he kept their path true to the trajectory of Fetch's flight? He thought so, but it was hard to tell in the featureless desert. They had been too long on the march, and their waterskins were dwindling toward empty. Nearby he could hear Krolgun still panting, his steps beginning to drag. The others were little better and, crane his neck though he would, there was no sign of the raven.

Only the empty blue skies, filled with the glare of Haomane's Wrath.

"Lord General?" Speros' voice, cracked and faint.

"Not now, Speros," he said impatiently.

"Lord General!" The Midlander's hand clutched his arm, dragging his attention from the empty skies. Speros' mouth was working, though no further words emerged. With his other hand, he pointed westward, where a line of twisted forms broke the horizon. "Look!" he managed at length.

Frowning, Tanaros followed his pointing finger. "Are those . . . trees?"

"Aye!" Releasing his arm, Speros broke into a mad, capering dance. "Jack pines, Lord General!" he shouted. "Good old Midlands jack pines! General!" There were tears glistening in his eyes, running down his sunburnt face. *"We've reached the edge!"*

It was the Gulnagel who broke ranks with an exuberant roar, abandoning his command to race toward the distant treeline. What sparse reserves of energy the Lowland Fjel had hoarded, they expended all at once. Their packs bounced and clanked as they ran, powerful haunches propelling their massive bodies in swift bounds. With a wordless shout, Speros discarded his near-empty waterskins and followed them at a dead run, whooping in his cracked voice.

Four figures, three large and one small, raced across the barren landscape.

Tanaros Blacksword, Commander General of Darkhaven, shook his head and hoped his army of four would not expire before reaching the desert's edge. He gathered up Speros' waterskins and settled them over his shoulder, then touched the hilt of the black sword that hung from his belt. It was still there, the echo of his Lordship's blood whispering to his fingertips. Back on course, the compass of his branded heart contracted.

Westward.

He set out at a steady jog, watching the treeline draw nearer, watching the racing figures ahead of him stagger, faltering and slowing. It was farther than they thought, at least another league. Such was always the case. Though his feet were blistered and his boots were cracking at the heels, he wound his way across the stony soil and kept a steady pace, drawing abreast of them in time. He dispensed waterskins and an acerbic word of reprimand, accepted with chagrin. They kept walking.

Their steps grew heavier as they walked, all energy spent. Heavy, but alive.

Tanaros' steps grew lighter, the nearer they drew.

Jack pines, stunted and twisted, marked the western boundary of the Unknown Desert. Beyond, sparse grass grew, an indication that the content of the soil was changing, scorched desert slowly giving way to the fertile territories of the Midlands.

In the shadow of the jack pines, Fetch perched on a needled branch, bobbing his head in triumphant welcome. His black eyes were bright, as bright as the reflection of sunlight on the trickling creek that fed the pines.

A small kindness.

CROUCHED UPON THE BACK OF the blood-bay stallion, Ushahin Dreamspinner floated above the horse's churning stride, borne aloft like a crippled vessel on the waves of a wind-tossed sea. And yet, there was power in him, far beyond the strength of his twisted limbs. Riding, he cast the net of his mind adrift over the whole of Urulat, and rode the pathways between waking and dreaming.

It was a thing he alone knew to do.

The Were had taught it to him; so many believed. It was true, and not true. The Grey Dam Sorash had taught him the ways of the Were, in whose blood ran the call of Oronin's Horn. Because there was Death in their Shaping, there were doors open to them that were closed to the other races of Lesser Shapers.

Ushahin had heard Oronin's Horn. It had blown for him when he was a child and his broken body had lain bleeding in the forests of Pelmar. Somewhere, there was a death waiting for him. But the Grey Dam had claimed him, grieving for her lost cubs, and whispered, *not yet*.

So she had claimed him, and taught him. Yet he was not Were, and their magic twisted in his usage. The Were, like the Fjeltroll, could smell Men's fear; unlike the Fjel, they could hear a Man's heart beat at a hundred paces and taste the pulse of his fear. Ushahin, in whose veins ran the blood of Haomane's Children, could sense Men's *thoughts*. And it was their thoughts—their dreams, their unspoken terrors and wordless joys—that formed the pathways along which he traveled. It was a network as vast and intricate as the Marasoumië, yet infinitely more subtle. He had walked it many a time. This was the first time he had ridden it.

Ushahin-who-walks-between-dusk-and-dawn.

Thus had the Grey Dam Sorash named him in the tongue of the Were, who had no other words for what he was. It was his name, the one he had borne for many times the length of a mortal lifespan. Although the Were reviled him and the Grey Dam Vashuka had repudiated his claim upon their kinship, it was the name he would keep.

It had been given him in love.

Once, he had had another name; a Pelmaran name, given

him by one long dead. His father's mother, he thought; there was some vague memory there. A widow of middle years, with hair gone early to grey, a lined face and a sharp tongue. *After all, we've got to call him something.* His father, a tall shadow, turning away with averted face. The Pelmaran lordling, his life ruined for a moment's passion, did not care what his son was called. He retreated into memory, reliving the moment. It was something few Men could claim, to have expended a lifetime of desire on Ellylon flesh.

That, Ushahin remembered.

Not what they had called him.

When he tried, he saw light; bright light, the light of Haomane's sun. It had stood high above the marketplace in Pelmar City the day the other children had run him down and held him at bay. He'd stood his ground for a long time, but in the end there had been too many of them. The children of Pelmar City did not like his bright eyes, that saw too keenly their squalid thoughts; they did not like his pale hair, the way his limbs moved or his sharp cheekbones; slanted, strange and unfamiliar. It made them afraid, and they knew, in the way children know things, that his father's guilt would keep his lips sealed, and his mother's people had gone far, far away.

Better none of it had ever happened.

So, with cobblestones wrenched from the market square, they had set out to make it so. The first few were thrown, and he had dodged them. If they had not cornered him, he would have dodged them all; but they had. They had run him to ground.

He remembered the first blow, an errant stone. It had grazed his cheek, raising a lump and a blueish graze, breaking his fair skin. Had it cracked the bone? Perhaps. It didn't matter. Worse had come later. They had closed in, stones in fists. There had been many blows, then. Ushahin did not remember the ones that had broken his hands, raised in futile defense. He had curled into a ball; they had pounced upon him, swarming, hauling his limbs straight. A trader's shadow had darkened the alley, and withdrawn. There would be no intervention in the quarrels of children. Someone—he did not remember who had done it, had never even seen their face—had stomped gleefully on his outstretched arms and legs, until the bones had broken with sounds like dry sticks snapping in half.

The last blow, he remembered.

There had been a boy, some twelve years of age. Kneeling on the cobblestones, a mortal boy on scabbed knees. A rock in his fist, crashing down upon Ushahin's temple. At that blow, bone had shattered, a dent caving the orbit of his eye. The boy had spat upon his broken face and whispered a name. What it was, he didn't remember. Only the long crawl afterward, moving his broken limbs like a swimmer on dry land, and the trail of blood it left behind him in the marketplace; the gentle succor of the forest's pine mast floor, and then the Grey Dam, giving him a new name.

Ushahin-who-walks-between-dusk-and-dawn.

The blood-bay's muscles surged beneath him, compressing and lengthening, stride after stride. It should have grown weary, but there was no weariness in dreams. Somewhere, distantly, Ushahin felt its astonishment. His power had grown during his sojourn in the Delta. He wondered why Satoris had never returned to the source of his birth, if his Lordship had ceded it to Calanthrag the Eldest as the price for the dragons' aid during the Shapers' War. Whatever regenerative mystery remained, it had infused him with strength. Even now he felt it course through his veins. The bay's nostrils flared, revealing the scarlet lining; still, it ran, its strides consuming the leagues. Beneath the dim starlight the marshes of outer Vedasia fell behind them, and they continued onward.

They ran as swift as rumor, following the curve of Harrington Inlet. The road was pale dust under their hooves,

and before them flew ravens in a wedge. To their left and to
their right ran a riderless horse; one ghost-grey, and one
night-black. In their wake, they left nightmares, and along
the coast the Free Fishermen of Harrington Inlet tossed in
their beds, waking upon sweat-dampened pallets to their
wives' worried faces and the cries of fretful children.

It made Ushahin smile.

But there was bigger game afoot. Casting his nets, he
caught Men's dreams in a seine, sifting through them. Behind him, yes. Behind him was that which was known, Aracus Altorus and his company, riding hot toward the west.
Ellylon blood and Ellylon pride ran high and hot, as did that
of the Men of Curonan. Still, they would not dare to cross
the Delta. Their thoughts veered away from it, filled with
fear. They would lose time crossing open water rather than
chance the Delta. Thinking of Calanthrag the Eldest, who
dwelled in its heart, Ushahin smiled again. He spared a moment's hate for Aracus Altorus, who had won a bitter victory from the Were. He spared a moment's pity for the
Sorceress of Beshtanag, doomed to rot in mortal flesh. He
spared a moment's curiosity for Blaise Caveros, who so resembled his ancestor, Tanaros.

Then, he gazed ahead.

To Meronil, he did not dare look. Ingolin the Wise kept
its boundaries with care, maintaining all that remained of
the old Ellyl magics, and even Ushahin Dreamspinner
dared not walk the dreams of the Ellylon who dwelt within.
But before Meronil was Seahold, a keep of Men, and north
of Seahold lay the fertile territories of the Midlands.

There, rumor stalked.

It came from the north; from the mountains of Staccia,
winding its way in a whisper of thought, passed from lip to
ear. Curious, Ushahin followed it to its source, tracing its
path through the mountains, back to the ancient battlefield
of Neherinach, where a node-point of the Marasoumië lay
dead and buried. Dead, yes, but no longer buried. The node-
point lay raw and exposed, granite cooling in the northern

sun. Something had disturbed it, blasting it from the very earth.

The *Galäinridder.*

Such was the word in the Staccian tongue; such was the image that disturbed their dreams, filtering its way from the mountains to the plains, distant as a dream. A rider, a warrior; the Shining Paladin, who rode upon a horse as white as the foam on the crest of a wave. Although his hands were empty, brightness blazed from his robes and the clear gem upon his breast, which shone like a star. His beard crackled with lightning, and power hung in every syllable of the terrible words he spoke, catching their consciences and playing on their fears of Haomane's Wrath.

Ushahin frowned.

What he had found, he did not like; what he had failed to find, he liked less. Where, in all of this, was the Bearer? A little Charred lad, accompanied only by his mortal kin. He should have been easy to find, his terrors setting the world of dreams ablaze. Only Malthus' power had protected him, enfolding him in a veil. If the Counselor were truly trapped in the dying Marasoumië, his power should be failing, exposing the Bearer. Yet . . . it was not.

"Malthus," Ushahin whispered. *"Galäinridder."*

East of Seahold, his thoughts turned. Was it Haomane's Counselor they feared? He would give them something better to fear, the grief of their mortal guilt, come back to turn their dreams into nightmares. Ushahin's lips twisted into the bitter semblance of a smile. Were Arahila's Children so sure of *right* and *wrong?* So. Let their nights be filled with mismatched eyes and shattered bone, the terrible sight of a rock held in a child's fist, descending in a crushing blow.

Let them awake in the cold sweat of terror, and wonder *why.*

The flying wedge of ravens altered its course, forging a new path through the twilight, in the borderlands between waking and sleeping. One heel nudged his mount's flank, the rope rein of the hackamore lying against a foam-flecked neck. Obedient, the blood-bay swerved; obedient, the riderless horses followed, shadowing his course.

Together, they plunged into the Midlands.

"THEY ARE COMING, VORAX."

"Very good, my Lord." If he had thought it hot in the Throne Hall, it was nothing to the Chamber of the Font. Sweat trickled down his brow, stinging the half-healed blisters he had sustained in the burning rain. Vorax swiped at it with a gauntleted hand, which only made it worse.

"Do you hear me?" Lord Satoris, pacing the perimeter of the Font, gave him a deep look. "Ushahin Dreamspinner comes. Tanaros Blacksword comes. It is only a matter of time. My Three shall be together once more, and then my Elder Brother's Allies shall tremble."

"Aye, my Lord." He tugged his jeweled gorget, wishing he were not wearing ceremonial armor. It would have been better to meet in the Throne Hall. At least his Lordship had not donned the Helm of Shadows. It sat in its niche on the wall, the empty eyeholes measuring his fear. He was glad nothing worse filled it, and glad he had not had to wear it himself since the day Satoris had destroyed the Marasoumië. Still, it stank of his Lordship's unhealing wound in the Chamber, a copper-sweet tang, thick and cloying, and Vorax wished he were elsewhere. "As you say. I welcome their return. Is there something you wish me to do in preparation?"

"No." Lord Satoris halted, staring into the coruscating heart of the Font. His massive hands, hanging empty at his sides, twitched as if to pluck Godslayer from its blue-white fire. "What news," he asked, "from Staccia?"

Vorax shook his head, droplets of sweat flying. "No news."

"So," the Shaper said. His head bowed and his fingertips twitched. But for that, he stood motionless, contemplating the Shard. Dark ichor gleaming on one thigh, seeping downward in a slow rill to pool on the flagstones. "No news."

"No news," Vorax echoed, feeling a strange twinge in his branded heart. "I'm sorry, my Lord, but I'm sure naught is amiss. It will take some time, finding a pair of errant mortals in all of the northlands. We expected no less." He paused. "Shall I send another company? Do you wish me to lead one myself? I am willing, of course."

"I . . . no." Lord Satoris shook his head, frowning. "I cannot spare you, Vorax. Not now. When Tanaros returns . . . perhaps. And yet, I am disturbed. There is . . . something. A bright mist clouds my vision. I do not know what it means."

Vorax scratched at his beard. "Have you . . . ?" He nodded at Godslayer.

"Yes." The Shaper's frown deepened, and he continued to gaze fixedly at the dagger, hanging pulsing and rubescent in the midst of the blazing Font. "To no avail. If something has passed elsewhere in Urulat, it is a thing not even the Souma may show me. And I am troubled by this. Godslayer has never failed me, when I dared invoke its powers in full. Not upon Urulat's soil."

"Break it," Vorax shrugged. "Maybe it's time. It would solve a lot of problems."

The words were out of his mouth before he knew he meant to speak them. In the brief, shocked silence that ensued, he knew it for a mistake. Certain things that might be thought should never be spoken aloud, not even by one of the Three.

"What?" Lord Satoris' head rose, and he seemed to gather height and mass in the sweltering Chamber. He took a step forward, hands clenching. The flagstones shuddered under his feet. Overhead, massive beams creaked. Shadows roiled around Satoris' shoulders and red fury lit his eyes. *"WHAT?"*

"My Lord!" He backed across the Chamber and raised

his gauntleted hands; half pleading, half placating. "Forgive me! I am thinking of us, of all of us . . . of you, my Lord! If Godslayer were shattered, if it were rendered into harmless pieces . . . why, it would no longer be a threat, and . . . and the Prophecy itself couldn't be fulfilled!"

"Do you think so?" The Shaper advanced, step by thunderous step.

"I, no . . . aye, my Lord!" Vorax felt the edge of a stair against his heel, and retreated up one spiraling step, then another, and another. He was sweating under his armor, sweat running in rivulets. "It could be like the Soumanië!" he breathed, clutching at the idea. "A piece for each of us, for each of the Three, and we could wield them in your defense, aye; and the largest one for you, of course! We would have more than they, yet no piece keen nor large enough, no dagger left to, to . . . " His words trailed off as Lord Satoris reached the base of the stair, leaning forward and planting his enormous hands on either side of it. His dark face was on a level with Vorax's, eyes blazing like embers. The reek of his blood hung heavy in the close air.

"To slay a Shaper," Lord Satoris said. "Is that it? Only pieces, broken pieces of the Souma. Is that what you propose, my Staccian?"

"Aye!" Vorax almost laughed with relief, wiping his brow. "Aye, my Lord."

"Fool!"

For a long moment, his Lordship's eyes glared into his, measuring the breadth and depth of his loyalty. A miasma of heat emanated from his body, as if Haomane's Wrath still scorched him. It seemed like an eternity before the Shaper turned away, pacing back toward the Font. When he did, Vorax sagged on the spiral stairway, damp and exhausted.

"It is Godslayer that keeps my Elder Brother at bay," Satoris said without looking at him. "Have you never grasped that, Staccian? *Because* it is capable of slaying a Shaper. That which renders me vulnerable is the shield that protects all of Darkhaven. Without it, Haomane would have no *need* to work through Prophecy, using mortal hands as his weapons." His voice held a grim tone. "Do you think the gap that Sunders our world is so vast? It is nothing. The Lord-of-Thought could abandon Torath and cross it in an instant, bringing all of my siblings with him onto Urulat's soil. But he will not," he added, reaching one open hand into the Font to let the blue-white flames of the marrow-fire caress it, "nor will they, while I hold *this*."

His hand closed on Godslayer's hilt. Vorax's heart convulsed within its brand, sending a shock of ecstatic pain through his flesh. Halfway up the winding stair, he went heavily to one knee, feeling the bruising impact through his armor. "Aye, my Lord," he said dully. "I am a fool."

"Yes," Satoris murmured, contemplating the dagger. "But a loyal one, or so I judge." He released the hilt, leaving the Shard in the Font. "Ah, Haomane!" he mused. "Would I slay you if I had the chance? Or would I sue for peace, if I held the dagger at your throat? It has been so long, so long. I do not even know myself." Remembering Vorax, he glanced over his shoulder. "Begone," he said. "I will speak to you anon, my Staccian. When my Three are united."

"Aye, my Lord." He clambered to his feet with difficulty, and bowed. "I will await your pleasure." There was no response. Vorax grunted with relief and turned around, making his way up the spiral stair. He kept one gauntleted hand on the glimmering onyx wall, steadying himself until he reached the three-fold door at the top of the stair.

Which way? The Staccian hesitated. The door to the right was *his* door, leading through the back passages of Darkhaven to his own quarters. He thought of them with longing; of their rich appointments, booty gained by right of spoil over the centuries. All his things were there, all his luxuries.

No. It was too soon. He stank of fear and dripped with sweat under his armor, and he did not want to bring it into his quarters. That had been a bad misstep in the Chamber.

He needed to walk the back ways, to clear his mind and temper his heat.

There was the middle door; Tanaros' door.

No. He did not wish to meet Tanaros Blacksword's Fjel guards upon emergence, and watch their nostrils widen at his stink. Not now.

Vorax laid his gauntleted hand upon the left door, Ushahin's door. Recognizing his touch as one of the Three, the veins of marrow-fire within it brightened. It swung open, then closed behind him as he stepped through it, sealing without a trace.

The air was markedly cooler, and he breathed it in with gratitude, letting his eyes adjust to new darkness. Only a faint trace of the marrow-fire lit his way, veins buried deep in the walls. Sounds filled the dark corridors; Ushahin's madlings, scratching, babbling, scrambling. Vorax smiled, setting out in the direction of the sounds.

The Dreamspinner's folk understood fear. They would forgive.

How many years had it been since he had ventured into Ushahin's passageways? He could not remember. Ten? More like fifty, or a hundred even. There had been no cause, during the long years of peace; or neutrality, which passed for peace. While Haomane's Allies sulked and left Lord Satoris unmolested, the Three tended to their separate ways, keeping Darkhaven's affairs in order. Vorax limped on his bruised knee and counted his strides, one hand hovering over his hilt. At a hundred paces, the corridor forked. He paused, listening, then took the right fork.

It forked, again and again.

Vorax followed the voices.

It was the Fjel who had built Darkhaven, in accordance with his Lordship's design; but these passages were not built to a Fjel's scale. They were behind the walls, the province of rats and scuttling madlings. Rats, Vorax had expected. He was amazed at the progress Ushahin's madlings had made; widening breaches in the masonry to open connections between passages where none were meant to exist, forging exits and entrances where none were intended. There was no danger to his Lordship, of course; no madling would touch dare the three-fold door and risk his wrath. Still, it made him uneasy to think how extensively they had penetrated the fortress. He wondered if Ushahin knew.

At one point he encountered a deep chasm in a passage-way, and had to sidle across the verge of it on his heels, both hands outflung to grasp the dimly veined walls, toes hanging out over empty nothingness. His knees creaked with the effort of balancing. Pausing to steady his nerves, Vorax looked down, gazing past his boot-tips. Dry heat blasted upward in a column.

The chasm went down and down, deeper than a mine-shaft. Somewhere, far below, was a flickering light cast by blue-white flames and a roar like that of a distant forest fire, or dragons. Vorax shuddered, and edged clear of the chasm, back onto solid ground. That was no work of madlings. He wondered what fault in Darkhaven's foundation had permit-ted the chasm to open. It was as close as any man should get to the Source; and a far sight closer than any Staccian ought. He'd had enough infernal heat to last him an immor-tal lifetime. It was *cool* in Staccia.

Betimes, he missed it.

Perhaps, when this latest threat had passed, it would be time to consider passing on his mantle. To retire to a pleas-ant estate, where the sun shone in a blue sky over a white, wintery landscape, and the wolf tracked the hare through new-fallen snow. He could continue his duties in Staccia, binding the earls and barons in fealty, negotiating lines of supply and men for Darkhaven, negotiating the companion-ship of their pretty younger daughters for himself, spinning out his days in soft, blissful comfort, freed from the con-straints of his vow-branded flesh to age his way into easeful death, pillowing his head in the laps of Staccian maidens. It was not a bad idea, after all, to have a presence in Staccia. It had been too long since he had made himself *known* there.

The path took an upward turn. Trudging doggedly up the steep incline, he tried to imagine if his Lordship would ever agree to such a thing. He rather thought not. After all, Staccia's very peace and prosperity were dependent upon the bargain Vorax had struck with his Lordship so many years ago. He had not imagined, then, that there could ever come a day when immortality would become burdensome.

Ah, well. It was a pleasant thought.

Ahead, voices echoed; a madlings' clamor, but with something else running through it, a single voice like a silver thread. The incline had ended at last, the path level beneath his feet. Frowning, Vorax quickened his stride. There was light ahead; not marrow-fire, but candlelight, warm and golden. Through a narrowing passage, he glimpsed it. He picked his way with care, easing shoulder-first into the gap. His armor scraped along the rocks, getting scratched and dented in the process.

Unexpectedly, the passage widened.

Vorax stumbled into open space, catching himself. It was a rough-hewn chamber, a natural space vastened by the efforts of a hundred generations chipping at the stone walls. Everywhere, butt-ends of tallow candles burned, wedged into every available niche and crevice. Scraps and oddments of carpet covered the floor, and the walls were covered with scratched messages; some legible, most a garble of words. There must have been a dozen madlings gathered, light glimmering from their eyes. All of them whispered, hissing and muttering to one another.

One was kneeling before the figure who stood in the center of the chamber, grimy fingers plucking at the hem of her blue robe as he raised a face filled with hope. "Me?" he said. "Me? Lady see me?"

The Lady Cerelinde bent her head, cupping the madling's face with both hands. Her hair spilled forward, shimmering in the candlelight, veiling her features. "Ludo," she said softly, her silvery voice ringing. "You were a wheelwright's son. I see you, Ludo. I see what might have been. I see you with a plump wife, smiling, and laughing children chasing one another in your father's yard."

"Lady!" He gasped the word, face shining and distorted with tears, and rocked back and forth, wringing the hem of her robe. "Lady, Lady, yes!"

Cerelinde released him with a gentle smile, lifted her head—and froze.

The madlings wailed in chorus.

"*Lady.*" Vorax took a further step into the chamber, his sword rasping free of its scabbard. He met her oddly fearless gaze, and the blood seemed to sing in his veins, a high-pitched tone ringing in his head. He raised the blade, angling it for a solid blow, watching her expose the vulnerable column of her throat as her gaze followed the sword. His voice, when he spoke, sounded strange to his ears. "What is it you do in this place?"

"I might ask you the same," she said calmly. "Do you desire a glimpse of *what might have been*, Lord Vorax? It is a small magic, one of the few which the Rivenlost are afforded, but I am willing to share it. All you must do is consent in your heart to know."

He gritted his teeth. "That, I do not."

"So." She watched the candlelight reflecting on the edge of his sword. "I do not blame you, given what you have chosen. They do. It gives them comfort to know, poor broken creatures that they are. Is there harm in it, my Lord? Have I trespassed? I was brought to this place."

"Who—?"

"Get out!" From the shadows a figure flung itself at him, wild-eyed, arms windmilling. Astonished, Vorax put up his sword, taking a step backward. He had a brief impression of sallow features beneath a mat of tangled hair. "Get out!" the madling shrilled, flailing at him. "*You* brought her here, but this is *our* place! *Ours!* Get out!"

Catching her thin wrists in one gauntleted hand, he held

her at bay. It took a moment to put a name to her, but he had seen her before; one of Tanaros' favorites, or one who favored him. There was no telling, with madlings. "Meara," he said. "What do you do here? *Why?*"

She sagged in his grasp, then twisted to scowl at him through her dark, matted hair. "We batter our hearts, my lord, against the specter of what might have been. Don't you see?" There were tears in her eyes, at odds with her expression. "I warned him, my lord," she said. "I did. I tried to tell him. But he didn't want to know, so he left, and Ushahin left, and we were left alone. Isn't it clear?"

"No." Vorax released his grasp, letting her crumple on the chamber floor. "No," he said again, "it's not." He eyed them; Meara, her face averted, the lad Ludo, weeping. Others wept, too. Only the Lady Cerelinde stood, dry-eyed. "Listen," he said to the madlings. "This place, all places, belong to Lord Satoris. What might have been . . . is not. Do you understand?"

Wails of assent arose in answer. One of the madlings was banging his head against an outcropping of rock, bloodying his forehead. "His blood!" he moaned. "His Lordship's blood!"

"Aye." Vorax gave them a hard look. "That which he shed to defend us all, and sheds every minute of every day in suffering. Do you disdain it?" They wailed denial. "Good," he said. "Because Ushahin Dreamspinner, who is your master, returns anon. And, too, there will come Tanaros Blacksword, who makes his way home even now. Do you wish them to find you weeping over *what might have been?*"

Perhaps it was the right thing to say; who could tell, with madlings? They dispersed, wailing, into the passageways of Darkhaven. Only Meara and the Ellyl woman were left, the one still huddled, the other still standing.

Vorax exhaled hard, dragging his arm across his brow, and sheathed his sword. "Meara," he said conversationally, "I suggest you return the Lady to her chambers, and do not allow her to venture out again unless his Lordship summons her. If I find you here again, I will not hesitate to strike. And if you think my mercy is cruel, remember what Ushahin Dreamspinner might do to her. He has no love for her kind."

"Aye, my lord." Meara stood sullenly, plucking at Cerelinde's sleeve.

The Lady of the Ellylon stood unmoving. "General Tanaros is coming?"

"Aye."

There was a change; a subtle one. She did not move, and even her lids did not flicker. Yet beneath her fair skin, a faint blush arose, tinting her cheeks. Something knotted in Vorax's belly, and he stepped into her space, crowding her with his bulk.

"Lady," he said softly. *"Leave him be."*

Her chin rose a fraction. "You were the one to offer me Lord Satoris' hospitality, my lord Glutton. Will you break it and be foresworn?"

"I would have slain you the instant Beshtanag fell." He watched fear seep into her luminous gaze, and favored her with a grim smile. "Make no mistake, Lady. Neither hatred nor madness drives me, and I know where the margin of profit lies. If his Lordship heeded me, you would be dead." He drew his sword a few inches clear of the scabbard, adding, "I may do it yet."

"You wouldn't dare!" Her eyes blazed with terrible beauty. "Aracus—"

"Aracus!" Vorax laughed, shoving the hilt back in place. "Oh, Lady, whatever happens, we've ages of time here behind the walls of Darkhaven before the Son of Altorus becomes a problem. No, if you want to invoke a protector, I suggest you stick with his Lordship. And mind, if I find you plying Tanaros with Ellylon glamours and magics, I *will* see you dead."

The Lady Cerelinde made no answer.

"Good." Vorax nodded. "Get her out of here, Meara, and

do not bring her again. Mind, I will be speaking to the Dreamspinner."

He watched them go, the madling leading, tugging at the Ellyl's sleeve. The sight did nothing to dispel the knotted, sinking feeling in his belly. It was providence that had made him choose the left-hand door, alerting him to untold danger. On the morrow he would assemble a patrol of his own men to scour the passages behind the walls, sealing off the madlings' secret corridors, or as many as they could find. Something was wrong within the edifice of Darkhaven, crumbling even as the chasm had opened in the floor under his feet. He remembered the moon-garden by half-light, a shining figure beneath the stars, the heady scent of vulnus-blossom mingling with sulfur in the damp air, evoking painful memory.

Lord Vorax, what do you see?

Vorax shook his head and blew out the candle-butts. By the glimmer of the marrow-fire he pressed onward, leaving the chamber behind and picking his path through the tangled maze of narrow passages until he reached an egress. It was a sanctioned door, opening to his touch behind a niche in one of Darkhaven's major hallways. One of the Haven-guard snapped to attention as he emerged; a Mørkhar Fjel, axe springing into one hand, shield raising, dark bristles prickling erect. "Lord Vorax, sir!"

"At ease," he sighed.

The Mørkhar stared straight ahead. Ignoring him, Vorax made his way down the towering halls, limping steadily back to his own quarters. It was a blessed relief to reach the tall ironwood doors, carved with the twin likenesses of a roaring Staccian bear, and a pair of his own Staccian guardsmen lounging against them. The fear-sweat had dried to a rime beneath his armor, and he was only tired, now. Beyond those doors lay comfort and easement. His belly rumbled at the thought of it.

"Let me in, Eadric."

"Aye, sir!" The senior guardsman grinned, fumbling at his belt for a key. "Good ease to you, sir!"

The tall ironwood doors swung open, and Vorax entered his quarters. Within, it was another world, rich and luxuriant, far removed from everything in Darkhaven; the stark grandeur of its halls, the fearful heat of the Chamber of the Font, the scrabbling mysteries behind its walls. Lamplight warmed rich tapestries, gleamed upon gilded statuary, sparkled on jewel-encrusted surfaces. He had had ten mortal lifetimes to amass the treasures contained within his quarters. Somewhere, music was playing. It paused as he entered, then resumed, the harpist bowing her head over the ivory-inlaid curve of her instrument, fingers caressing the strings. Three Staccian handmaids rose to their feet, surrounding him with solicitous care, their deft fingers unbuckling his ceremonial armor.

"My lord, you are weary!"

"My lord, you must rest!"

"My lord, you must eat!"

It was not, after all, so much to ask. For a thousand years he had guaranteed the safety of their nation. In the bathing-room, Vorax let them strip him and stood while they brought warm water and sponged the stink of sweat and fear from his skin. Water ran in rivulets, coursing through the ruddy hair on his chest, over the bulge of his stomach, down the thick columns of his legs. Their hands were gentle. They understood his needs and were paid well for their terms of service, their families recompensed in titles, lands and money. Did a man deserve any less, after a thousand years?

They robed him and led him, gently, to his great ironwood chair. It, too, was carved in the likeness of a bear. That had been his family's insignia, once. Now it was his, and his alone. He sank into it, into the familiar curves, the ironwood having conformed over long centuries of wear to his own shape. One of his handmaids fetched a pitcher of

Vedasian wine, pouring him a brimming goblet. He quaffed half at a gulp, while another handmaid hurried to the door, her soft voice ordering a message relayed to the kitchen. A meal in nine courses, including soup to whet his appetite, a brace of pigeon, a whole rack of lamb, grilled turbot, a cheese course and sweets to follow. His belly growled plaintively at the prospect. This day called for sustenance on a grand scale. He drank off the rest of the goblet's contents, held it out to be refilled, and drank again. Warmth spread throughout him from within. The wine began to ease his stiff joints, rendering the throbbing bruise on his knee a distant ache. His free arm lay in magisterial repose over the top of the chair's, fingers curling into the bear's paws. His feet were propped on soft cushions. He groaned as another of his handmaids knelt, kneading his stockinged soles with her thumbs.

"Is it good, my lord?" Her blue-grey eyes gazed up at him. There was a spattering of freckles over the bridge of her nose. They would have been innocent, those eyes, save for a reflection of gold coin held cunning in their depths. The youngest daughter of a Staccian lordling, she knew where her family's margin of profit lay. "Your supper will arrive anon."

"Aye," he said gently, thinking of the Lady Cerelinde's blush, of her terrible beauty, and the scent of vulnus-blossom. Some things were better measured in coin. "'Tis good, sweetling."

A scratch at the door announced the arrival of his supper. Vorax inhaled deeply as the dishes were uncovered and the savory aroma of food filled his quarters. His Staccian handmaids helped him to the table, filled to groaning with his repast. They brought the wine-pitcher, placing his goblet in easy reach. Eyeing the repast, he selected a bowl of consommé and raised it to his lips with both hands.

It would take a mountain of food to ease the memory of his misstep in the Chamber, of Lord Satoris' anger, of the

silence out of Staccia, of the madlings' gathering, of the
Lady of the Ellylon's presence among them, and above all,
of that gaping chasm in the secret heart of Darkhaven.

Drinking deep from the bowl, Vorax began.

"Go, LADY, GO!" MEARA ACTUALLY shoved her from behind, then snatched her hands back as if the touch burned.
Caught unawares, Cerelinde stumbled over the threshold of
the hidden door, pushing the heavy tapestry aside to enter
her quarters.

It was blessedly quiet within.

She sat on the edge of her bed, willing her heartbeat to
slow, remembering candlelight reflecting from the edge of
Vorax's sword and meditating upon the nearness of death.
This must be, she thought, the way warriors felt in the aftermath of battle; a strange mix of latent terror and exhilaration. Meara paced the boundaries of the room, peering
anxiously into every corner. Where she trod upon the soft
carpets, the scent of bruised heart-grass followed in a
ghostly reminder of the Ellylon weavers who had woven
them long ago.

"It is safe," she pronounced at length. "No one is here."

"That is well." Her calm restored, Cerelinde inclined her
head. "Forgive me, Meara. Perhaps the venture was ill-
advised. I would not wish any of you to be placed in danger."

The madling shot her a glance. "He's right, you know.
Lord Vorax is. You should leave the Lord General alone.
There's nothing but death in it, death and blood and more
madness. You should leave *us* alone. Why don't you? Why
did he have to bring you here?"

"Meara." She spread her hands, helpless. "To that, I cannot speak. You know I am a hostage here. It is a small gift, a
small kindness. You asked me to share it. Since it is all I
have to offer, I did."

"I know." Meara hunkered at the foot of the bed. "Aye, I know, I did. We are the broken ones, we who want to know. They should not have left us, and they should not have brought you. They should have known better, and you should never have shown me kindness, no." She gnawed on her thumbnail, then asked abruptly, "Lady, what would you have seen for Lord Vorax? Would you have shown him what the shape of Urulat would be if he had chosen elsewise?"

"No." Cerelinde shook her head. "A glimpse of the life he might have had, nothing more; a life that would have ended long, long ago. More than that, I cannot say. We are only afforded a faint glimpse, Meara, beyond the greatest of branchings in a single life. It is a small gift, truly."

"Why?"

She gazed at the madling with sorrow and compassion. "We are Rivenlost, Meara. We were left behind upon the shores of Urulat, while the Bright Ones, those among his Children whom Haomane held dearest, dwell beside him upon the crown of Torath. In curiosity, in innocent desire, those of us who are the Rivenlost wandered too far from Haomane's side, and we were stranded when the world was Sundered. This small gift was won in bitter hours, when the eldest among us wondered and sought to pierce the veil. What if we had been more diligent? What if we had stood at the Lord-of-Thought's side during the Sundering? It has been passed down, this gift. We, too, batter our hearts against *what might have been*."

"What do you see?" Meara whispered.

"Brightness." Cerelinde smiled, glancing westward. "Brightness, and joy."

"So." Squatting, Meara wrapped both arms about her knees and tucked her chin into her chest, hiding her face. "You cannot see the *small* might-haves."

"No." She thought, with regret, of a myriad small might-have-beens. What if she had consented to wed Aracus in the sturdy mortal confines of Seahold? What if Aracus had consented to their wedding vows being held in the warded halls of Meronil, under the aegis of Ingolin the Wise? What if . . . *what if* . . . she had never agreed to wed him at all? "I would that I could, Meara. But, no. The tapestry is too vast, and there are too many threads woven into it. Pluck at a small one, and others unravel. Only Haomane the Lord-of-Thought is vouchsafed that knowledge."

Meara tilted her head. Her eyes, peering through a thicket of hair, held a cunning gleam. "What about his Lordship?"

"Lord . . . Satoris?" Without thinking, Cerelinde stiffened. In memory's eye, she saw the Shaper's form blotting out the stars, the shadow of his extended hand lying stark and black on the desiccated grass of the moon-garden, patiently proffered for her inevitable refusal.

"Aye." Meara nodded sharply.

Cerelinde shook her head. "He is a Shaper. He is beyond my ken."

"There was a . . . what do you call it? A great branching." Studying the floor, Meara plucked at the carpet, then sniffed at the sweet odor of heart-grass on her fingertips. "When he refused, three times, to withdraw his Gift from Arahila's Children." Her sharp chin pointed upward, eyes glancing. "What might have been, had he not? You could see *that* for him."

A chill ran the length of Cerelinde's spine. "I do not think," she said gently, "his Lordship would consent to seek this knowledge."

"You could ask." Meara straightened abruptly, tossing back her hair. "It would be interesting to know, since *some* of Arahila's Children disdain it. His Lordship's Gift, that is. Which is odd, since it is all they have that *you* do not; and all I do, too. I do, you know." Placing her hands on her hips, she fixed the Lady of the Ellylon with a disconcerting stare. "I will go now. Thank you, for what you did. It meant very much to some people. I am sorry to have placed you in danger, but I do not think Lord Vorax will kill you. Not yet, anyway."

"Good," Cerelinde said simply, staring back.

When the madling had gone, Cerelinde buried her face in her hands and took a deep, shuddering breath. When all was said and done, there was too much here beyond her comprehension. She had been grateful for Meara's request. She had hoped, in sharing this small gift, to bring a measure of compassion to the stark halls of Darkhaven, to the meager lives of those who dwelled within its walls. It had seemed a kindness, a simple kindness, to offer comfort in lieu of the healing she could not effect.

Now, she was not so sure.

Seeking comfort of her own, she thought of Aracus, and tried to imagine his understanding. There was nothing there, only the memory of his gaze, wide-set and demanding, stirring her blood in unaccustomed ways, filling her with hope and pride and the dream of the Prophecy fulfilled.

In this place, it seemed very far away.

She thought of Tanaros instead, and remembered the old madling woman Sharit they had met in the halls of Darkhaven, and how gently he had taken her hand; how proudly she had stood, gripping it tight. Whatever had passed here this day, Tanaros would understand it.

He was not what she would have expected him to be, at once both less and more. Less terrifying; a Man, not a monster. And yet he was more than a Man. Immortal, as Aracus was not. Like the Ellylon, he understood the scope of ages.

Cerelinde wondered what he had been like, so long ago, as a mortal Man. Not so different, perhaps, from Aracus. After all, Tanaros was related by ties of distant kinship and fosterage to the House of Altorus. He must have been as close to his liege-lord as Blaise Caveros was to Aracus. Had he been as fiercely loyal? Yes, she thought, he must have been. The betrayal would not have wounded him so deeply if he were not.

He must have loved his wife, too. What manner of passion had led her to commit such a grievous betrayal? She thought about Aracus, and the quick, hot drive that blazed within him. And she thought about Tanaros, steady and calm, despite the ancient, aching grief that lay behind his dark gaze. Though he was her enemy, he treated her with unfailing courtesy. She did not know the answer.

He was coming.

They were all coming. Vorax the Glutton's words had confirmed it. Somewhere, in the world beyond Darkhaven's walls, the tides of fate had shifted. Beshtanag had fallen. Tanaros Kingslayer and Ushahin the Misbegotten were on their way, soon to reunite the Three. And on their heels would be Aracus Altorus, the Borderguard and her kinsmen in his train, intent on storming Darkhaven.

She was the Lady of the Ellylon and his betrothed, the key to fulfilling Haomane's Prophecy. They would not relent until she was freed or the plains of Curonan were churned to red mud with the last of their dying blood.

And Lord Satoris in his immortal pride and folly would revel in it.

Death was the only certainty. Whatever else transpired, the ravens of Darkhaven would feast on the flesh of foes and allies alike. The thought of it made her shudder to the bone. The hand of Haomane's Prophecy hovered over her, a bright and terrible shadow, filled with the twinned promise of hope and bloodshed. Although she wished it otherwise, she could see, now, how they were intertwined.

All things were as they must be. Light and dark, bound together in an inextricable battle. The paths that led them here were beginning to narrow. Soon, it would not matter *what might have been*. Only what *was*.

She was afraid, and weary of being alone with her fear.

Hurry, Cerelinde prayed. *Oh, hurry!*

And she was no longer sure, in that moment, to whom or for what she prayed.

Of all the things that had befallen her in Darkhaven, this was surely the most fearful.

A preview of

GODSLAYER

by
Jacqueline Carey

Now Available in Hardcover
from Tom Doherty Associates

ONE

❖

ALL THINGS CONVERGE.

In the last Great Age of the Sundered World of Urulat, which was once called Uru-Alat after the World God that gave birth to it, they began to converge upon Darkhaven.

It began with a red star rising in the west; Dergail's Soumanië, a polished stone that had once been a chip of the Souma itself—that mighty gem that rested on the sundered isle of Torath, the Eye in the Brow of Uru-Alat, source of the Shapers' power.

Satoris the Shaper took it for a warning, a message from a sister who had loved him, once upon a time; Arahila the Fair, whose children were the race of Men. His enemies took it as a declaration of war.

Whatever the truth, war ensued.

Haomane, First-Born among Shapers, long ago uttered a Prophecy.

"When the unknown is made known, when the lost weapon is found, when the marrow-fire is quenched and Godslayer is freed, when a daughter of Elterrion weds a son of Altorus, when the Spear of Light is brought forth and the Helm of Shadows is broken, the Fjeltroll shall fall, the Were shall be defeated ere they rise, and the Sunderer shall be no more, the Souma shall be restored and the Sundered World made whole and Haomane's Children shall endure."

It began with the rising of Dergail's Soumanië. Cerelinde, the Lady of the Ellylon, a daughter of Elterrion's line, plighted her troth to Aracus Altorus. It was the first step toward fulfilling Haomane's Prophecy; Arahila's Children and Haomane's conjoined, their lines inextricably mingled. But in Lindanen Dale, their nuptials were disrupted.

Bloodshed ensued.

It was a trap; a trap that went awry. It seemed at first that all the pieces fell into place. Driven by vengeance, the Grey Dam of the Were spent her life in an attack, and the half-breed Ushahin Dreamspinner unleashed madness and illusion. Under its cover, Tanaros Blacksword abducted the Lady Cerelinde and took her to Darkhaven.

Haomane's Allies were misled. Pursuing a rumor of dragons, under the command of Aracus Altorus, they raised an army and launched an assault on Beshtanag and Lilias, Sorceress of the East. And there the trap went awry. The Ways were closed, and the Army of Darkhaven was turned back, their company's leadership scattered. In Beshtanag, Haomane's Allies took to the field.

There, they prevailed.

They were not supposed to do so.

They were coming; all of them.

They came on foot and on horseback and by sailing ship, for the Ways of the Marasoumië had been destroyed. Lord Satoris had done this in his wrath. The Dragon of Beshtanag was no more, slain by the Arrow of Fire; the lost weapon, found. Bereft of her Soumanië, the Sorceress of the East was nothing more than an ordinary woman; Lilias, mortal and powerless. The Were had struck a bitter bargain with Aracus Altorus, ceding to his terms; defeated ere they rose. Aracus was coming, his heart filled with righteous fury, knowing he had been duped.

Malthus the Wise Counselor, trapped in the Ways, had vanished beyond the sight of even Godslayer itself . . . but rumor whispered of a new figure. The Galäinridder, the Bright Rider, whose words bred fear in the hearts of Men, inspiring them to betray their ancient oaths to Lord Satoris.

But Haomane's Allies had not won yet.

On the westernmost verge of the Unknown Desert, Tanaros Blacksword, Commander General of the Army of

Darkhaven, made camp alongside a creek. There he slaked the thirst of his long-parched flesh and made ready to rally his surviving troops and set his face toward home. Immortal though he was, he could have died in the desert. Thanks to a raven's gratitude, he lived.

When he dreamed, he dreamed of the Lady Cerelinde.

On the back of a blood-bay horse, Ushahin Dreamspinner rode the pathways between waking and dreaming, plunging into the Midlands and leaving a trail of nightmares in his wake. A wedge of ravens forged his path, and on either side, a riderless horse flanked him; one a spectral grey, the other as black as coal.

If he had dreamed, which he did not, he would dream of the counsel of dragons.

Vorax the Glutton, muttering over his stores, awaited them in Darkhaven.

The immortal Three were soon to be reunited.

Haomane's Prophecy was yet to be fulfilled.

In the mighty fortress of Darkhaven, where the Lady Cerelinde endured imprisonment and fought against a rising tide of doubt, the marrow-fire yet burned. Within it hung the dagger, Godslayer; ruby-red, a Shard of the Souma. Once, it had wounded Satoris; the wound that would not heal. Godslayer alone could end a Shaper's life; the life of Lord Satoris, the life of any of the Shapers. And while the marrow-fire burned, no mortal hand could touch it. None but a Shaper would dare.

Only the Water of Life, drawn from the Well of the World, could extinguish the marrow-fire. The Water had been drawn, but its Bearer was lost.

Thrust out of the Ways by Malthus the Counselor in a desperate gambit, abandoned and lost, Dani of the Yarru wandered the cold lands of the Northern Harrow, deep in Fjeltroll territory, with only his uncle to guide him. Together, they sought to follow the rivers, the lifeblood of Urulat, to Darkhaven.

And they, too, were being hunted. . . .

Led by Skragdal of the Tungskulder, the Fjel were on the hunt. Their loyalty to Lord Satoris was beyond question. Haomane's Prophecy promised them nothing but death. No matter where it led them, they would not abandon their quest. They would succeed or die trying.

All things converge.

NEHERINACH WAS A GREEN BOWL cradled in the mountain's hands. Here and there, small boulders breached its surface; elsewhere, a half dozen small hillocks arose, covered in flowering ivy. A small river, spring-fed, wound through the center of it, meandering westward to sink belowground. Low mountains, sloping upward with a deceptively gentle grade, surrounded it. Patches of gorse offered grazing to fallow deer, shelter to hare that crouched in the shadow of small crags.

It was a peaceful place, and a terrible one.

On the verges, the Kaldjager scouts waited, glancing sidelong out of yellow eyes to watch the others' straggling progress. Skragdal, leading them, knew what the Kaldjager felt. This was where it had begun.

They assembled in silence on the field of Neherinach. The green grass was soft beneath their feet. Water sparkled under the bright sun. Birds stirred in the trees, insects took flight from grass stems.

"Come," Skragdal said quietly.

They crossed the field together, and the grass flattened beneath their approach, springing back once they had passed. It smelled clean and sweet. Skragdal felt his talons breach the surface of the soil beneath, rich and crumbling. It filled him with an ancient fury. There was old blood in that soil. Thousand upon thousand of Fjel had died in this place, fighting without weapons against a vast army of Men and Ellylon, attacked without quarter for the crime of giving shelter to the wounded Shaper who had taught them the measure of their own worth. The ivy-covered hillocks that dotted the field marked the cairns of Fjel dead; one for each of the six tribes.

In the end, they had won; by treachery and stealth, according to the songs of Haomane's Allies. It was true, they had laid traps, but what was treachery to a people invaded without provocation? It had been a bitter victory.

Near the riverbank, where the ground was soft enough to hold an impression, they found a trace of old hoofprints. Skragdal frowned. Only Men and Ellylon rode horses, and he did not like the idea of either despoiling Neherinach.

"A rider," Thorun said.

"Aye."

"The earl's Galäinridder?"

"Perhaps."

Led by the Kaldjager, they followed the tracks to their origin. At the northern tip of Neherinach, a node-point of the Marasoumië had lain buried in a hollow place. Now, a great crater had been gouged from the earth. Splintered rock thrust outward in every direction. Whatever had emerged had done so with great force. The innermost surfaces of the granite were smooth and gleaming, as if the rock itself had become molten. It had not happened all that long ago. There were fresh scratches on the rock, and the remnants of hoofprints were still visible on the churned ground.

"That's not good," Thorun said.

"No." Staring into the hole, Skragdal thought of Osric's Men gossiping in the tunnels, and of Osric in Gerflod Hall, grinning his dead grin at the ceiling. The ragged hole gaped like a wound in the green field of Neherinach, exposing the ashen remains of the node far below. Earl Coenred's final words echoed in his memory, making his hide crawl with unease. *Dead, and you don't even know it!* "It's not."

He thought about changing their course, setting the Kaldjager to track the Galäinridder; but General Tanaros had told them, again and again, the importance of obeying orders. It was important to obey orders, even those Lord Vo-

rax had given. Anyway, it was already too late. Gerflod
Keep lay a day behind them, and the Rider had some days'
start. Not even the Gulnagel could catch him now.

But they could warn Darkhaven.

"Rhilmar," he said decisively. "Morstag. Go back. If
General Tanaros has returned, tell him what we have seen
here. Tell him what happened in Gerflod. If he is not there,
tell Lord Vorax. And if he will not listen, tell Marshal Hyrgolf. No; tell him anyway. He needs to know. This is a matter that concerns the Fjel."

"Aye, boss." Rhilmar, the smaller of the two, shivered in
the bright sun. In this place of green grass, sparkling rivers,
and old bones, fear had caught up to him; the reek of it oozed
from him, tainting the air. "Just . . . just the two of us?"

One of the Kaldjager snorted with contempt. Skragdal
ignored it. "Haomane's Allies didn't fear to send only two,
and smallfolk at that," he said to Rhilmar. "Go fast, and
avoid Men's keeps." He turned to the Kaldjager. "Blågen,
where is the nearest Fjel den?"

The Kaldjager pointed to the east. "Half a league." His
yellow eyes gleamed. "Are we hunting?"

"Aye." Skragdal nodded. "We follow orders. We will
spread word among the tribes until there is nowhere safe
and no place for them to hide. Whoever—whatever—this
Galäinridder is, he did well to flee Fjel territories and put
himself beyond our reach." Standing beside the desecrated
earth, he bared his eyetusks in a grim smile. "Pity the
smallfolk he left behind."

THEY SPENT AN ENTIRE DAY camped beneath the jack pines,
reveling in the presence of water and shade. Red squirrels
chattered in the trees, providing easy prey for the Gulnagel.
Speros, ranging along the course of the creek, discovered a
patch of wild onion. Tanaros' much-dented helmet, having
served as bucket and shovel, served now as a makeshift
cooking pot for a hearty stew.

By Tanaros' reckoning, they had emerged to the south-east of Darkhaven. Between them lay the fertile territories of the Midlands, then the sweeping plains of Curonan. It was possible that they could locate an entrance to the tunnels on the outskirts of the Midlands, but there was still a great deal of open ground to cover. It would be an easy journey by the standards of the desert; but there was the problem of the Fjel. Two Men traveling in enemy territory were easily disguised.

Not so, three large Gulnagel.

"We'll have to travel by night," Tanaros said ruefully. "At least we're well used to it." He eyed Speros. "Do you still remember how to steal horses?"

The Midlander looked uncertain. "Is that a jest, sir?"

Tanaros shook his head. "No."

They passed a farmstead on the first night and stole close enough to make out the shape of a stable, but at a hundred paces the sound of barking dogs filled the air. When a lamp was kindled in the cottage and silhouetted figures moved before the windows, Tanaros ordered a hasty, ignominious retreat, racing across fields, while the Gulnagel accompanied them at a slow jog.

Not until they had put a good distance between themselves and the farmstead did he order a halt. Back on the dusty road, Speros doubled over, bracing his hands on his thighs and catching his breath. "Why . . . not just . . . kill them? Surely . . . farmers wouldn't be much trouble."

Tanaros cocked a brow at him. "And have their deaths discovered? We've leagues to go before we're in the clear, and all of the Midlands standing on alert. You were the one served in the volunteer militia, Speros of Haimhault. Do you want one such on our trail?"

"Right." Speros straightened. "Shank's mare it is, General."

They walked in silence for several hours. After the desert, Tanaros reflected, it was almost pleasant. Their waterskins were full, and the fields provided ample hunting for

the Gulnagel. The air was balmy and moist, and the stars
overhead provided enough light to make out the rutted road.
On such a night, one could imagine walking forever. He
thought about the farmstead they had passed and smiled to
himself. While his motive for having done so was reasoned,
there was a luxuriant pleasure in having spared its inhabi-
tants' lives. Such choices seldom came his way. He wondered what story they would tell in the morning. They'd
pass a sleepless night if they knew the truth. Likely the
scent of the Gulnagel had set the dogs to barking; better to
send Speros alone, next time. He wondered if Fetch, who
had flown ahead, might be able to scout a likely candidate
for horse-thievery.

"It's funny, isn't it?" Speros remarked. "I never could
have imagined this."

"What's that?"

"*This.*" The Midlander waved one hand, indicating the
empty road, the quiet fields. "Us, here. Tramping across the
country like common beggars. I'd have thought . . . I don't
know, Lord General." He shrugged. "I'd have thought
there'd be more *magic.*"

"No." Tanaros shook his head. "There's precious little
magic in war, Speros."

"But you're . . . one of the Three, sir!" Speros protested.
"Tanaros Blacksword, Tanaros . . ." His voice trailed off.

"Kingslayer," Tanaros said equably. "Aye. An ordinary
man, rendered extraordinary only by the grace of Lord
Satoris." He touched the hilt of his sword. "This blade cannot be broken by mortal means, Speros, but I wield no
power but that which lies in reach of it. Are you disappointed?"

"No." Speros studied his boots as he walked, scuffing the
ruts in the road with cracked heels. "No," he repeated more
strongly, lifting his head. "I'm not." He grinned, the glint of
starlight revealing the gap amid his teeth. "It gives me hope.
After all, Lord General, *I* could be you!"

As Tanaros opened his mouth to reply, one of the Gulnagel raised a hand and grunted. The others froze, listening. Motioning for silence, Tanaros strained his ears. Not the farmsteaders, he hoped. Surely, they had seen nothing. There had been only the warning of the dogs to disturb their sleep. Like as not, they had cast a weary gaze over the empty fields, scolded the dogs, and gone back to sleep. What, then? The Fjel had keener ears than Men, but all three wore perplexed expressions. Speros, by contrast, bore a look of glazed horror.

Tanaros concentrated.

At first he heard nothing; then, distantly, a drumming like thunder. Hoofbeats? It sounded like, and unlike. There were too many, too fast—and another sound, too, a rushing, pulsating wind, like the sound of a thousand wings beating at once. It sounded, he realized, like the Ravensmirror.

"Fetch?" Tanaros called.

"Kaugh!"

The fabric of the night itself seemed to split beneath the onslaught as they emerged from the dreaming pathways into the waking world; ravens, aye, a whole flock, sweeping down the road in a single, vast wing. There, at the head, was Fetch, eyes like obsidian pebbles. And behind them, forelegs churning, nostrils flaring . . .

Horses.

They emerged from darkness as if through a doorway, and starlight gleamed on their sleek hides. All around them, the ravens settled in the fields; save for Fetch, who took up his perch on Tanaros' shoulder. Their iron-shod hooves rang on the road, solid and real, large bodies milling. There were three of them; one grey as a ghost, one black as pitch, and in the middle, a bay the color of recently spilled blood.

And on its back, a pale, crooked figure with moonspun hair and a face of ruined beauty smiled crookedly and lifted a hand in greeting.

"Well met, cousin," said Ushahin Dreamspinner. "A little bird told me you were in need of a ride."

"Dreamspinner!" Tanaros laughed aloud. "Well met, in-

deed." He clapped one hand on Speros' shoulder. "I retract
my words, lad. Forgive me for speaking in haste. It seems
the night holds more magic than I had suspected."

Speros, the color draining from his desert-scorched skin,
stared without words.

"I have ridden the wings of a nightmare, cousin, and I
fear it has brushed your protégé's thoughts." Ushahin's
voice was amused. "What plagues you, Midlander? Did you
catch a glimpse of your own mortal frailties and failings,
the envy to which your kind is prey? A rock, perchance,
clutched in a boyish fist? But for an accident of geography,
you might have been one of *them*." His mismatched eyes
glinted, shadows pooling in the hollow of his dented temple. "Are you afraid to meet my gaze, Midlander?"

"Cousin—" Tanaros began.

"No." With an effort of will, Speros raised his chin and
met the half-breed's glittering gaze. Clenching one hand
and pressing it to his heart, he extended it open in the ancient salute. His starlit face was earnest and stubborn. "No,
Lord Dreamspinner. I am not afraid."

Ushahin smiled his crooked smile. "It is a lie, but it is one
I will honor for the sake of what you have endured." He
nodded to his left. "Take the grey. Do you follow in my
footprints, within the swath the ravens forge, she will bear
you in my wake, Tanaros." He pointed to the black horse.
"You rode such a one, once. Here is another. Can your Gulnagel keep pace?"

"Aye," Tanaros murmured, his assent echoed by the grinning Fjel. He approached the black horse, running one hand
along the arch of its neck. Its black mane spilled like water
over his hand, and it turned its head, baring sharp teeth, a
preternaturally intelligent eye glimmering. Clutching a
hank of mane low on the withers, he swung himself astride.
Equine muscle surged beneath his thighs; Fetch squawked
with displeasure and took wing. Using the pressure of his
knees, Tanaros turned the black. He thought of his own stallion, his faithful black, lost in the Ways of the Marasoumië,

and wondered what had become of it. "These are Darkhaven's horses, cousin, born and bred. Where did you come
by them?"

"On the southern edge of the Delta."

Tanaros paused. "My Staccians. The trackers?"

"I fear it is so." There was an unnerving sympathy in
Ushahin's expression. "They met a . . . a worthy end,
cousin. I will tell you of it, later, but we must be off before
Haomane's dawn fingers the sky, else I cannot keep this
pathway open. Night is short, and there are . . . other con-
siderations afoot. Will you ride?"

"Aye." Tanaros squeezed the black's barrel, feeling its
readiness to run, to feel the twilit road unfurling like a ribbon once more beneath its hooves. He glanced at Speros and
saw the Midlander, too, was astride, eyes wide with excitement. He glanced at the Gulnagel and saw them readying themselves to run, muscles bunching in their powerful
haunches. "Let us make haste."

"Boss?" One held up Tanaros' helmet. "You want this?"

"No." Thinking of water holes, of shallow graves and
squirrel stew, Tanaros shook his head. "Leave it. It has
served its purpose, and more. Let the Midlanders find it and
wonder. I do not need it."

"Okay." The Fjel laid it gently alongside the road.

Tanaros took a deep breath, touching the sword that hung
at his side. His branded heart throbbed, answering to the
touch, to the echo of Godslayer's fire and his Lordship's
blood. He thought, with deep longing, of Darkhaven's encompassing walls. He tried not to think about the fact that
she was there. A small voice whispered a name in his
thoughts, insinuating a tendril into his heart, as delicate and
fragile as the shudder of a mortexigus flower. With an effort, he squelched it. "We are ready, cousin."

"Good," Ushahin said simply. He lifted one hand, and a
cloud of ravens rose swirling from the fields, gathering and
grouping. The blood-bay stallion shifted beneath his
weight, hide shivering, gathering. The road, which was at

once like and *unlike* the road upon which they stood, beckoned in a silvery path. "Then let us ride."

Home!

The blood-bay leapt and the ravens swept forward. Behind them ran the grey and the black. The world lurched and the stars blurred; all save one, the blood-red star that sat on the western horizon. Now three rode astride, and two were of the Three. The beating of the ravens' wings melted into the drumming sound of hoofbeats and the swift, steady pad of the Gulnagel's taloned feet.

And somewhere to the north, a lone Rider veered into the Unknown Desert.

In the farmsteads and villages, Midlanders tossed in their sleep, plagued by nightmares. The color of their dreams changed. Where they had seen a horse as white as foam, they saw three; smoke and pitch and blood.

Where they had seen a venerable figure—a Man, or something like one—with a gem as clear as water on his breast, they saw a shadowy face, averted, and a rough stone clenched in a child's fist, the crunch of bone and a splash of blood.

Over and over, it rose and fell.

Onward, they rode.